"*Not the Witch You Wed* is breezy, warm, and a pleasure to read. I adore smitten, supportive heroes like Lincoln, and watching Violet grow into her own power—both personal and magical—is delightful."

—Olivia Dade, nationally bestselling author of *Spoiler Alert*

"Wow! I was not expecting *Not the Witch You Wed* to be such a fun, sexy romp! Sweet and sizzling at the same time, this book brought true joy to my heart. Vi and Lincoln are adorable together, their attraction magical, and reading this made my day all the brighter. If you like laughing out loud, scorching chemistry, and falling in love, pick up this book now!"

—Darynda Jones, *New York Times* bestselling author of *A Bad Day for Sunshine*

"*Not the Witch You Wed* is a wickedly delicious brew of juicy conflict, sizzling chemistry, and one-liners that made me smile so hard. Plus, the hero's literally an Alpha (wolf shifter, that is), and I couldn't get enough of his sweet and sexy ways. A paranormal rom-com, you say? Well, Ms. Asher, I am ALL IN."

—Mia Sosa, *USA Today* bestselling author of *The Worst Best Man*

Not the Witch You Wed

A SUPERNATURAL SINGLES Novel

APRIL ASHER

ST. MARTIN'S GRIFFIN

NEW YORK

First published in the United States by St. Martin's Griffin, an imprint of St. Martin's Publishing Group

NOT THE WITCH YOU WED. Copyright © 2022 by April Schwartz. All rights reserved. Printed in the United States of America. For information, address St. Martin's Publishing Group, 120 Broadway, New York, NY 10271.

www.stmartins.com

The Library of Congress Cataloging-in-Publication Data is available upon request.

ISBN 978-1-250-80799-1 (trade paperback)
ISBN 978-1-250-80800-4 (ebook)

Our books may be purchased in bulk for promotional, educational, or business use. Please contact your local bookseller or the Macmillan Corporate and Premium Sales Department at 1-800-221-7945, extension 5442, or by email at MacmillanSpecialMarkets@macmillan.com.

First Edition: 2022

10 9 8 7 6 5 4 3 2 1

To my #GirlsWriteNight: Tif, Jeanette, Annie, and Rachel—there is nothing more powerful than the Magic of true friendship . . . except chocolate.

(Just kidding.)

Not the Witch You Wed

1

Son of a Witch's %$@!

When most people envisioned hell, they conjured images of wicked, soul-destroying flames and near bottomless abysses bursting with spirits of the damned. The Head Honcho himself, either in his horn-to-hoof birthday suit or a red satin Armani three-piece, usually sat on a throne built from the charred skeletal remains of his victims.

That wasn't Violet Maxwell's brand of hell.

Far, far worse, hers was a triple-threat combo of Whispering Pines Ski Resort, her sister Rose's Witch Bond Announcement weekend, and the three-inch heels said sister had strong-armed her into wearing that morning.

A hell-break was long past due.

Her torture stilts abandoned in the hotel foyer, Vi hustled to the nearest corridor as if Lucifer himself was hot on her tail. If luck—and Mrs. Bender's gift of gab—was on her side, she'd get a five-minute head start before Rose realized she'd ducked out of the meet 'n' greet.

It wasn't like she hadn't done her sisterly duty. She'd met. She'd greeted. She'd smiled, unhinging her jaw more with each guest who poured into the lobby. For Goddess's sake, she'd withheld her gag response while their gran's coven friend described her recent bunion surgery in explicit, gory detail and offered to show her pictures.

Since their gran, Edie Maxwell, the Prima Witch herself, sat on the Supernatural Council that had been responsible for Supes stepping out from the shadows fifty years ago, anything having to do with a Maxwell was a big deal.

A sneeze? *Report it in the paper.*

A shopping trip? *Buy stock from the visited stores.*

A Witch Bond between a Maxwell triplet and Valentin Bisset, the notorious European Alpha? *Hold the presses, hold your wallets, and party like it's the event of a lifetime.* People had come out of the woodwork to celebrate, and the ceremony itself was still months away.

Now *that* was a three-ring circus she wasn't looking forward to.

As Vi turned at the indoor swimming pool, her cell phone vibrated against her left boob. Going against her better judgment, she tugged it from her DD cup and immediately regretted reading Rose's message.

You can run, but you can't hide. You and Olive owe me.
🔪🌋🔪

Hell's Spells, it hasn't even been a minute and the witch broke out the emoji threat.

Those little icons sat on Vi's chest like an anvil. This was *bad*. This was *Dirty Dancing* remake bad. *This* brand of bad called for triplet backup.

She didn't need to ping her younger-by-four-minutes sister's phone or use her nonexistent Magic to track Olive down. Where there'd be no people, there'd be an Olive, and no one in their right mind would hit the library while at a state-of-the-art ski resort except for her sister.

It took four minutes at a mall-walker pace to reach the H. Kline

Library and all of two seconds to spot the youngest triplet, sitting on the leather corner sofa with her legs curled beneath her and surrounded by no less than a dozen books. Olive didn't even look up when Vi closed the door.

"You know I hate interrupting your literary vacation, but unless you want to be subjected to one of our sister's bright ideas, we need to relocate you. Pronto." Vi snatched Olly's bag and waited by the door. "Like five minutes ago pronto. Fifteen to give us a comfortable cushion."

Behind her thick-framed glasses, Olive's blue-eyed gaze finally flickered off her book and transferred to Vi. "What happened to Rose greeting guests with the Tiger King all morning?"

"Olly, what time do you think it is?"

"Ten? Maybe eleven?"

"Try three in the afternoon. You missed the brunch. When she brought up outdoor excursions over the omelet station, there was a *look* in her eye. She means business."

"There's always a look in her eye. She claims it's from determination, but I'm ninety percent sure it's the uncorrected astigmatism." Pushing her glasses higher on her nose, Olive turned back to the book in her lap.

Vi stole it. "You're not grasping the severity here, babe. It was worse than the look that led to the skinny-dipping incident freshman year."

"That was your idea. So was the triple date I still have nightmares about, and the hair dye fiasco Mom still won't forgive us for."

"Oh. Yeah. Those were . . . me . . ." Vi paused, thinking, then snapped her fingers. "It was worse than the time she bulldozed us into being the Sanderson sisters for Halloween. Remember? *That* was not me."

Olly's face paled. "Why the hell didn't you lead with that? I am *not* being Winifred again. She's way too cutthroat for my blood." Jumping up from the couch, Olive carefully crammed her dusty book friends back into their empty shelf slots. "Let's get the hell out of here before—"

"Before what?" Rose's voice startled them both.

"Son of a witch's tit!" Vi clutched her chest, her pounding heart practically tickling her tonsils. "For the love of Goddess, Ro, my purple highlights just turned white. Do you know how much experimenting I had to do to find the perfect shade?"

Olive frowned. "Did Gran teach you how to do her poofy ninja-appearing thing? Because we've discussed how that trick is to never be used for evil . . . or against your sisters."

"No, you both were too busy plotting your escape to notice me." Rose cocked a meticulously microbladed eyebrow. "Or are you denying trying to make a break for it?"

"Would you believe us if we did?"

"We're at a ski resort. What did you think we'd be doing in our downtime?"

"Truthfully?" Vi ticked the list off on her fingers. "Avoiding our parents. Avoiding our parents' friends. Avoiding the people pretending to be our parents' friends." She slid a questionable look to Olive, knowing her younger sister loved Supernatural societal nonsense nearly as much as she did—*insert sarcasm*. "Did I leave anything out?"

"Avoiding people in general?" Olly quipped.

Vi playfully tugged a strand of her dirty-blond hair. "Ah, our little introvert."

Rose huffed, not amused. "You can't possibly avoid everyone all weekend."

"See, I beg to differ, because this place has a seriously decadent room service menu. I can't tell you the last time I ate seared scallops that didn't make me feel as though I had sand in my teeth."

"You want to spend all your time at this incredible mountain resort holed up in your room? Or here?" Rose looked around the small library in distaste. "How did we share a womb for eight months?"

"I ask myself that every day," Olive muttered under her breath.

That got a stern look from Rose. Yeah, she'd definitely been taking lessons from their grandma, because her glare was all Prima.

It was common knowledge that the Maxwell triplets couldn't be any less alike . . . in temperament, magical abilities, *and* looks. While Olive had their mother's blond locks and their father's mountain lion–shifter smarts, Rose was the perfect physical blend of both parental gene pools. Tall, with an athletic build and gorgeous caramel-highlighted hair, she could've strutted down any runway and not looked out of place.

Violet, on the other hand, could trip over her own feet standing stationary, and while she'd inherited their gran's dark hair and petite, curvy figure . . . she did *not* possess the same magical ability.

As the eldest in their Magical Triad, Vi *should've* been the strongest of her sisters, which *should've* prepped her for stepping into the Prima role. That Witch Bond Rose was about to enter? It *should've* been Vi's duty to uphold.

Instead, she'd been born the Maxwell Dud, or to those in other circles, the Magicless Maxwell, unable to hex anyone with so much as a hearty pimple. Vi had long ago relinquished her role as the Prima Apparent, and Rose, as the second eldest, had stepped forward in her place.

Her photogenic sister was born to be the next Prima—just not literally. The spotlight loved her, and Rose adored all the power, clothes, and attention that came along with it. It was her happy place, while Vi's happiness would forever lie with her favorite pair of Chuck Taylors, an endless supply of chocolate . . . and out of whatever her triplet had planned.

With a heavy sigh, she sank onto the arm of the couch. "We're not escaping this, are we?"

"You could try to Magic your way out of it and see what happens." Rose held direct, probing eye contact. "You might get lucky."

"That was a low blow."

"So was siccing Mrs. Bender on me. It's skiing. It's not like I'm asking you to risk life and limb."

✦ ✦ ✦

Forty-five minutes later, Vi had risked not only all her limbs and her own life, but the lives of everyone on the mountain. She'd accidentally stabbed her skis into the back of no less than six pairs of legs and nearly removed the eye of one ridiculously patient equipment valet. And if she hadn't been graced with her gran's curves, she'd have a bruised tailbone from the number of times she'd already fallen on her ass.

Rose eyed the far left slope, where a handful of expert skiers whipped down a steep section of the mountainside at Mach speed. "Anyone want to take on the Black Diamond Slope with me?"

Vi stabbed her ski poles into the snow-covered ground and held so tight her knuckles cracked. "I'll pass. But you feel free to go ahead and cheat death. Or not."

"Fuddy-dud." Ro's lips curled into a coy grin.

"I will stand right here and dud myself all damn day, but at least I'll be alive." She released her grip long enough to shoo her sisters away, and immediately slipped, falling on her ass for the one millionth time.

They all laughed.

"Okay, I'll be *sitting* right here dudding myself all damn day," she corrected, laughing harder. Olive reached out to help her up, but Vi waved her off. "Seriously. You two go."

"Are you sure?" Olive frowned, conflicted.

"I'm sure. Trust me."

Her sister didn't. Olly looked back no less than twelve times before she and Rose jumped on the black diamond ski lift and disappeared from view.

Vi flopped onto her back and stared at the clear sky, which seemed ridiculously blue even through her gray-tinted goggles.

Views like this weren't possible in New York City, with its sky broken up by a sea of rooftops. But while she loved nature and the fresh, clean air of the Poconos, the longer she stayed away from the city, the more she longed for the questionable camaraderie of the subway and the sound of her upstairs neighbors clog dancing at three o'clock in the morning.

Literal clog dancing, not sarcastic clog dancing, because they were both in the ensemble of a Broadway musical.

In New York, it was easy to disappear. Even as a Maxwell. Unless you did something outrageously stupid, no one gave you a second look, and if they did, most people shrugged it off and moved on with their day without another thought.

It sucked for dating prospects, but Vi was no longer thirty, not so flirty, and totally fine with not getting her hands dirty in the dating trenches. Being sexy, single, and sorta-supernatural in the city was fine with her, and on the rare nights that it wasn't, she had Roger.

Best. Purchase. Ever. There wasn't a bad mood or dry spell Roger the Rabbit Vibrator couldn't end when on mode number five.

"I'm not sure if I should offer to help you up, or leave you because you look so damn comfortable," a husky voice teased with thinly veiled humor.

Decked out in black-and-silver snow gear that in no way hid the tall, fit body beneath, a broad-shouldered shadow slowly transformed into a mouth-watering man specimen. Mirrored goggles and a knit beanie obscured the upper half of his face, but not the dark stubble peppering his strong, angular jaw or the crooked half smirk that immediately put her lady bits on defrost.

I really regret not stuffing Roger in my suitcase when I packed.

A vague sense of familiarity stirred something in her memory vault . . .

Mr. Sexy Voice chuckled. "Or maybe I've misjudged things and you're asleep behind those goggles."

Ah, right. He couldn't *see* her visually objectifying his body.

She subtly ran a gloved hand over her face to collect any drool. "Not asleep, but I'm not sure I have the sufficient mental capacity to get back on my feet."

In the distance, Vi heard her mother's high-octave voice, the sound wrenching a groan from her own throat.

Christina Maxwell, looking every bit the part of a *Real Housewives* snow bunny in her fuzzy angora earmuffs, strode from group to group, playing hostess-with-the-mostess with her typical high-energy pizzazz.

Vi hadn't been spotted—yet—but that would change if she didn't move. "On second thought, I'll take you up on that offer to help me up, if it's still on the table."

"It would be my pleasure." Tucking his poles beneath his arms, her savior grasped her gloved hands and, with a gentle tug, effortlessly brought her to her feet.

Her skis locked with his and she immediately flailed. "Hex me sideways."

Mr. Sexy Voice banded a tree-trunk arm around her waist and tugged her flush against his sturdy chest, his perfect mouth twitching into a grin. "'Hex me sideways'?"

She shrugged. "I don't have much of a filter. Sorry."

"Don't be. I like it."

And she liked *him* . . . or at least she liked the fluttery feeling that got stronger the longer she stayed in his arms. "Then I guess I'm sorry for nearly taking you out."

"Not your fault. I have a tendency to quake the knees of beautiful women."

It was on the tip of her tongue to call him out on the corny line when the flutter in her stomach went supernova. Tingling heat unlike anything she'd ever felt rushed through her, stealing not only her breath, but her ability to remain upright.

Her knees buckled . . . *for real this time.*

"Whoa. Hey. Are you okay?" Concern deepened Sexy Voice's voice as his arms tightened. "You sure you didn't fall and hit your head or something? Should I be calling for the medic?"

"Yes . . . I mean, no. No medic. I'm sure I didn't hit my head." Breathing slightly heavier than publicly appropriate, she pulled away and fought against the abrupt spin of her head. "I—I'm fine."

"You don't look fine."

"Thought you said I was a gorgeous woman." Her tease fell flat.

The sudden downturn of Mr. Sexy Voice's gorgeous lips told her he didn't believe her any more than she believed herself. That had *not* been the result of the breakfast burrito she'd inhaled this morning, and now that she took a small step back, and then a second, the charged buzz hanging in the air slowly diminished.

Her gaze darted left and right, searching for an escape route. *Any* escape. "Th-thank you for the save, but I have to go."

"I'm sorry. Did I—?"

"No. No, you were real superhero material." Gaze landing on an empty ski lift, she picked up her poles and pushed off. "Thanks again!"

It took a twenty-foot distance before Vi's heart rate finally settled, but while *it* dissipated, the heated gaze Mr. Sexy Voice burned into the back of her puffer jacket did not. She refused to look back, only glancing up as the ski lift's safety bar fell over her lap.

He stood in the same spot she'd left him, his attention catapulting another swarm of goose bumps over her body. She couldn't tear her eyes away from his goggled face until an oversized pair of angora earmuffs stepped into her line of view, breaking contact.

He and Christina chatted amicably, which meant he was a party guest and, judging by the sheer size of him—which Vi could now appreciate from a distance—probably one of Valentin's shifter friends. Her mother didn't break out the musical laugh for anyone, and the older witch was practically belting out a symphony.

An electricity-induced dizzy spell. Her mother. Mr. Sexy Voice.

Vi was still attempting to piece everything together when the lift screeched to a halt at the first summit.

The operator looked at her as if waiting for her to do something. "Ma'am?"

"What just happened?" For the first time, she realized no one else was on this particular slope.

"You're the last person."

"The last person for what?"

"Did you not see the sign at the bottom of the lift? We're performing maintenance to get ready for the busy weekend. You were the last person up the mountain."

"The last person . . ." Flinging her gaze to where she'd left her mother and Mr. Sexy Voice, she whimpered. She didn't even know which ant-size dots they were anymore. "Oh no. You have to take me back down."

"Repairman's already started working on the other end, so the only way down is on those skis attached to your feet."

"I can't do that." At least not without losing her life. "How long will the maintenance take?"

"Hard to say. At least a few."

"Minutes? That's not so bad. I can wait."

"Hours. If we're lucky, only four."

Four. Hours. That was less good, and while she could wait in theory, her bladder most definitely would not have gotten the memo.

Although not as pampered as Rose, she drew the line at squatting in the woods. Not that many plants were growing at this time of year, but with her luck, she'd hover over the only hardy poison ivy vine on the whole mountain and walk away with a rash in an unfortunate—and hard to itch—area.

With a push of his ski poles, the lift operator took off down the slope. "Enjoy your run!"

Yeah, that wasn't likely.

"This cannot be happening." She couldn't ski her way down the hill without becoming a witch-size boulder and taking out anyone unfortunate enough to be standing in her way. She couldn't stay . . . because *bladder*.

Summoning every ski lesson she'd ever taken—which obviously never "took"—Vi glanced down the hill and gulped. "I can't believe I'm about to do this."

With a silent prayer to Goddess, she gently pushed off . . . and immediately knew she was in a witch-heap of trouble.

✦ ✦ ✦

The only highlight of Lincoln Thorne's weekend had sped away from him as if a pack of rabid wolves were hot on the back of her skis. He hadn't laid eyes on Violet Maxwell in years, and while he knew his chances of running into the gorgeous witch this weekend had been pretty damn good, he hadn't been prepared to run into her on the slopes while escaping monotonous Pack duties.

Despite her being bundled up from head to toe, he'd recognized her. His *Wolf* had recognized her, practically sitting up and whimpering as he honed in on her sweet flowery scent. But less than two seconds into their conversation, it had become obvious *she* hadn't identified *him*.

If she had, he'd still be wiping snow from his face.

In preschool, they'd fought for the same sandbox toys, and in junior high, they'd faced off in a heated race for class president. High school was pretty much more of the same. He'd be hard-pressed to think of a time they hadn't been trying to get one over on each other.

Except their senior year . . .

For him, that year had been filled with a lot of ups and downs, the latter usually involving his father, the then Alpha of the North American Pack, or NAP.

The ups?

Ninety-five percent of them involved Violet . . . until his bastard of a father destroyed that, too.

"Alpha Thorne! There you are!" Christina Maxwell approached, a gloved hand waving.

Linc quickly threw on a smile. "If it isn't the proud mother of the Prima Apparent. Christina, it's good to see you. Where's that elusive mate of yours?"

"Oh, you know Peter. He'll hide until his presence is absolutely required. I heard you'd arrived, but that handsome Second-in-Command couldn't tell me where you'd gotten to." She tugged him into a hug. "And 'proud' doesn't cover how I feel right now. As a mother, you always want what's best for your children, and it's an amazing feeling to see it coming true."

Linc bit the inside of his cheek. He'd never call Valentin Bisset the best of anything, except maybe asshole, philanderer, and general disgrace to the shifter community.

Step by agonizingly slow step, Linc had worked hard to dismantle the broken, bloodthirsty Pack system his father had led and put one in its place that was based on mutual respect and personal responsibility. One where it didn't matter if the shifter was wolf, beaver, bear, or eagle. Predatory or not. An old NAP member or a new one.

No one was more important, or more expendable, than any other.

Everyone was on the same level.

Everyone was *Pack*.

But not all the Alphas held the same beliefs. Like Bisset. The pretentious French tiger bastard—and head of the European Pack—made Gregor Thorne look like a kitten when it came to leadership tactics, and he was one of the largest obstacles Linc had in getting the seven highest-ranking Alphas on board with his new vision.

"What on earth is that girl doing?" Christina's gaze locked on something over Lincoln's shoulder.

He followed her line of sight to the lone figure skiing down the mountain. Strike that—*flying* down the mountain, and going faster with each passing second. He immediately recognized the bright purple hat.

"I didn't know Violet skied," Linc heard himself say.

"Vi?" Christina chuckled. "Goddess, no. That girl could trip over her own two feet while standing still. I'm not sure what she's trying to accomplish."

The flailing hands and out-of-control weaving indicated she was trying to not break her neck.

Lincoln pushed off on his skis, keeping an eye on her trajectory and bypassing a few spectators who'd stopped to watch the show.

"Violet Ann Maxwell," Christina bellowed. "For the love of Goddess, stop playing around!"

No way in hell was she playing.

People scrambled out of the way, leaving behind a line of abandoned snowmobiles like a snow-equipment barricade. The second Violet saw it, magical-themed curses spewed from her lips at an alarming rate. She dropped to her ass in an attempt to slow her descent.

It didn't work.

Linc popped off his skis and ran as fast as his legs, and his inner Wolf, would take him. When she was two seconds away from impact, he leaped, cocooning her smaller body against his, and dropping them into a controlled roll. They log-rolled ten feet before coming to a stop.

Her face burrowed into his chest, Violet's breath came out in quick pants. "I'm alive. I'm not witch splatter. Wait . . . am I?"

Hearing the humor in her voice, Linc chuckled. "You're all in one piece."

Her legs automatically draped on either side of his waist as she slowly pushed herself upright. He sucked in a groan and told Linc Junior to behave, but his cock had a mind of its own.

At some point during their tumble, Violet's goggles and hat had come off, and her rare periwinkle eyes twinkled down at him. Snow wet the ends of her silky, purple-streaked dark hair, and both cold and adrenaline had long since pinked her cheeks.

She'd been a beauty when they were teenagers, but now she took his breath away.

"You have a hero complex or something, huh?" Her lips twitched into a teasing smirk. "You know what? I don't even care. Thank you."

He dragged his attention away from her mouth—barely. "You're very welcome. You sure you're okay? Nothing broken?"

"Only my pride." Tilting her head, she peered down at him as if he was a bug under a microscope. "Do I kn—?"

"Oh my Goddess!" Christina Maxwell rushed forward. "Are you all right? Please tell me nothing's broken!"

Violet glanced up at her mother. "I'm okay. Thanks to—"

"That was an incredibly brave thing for you to do, Alpha Thorne. Goodness, my heart is still pounding." Christina wasn't even talking to her, her concern directed at him.

"It was a matter of being in the right place at the right time." Keeping his gaze locked on Violet's face, he witnessed the exact moment she connected the dots.

Her purple eyes narrowed.

Her lips tightened into a thin, hard line.

Prying his dark-tinted goggles away from his face, she scowled at him. "*You.*"

Linc smirked. "Hello there, Violet. Long time no see."

"Not nearly long enough." She released his goggles.

The heavy frames smacked back into his face with a loud *thwack*, earning a soft gasp from Christina and a handful of spectators. Vi pushed off him and stalked away.

"Come on now, princess. Don't be like that," he called after her, failing to hide his amusement. "Maybe we could get a bite to eat or something. Are vanilla shakes with fries still your weakness?"

She turned as if in slow motion and drilled him with the Violet Maxwell glare he remembered so fondly from their childhood. "You want to grab a bite to eat."

"I asked, didn't I?"

She scooped up a handful of snow, and after shaping it into a large ball, hurled it with the tenacity of an MLB pitcher. "Eat *that*, Lincoln Thorne."

The projectile nailed him square in the face, snow exploding in every direction, including straight up his nose. He sputtered, his laughter angering her more as she whirled and continued her exit.

"So I take that as a no?"

She volleyed back with a gloved middle finger in the air, and he laughed harder. Back when everyone treated him like the future Alpha, making nice and giving him leniencies they shouldn't have, she hadn't.

If anything, she'd gone out of her way to be a pain in his ass, and while he hadn't appreciated it at first, he did now. It kept him humble and his ego in check. Hell, it was one of the things that had made him contemplate changing the status quo in Pack life.

Violet Maxwell was the one who got away. And he wasn't just the bastard that let it happen.

He was the idiot who hadn't run after her.

2

To Bae, or Not to Bae

One hour. Fifteen minutes. And twenty-three seconds. That's how long Linc had been trapped in the Supernatural hell that was the first official Bond Announcement event scheduled for the weekend.

He couldn't wait to break free, shift into his Wolf, and hunt something. Hell, he'd be good with a human run in the fresh air at this point.

It was in and out, Adrian had said. No need to talk to anyone, Adrian had insisted. Neither turned out to be true, because he'd already been here way too long and had been forced to make nice with more people than he cared to count . . . except the one he really wanted to see.

Call him a masochist, but he couldn't stop thinking about his earlier run-in with Violet, and found himself standing in the corner scanning the room in hopes of scoring another.

Adrian interrupted his solitude, handing him a flute of something sparkly. "Please tell me you haven't bitten anyone's head off their shoulders while I've left you unsupervised."

Linc shot his friend a glare. "I'm not completely lacking in social graces, you know."

"Yeah, just mostly. Why else would a five-foot witch nail you in the face with a snowball?" His Second-in-Command surveyed the room. "Speaking of our pretty little snowball wielder, have you seen her tonight? I was hoping to secure myself an intro . . . compliment her on her throwing arm."

Linc's inner Wolf growled at the idea of his friend seeking out Violet. Listed as one of the top ten Sexiest Supernaturals Alive five years running, the lion shifter was a self-proclaimed charmer who made a young Hugh Hefner look virginal.

"I haven't seen her," Linc said truthfully.

He'd looked. Even when he hadn't been actively searching for Violet, his gaze had lingered on the back of every curvy-bodied brunette until they turned for him to see it wasn't her. Knowing Violet as he did, she'd be on the opposite side of the room from her mother, away from large crowds, and near a viable exit.

She probably wanted to be here less than he did.

More of a beer man, Linc dumped his champagne in the nearest planter. "How much longer until I'm allowed to disappear?"

"Have you wished the happy couple congratulations from the North American Pack yet?"

"No, and I don't think it would be a wise thing to do . . . unless you don't mind posting my bail money."

Their gazes skated across the room to Bisset. The French thorn in Linc's side stood with Flores, the South American Alpha, the two of them talking in hushed tones. Smarmy bastard was already trying to undo every inch Linc had fought to gain with the panther shifter earlier that morning.

Saying shifters resisted change was an understatement. It was practically engrained in their DNA. But dissolving the Elder Board? That wasn't a change . . . that was a life-altering move that would not only benefit his own Pack, but *all* of them.

At least that's what he had five more weeks to prove to the six other Alphas.

He had just over a month to shift Pack life a step closer to a democracy . . . and for him to avoid a forced mating with someone of the Elders' choosing. Bisset's personal mission seemed to ensure democracy didn't happen.

The tiger shifter broke away from his conversation with Alpha Flores and flashed Linc a knowing wink.

"You know what that asshole's doing, don't you?" Linc said to Adrian. "I'll have to video call with Flores for an entire weekend to undo whatever the hell he did in just five minutes."

"And if that's what it takes, that's what you'll do. We both knew this wouldn't be easy. Don't let the bastard get into your head."

Easier said than done. Especially since if he failed to dissolve the Elders' stronghold over the Packs, on his thirty-third birthday, he'd have two choices: relinquish both his Pack title and his seat on the Supernatural Council, or accept a mate the Elders chose for him.

If he chose the first option, everything he'd fought so hard to change for his people would be for nothing. If he chose the second, he'd very literally be locked in a marriage from hell, much like the one to which his mother had been subjected.

"There is one other option," Adrian added, as if reading Linc's thoughts. "You're in a room filled with a *Who's Who* of both Supernatural and Norm socialites. Eenie-meenie-mo your way to a mate of your *own* choosing."

"For the love of God," Linc muttered, pinching the bridge of his nose.

"I'm not a god, but I see how it could be a little confusing." Adrian smirked. "And don't look at me like I pissed in your food bowl. We both know you're not relinquishing your title, so it's either Mate Bond with the Elder's pawn piece, or find your own leading lady."

"I choose to dissolve the Elder Board before I'm forced into a decision."

"And that's my hope, too, but do you want to fuck this up by not preparing for all contingencies?" Adrian flashed him a sympathetic look. "I get that you're waiting for *her*, but be realistic here, man. She may not exist."

Her. His *True* Mate.

The chance both his human and Wolf souls found their perfect matches in the same person was practically a thing of fairy tales. Hell, the reigning Prima finding hers in a bear shifter had been nothing short of divine intervention.

"You know I'd go to war for you, right?" Adrian's tone got serious. "If you want the Elders off your back about the mate thing, give them *something*. Or at the very least, make them *think* you're about to give them something. It's not a long-game plan, but it'll give you extra time to figure shit out."

Linc opened his mouth, about to ask Adrian if he had any ideas on how to make that happen, when his Wolf stirred. He looked over to the dance floor, already knowing what he'd see, and he was right.

Violet Maxwell stood to the left of the patio doors, looking damn near edible in a dark purple dress that hugged her glorious curves to perfection. Her hair, swept up in a stylishly messy twist, left her shoulders bare and exposed a sexy tattoo for all to see.

As familiar as she was to him and his Wolf, it was like seeing her for the first time. The beauty slowly walking the length of the room, careful to keep her back toward the wall, was not the teenager he'd been enamored with fourteen years ago.

This Violet Maxwell was all woman ... and a vision from which he couldn't seem to tear his eyes away.

✦ ✦ ✦

Vi stood adjacent to the party and studied her sister in a noncreepy way. Hanging off the arm of her fiancé, Valentin Bisset, Rose tossed her head of caramel curls and laughed at something he said.

Was that her fake laugh? Vi couldn't tell from this far.

She *looked* every bit the excited, newly engaged Prima Apparent, but looks deceived—especially Rose's. The middle triplet could have an internal Doomsday Clock ticking away and no one would see her sweat; her ability to mask emotions was directly responsible for her poker night winning streak.

But something didn't feel right, and Vi learned long ago to never pooh-pooh a gut feeling. Sure, the European Alpha checked all the boxes for a lot of people: gorgeous, rich, and able to turn into a freakin' jungle cat on a whim. But as alluring as that might be to some, her sister's future Bond Mate looked too much like a sleazy Wall Street guy to put Vi at ease.

A Witch Bond was "Marriage: Prima Edition." They only happened with the emergence of a new Prima, and prior to Edie Maxwell's birth seventy-four years ago, there hadn't been either in nearly a hundred and fifty years. A link of body, soul, and Magic, a Witch Bond anchored a Prima's powers so the world didn't go *kaboom* and quite literally blow up in everyone's faces.

It gave a whole new spin to "till death do us part," because with a Witch Bond, death wasn't always a deal-breaker. Edie swore up and down that she still spoke with her departed husband every evening before bed.

"Violet Maxwell! You've been hiding from me!"

Evidently not well enough . . .

Mrs. Bender, one of her grandmother's coven friends, jerked her into a hug that nearly knocked Vi out of her kitten heels. The older woman's gaze skated over her tattoo, a Celtic knot representing the unbreakable bond between her and her sisters.

The triplets had designed the intricate latticework of curves when they were teenagers. The very minute they turned eighteen, they'd gotten their tattoos, Olive's on the back of her neck and Rose's on her inner wrist. Vi's, on her left shoulder, was—by far— the largest and most noticeable, because she didn't give a flying broomstick about Supernatural social graces.

She hadn't bothered hiding it tonight, and the teenage rebel in her still giggled when she remembered her mom's reaction on first seeing it on display.

Mrs. Bender regaled her with story after story, the woman's voice slowly fading into the background as Vi smiled and nodded at the appropriate times. Unfortunately for her, she resumed attention around the time Mrs. B mentioned Valentin's virility and how lucky Rose was to be able to take advantage of it.

Vi threw up in her mouth a little bit.

"Oh, sweetheart. I'm so sorry." Misinterpreting her sudden bout of nausea, the older woman laid a gentle hand on her arm, pity softening her eyes. "This must be bittersweet for you. After all, it should be you over there on the arm of that impressive young man."

Thank. Goddess. Not.

Vi forced a smile. "The right triplet definitely got the part. Olive and I couldn't be happier for her."

And happy for themselves, because now that Rose was the official Prima Apparent, they could stay as far away from magical drama as their parents—and their gran—physically allowed.

By the grace of Goddess, someone called Mrs. Bender away, and not leaving anything to chance, Vi abandoned one wall for another in case she decided to return.

Normally, she and Olive made a sisterly appearance together at these functions, but the traitor was currently boarding a plane to Scotland to intercept an important magical text on behalf of NYU, where she taught.

At first Vi thought it a not-so-well-thought-out lie in an attempt not to *people*, but she'd read the email from Olive's boss herself. In the subject line, the eccentric head of Supernatural Studies had even dubbed it a "Scholarly Emergency," almost giving her sister a run for her money in his love of dusty old books.

Right now, Vi wished she was into old books, or anything that would've prevented her from being subjected to hundreds of stares.

Being the Maxwell Dud, she was used to whispers, but it wasn't her lack of magical prowess people were discussing tonight.

News of her *assault* on the poor North American Alpha had spread like wildfire through the resort, so much so that eight hours later, people were still giving her a wide berth.

It would be kind of nice if it weren't for the judgy stares.

Glancing around the ballroom, Vi cased the exits. She counted three, maybe four, if the mayor ever left the chocolate fountain. Until he did, the back patio was her last option, because the man could—and would—talk to anyone with ears.

"The only way you're getting out of here is if you pull one of the fire alarms." Vi's favorite person in the world came to stand next to her, her head of gray hair, pinned up in an elaborate twist, barely reaching Violet's chin. "You might have staged a successful breakout ten minutes ago, but your window has long since passed. Snooze, you lose, bae."

With a low chuckle, Vi rolled her eyes. "How many times have I told you to stop saying *bae*, Gran? It's very much over."

"It's not over if I continue to use it, now, is it?" A slender silver eyebrow shot up in a silent challenge.

No one openly disagreed with Edie Maxwell, not even Violet. There was a reason you couldn't read a supernatural textbook without seeing the Prima's name. The power the Maxwell matriarch had in her pinkie finger could light up not only all of New York City, but the entire Northeast electric grid. She'd stopped countless wars—and maybe started a few minor skirmishes—and had saved more lives throughout the years than anyone could count.

Move over, Superman, because Super Gran is in the house.

"On a scale of one to ten, how noticed do you think it'll be if I jump ship before the rest of the dessert is brought out?" Vi asked.

"Look at the exits, sweetheart, and look closely." Gran nudged her gaze to the nearest doorway, located a few feet beyond the coat check.

Vi didn't see anything except freedom and a future involving the pint of Ben & Jerry's Chocolate Fudge Brownie sitting in her freezer back home, but knowing her grandma had told her to look closer for a reason, she narrowed her eyes and squinted.

It took a full thirty seconds to see the faint glimmer sliding over the tall archway. She lasered her attention to the patio doors behind the mayor and . . .

Narrow eyes, unfocus, and stare.

Violet cursed. "I should've left when Olive did."

Edie chuckled, not fazed by her colorful vocab. "I knew you'd see it."

"Mom put alarm charms on the doorways? She went way too far this time," Vi grumbled before shooting her gran a beamingly bright smile. "But luckily, I have a wickedly awesome granny who would do anything for her favorite granddaughter. Right, *bae*?"

"You know I don't have favorites." Edie patted her arm affectionately, a half smile pulling on her lips. "And don't say *bae*. It doesn't have the same oomph when you say it, dear. As for the jailbreak, as much as I'd love to help you bust out of this joint, I'm afraid my Magic is tied up at the moment. Whoever put up those charms learned from the last time."

Last time. That would be her father's birthday party three years ago, during which her mother had introduced her to the son of a friend's hairdresser, who, at the ripe old age of thirty-five, still lived in the basement of his parents' home with no intention of ever leaving.

Vi didn't know if she should be annoyed at her mom for throwing up the charms, or at Rose for keeping her busy while she did it.

"Oh, come now. Don't look like someone killed your familiar,"

Edie joked, knowing full well that witches didn't have familiars. "It can't be all that bad."

"I don't know how else to look, Gran." Vi felt more out of place than ever, not to mention outnumbered. "Do you realize that if my last name weren't Maxwell, I wouldn't even be invited to this little shindig?"

She'd convinced her best friends to party-crash as her wing-persons, but Bax had been called away on last-minute Guardian Angel business, and Vi's boss at Potion's Up—the magic-themed bar in downtown Manhattan where she was brewmaster—had guilted Harper into working Vi's open shift.

No friends. No sister. It left Vi well and truly alone, not to mention vulnerable in a way she really, really didn't like . . . especially when she half expected Lincoln Thorne to pop up like a bad rash.

"You're worried about something." Edie watched Violet with hawklike eyes. "Does it have something to do with the wolf shifter?"

Vi snorted. "Only you could call the North American Alpha a *wolf shifter*. But no, it has nothing to do with Lincoln."

"Are you sure? Because my eyesight may not be what it was ten years ago, but my hearing's still sharp as ever."

"Are you going to scold me, too?"

"When have I ever scolded you?"

"Never, but that's because one disapproving frown from you is ten times worse than any of Christina's bellowing rants—which I was already subjected to for a solid twenty-five minutes. She could've gone longer, but she was called away about an hors d'oeuvre issue."

Edie's brow lifted. "*Christina?* Please tell me she's not still insisting you call her by her given name."

"Only for the last ten years . . . but at least now it's only required in public."

Her gran sighed. "Back to your little one-sided snowball fight . . . Did he deserve it?"

"Without a doubt," Vi said adamantly. "Stealing my milk straw. Commandeering my favorite swing on the playground. And let's not forget the class presidency debacle. I had that election in the bag until His Royal Alpha-ness got bored one afternoon and decided to run."

But the biggest pièce de résistance had come when they were eighteen.

With the ink barely dry on their high school diplomas, she'd stood on the riverbank with her nerves, a near bursting duffel, and naive dreams of forever as she'd waited for him at their rendezvous point. Agreeing to leave her family—especially her sisters—had been a pretty damn big deal, and not a decision she'd taken lightly.

She'd waited for Lincoln until the sun broke over the horizon . . . and he never showed.

She'd worried. She'd called. Pulling up her big-witch panties, she'd even braved a visit to the Thorne house, to find that not only had he no intention of escaping his dick of a father like they'd carefully planned, but that he'd wholeheartedly immersed himself in the Alpha limelight.

Fool me once, shame on you. Fool me twice, shame on me . . .

Betrayed and hurt, she'd vowed to never let Lincoln Thorne that close to her heart—or any part of her body—ever again. And up until earlier that afternoon, she'd done a pretty damned good job keeping that promise.

Vi glanced at Edie, the older witch watching her expectantly. "What?"

"Did Alpha Thorne do anything in this last decade to deserve your animosity?"

"He . . . saved me from a trip to the emergency room." *Well, crap.* Said out loud, it did sound like a pretty dick move.

Edie gifted her *the look*.

"See! Right there!" Vi pointed at her gran's face. "That's the exact frown I'm talking about. Okay, fine! Yes! I probably shouldn't have lobbed a snowball at his face, but in my defense, it's not like he hasn't deserved it a few dozen times in his lifetime."

"I see," Edie said cryptically.

"You see what?"

"Myself and your grandfather—Goddess rest his soul—had almost the same dynamics in the beginning stages of our courtship."

"Whoa, whoa, whoa. Slow your roll there, Gran, because what Lincoln Thorne and I have is *not* a courtship, or anything close to what you had with Pappy. Seriously, you two were True Mates. Lincoln and I are practically mortal enemies."

"Thanks to their strong, visceral reactions, love and hate are often mistaken for one another," Edie teased.

"I just threw up in my mouth for the second time today."

"Sorry to hear you're not feeling well, Violet. Hope it's only a twenty-four-hour bug." Spoken behind her, Lincoln's deep voice sent a small, heated shiver down her spine.

She shot her gran a fierce look. No way had Edie missed the Alpha slithering up on Vi's backside.

Edie grinned over her shoulder. "Alpha Thorne, it's a pleasure to see you outside of the Council chambers."

"It's always a pleasure to see you, Prima. In the chambers or not. I trust everything has been to your family's liking so far this weekend?"

"My daughter has done most of the planning for the event, but from what I understand, she's given your staff excellent praise . . . and that's saying something, as Christina is not easily pleased."

"Then that's definitely a win."

Not liking him at her back, or maybe liking it a little too much, Vi shifted closer to her grandmother. The jerk flashed her a shit-eating grin as if knowing exactly why she'd moved. "Your staff? You own Whispering Pines?"

Lincoln slid his hands deep into his pockets, the move fanning out his already open tux jacket and emphasizing his broad chest. "I do."

"I'd think you'd be too busy with Alpha duties to waste your time running a resort."

"Whispering Pines isn't just a resort. We work with local officials to help with conservation and wildlife protection. Money earned above operating costs goes right back into conservation education, as well as frontline ecosystem preservation efforts."

Lincoln Thorne, conservationist? She'd never seen that coming.

"But you're right." He grinned. "My time is pretty limited, which is why I hire smart people to run it for me . . . many of whom happen to be members of my Pack."

"You know, Alpha Thorne," Edie interjected, "I was hoping you could do me a small favor."

"Name it. If it's within my power, consider it done."

"I think my granddaughter's sour stomach has something to do with a guest who went a little heavy with the perfume. Do you have a free moment to escort her outside for a quick breath of fresh air?"

Vi whipped her head toward her grandma. "What are you doing?"

"Proving a point, bae. Roll with it," Edie whispered.

Locking his gaze on Vi, Lincoln extended his arm. "It would be my pleasure."

He waited.

Edie waited.

Clenching her jaw, Vi reluctantly slipped her arm through Linc's. "Oh . . . I can't. The charms."

Edie waved her hand in the air, and in an instant, the glimmers shielding the patio doors fell away. "What charms?"

"You little sneak! You said my mother put those on the exits!"

"Did I? You two kids enjoy the fresh air." Edie grinned over her shoulder, already leaving them alone.

Lincoln guided her through the doors and onto the gray-stoned patio, where thanks to a few strategically placed outdoor heaters, a few couples danced to the music filtering out through nondescript speakers. Potted trees twinkled with tiny white lights and scented flowers overfilled large, elaborately sculpted flowerboxes.

It would've been romantic if it weren't for her present company.

"You're enjoying this, aren't you?" She threw him an accusing glare.

"That your grandmother basically Violet-proofed the ballroom? Immensely. Do you have childproof locks on all your cabinets and those little padded bumpers on sharp corners?"

She dropped his arm. "Consider Operation Fresh Air complete. Go about your merry way, have fun, and please forget to write. You're adept at forgetting things. It shouldn't be too hard."

He winced. "You have every right to hate me—"

"I'm so glad I have your permission to think you're a pompous, opportunistic jerk-turd."

She turned to find the nearest path back to her room and came to an abrupt stop. Mayor Ruddick was approaching, pursuing her like a man on a mission, and the city official was way too clingy, too talky, and too adverse to personal hygiene for her now diminished patience.

Twenty feet.

Ten.

Spittle clung to the corner of his mouth, getting more noticeable the closer he got. Less than a few seconds from contact, a solid arm banded around her waist and guided her onto the dance floor.

"My apologies, Mayor Ruddick," Lincoln said, nodding at the older man in acknowledgment. "I've been trying to get this beautiful woman to myself all night. I'm sure you understand she'll have to take a rain check."

Ruddick waved his hand in a noncommittal gesture. "Suppose that's what I get for waiting too long. But now that I've bumped into you, though . . . I've been meaning to give your office a return call about that project I spoke with you about a few weeks ago."

"That sounds suspiciously like business, and tonight is all about a celebration. Call my office on Monday and I'll have my assistant set up an appointment."

"I'll do that. Thank you. Miss Maxwell . . ." The mayor smiled, looking appeased as he walked back the way he'd come.

"Two saves in the same day. You're welcome."

"Thank you," Vi forced out, her jaw clenching.

A chuckle rumbled through Lincoln's chest. "I'm sorry, what was that? I must have heard you incorrectly, because I could've sworn Violet Maxwell just thanked me. And here I was expecting another snowball to the face."

"The night's still young."

Lincoln's thumb caressed her knuckles in slow, gentle strokes. Evidently there was a direct pleasure line from her hand to her lady bits, because she damned near ruined her panties, the threat worsened by their close proximity.

Goddess, they were so close, and with every sway of their bodies, closer still. She drilled her gaze into his tux jacket, hesitant to look him in the face as heated arousal crept to her cheeks—and to places she shouldn't be feeling anything as far as the wolf shifter was concerned.

"Will I see those pretty eyes of yours again tonight?" he asked, his voice a soft, rumbling growl.

Nope.

She shouldn't.

It was in her best interests to keep her gaze fixed on his tux, his chest, or any other part of his anatomy that was not his golden brown eyes, but she looked up anyway.

Alphas—by nature—didn't like being stared dead in the eye. Their inner animals saw it as a challenge or a play for power, so most Supernaturals chose not to do it and risk pissing them off.

But Violet *couldn't* look away. Not now, and not when they were kids.

She didn't realize they'd stopped dancing until that tingling heat low in her stomach stirred. Unlike earlier on the ski slope, this time, it didn't rush—it glided, rising through her core until it warmed her veins, then her skin.

The tips of her fingers tingled.

Sure enough, a faint purple mist crackled along their surface.

Magic . . .

She yanked away. "What are you doing?"

"Dancing . . . or at least I was, until a second ago."

If she didn't know him so well, she might have bought his innocent act. None of this made sense. For thirty-two years, she hadn't had an ounce of Magic, and suddenly it had made itself known twice in less than twenty-four hours?

Coincidences broke her into hives.

"I don't know what your agenda is, but it stops right now," she demanded.

"Violet, I don't know what—" He reached out to her.

"Don't touch me." She stepped back, not sure what her Magic would do to either of them if they made contact again.

The more distance she put between them, the less her hands glowed, which proved that Lincoln Thorne was bad for her health. "Do me a favor. Next time you see me hurtling down a mountain, or about to be subjected to one of Ruddick's long-winded stories, and want to get involved, *don't.*"

She'd much rather crash into a snowmobile a thousand times and suffer through whatever injuries she obtained in the process than subject herself to the pain and humiliation she'd suffered at the hands of the wolf shifter fourteen years ago.

Lincoln Thorne had broken her fragile teenage heart once. She'd be damned if she let him have a go-round at her battle-scarred adult one, too.

3

Abra-Freakin'-Cadabra

Vi cursed herself for not calling in sick and turning her two nights off into three. After the Bond Announcement weekend from hell, she wasn't up to dealing with people. Not that she was an extrovert any other day of the week, but after all the smiling and small talk—not to mention the unexpected reappearance of her childhood nemesis . . . and *Magic*? She deserved an extra recovery day, damn it.

Instead, she got a double shift, a cantankerous boss, and a full Blood Moon to put that special amount of bizarre in an already otherwise bonkers establishment.

If it was supernatural, it was represented somewhere within Potion's Up, the supernatural-themed watering hole where she was brewmaster (aka bartender). Menu items. Drink names. Décor. For parties and special occasions, they broke out the oversized cauldron and bottle-flipped their way to some pretty decent tips.

As sad as it might seem, Potion's Up was her home away from home.

"I need five more Love Spells for table nine." A tray clanked down on the counter and one-half of Vi's best friend brigade sighed, the move pushing out her perfect C-cup boobs.

A redhead with curves to make a pinup envious, Harper Jacobs's thirst for fun rivaled only her wicked smarts. Not only did she have a master's in psychology and certification in sex therapy, but she also happened to be the only adult virgin succubus—as in, *sex demon*—in the tristate area.

Maybe in the country.

Possibly in the Western Hemisphere.

Both Harp's virginal status and the fact that she moonlighted as the anonymous host of the radio show *Sex Talk with Savannah* were well-kept secrets known only to Violet and her sisters, and ones the succubus protected above all else.

Temporarily ignoring the bachelorette party attempting to flag her down from the other end of the bar, Vi worked on her friend's refills. "Does table nine know these aren't *actually* love potions?"

"Beats me. As long as they tip well, they can believe whatever the hell they want." Harper dropped her chin into her hand and studied Vi as she filled the shaker. "Don't think I've forgotten about the party. You owe me details, witch. Who was wearing what, or more importantly, who was wearing who? And I need to hear the grand tally."

"What grand tally?"

"How many people Edie made pee their pants. My bet is three. Was it three?"

Vi confined her laugh to a snort. "That happened *one* time, and although she claims to be proud of it, I'm not sure it was on purpose."

"It was." Bax dropped into the only vacant seat. "Hit me with a Goblin Drop."

Vi and Harper exchanged looks. Down the bar, the bachelorettes salivated at the Guardian Angel's presence, and she couldn't blame them. A bronze gift from the heavens, the other member of their best friend trio had dual full-sleeve tattoos and Jason Momoa–inspired hair that would lure a nun to the lusty side.

Keeping her tone light, Vi slid him the shot. "I take it you're not on Guardian duty tonight?"

"Nope." He downed the frothy green liquid in one gulp and grimaced before nodding for a refill. "Currently in between assignments."

That wasn't good.

Guardians usually stuck with an assignment for a few years—minimum. He'd had two this year alone.

"So if I did my bartender duty and asked if you wanted to talk about it . . . ?"

He shot her a look. "Refill, babe. Just the refill."

Evasion. A typical Bax maneuver, and one she'd expected. In true angel fashion, he never unloaded on them. He never flung himself on the couch with a *Boy, it was one of those days*, then blathered on about a brewing office romance or the latest in a string of his supervisor's ridiculous expectations. It was an angel thing.

Private. Quiet. And Deny It.

Flashing him a teasing smile, she slid him his refill. "Well, two's your limit, angel-cakes. We can't have you flying under the influence. Gage would sink his vampire fangs into me if I enabled angelic inebriation."

Bax scowled at her and changed the subject. "So how was the grand ball?"

"Pretty dull stuff," she half lied. "Perfectly dressed people—who, blessedly, mostly ignored me. Perfect music. Perfect food. And of course, Rose, the perfect witchy princess with her perfectly charming soon-to-be mate."

Harper scrunched her nose, showcasing her freckles. "Is the bastard as drool-worthy in person as he is in pictures? Because I don't know how that's physically possible."

"It is. He's so pretty it almost hurts to look at him. And he seems pretty enamored with Rose."

"Well, yeah! Hitching yourself to the next Prima would enamor anyone." Harper's face fell as if realizing what she'd said. "Shit. Vi,

I am *so* sorry. I mean, by all rights you should be the one on Prima deck and about to boink the hot French dude, but . . . crap. I'm making this worse, aren't I?"

"Yes," Bax said at the same time Vi disagreed with a strong "no."

Grabbing a rag, she cleaned a small spill on the bar top and continued polishing even after it disappeared. "It's fine. I've long since come to grips with Rose getting the fancy Magic, and could you seriously see me tied down with a Valentin type?"

Harper raised a finely plucked eyebrow. "You mean one who's hot as hell and looks like he knows how to work a tongue? Uh, yeah."

"I meant a growly, bossy alpha type . . . not to mention an *actual* Alpha." Vi shivered. "I barely made it through Ro's party without breaking into hives. I can't imagine attending things like that on a daily basis."

"Pretty clothes. Great food. Hot, animalistic shifters and other stunning Supernaturals," Harper said. "Yeah, I could see how that would be considered a drawback . . . in an alternate world, or to someone who is evidently my best friend."

Harper was teasing, but Violet loved her Norm life, free of Supernatural drama. And her as Prima? Less than ten minutes into having the title, she'd insult someone in the higher echelon of Supernatural society, probably not by accident, and cause an international incident.

But as much as she kept away from the Supernatural side of things, she hadn't stopped thinking about Lincoln Thorne, who was very much an Alpha. And a shifter. And the physical embodiment of drama. Going by how many times he'd graced the cover of magazines, the man couldn't squeeze an avocado at the grocery store without paparazzi documenting it for all to see.

They'd been opposites in every way, even as kids. He'd been the athletic to her bookwormy, the popular to her not. He'd soaked up attention like vitamin D while she'd done her damned best to stay in her own secluded bubble . . . until the jerk popped it with his damn smile and wolfy charm.

Harper's gaze shifted nervously through the room before settling on her again. "Uh . . . Vi?"

"Yeah?"

"You do remember there's not supposed to be real Magic in those Love Potions, right?"

"Huh?" She stared at her friend blankly.

Harper nodded to where Vi's hands, wrapped around the last two cocktails, crackled and sparked with a hazy mist of near purple Magic.

Vi jolted, knocking over all but one of the Love Potions. "What the magical shiitakes?"

She shook her hands as if trying to air-dry them, but the more she flicked, the larger the magical mist grew. People turned their way, curious about the commotion.

Harper kicked open the swinging gate at the end of the bar. "Bathroom! Now!"

Ignoring her boss's shout from somewhere behind her, Vi rushed into the thankfully empty women's restroom. By the time the door closed, her hair was sticking out as if she'd plugged her finger into an electrical socket.

"No, no. *No*." She braced her hands on the sink and glared into the mirror. "You are not doing this right now, Sparky. Chill the hex out."

Her Magic hovered beneath the surface of her skin and, at her firm demand, pushed higher as if saying *oh yeah we are, bewitch*.

Even her Magic had a damn attitude.

Bax slipped into the bathroom, his gaze flickering to her still glowing hands. "Of course it's purple."

Her eye twitched as she threw him a dirty look.

"Because your name's Violet . . ."

"Yeah, I got it, Bax. There's a reason I didn't laugh. You shouldn't be in here. Hell, you and Harper should be evacuating the building."

"I'm right where I should be." Slipping into Guardian Angel mode, he reached for her hands.

She yanked them away. "Are you off your rocker? There's no telling what these things will do to you. Did you not see what damage the Infinity Stones caused in *The Avengers*?"

"Then what will help you control it?"

"Do you think I would've hidden in the bathroom if I knew?" She immediately regretted her snap. "I'm sorry. I just . . . wish I knew why the hell this keeps happening."

Bax smirked. "Witch puberty?"

"At thirty-two years old?"

He shrugged. "Just a thought."

Goddess, she wanted to talk to her sisters, but this wasn't the type of thing you discussed over video chat, and with Olive still overseas and Rose either Prima training with their gran or smooching it up with her shifter fiancé, she had no choice but to deal with it alone.

Vi sighed. "You best get started with that evacuation."

"We don't need an evacuation. Let's think about this logically." Not listening to her, Bax leaned against the counter. "To make this go away, we need to figure out what brought it on. What were you thinking about when your hands turned into flashlights?"

"Harp's cocktails."

"You make those drinks on autopilot. Try again. We were talking about the party, and . . ."

Vi sighed again. "Harper mentioned Valentin and I guess I flashed back to this other Alpha I knew when I was a kid."

His ridiculously blue eyes never left her face.

"Why are you looking at me like that?" Fidgeting, she fixed her shirt, although it didn't need it. "It feels like you're spelunking your way into my soul or something. Seriously, put those things away."

"They know when someone's bullshitting me, and you, sweetheart, dropped quite the odoriferous deuce. Who was the Alpha you were thinking about, and what made you think about him?"

"Because he was at the weekend from hell."

Bax waited expectantly.

Vi growled. "There may or may not have been mild flirting, or what I first thought was flirting—but way before I realized who he was. And then there was a thwarted assassination by snowmobile, and later a dance with pretty-eye compliments and wonky Magic and—"

Clearing his throat, Bax nodded to her hands.

Sure enough, the flames brightened and sizzled with gold flecks shooting off like mini fireworks. "Hell's Spells, I'm going to end up burning down the entire building. Gage will be *really* livid then."

"You're not burning down the bar." Bax eased her shoulders into a parallel position with his. "Close your eyes, and put Mr. Alpha out of your mind. Empty it of everything and take a couple deep, slow breaths. In for two seconds. Out for four."

"This is a waste of time."

"Vi," he warned.

"Fine." She closed her eyes. "Now what?"

"Picture the last place where you'd ever lay eyes on Mr. Alpha."

The last place? She tried, but in every image she conjured in her head, Linc popped up.

Her parents' house. *Linc*. Her gym. *Linc*. Even the Kids' Community Center where she volunteered. *Linc*. Evidently no place was Lincoln-proof.

The last place she'd ever see Lincoln Thorne . . .

Her bed.

✦ ✦ ✦

Linc had woken up with a tension headache pulsing behind his eyes, and he'd done his damned best to get rid of it ever since. He'd downed water. Popped ibuprofen. Pommeled his heavy bag for nearly two hours in an attempt to work it out of his system.

All this accomplished was making him late for his first morning appointment, and it had been downhill ever since.

"Marie!" Linc shouted through his open office door to his assistant. "Where's that party invitation from the Australian Alpha? It was here one minute and now it's gone! *Marie!*"

"I heard you! Honestly, are you a wolf or a howler monkey?" She stepped into the office, her purse already draped on her shoulder. "And the invitation is in the same place you left it."

Marie Hansen was one of the only shifters—other than Adrian— who didn't hesitate to give him shit. One afternoon, after he'd fired his third assistant in two weeks, the bear shifter had shown up at the office with his lunch order, and she hadn't left since.

That was five years ago, and he'd lose the head on his shoulders if it weren't for her keeping him organized and in line.

He chuckled at the obvious annoyance on her face, and gentled his voice. "Marie, do you *know* where the invitation is at this very moment?"

"I do."

He waited, and when it was obvious she wasn't volunteering any more information . . . "And that would be where?"

"It's on my desk."

"How is that—?"

"You Frisbeed it across the room and asked me to deal with it. Well, I dealt with it, so you and your plus-one have officially told the Australian Alpha and her family you would be delighted to take part in her grandcub's first birthday celebration. It's a beach party, by the way, so dress appropriate."

The headache behind his eyes pulsated. "Of course you did."

"I think the phrase you're looking for is 'Thank you, Marie,' and you're very welcome. It is, after all, why you gave me a nice big raise."

"I didn't—"

"Now, if you don't need me for anything else, I'm heading out." She turned to leave.

"Marie?"

"Yes?" She glanced back at him.

Linc flashed her a tired smile. "Thank you. I know I've been a little difficult to deal with today."

"Really? I haven't noticed." Sarcasm weighted her words to the floor, making Lincoln laugh as she winked and left with a small wave.

Adrian strutted in a minute later. "I think Marie gets prettier every time I see her."

"That's because she keeps turning down your dinner offer."

His Second-in-Command laughed, knowing there was truth to the joke. "Lay it on me. What's put that pinched expression on your face?"

"Pick a shit-storm. Any one of them could be the cause." As expected, he'd spent the last four hours of his morning on the phone with Alpha Flores trying to reassure the panther shifter that dissolving the Elder Board wouldn't bring about a Supernatural end-of-days situation.

"How about we talk about the one Marie mentioned on her way out? Something about a party?"

"Marie RSVP'd to the birthday party for Alpha Benson's grandson . . . for me, with a plus-one."

"Ah." Adrian fought not to smirk. "The Party Down Under."

"You think this is funny? That *party*—which we both know is a Supernatural political event decorated in balloon animals, is *four days* before my birthday. Anyone I bring will automatically be scrutinized as the future Mrs. Lincoln Thorne."

"So play hooky and stay home."

"And potentially piss off the Alpha whose vote on the Elder Board I'm most worried about? Smart idea." He stuck his to-do list for the next morning—which was heavy on phone calls—on his computer before shutting it down. "Don't you have a club to be hitting up or a woman to be hitting on?"

"Both are happening later. I wanted to see if you've given any thought to my earlier suggestion."

"This is the first time I've seen you since yesterday. What suggestion?"

"The link I emailed you."

Email? His inbox was a fucking disaster, but he mentally plowed through its million and one contents. "You mean the one about the game show?"

"Reality *mating* competition," Adrian corrected. Sitting, he kicked his booted feet onto the desk. "What do you think?"

"I think it's a ridiculous scam meant to cater to Normal curiosities about shifter society. Could you seriously imagine being mated to someone who'd put themselves in that situation? It's nothing more than a sad plea for attention."

Linc grabbed his leather jacket from the wall hook and shrugged into it. Adrian hadn't moved. He lasered his attention to his best friend, who had gone way too silent for a man who loved hearing himself talk. "What did you do?"

"I may have inquired about—"

"*No,*" Linc growled.

Adrian raised his hands. "Hear me out . . ."

"I'll *see* you out." He held open his office door.

"My job as your SIC is to make sure your stubborn ass is covered on all sides. Right now, you have a gaping glory hole waiting for someone to fuck you over."

"And your solution is to throw me on some reality show and prance me around like a show pony? It's not happening."

"You're not giving me many ideas! You don't date—"

"Because I have more pressing things to do with my time."

"Your time is running out, Linc!" Adrian bellowed, his smirk now gone as he rose to his feet. "And what happens if Benson never gets on board? You're asking the Alphas to go against hundreds of years of tradition and essentially give up every Pack perk they've grown to depend on."

"I'm asking them to realize we can't build a modern society with a belief structure that's rooted in the past. Our familial lines shouldn't be the lone voice for thousands of shifters simply because of our names."

A name didn't give someone the ability to lead with the best interests of their people in mind. Cases in point: Linc's father. *Bisset.* The only interests they served were their own. It was why next up on Linc's agenda, after dismantling the Elder Board, was transforming the Alpha role from a position of birth to one of service.

Service *to* the Pack.

Packs would *vote* for who they wanted to lead them, and if that was someone other than the reigning Alphas, it meant those Alphas willingly stepped aside. Goodbye, shifter fear tactics. Hello, shifter democracy.

Adrian sighed. "Look, you know I'm with you on this. One hundred percent. But what will you do if the other Alphas don't come through? What if you can't dissolve the Elders' positions in time?"

"Maybe I'll step down and let you do the heavy lifting for a while." His lips twitched. "It's about time you worked for your title."

His best friend's face drained of color. "Fuck. Don't even joke about that, man. I'm a lover, not a fighter."

They laughed, the tension slow to fade. Linc scrubbed his palm over his face, his tired muscles craving his bed. "What do you want me to do? Besides that damn reality show."

"Look for potential mate prospects. You need to *date*."

"Date."

"Yeah, date. Wine, dine, and woo. Be yourself. No, don't do that. Be . . . nice."

Linc glowered. "I can be nice if I fucking want to be."

Adrian snorted.

Being nice wasn't Linc's issue. What concerned him was potentially hurting someone who didn't deserve to be hurt. Fourteen years ago, he'd done exactly that to Violet. By not fighting for them and standing up to his father, he'd walked away, hurting them both. If they'd been True Mates, that never would've happened.

If they *had* been True Mates, he never would've been physically *able* to walk away. His father's threats, his intimidation, even magical interference wouldn't have worked.

Nothing would've kept them apart.

Adrian meant well, and dating made logical sense, but Linc wasn't so much of a bastard that he'd risk history repeating itself.

He couldn't afford to get distracted by a real romance.

But a fake one . . .

He could do that. He just needed the right woman.

4

Kibble & Yips

At this point in her shift at the Kids' Community Center, Vi would perform indecent favors in exchange for a venti mocha Frappuccino with two extra shots of caramel sauce.

Usually she didn't mind busy days. Busy meant they'd helped a lot of kids. Activities. Recreation. Education. The center did it all, and she loved doing her part to help the community in Astoria, Queens. But after today, what she'd love more was if everyone went home breathing.

Two volunteers out sick left the center shorthanded, and those who showed up were stressed about their afternoon visit from someone on the Supernatural Council. It had to go well, because those annual visits, which their director, Isaac, jokingly called a "Puff-n-Parade," dictated what funding the center would receive next year. Of course, he hadn't bothered showing his face this morning, but that was beside the point.

Vi had already broken up three fights, one of which resulted in a little boy getting trapped in the walk-in freezer, and thwarted a duo of mean witches from slipping Goddess only knew what into the new girl's thermos. Now, less than twenty minutes later, another commotion was brewing outside her office in the gym.

This day needed to be over. *Pronto.*

Harper slipped her head through the door, a wary smile on her face. "So . . . funny story."

"I can't take any more funny, Harper." Vi dropped heavily into the chair, her clothes squishing, still wet from an earlier bathroom mishap. "I'm all funnied out. Seriously. Can't it wait until Isaac comes in?"

"You mean he's gracing us with his presence? Who's granting miracles?"

Yeah, it was pretty far-fetched. Although he was the center's only full-time paid employee, the director rarely came into the office, often stating he'd be "off-site" for meetings. Unless those meetings happened in his pj's and in the comfort of his own apartment building, Vi—and anyone else who knew Isaac Ziegler—called bullshit.

With a heavy sigh, she lifted herself from the chair. "Lead the way to the funny."

"So it's not so much funny-ha-ha as it is funny-oh-shit," Harp said as she led the way into the gym. "I already dragged the ladder from the storage room and tried reaching him myself."

In the gym, Vi came to a dead stop. "What the . . . ?"

Kids swarmed the far end of the basketball court, some watching in quiet concern while others enjoyed the sight of Timmy Elias sitting inside the ten-foot-high hoop. But no one seemed to enjoy it more than the three teenage shifters she already knew were to blame for Timmy's predicament.

The wolf, bear, and cougar shifters had taken to tormenting the young eagle whenever they thought staff wasn't watching, and because the trio were larger and scarier than most of them, volunteers included, no one usually tried stopping them.

Except for Misha Sharma.

The eight-year-old witch faced off against the much larger boys, her hands, held out in front of her, emitting a soft pink glow. Tony, the wolf shifter, attempted to peg Timmy with a basketball, and with a flick of her wrist, Misha sent the ball right back, nailing the teen in the side of the head.

"You'll regret that, witchling," Tony growled. Nearly double the little girl's height, he stepped forward as if to follow through on his threat.

Another ball whipped past her shoulder and pegged him between the legs.

"And if *you* don't leave Timmy alone, you'll be peeing through your nose, fleabag," Misha warned.

"All he has to do is shift," Cameron, the bear shifter, taunted a teary-eyed Tim. "You birds are good at flying away when the going gets tough, right? So fly, little bird! Flap those chicken wings."

"Enough is enough." Vi gently pushed her way through the crowd until she stood directly between the three teens and the little girl. "I don't need to ask what's happening here. Do I?"

Nathan, the stocky cougar shifter, grinned wide, not the least bit intimidated by her presence. He already dwarfed her in size, and the big little jerk knew it. "We're just having a bit of fun, Vi. It's all good."

"It's Miss Violet to the three of you. And it's not all good, nor do I think Timmy's having much fun. Does one of you want to tell me how he got up there in the first place?"

"Guess he had a wicked slam dunk."

The three shifters laughed as if the joke was the funniest thing they'd ever heard, taking turns giving each other high-fives.

She didn't have time for this crap. "Harper, take them into the office and call their parents to come pick them up. They're suspended from Center grounds until further notice."

Cameron snorted. "You think our parents will let you ban us? There wouldn't be a community center if it weren't for our parents."

Violet's anger, more combustible from the lack of caffeine, surged as she stepped close. She looked each shifter in the eye. They *hated* it . . . especially the ones who put stock in their alpha-ness.

"There wouldn't be a community center without kids who feel comfortable enough to step through our doors," she corrected Cam. "I don't give a bear's furry backside who your parents are or what they've contributed to the KCC. This behavior will not be tolerated here."

Tony eased in closer on her left. "Big talk for the Maxwell Dud. How do you plan on making us do anything, much less go to the office?"

Behind her, Harper sucked in a quick breath.

As if it sensed being questioned, Vi's Magic stirred in its little hidey-hole. She held it at bay—barely. These brats' parents would be pissed enough at her attempt to discipline them in their absence. She couldn't imagine how angry they'd be if she accidentally hexed them each with pigs' tails, too.

Summoning every ounce of her gran's badassery—sans Magic—Vi glared at the teen wolf. "And your attitude is pretty big for someone who eats kibble and yips. Get into the office and plant your behinds in the chairs, or I'll show you what this magicless witch can do."

She didn't blink, flinch, or breathe, half expecting the guys to push back. Instead, they followed Harper and drilled her with death glares until the office door closed behind them.

With one problem solved, she turned to the other, giving the nine-year-old in the net what she hoped was a comforting smile. "We'll get you down from there, Timmy. I promise."

He nodded, his tears slowly drying. "I couldn't shift and I—"

"It's okay. Stay put until I figure out how we're doing this."

Vi eyed the ladder. She *so* didn't want to climb, but short of growing five feet taller, there was no way she'd reach him otherwise. After directing two of the larger kids to steady the ladder, she slowly climbed toward the redheaded boy.

At the top, she flashed Timmy a grin, pointedly not looking down. "See? Easy as pie."

"My aunt says pie is too hard to make and that's why she always gets ours at the store."

Vi chuckled. "I guess it depends on the pie, but since you're a smart kiddo, this will be easy. Lift your rump out of the basket and swing your legs toward me. I'll help guide your feet to the ladder, okay?"

He worked slowly, following her directions. She didn't breathe until they were both on their way down. At the halfway point, Timmy picked up his pace.

"A little slower, Tim. Take it easy," Vi urged.

The ladder wobbled and the little boy, anxious, stepped on the rung her fingers hadn't yet left. Vi yelped. Timmy startled.

And that was all it took.

Violet's foot slipped. Too busy falling to register the loud cacophony of warning shouts, she braced for impact . . . and fell into a pair of ridiculously strong arms.

Both the arms and the man attached to them smelled really good.

Like pine and leather.

Like wolf and rebel.

Like Lincoln freakin' Thorne.

Vi pried her eyes open one at a time, and sure enough. Somehow. Some way. She was cradled in the damn shifter's arms.

Again.

"I think I would've preferred hitting the floor," she muttered.

Lincoln's mouth twitched. "Your wish is my command, princess."

He dropped her onto the cushioned mats someone had laid out beneath the basketball hoop. "Ow! Hey! What was that for?"

"I firmly believe in giving women what they want."

Glaring, she pushed to her feet. The second she was upright, Timmy wrapped his arms around her waist in a tight hug. "Thank you, Miss Violet. I'm so sorry I rushed, but I needed to get down and . . . I'm so glad you're okay."

"It's not a problem, buddy. Don't worry about it." She ruffled his mop of orange hair. "Go ahead and clean up before snack time, okay?"

He nodded and all the kids dispersed, including Misha, who took a protective position on Timmy's left.

Harper hustled out of the office and came to an abrupt stop. "Oh, um, so you already know . . ."

"Know? Know what?" Vi asked her best friend.

The succubus nodded toward Lincoln and the tall, broad-shouldered man on his left. "Officials from the Supernatural Council are here for their tour. Alpha Thorne and—"

"Adrian Collins." The dark-haired shifter held his hand out for her to shake. "Although I'm not on the Council. I'm the SIC—Second-in-Command—of the North American Pack. It's a pleasure to finally meet you, Violet Maxwell. I've heard a lot about you."

Something that sounded suspiciously like a growl rumbled from Lincoln as Vi shook Adrian's hand. "And I've heard a lot about you, but all of it came from the tabloids."

Adrian chuckled. "Eh, it was probably still true."

"Harper can give you and Lincoln a tour of the center and answer any questions you may have."

Harper volleyed with a questioning look but kept her mouth closed. "Sure. Yeah. I can do that."

"You're not joining us?" Linc almost sounded disappointed.

"Nope. You'll be in good hands. I have a few pups to muzzle."

Lincoln's look was impossible to translate. Not that she wanted to. But the more she tried ignoring it—and his heated gaze on her ass as she walked away—the more her skin hummed.

Purple wisps of Magic hovered over her fingertips.

This time, it didn't send her running to the bathroom. This

time, she lifted her chin and prepared to show three mouthy teen-agers how much a near magicless Maxwell witch could do.

✦ ✦ ✦

Muzzling pups.

Violet disappeared into the main office before Linc could ask her what she'd meant, leaving him and Adrian with Harper as their tour guide. Drool practically dripped from his friend's chin as Adrian hung on every word that came out of the petite redhead's mouth, but the succubus—if Linc's nose guessed right—didn't seem as impressed with his Second-in-Command.

Little did she know that would make the bastard try that much harder.

"Is Violet the KCC's director?" Linc asked. "I could've sworn I'd seen another name in our files."

"That would be Isaac Ziegler, but Vi oversees the place when he's not in the office."

Something in her tone made him ask, "Does he not come into the office a lot?"

Considering that the Council paid the man's salary, it was something he wanted to know.

Harper bit her lip as if trying to figure out how much she should share. "He's in the office unless he has something to handle off-site."

A perfect non-answer, which answered his question enough for him to make a mental note to have Marie dig into Isaac Ziegler's work habits. His gut told him the man was off-site a hell of a lot more than he was on it.

Harper ended up being a great tour guide, and the KCC impressed him more and more with each thing he was shown. She guided them around the building and out onto the grounds, where

Adrian attempted winning her over by stacking a few patio chairs someone had left out.

By the time they headed back indoors, kids with healthy snacks and textbooks sprawled open in front of them occupied rows of tables, everyone working together quietly.

Linc watched a teen girl walk a six- or seven-year-old through a math problem using the small mound of pretzels in front of them. "What are they up to here?"

Harper beamed wide. "It's Study Buddy Hour. We instituted it a while back to help foster relationships between the kids, and to help with their academics. It's so popular now that some neighborhood kids come here specifically for Study Buddy."

"Peer tutoring. I like it. More of the city's centers should have programs like this."

"Vi tried convincing Isaac to take it to the city council, but I don't know if he ever did."

Another thing for him to look into.

He had just opened his mouth to thank Harper for showing them around when a male shout echoed off the walls, quickly followed by another, and then a third. Linc's head snapped in the direction of the growing commotion. *The office.* "What the hell's happening in there?"

Harper cast a nervous glance toward the door where Violet had disappeared. "We called the parents of the boys who were involved with the earlier . . . incident. They're shift—uh . . . not used to being told what to do. We've tried suspending them before, but it never lasts. Their parents have pull, and Isaac always gives in to the pressure."

Adrian chuckled. "I think what Miss Jacobs is trying to say is that a few someones from the North American Pack think they and their little cubs are beyond reproach."

Harper snorted. "That's the nice way to phrase it."

"What's the real version?" Linc asked, curious.

"That those three hormonal, not-so-little brutes have been ter-rorizing the kids and the staff in this building because they know they can get away with it."

"Why don't we go ahead and make sure that changes?" He strode toward the office and, with each step, let his Alpha powers leak out a bit more. By the time he reached the door, there was no way the shifters on the other side didn't detect him coming.

"This will be fun," Adrian muttered gleefully.

Harper stepped in front of Lincoln. "I don't think you should go in there. Vi can handle it, and she won't like you getting involved."

Linc paused with his hand on the knob. "Me specifically, or any male in general?"

"Both?"

"Too bad." He stepped into the office and, as expected, five shifter heads whipped his way—eight, if he included the three teens smugly sitting to his left.

"Alpha Thorne. It's a pleasure to see you again." The man near-est him, burly and gruff but dressed in a designer suit, stretched his hand out in greeting.

Linc recognized the bear shifter right away as one from the New York clan, which had deep pockets in the city's bank industry. He pointedly ignored the man, and the rebuff hit home, slowly melt-ing any excited smiles remaining in the room.

Linc's eyes landed on the curvy witch behind the desk. "Miss Maxwell."

Violet's periwinkle eyes narrowed on him, sparking with anger. "What the hell are you doing in here?"

The shifters in the room gasped, but it didn't faze Linc. "Harper was extremely thorough with the tour, but she mistakenly skipped your office."

"It isn't *her* office," the adult cougar shifter huffed. "Isaac Ziegler runs point on the KCC and has for the last few years."

"I see." Linc slowly turned to the man. "And where is Mr. Ziegler today? And how many days has he been in the center this week?"

"I don't see how—"

"No, you're right. You don't see, and I have to admit, neither did I, but I'm now making it a point to do just that." He turned a hard glare on the three boys. Their shit-eating smirks instantly vanished, the one on the end letting out a small whimper. "From what I understand, these three cubs endangered the well-being of not only another child here at the center, but Miss Maxwell herself."

"It's not like anyone was in mortal danger. It was just a matter of boys being boys," the bear shifter scoffed.

"Boys being boys." Linc clenched his jaw. Something cracked, but he didn't give a damn.

A shit-ton of what was wrong in the world could be linked directly to that exact toxic belief system, one his father had also adhered to. As a matter of fact, Gregor Thorne had said it so damn often, it had practically become a fucking Pack motto.

Someone kicked the shit of your kid? *Boys will be boys.*

Someone taunted your daughter? *Boys will be boys.*

Boys eventually turned to men and then their actions, fueled by a childhood of getting away with shit, amplified by ten.

The bear, missing Lincoln's mood shift, nodded. "Yes. And shifter boys especially are known to be—"

"Brutish little shits?" Vi muttered. In a room full of shifters with exceptionally sharp hearing, it wouldn't have mattered if she'd whispered, but it was obvious she didn't care about being heard. In a louder voice, she continued, "Your boys have bullied other children here since the day they stepped into the building, and they do it because there won't be any repercussions."

"They are from high-standing clans." The bear shifter's chest puffed out like a damn peacock's.

"And that gives them the right to prey on people *they* deem less powerful?" Violet's voice gradually rose as she scowled at each shifter, Linc included. "This community center is supposed to be a place where kids—Norm and Supe—can come to feel safe and secure. Your boys have done the exact opposite, and frankly, I'm getting damn sick of it."

The bear shifter's face reddened. "I demand your resignation, as well as the resignation of everyone currently working here. It's obvious you're unable to handle the children or the responsibilities of a place like this."

Linc's growl brought everyone to a quick, abrupt silence. *"No one is resigning.* And even if Miss Maxwell wasn't an unpaid volunteer, the KCC's primary funds are gifted from both the Supernatural and Norm Councils. You have no say over staffing."

"I've sponsored this center's education fund since the doors first opened. I'll be damned if I don't have a say in how it's run."

"I think there's a simple fix for that. Take it back."

"Excuse me?" His Pack member blustered.

"Get a full accounting of all your KCC donations and contributions on my desk at Thorne Enterprises by end of business today, and I *might* be gracious enough to put those monies back into your hands. In the meantime, you can take your entitlement, your disrespect, and your cubs, and walk out the door. Now."

Mouths opened and closed, not used to being talked to in such a way.

"One more thing," Linc added as the first shifter parent reached the office door. "Attendance at the next Pack meeting is mandatory for your entire families. We'll be addressing how NAP shifters are expected to conduct themselves, and I expect all of you to be right in the first row."

No one had anything to say as they hustled out.

"Fuck me," Harper muttered, not quietly enough. "I don't care what you say about alpha shifters, Vi. That was fucking hot."

Adrian clapped him on the back, grinning like a fool. "That was a thing of beauty. Totally worth the aggravation we'll have to deal with later."

"Make sure Marie knows to expect their financial logs, and if they don't submit them, I want to know about it. I'll meet you out front in a few."

"Sure thing." His friend bounced his gaze from Violet to Linc. "Good luck, man. It's been nice serving under you."

Adrian chuckled as he followed Harper back into the gym, leaving Linc and Violet alone.

He couldn't read her. Sensing emotions from miles away was something a shifter excelled at, but hers were jumbled into one large, knotted mess. There was anger and relief, and something that smelled suspiciously like arousal.

Folding her arms, she rounded the desk and admonished him from a closer distance. "You doomed the entire future of the KCC in less than five minutes. Congratulations, Wolfman. That must be a record."

"I didn't doom the center."

"No? Because those shifters, while complete jerks, are pros at writing nice fat quarterly checks that fund educational field trips like our campout at Cheesequake in a few weeks. Because if you think we can do everything we do here on what the Supernatural and City Councils give us, you're smoking wolfsbane."

"You'll still get quarterly donations. You'll just be getting them from Thorne Enterprises."

"From you?"

He leaned against the edge of the desk, folding his arms over his chest. "You keep sounding surprised when I tell you things about myself. Keep it up and I'll start thinking you consider me a grade-A asshole."

Gorgeous eyes narrowing into a death glare, she hurled back, "If the wolf tail wags . . ."

"We were friends once, princess. We were more than friends." Once upon a time, she'd been his fucking lifeline.

When he'd told her that he couldn't stay under his father's barbaric rule any longer, she'd agreed to leave with him. He'd been both floored and awed at her willingness to abandon her supportive family so he could escape his toxic one.

They'd been so damn close to having a life together . . . and then the night before they'd planned to leave, Violet had broken a Pack law without even realizing it: she'd followed him home after a graduation party and witnessed one of his father's Blood Matches.

Gregor Thorne had taken an arcane ritual that had once been used to establish Pack hierarchy and turned it into a bloody sporting event, one which often led to a clear victor—and lone survivor. Two walked into the ring and only one walked—or limped—out.

No interference. No retaliations. And the only rule was *no outsiders.*

Death was the punishment if someone broke it, and Linc's father hadn't been about to make exceptions for the girl his son had fallen for, so Linc had bartered: Violet's life, for him to walk away from her. Except his father had gone one step further to ensure Lincoln never talked about that night, or their deal.

Even now, despite wanting to tell Violet every damn thing that had happened fourteen years ago, he couldn't. Moisture dried his throat like a puddle in the Sahara. A warning: *Tread lightly, or feel your tongue blow up to the size of a watermelon.*

"Friends?" Violet covered a flash of hurt with a humorless scoff. "Friends don't do what you did, Lincoln. Hell, I had childhood bullies who treated me with more respect."

"That wasn't my intent—"

"You didn't intend to leave me waiting by the river—alone—for hours?" Her look of indignation—and anger—catapulted through the room as she slowly approached, stopping a few inches shy of bumping into his feet. "Or maybe you didn't intend to tell me that

I no longer fit in your life when I showed up at your door, worried your father had found out about our plan and done something to you?"

A vise squeezed the breath from Linc's chest.

"I was willing to leave my parents, my grandmother . . . my *sisters* . . . to get you away from your bastard father, and what did you do?" Violet asked softly. "You became his fucking puppet. And then for good measure, you washed me from your life . . . which, by the way, isn't something one usually does when they feel *more* than friendship for someone."

"I didn't have much of a choice." Linc's tongue itched as it slowly swelled.

"Oh, you had a choice, and you made it. It wasn't me."

His choice had *always* revolved around her. Around protecting her . . . both from his father's threats and from Lincoln himself. But even when Gregor finally pissed off the wrong person and took a talon to the throat, it was too late. She hated him. And his father's insurance policy ensured that he could never make amends.

Violet pushed past him.

An electric current zipped down from the point of contact, straight to his fingers. It had happened that day on the ski slopes, and again when they'd danced at the party. And it woke up his inner Wolf.

Violet held the door open for him. "The center will gladly take your money, but we won't take more of your time. Thanks for dropping by. I'm sure you have a full day of meddling in other people's affairs. Don't let us keep you."

He paused at the threshold. "Just so you know, I'm not only taking over the quarterly donations. I'll be volunteering my time here, too."

Her pretty mouth slackened. "Excuse me?"

"On the tour, Harper mentioned that your current child-to-staff ratio is pretty high. I'm lowering it. Go ahead and place me and Adrian on the rotating schedule, and you can count on us for the camping weekend at Cheesequake, too."

Violet's frown deepened, her chin lifting to hold his gaze. "Why are you doing this?"

"Because as Alpha of the North American Pack, it's my duty to make an active difference in my community, and what better way to do that than leading by example?" He curled his lips into a small smile. "And maybe I'd like to get reacquainted with an old non-friend."

She stared at him as if he'd shifted into a unicorn, then, with a muttered curse, hustled into the gym, where she collected a waiting Harper and promptly disappeared.

Adrian approached with a smirk. "I know you're a pro at clearing a room, but what the hell did you say to have them practically teleporting out of here?"

"How do you feel about volunteering here a few hours a week?"

"I think I know why *I* would want to do that, but the real question is, why would *you*? See something you like, Alpha Thorne?" Adrian wiggled his eyebrows.

Linc stared at the doorway through which Violet had vanished.

Violet Maxwell intrigued him as much as she had fourteen years ago. Hell, even more. She argued. She pushed back. She dared look him in the eye and question his tactics, something no Supernatural in their right mind would feel comfortable doing.

Did he see something he liked?

Hell to the yes.

5

Put a Leash on It

Violet should've opted for the large purse instead of the small clutch her mother had insisted she bring. All the damn thing fit was her ID and a chapstick, when what she needed was an extra-large barf bag.

For years she'd avoided standing in front of the Supernatural Council, and she'd have been happy with that streak lasting a dozen years more. No such luck. The summons had shown up that morning, and any hope that it had been a Harper-instigated gag after what happened with Lincoln at the KCC went out the window with the dozen panicked texts from Christina that followed.

It wasn't as if she'd done anything wrong. If the Alpha of the North American Pack couldn't handle a little witchy snark, he needed to get a new occupation.

"Will you please stop fidgeting?" As they stood in the corridor outside the Council chambers, Christina checked her lipstick for the third time. "Maxwells don't show nerves."

"Maxwells also don't get summoned to stand before the Supernatural Council, and yet I had to navigate the C train this afternoon."

Her comment earned her a scowl. "I'm so thrilled you're taking this seriously."

Violet was about to toss her meager breakfast on her shoes. How much more serious did her mother want her to take it?

Standing in front of a panel of the world's most influential Supernaturals wasn't high on the list of things she enjoyed. They stared. They judged. They made her wish for a damn barf bag again. All except Edie.

Her gran didn't count. Although she was the Prima and the formal Council leader, she was always *Gran* first. Vi's greatest cheerleader. Her wing-woman. Her biggest protector. And *that's* what made her nervous. There'd been no call or text giving her a heads-up.

A sudden thought drained all the blood from her face.

Her *Magic*.

Did they know? Had someone seen something? Said something? She'd tried damn hard to keep that shit locked away, but sometimes it . . . oozed out.

"Violet." Her grandmother glided down the corridor, no hint of a smile on her face as she approached. "How are you doing, sweetheart?"

"I'd be better if I knew what the hell was happening."

Christina huffed. "Yes, Mother. What *is* the meaning of all this? A summons from the Council? What in Goddess's name for? It's not as though Violet has Magic to misuse."

Her mother's comment stung. "Gran? What *is* this about?"

Edie sighed. "Something I've tried staving off, but it appears my attempts have been in vain."

The more Vi heard, the more this sounded like tenth-level-of-hell bad.

Her gran gave her hand a gentle squeeze. "Whatever happens in that room, I'm on *your* side. Forever and always."

Maybe the twelfth level . . .

"Your best interest is always at the forefront of my mind."

And now it was the fourteenth . . .

"Trust that I know how to handle this."

Fuck it. We're now in hell's freakin' basement . . .

"I trust you with my life, Gran," Vi admitted truthfully. Other than her sisters, Bax, and Harper, her grandma was the only person who'd never treated her differently when her powers didn't manifest.

"Good. Then keep your spine straight, your chin high, and don't let that mouth of yours run away."

"It doesn't run. Sometimes it . . . skips."

Edie cocked a silver eyebrow.

"Saunters?" Vi corrected. "Okay. On occasion, it may speed-walk, but I can't always control it. It has a mind of its own."

"Put a leash on it, and remember, no matter what I say or do in the other room, I have a plan." The doors opened, and Edie disappeared with a small wink.

The Council room wasn't unlike most courtrooms. In the place of a judge's bench, and lifted on a small riser, sat a long, rectangular table that accommodated the five members of the Supernatural Council. Spectator chairs filled the rest of the space, and soon after Vi and her mother grabbed middle seats in the back row, there wasn't an empty one to be found.

The Council filed in, her grandmother first in line. Next to her walked the angel representative, Angel Ramón Vega; between Ramón and the demon prince, Julius Kontos, was Xavier Hastings, the spokesman for the vampire community.

Taking the last seat was Lincoln Thorne himself.

Years of not running into each other, and now the man was freakin' everywhere. As if sensing her glare, his golden brown eyes scanned the room, sliding over her once before quickly snapping back.

He hid his shock well, but it was there, and it gave her a smidge of hope. *If he'd filed a complaint against me, he wouldn't look surprised, right?*

"If everyone would please take a seat and be quiet, we will begin our day," the Prima addressed the room.

And she'd meant the *day*. Hours passed as Vi sat and listened to the Council review case after case. Magic misuse. Underage blood-drinking. Eventually, she and Christina were the only two people—besides the Council members—left in the room.

"Next up is the matter of the Maxwell Firstborn." Angel Ramón's gaze settled on her like a heavy weight. "Miss Violet Maxwell, please come to the front."

Vi nervously pushed herself to standing and forcing her feet to move, snuck a quick look toward her gran. Edie gifted her a faint nod of support as Violet stepped up to a small podium and lifted her chin.

"Violet Maxwell," the angel said formally, "as you are a descendent of the reigning Prima—and leader of this Council—I'll be the one taking the lead in your deliberation."

Well, hex me.

"Oh-kay." Vi cleared her throat, wincing at the sudden dryness.

"You are the Firstborn of the Supernatural community's only remaining Magical Triad. Is that correct?"

"I . . . guess. Technically."

"And as it states in the Supernatural Codex, all Firstborns of Magical Triads are to enter a Witch Bond. It's a law that was put into place and followed long before anyone on this Council even walked the earth . . . followed, that is, until you. Today, it's this Council's duty to ensure one is put into place posthaste."

Vi slid a glance to her grandmother's impassive face and back to the angel. "I'm sorry, sir, but I don't understand. Witch Bonds are only required of Primas, and, as I'm sure you know, that honor will go to my sister. Her Bonding to the European Alpha has already been announced."

"Actually, you're mistaken." Julius Kontos, the demon prince sitting on Lincoln's right, stared at her with cool, calculating eyes.

She would've considered him good-looking if he didn't scare the witch-dust out of her. "Supernatural law specifically dictates that it's the *Firstborn* of a Triad who shall undergo a Witch Bond. Your sister is the Secondborn."

"By two minutes."

"Whether it be two minutes, two years, or two decades. *You* are still the Firstborn witch." Xavier—the vampire—bristled, sending a rush of Magic through the room strong enough to buckle her knees. *Asshole.*

A few rows back, Christina cleared her throat, gaining the Council's attention. "Are you trying to say that despite my daughter not being blessed with magical gifts, you're still requiring that she secure a Witch Bond?"

"That is exactly what I'm saying, Mrs. Maxwell."

Vi's mouth opened and closed. She hoped the vampire developed an abscessed cavity in his right fang, but her gran's warning chimed in her head: *Put a leash on it.*

But that didn't mean she couldn't give her tongue a little exercise.

"May I address the Council directly, Madam Prima? I have something I'd like to say." Violet turned her attention to her grandmother, immediately seeing the twinkle of laughter dancing in the older witch's eyes.

"Why, thank you for asking, Miss Maxwell." Edie's lips twitched—barely. "Address away."

"The entire point of a Witch Bond is to aid in the magical control that comes with the heightened powers of a Firstborn witch. My sister is the Prima Apparent because I don't have any Magic to control."

Vi held her breath and prayed to Goddess a bolt of lightning didn't strike her for the little white lie. But for the majority of her life, she'd basically been a Norm.

"Law is law," Julius stated, sounding bored.

Vi's mother spouted, "But what Supernatural in their right mind would agree to Bond with a magicless Firstborn?"

A few Council members gaped at Christina, surprised a mother could speak so bluntly in the presence of her child. Vi wasn't. It was harsh, but true.

If she'd been a regular Firstborn—like her gran—Violet would've had a long list of suitors. Vampires. Demons. Shifters. And yeah, angels, too. Being Witch Bonded to a Firstborn had more magical perks than anyone could count, but the two most important ones?

Power and status, not to mention creating powerful little bundles of Supernatural joy.

But Violet *wasn't* a Firstborn like Edie. To every Supernatural, she'd forever and always be the Maxwell Dud. No one wanted to be bonded to a dud for eternity, or potentially have equally dud-like children and take on all the stigma that came with it.

The angel spoke over the demon, and the vampire was quick to interrupt both. Soon, everyone was trying to be heard over everyone else, with the exception of Lincoln and the Prima, both of whom were way too quiet.

"I'd like to propose a suggestion to be considered by the Council." Edie controlled the room without raising her voice so much as a decibel. "Due to the unusual circumstances Miss Maxwell has pointed out, I don't see any reason to push for an immediate Bonding. I propose a period of lenience during which a mutually beneficial Witch Bond can be arranged."

The vampire bristled. "Lenience now can lead to chaos later . . . or am I the only one who remembers what life was like prior to the Supernatural Codex? If we start doling out exemptions to laws that were put in place for a reason—what's next?"

"*Progress?*" Lincoln said, speaking for the first time, making sure to hit each Council member with the force of his stare. "The Supernatural Community has evolved since our time of warring factions and human slaughtering, and it's about time our laws evolved, too. It's up to us as members of the Council to not only keep our society in concordance with the law, but to recognize when certain laws no longer apply."

Angel Ramón pursed his lips, deep in thought. "And you think this law no longer applies to our society?"

"I think, as Miss Maxwell said herself, the point of a Witch Bond is to stabilize a Firstborn's Magic through the Bond itself. She doesn't have any Magic with which to even complete the ritual . . . not in the way it was meant to be executed."

"So you think we should grant an exemption?"

"I think we should at least be open to a discussion of it, yes."

Vi wasn't sure what the hell was happening, too busy trying to match the words coming from everyone's mouths with the reactions of the rest of the Council. Everyone talked. Everyone gave suggestions.

Finally, Ramón banged his honest-to-Goddess gavel. "It seems as though we are at an impasse. This leads me to make the only viable decision . . . one that steadfastly meets in the middle between immediate Bonding . . ." He glanced at Xavier. ". . . and the expunging of the ancient Witch Bond law." He looked briefly at Lincoln before turning his steel-blue gaze on Violet.

"Miss Violet Ann Maxwell, you are granted a three-month reprieve, after which you are expected to enter a Witch Bond—either with someone of your choosing, or someone who will be chosen for you. Any changes to your situation could—and will—alter this agreement."

Vi raised her hand. "I do have one quick question."

"Which is?"

"What happens if I *don't* enter a Witch Bond?"

All five Supernatural heads stared down from their perches.

"Then we'd be forced to place you with the other Supernaturals who openly defy the law—in prison, Miss Maxwell." Angel Ramón smacked his gavel again. "Meeting adjourned."

Violet finally unleashed her tongue when Edie approached her outside the Council room twenty minutes later. "*This* was your plan? To pimp me out as a broodmare, *but just not right now*? Am I living in an episode of *Handmaid's Tale*? Three months, Gran! It takes me longer to pick out a dress from Loft, and that's returnable!"

Edie reached for her hands. "I know the Supernaturals on the Council, and no way would they let us ignore the law once it was brought to their attention. Agreeing to a delay is the next best thing."

Maybe that's why this entire fiasco rubbed her the wrong way. "How *did* this come to their attention? The expectations of Magical Triads have been around forever, and no one saw this little loophole until now?"

"It came to the Council as an anonymous complaint, and you're not wrong. This law has been phrased the same way for hundreds of years, and until now, there's never been cause to question it."

Meaning before Violet, there'd never been a Firstborn who didn't need a Witch Bond. *Talk about the stifled, archaic thinking of our forefathers and mothers.* "That Witch Bond law needs to be strapped with C-4 and lit with a blowtorch."

Edie gave her an affectionate side hug. "Think on the positive side. We now have three months to regroup and figure out a plan. All it takes is one thing to fall into place and everything else will soon follow."

"Time and opportunity are often the best recourse for a lot of things." Lincoln's husky voice, way too sexy for Vi's own good, washed over her as he joined the party.

She re-leashed her tongue. After all, the man had suggested giving her a "Get Out of a Witch Bond Free" card.

He slowly transferred his attention from Edie to Violet. "Maybe the North American Pack can be of some assistance. We have a few social functions happening here in the city in the next few weeks, and we'd be honored to have you as our guest. You never know . . . you could find your perfect match."

He winked.

And tongue unleashed . . .

"Thanks, but no. Being paraded around a bunch of horny shifters like some walking fresh meat buffet isn't on my to-do list."

Lincoln's lips twitched . . . the bastard. "It would hardly be a buffet, Violet. I mean, you're only what? Five foot at the most? At best all you'd be is a midday snack."

Her entire body heated as if she'd stepped on a live wire. She didn't need to look down at her hands to know they were glowing purple. Her gran's fingers covered hers in a hard squeeze, but if the Prima had seen the little light show, she didn't let on. Thankfully, no one had. Vi took a deep breath and reminded herself that electrocuting the Council's shifter rep with Magic after she'd just claimed she didn't have any wouldn't put her in their good graces. Not to mention that they'd take back their three-month *reprieve* ASAP.

"Thank you for the offer, Alpha Thorne. Violet will take your invitation into consideration," Edie said, way too diplomatically.

Lincoln bowed his head. "My pleasure, Prima. Please let me know if I can be of service."

Service her Ben & Jerry's–loving ass. Everything about the wolf reeked of a hidden agenda, because after years of not running into each other, he was now everywhere. Like a bad rash.

Lincoln paid his respects to her mother, practically making Christina swoon as he placed a quick kiss on the back of her hand, then turned to Vi.

Pitching her voice low enough that only his wolfy ears would hear, she whispered, "Kiss my hand, and I will curse your lips to fall off your face, Wolfman."

His smirk grew as he slowly lifted her hands toward his lips, his eyes fastened on hers. His callus-roughened thumb brushed over her sensitive skin, the gentle touch sending a torrent of tingles straight to each one of her pleasure points.

But he didn't kiss the back of her hand like he had her mother's. Of course not.

An inch from making contact, he turned her arm and brushed his lips over the tender underside of her wrist.

Vi jolted, her Magic perking up its head as if hooked up to a car battery. *The little hussy.*

Lincoln's mouth eased into a lopsided grin. Bastard knew exactly what effect he'd had on her. "I'll be waiting for your call when you change your mind."

"You'll be waiting a long time, because you are the last person on earth I'd call for anything, much less something like this."

Vi left the infuriating Alpha with her grandmother and Christina, and refused to look over her shoulder. Not like it mattered. His gaze heated not only the back of her neck but her entire damn body—the traitorous five feet *two* inches of flesh.

A summons. A magical edict. And a cocky wolf in designer clothing.

Exactly how much worse could this day freakin' get?

✦ ✦ ✦

Council days drained Linc more than when he traveled for weeks on end, taking off from one airport and landing in another. More than when he had to Alpha at charity galas. He'd even be willing to say more than tearing down centuries-old traditions and erecting new ones.

He'd been surprised to see the Witch Bond law on the meeting's agenda, and even more floored to realize Violet had found herself caught up in it. Pushing someone into something because it was the way it had "always been done" didn't sit well with him, and like the Elder Board's edict that he take a mate by his thirty-third birthday, a Witch Bond for a magicless witch didn't make a damn bit of sense.

He wished like hell the Council had granted her an exemption instead of a mere grace period. Thinking about what she'd be forced to do at the end of those three months, his inner Wolf growled.

The human in him joined in, too.

Linc headed toward his SUV, parked alone in the alley behind the Council building. As if thinking about her had conjured her appearance, Violet's heady spring scent infiltrated his senses.

She was nearby.

His mouth reflexively slid into a smile . . . until he registered the second, very distinct fragrance of Magic.

A scream pierced the air, echoing down the alley.

Linc bolted. His Wolf surged close to the surface, pumping his legs as hard as they could go without shifting. The closer he got to the corner, the more Magic permeated in the air. By the time he turned, every hair on the back of his neck was standing up.

As quickly as he'd burst into movement, he froze, taking in the scene in front of him. "What the hell . . . ?"

Sparkling purple and gold light engulfed Violet's palms as she stood between an injured young woman and a tall, broad-shouldered man, both of whom appeared human.

Catching his movement, Vi softly nudged her chin toward the whimpering woman on the ground. *Get her out of here.*

He shot off a quick text telling Adrian to call the police, and slowly eased around a dumpster. The woman, dressed in a Maeve's Diner shirt and wearing a nametag that read "Gina," glanced up as he approached. With a finger to his lips, he instructed her to be quiet and coaxed her closer to him. The man was too focused on Violet to even notice.

Tears poured down the woman's face as she reached him. "You need to help her."

"What's going on?"

"My ex found out I emptied my things from the apartment and he just freaked and—"

"That's your ex? What's his name?"

"Johnnie. He grabbed me and I screamed, and then she came around the corner. You can't let her deal with him on her own. He's got a mean temper and he's got nothing against fighting dirty."

"I have no intention of letting her deal with him on her own. Get inside. The police are on their way."

She nodded and ran off. When Gina was safely inside the café, Linc turned to Violet and her new friend, who'd nearly backed her against the wall. Why didn't she blast him with her Magic?

And when the hell did she *get* Magic?

"I don't want trouble," Vi clarified.

"You should've thought about that before you stuck your nose someplace it didn't belong," Johnnie growled. Everything about the bastard's body language screamed "loose and unhinged." He was poised to do something stupid.

Linc edged closer, but a subtle head shake from Violet told him to stay back. Fine. She wanted to handle this on her own? That's exactly what he'd let her do . . . within reason.

He stopped far enough away to let her handle things, but not so far that he couldn't intervene if necessary.

"If my nose didn't belong here, then your fist most definitely didn't belong in your ex's face," Vi smarted back. "She left you. It sucks. Deal with it and find a roommate to split the rent."

"I don't think I like your tone."

"And I don't really care."

Johnnie advanced one small step at a time.

Linc prepped to move.

"You Supernaturals think you're free to say whatever the hell you want?" Johnnie nodded to her hands. "Making little purple sparks doesn't make you better than everyone else."

"Trust me, I know."

Gina's ex took another step, now putting him less than five feet away from Violet. "No, you don't, but maybe someone should show you firsthand."

And that was enough.

"Blast him already." Linc pushed off the wall.

Johnnie whipped around, not realizing they hadn't been alone. "Who the fuck are you?"

"Your worst nightmare, if you keep talking or take one more step closer to her."

Violet groaned. "Did you seriously say you're his worst nightmare? Who do you think you are? Batman?"

"Actually, Rambo was the first to say it, in *Rambo III*. Now blast him."

"Are you being serious right now? And no. I can't be sure it won't kill him."

"I never joke about John James Rambo. And if you don't make him take a magical nap, I'll make him take a non-magical one."

"By all means, he's yours." She stepped aside. The move shifted her one foot closer to Johnnie.

That was all the opportunity the Norm needed. Johnnie pounced, reaching a beefy hand to the knife stuffed in the waistband of his pants.

"Violet! Now!" Linc grabbed the man's knife hand a split second before he thrust it in her direction.

With a sharp squeak, Violet flung out her palms.

A million magical volts of electricity ripped through Lincoln's chest, dropping both him and Johnnie to the ground. His muscles clenched and twitched violently. *Fuck, this hurt like hell.*

"No, no, no." Violet's voice echoed, sounding far away. "Don't you dare go to sleep on me! Wake up, Wolfman, or I swear to Goddess, I'll . . . *Fuckity-fuck*. Lincoln!"

Darkness slowly claimed his vision. He couldn't speak. He could barely hear. And the last thought he mustered together before passing out was that if the witch who hated his guts was this concerned about him, he must be in really deep shit.

6

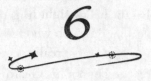

Magical Hot Spots

Vi paced the length of her six-hundred-square-foot studio apartment, her stomach churning more with each pass. Any lull in nausea ended with a quick glance at the unconscious man on her bed.

Actually, Lincoln wasn't only a man.

Or a wolf shifter.

Or the jerk she'd salivated over ever since she'd graduated from training bras.

He was Alpha of the North American Pack, a member of the Supernatural Council, and unofficial badass of the entire freaking Supernatural community . . . and she'd just shifter-napped him straight off the street.

"I think you killed him." Harper leaned over the bed where Lincoln had been lying unnervingly still for the past two hours, and held a mirror under his nose. Two agonizing heartbeats later, it fogged. "Nope. Still breathing. We're good."

Violet waved her hand toward the unconscious body, her voice cracking. "You call this *good*? I hit him with a bolt of *Magic*, Harper! A freakin' *bolt*! I didn't even think that was possible!"

She spun toward Bax, who'd been quietly holding up her bedroom wall with his back. "Can't you do something Guardian

Angel–like? Fan him with a feather plucked from your wing or sprinkle him with holy water? *Something?*"

He raised an eyebrow. "You've got to stop reading those Pre-Reveal romances. What the hell will a feather do? Besides hurt like hell and give me a bald spot?"

"Bax!"

"Sweetheart, you realize I'm not his Guardian Angel, right?"

"If you were, you did a pretty sucky job," Harper snickered.

Both Bax and Violet drilled the succubus with twin glares.

"Too soon?"

"I can't intervene," Bax said, bringing them back on topic. "I shouldn't even have helped you move him from the crime scene to bring him here."

"I couldn't very well let him stay on the ground until the police showed. Could you imagine if the rest of the Council got wind of me nearly killing one of their own? That little extra time they granted me would disappear like that." Vi snapped her fingers badly.

"But bright side . . . you and Rose could then have a double ceremony," Bax teased.

Vi grabbed the nearest object and threw it at his head. Unfortunately for Bax, it was one of her see-through bras. He plucked it off his nose and dropped it like a hot potato.

Right around the time she envisioned the Council dragging her out of her apartment in Magic-fortified handcuffs, her cell rang. Olive's smiling heart-shaped face popped up on a video call.

Vi swiped immediately. "Do they not have cell phone towers wherever the hell you are?"

"I'm in Scotland, not Neverland. This library has an unbelievable collection of ancient magical scrolls, and I have a lead on this ancient angel co—"

"You're getting busy with books, I know. I'm in crisis here, and I need your help. With *this*." Vi flipped her camera view so her sister could see Lincoln.

"Is that Lincoln 'The Jerk-Turd' Thorne?" Olive's blue eyes widened to silver dollar size. "What the fuck did you do?"

Vi aimed the camera back at herself. "Why do you immediately think *I* did something?"

"He's lying in your bed, and you're the one who's left ten messages on my voice mail in the last hour. Even if I didn't have a genius IQ, a law degree, and impeccable common sense, I'd have figured that out."

"Genius my way out of this mess, Olly, and preferably before members of his Pack come sniffing around my apartment. Literally."

"Tell me what happened . . . in as much detail as possible."

Taking a deep breath, Vi did exactly that. With Magic, the smallest, most minute detail—a feeling, a thought—could make the biggest difference. So she let it all out, and before the end of her play-by-play, her sister was struck silent.

Almost.

"You have Magic." Olive blinked.

"Olly?" Vi tried not to freak.

"Yeah?"

"Did you hear anything *else* I said?"

That seemed to snap her triplet out of her shock. "Yeah, but don't think we're not coming back to why I'm just hearing about this now. Wait . . . does Rose already know?"

"Olive!"

"Fine! Hold on." She flipped through pages of texts, humming as she scanned each page. A twelve-hour-long minute later . . . "It's what I thought."

"You found something? What? What should I do?"

"You should call Gran."

Hysterical laughter bubbled from Vi's chest, and once it started, it wouldn't stop. As tears poured down her cheeks, she mopped them up with her shirtsleeve.

Harper peered into the phone. "I think you broke her."

"Have you taken up recreational drugs while in Scotland, or flirted with Magic of Questionable Origin?" Vi asked. "Those are the only two reasons I can think of why you would say something so ridiculously outrageous."

Olive drilled her with a look from over the rim of her glasses. "Do you plan on using your Magic to reverse whatever you did?"

"Uh, no. I may not like the guy, but I don't want to kill him."

"Then Gran's your best bet."

Vi pinched the bridge of her nose, hoping it would help relieve a bit of the pressure before her head exploded. Her sister was right. The strongest witch around was her best bet to getting Lincoln back to his normal, frustratingly gorgeous self.

"Do you want me to call her?" Olive offered.

"No. I'll do it . . . the second I figure out how to say, 'Hey, Gran, can you do me a little favor? I nearly killed your coworker with the Magic I'm not supposed to have.'" She snuck a look at the clock. "I better get this done sooner rather than later. Thanks, Olly."

"Call me if you need anything, okay? I'll keep my phone right next to me . . . and I'll even take it off silent."

"How good are you at forging paperwork? If this doesn't go well, I may need a new identity."

"I made us those fake IDs when we were seventeen, didn't I? Go save your Alpha."

"He is *not* my Alpha."

Olive smirked. "Okay."

"I mean it, Olly."

"I know."

Vi hung up, and had no sooner brought up her contact list again when her doorbell buzzed.

Harper and Violet both jumped, the succubus paling. "You don't think his Pack would've tracked him this fast, do you?"

"Only one way to find out." Bax hit the intercom button. "Yeah?"

"'Yeah'? Is that how you kids answer doors and phones these days?" Edie Maxwell's voice crackled over the old speaker. "Let me up, Baxter Donovan. It's cold and wet and I'm not wearing the proper shoes for this weather."

Five minutes later, the Prima stepped into the apartment, dressed in a heavy housecoat and unicorn slippers.

"Gran . . . ?" Vi nudged her attention to the footwear.

"I told you I wasn't dressed properly." Edie shrugged out of the housecoat, revealing a silky red pajama set that thankfully covered her from head to toe. She glanced around the apartment. "Where is he?"

"Where is *who*?" Vi asked innocently. Maybe this was a bad idea.

"Sweetheart, I sensed a disturbance in the Force hours ago, and waited for you to call me—a call I'm still waiting for, mind you. I finally decided to come myself. Now, where's Lincoln?"

Violet nodded toward the privacy screen that half hid her bedroom.

"Come." Grasping Violet's hand, Edie tugged her toward the bed. "Well, he's been magically walloped nice and good, hasn't he?"

"You can fix him, right?" Vi stayed hopeful. "Please tell me you can fix him."

The older witch walked around the bed, assessing Lincoln from every vantage point. After five minutes of thoughtful noises, she held her hand inches shy of his serene face, her misty gold Magic filling the room. As quick as it came, it disappeared.

"No." Edie shook her head.

Vi startled. "No? What 'no'? You can't . . . Is he . . . ?"

Hell's Spells. She really was going to be put in handcuffs.

"It can't be me who does it," Edie clarified. "I'll walk you through every little step. It'll be fine."

It took a moment to catch her gran's meaning, and when she

did, her stomach nearly revolted. "Oh no, no, no. No way do you mean *me*. I don't fix things, Gran. I destroy. Take as evidence the very unconscious wolf shifter lying on my Target comforter."

Her grandma's hands dropped onto Violet's shoulders and gave an encouraging squeeze. "Darling, I staunchly believe you can do this."

"And I staunchly believe you've been drinking the same Kool-Aid as Olive," Vi muttered.

"What?"

Speaking louder, she added, "I appreciate the rah-rah cheer, Gran, but I've had my Magic for like, two seconds. I can't be expected to do something as important as . . . whatever needs to happen to help Lincoln."

"You, Violet Ann, are a Maxwell witch. Your Magic never would've surfaced if it didn't think you capable of handling it." The older woman nudged her side. "Enough wasting time. Jump onto the bed with the man and make sure all your magical hot spots touch all of his."

"I am not getting naked!"

Edie rolled her eyes with a little chuff. "Head, chest, and feet, sweetheart. It hardly warrants a birthday suit."

Harper swallowed her laughter, but Bax excused himself to the other side of the apartment to hide his. *Jerks.*

Gran gave her watch an impatient glance. "I'm not trying to rush you, dear, but when an Alpha's life hangs in the balance, the rest of the Pack goes on high alert."

"I want to go on record as saying that I think this is a disaster waiting to happen." Vi climbed onto the bed next to Lincoln.

Thanks to his massive bulk, she had to lie on her side in order to fit on her full-size mattress. Of all the times she'd mentally pictured sharing a bed with Lincoln Thorne, she'd never once imagined her grandmother and two best friends standing six feet away while she did.

Head. Chest. Feet.

Vi slid into the bed next to an eerily still Lincoln, put herself into the position of big spoon, and waited. "Nothing's happening. Is something supposed to be happening?"

Edie tapped a red fingernail against her chin. "Your Magic requires a little extra oomph. I think you need an additional transfer point. Go ahead and pucker those lips."

She snapped her head toward her grandmother. "I am not kissing an unconscious man who's unable to give his consent, Gran!"

Harper nodded emphatically. "She's not wrong. Even succubi need green lights to feed."

The Prima sighed heavily. "I'm not saying lay a hot one on his mouth. Put your nose on his knee or an elbow between his ribs for all I care. You just need another point of contact."

Another point of contact, all while keeping their heads, chests, and feet in close proximity. This Magic nonsense wasn't difficult to figure out at all—*insert sarcasm.*

"I'm already regretting this." Scooting closer, Vi tucked her head into the curve of Lincoln's neck and pushed her cheek against his collarbone.

Damn, he smelled good.

Her question on how to call her Magic died on her lips as she felt it stir. Closing her eyes, she envisioned it unfurling after a long nap, stretching its limbs and uncoiling its muscles. With each big unravel, it warmed her body from the inside.

She nearly hummed at the cozy sensation that wrapped around her like a magical blanket.

There you are, Sparky.

Vi lifted her head to ask her grandma what to do next, and found three sets of wide eyes and open mouths turned toward her. Instead of Edie's signature golden Magic filling the room, a misty purple haze hovered in the air.

Startled, she moved her body away from Lincoln's, and the Magic flickered.

"No, no." Edie stopped her. "You're doing great!"

"But it's not doing anything. It's just . . . relaxing here."

"Good. That's good." Edie flashed her a calm, reassuring smile. "Now, I want you to direct it where it needs to go—inside Lincoln."

"That's what got me into this mess."

"That was a knee-jerk reaction. It was protecting itself, and you. This is different. Direct your Magic where to go. Let it know what you want it to do."

All right, Sparky, you magical pain in my ass, you created this mess. Now you fix it.

As if in response to her demand, her Magic swirled around them, her hair whipping around her face as if she stood in the middle of Central Park instead of in her third-floor apartment.

Harper's mouth dropped. "Well, I'll be a succubus's sex toy. It's working."

It *was* working. Ounce by ounce, her Magic swarmed Lincoln, warming him as it had her a little bit ago. *Call the National Guard! Call the press!* It was doing something she'd meant it to do!

Now if she could only figure out how the hell she'd done it . . .

The sweet, intoxicating scent of lavender wrapped around Linc and his inner Wolf like a warm hug. He burrowed into the softness and dragged it closer, releasing a pleasure-filled sigh.

"Yeah, okay. That's enough." His delicious-smelling pillow pulled away.

He reached out to tug it back when something rapped hard against his knuckles. Linc instantly bolted to attention.

"Calm now, Alpha Thorne. You're among friends," a familiar voice soothed.

"I wouldn't say that exactly."

Linc gradually registered the unfamiliar bed . . . and Violet and the Prima standing at the end of it.

"Did you just slap me?" He directed the question to Violet, even though he already knew the answer, just as he knew she'd been the source of the incredible smell.

She shrugged. "Grab things that don't belong to you, and you'll eventually get worse than a slap on the hand."

"Yeah, she could've put you in a magical coma," Harper snorted.

A tall man he didn't recognize steered the succubus away. "Now that the crisis has been averted, let's get out of here before you start another one."

"Love you! Call me later!" Harper shouted as she and the guy walked out the door.

Linc's legs wobbled as he slowly got to his feet. "Why do I feel like I've been hit by a bullet train?"

"Because you were . . . if that train happened to be a magical bullet train," the Prima answered. "What do you remember before you passed out?"

"Not much." Slowly working his way through the fuzz, he vaguely recalled reaching his car and then thinking of Violet . . .

His gaze flew to the brunette witch and immediately did a visual inventory, looking her over for any bruises or signs she'd been hurt. "*You* have Magic."

Violet traded glances with the Prima.

The older witch cleared her throat. "I'm sure you understand that we're in a very delicate situation here, Alpha Thorne."

"You think?" He looked to Violet. "How long have you been able to do . . . *that*?"

"Honestly, that was a first for me . . . but if you're asking how long I've had Magic, the answer is not long. Rose's Bond Announcement weekend was the first time I felt so much as a twinge."

That made him feel better . . . and slightly not.

"What do you plan on doing about it?" Arms folded across her chest, Vi looked more guarded than he'd ever seen her look before.

"Are you asking me if I plan on telling the rest of the Council?"

"*Are* you?"

"I probably should. You zapped me unconscious . . . at least I'm assuming that's why I don't remember coming here."

"Technically, I zapped both you and the asshole ex, but for some reason Johnnie didn't stay out for long, and when he came to, he had no recollection of what happened immediately beforehand."

"Is that supposed to make me feel better?"

"I didn't knock you out on purpose."

"So you *almost* accidentally killed me. Not much of an improvement."

"If you hadn't tried to play Batman, you wouldn't have been in that situation in the first place. So really, you have no one to blame but yourself."

The Prima made a soft noise. "Only himself?"

"We both had a hand in it," Violet corrected before drilling him with a hard look, "but it never would've happened if you hadn't walked into that alley."

He snorted. "You're right. If I hadn't been there, Goddess only knows what that asshole would've done to you."

She rolled her striking eyes. "Is being overdramatic a wolf thing, or a Lincoln Thorne thing? Or maybe it's an Alpha thing? Newsflash, not every witch needs a wolf shifter to save their ass."

He didn't realize he'd closed the distance between them until he felt Violet's body heat warming him from less than a few inches away. "Except you do. I mean, I saved you from breaking your pretty neck on the ski slope. I saved your toes from breaking under Mayor Ruddick's two left feet. And correct me if I'm wrong, but don't you need me to be quiet about your little *magical affliction*? If I open my mouth, that three-month reprieve Ramón gave you will disappear in a flash. So that's save number three. You're really racking them up."

"Oh. My. Goddess. Do you work at being such a condescending megalomaniac or does it come naturally to you?"

"It comes pretty easily."

"No wonder you don't have a mate, *old man.*" His Wolf bristled at that, and she smirked. "Yeah, that's right. I know your bachelorhood is coming to the end of the line. You got about a month, right?"

He was both annoyed and thrilled that she remembered his birthday.

"All right, both of you to separate corners," Edie ordered sternly, her gaze bouncing between them. "Honestly, you're both in quite a predicament."

Linc grunted. "I'm just fine."

Edie's brow lifted toward her hairline. "You'd be a fool to think the Elders aren't aware that you have no intention of entering a Mate Bond with their chosen. They may be opportunistic and self-serving, but they're not stupid. They'll question why it is—with only a month until your thirty-third—that you're making *no attempts* to secure your own Bond. And that's if they don't already have suspicions about your plans with the Alphas."

Linc clenched his jaw until something popped.

Vi muttered, "Doesn't sound so *fine* to me."

Her comment earned her a hard glare from her grandmother. "You're not exactly free and clear, either, my dear. Have you given any thought to what will happen in three months? Or sooner, if you walk around the city oozing Magic everywhere you go? What's *your* plan?"

"I . . ." Violet shifted her feet awkwardly. ". . . don't know . . . yet. I'll figure something out."

"*Before* you find yourself backed into a corner from which you can't escape? You're both in a bit of a cluster. And both predicaments involve securing Bonds."

Edie Maxwell's pregnant pause put not only him on alert, but her granddaughter as well. Vi sensed, as he did, that there was something the older woman wasn't saying.

"Gran, it almost sounds like you're suggesting—"

"I'm not suggesting anything, child. I'm stating facts. What you conclude from them is your own doing."

"What are these facts, again?" Linc wanted to be clear he was hearing correctly.

"That not exhibiting an effort to find Bondmates will draw attention to yourselves that neither of you can afford. And unless I'm mistaken, there are no front-runners for either of you."

Violet busted out with a snort-laugh. "Form a Witch Bond with *him*? You're serious? Gran, he's not a front-runner, a middle-runner, or an in-last-place-runner. Hell, he's not even running. He's stationary."

Linc nodded. "Finally something we're in agreement about, princess."

"Call me 'princess' again and I won't hesitate to put you in another magical coma."

"Yeah? Think you can manage the same spell twice? Do you even remember how you did it the first time?"

Her hands sparked, and for a moment he thought he'd pushed her too far. "It would never work. We can't tolerate being in the same room for five minutes, much less spend the rest of our lives together. And let's not forget he's the freakin' Alpha of the NAP."

"And?" Edie waited for her to elaborate.

Violet swung her gaze to him and back, softly murmuring, "Even if people believe it, there's no way they won't have an issue with it."

"You're a *Maxwell*, and the Firstborn in the world's only remaining Triad."

"And I've spent half my life avoiding Supernatural life. There's bound to be haters out there who won't be thrilled with me trying to weasel my way back inside."

Adrian's suggestion about upping his dating game echoed in his head.

Linc cleared his throat. "It wouldn't have to be real. I mean, to those watching from the outside, it would be, but to us? It would just be a . . . business arrangement. A way to give us a little extra time to figure out our shit."

"*Fake*-date our way to a fake mating?" Violet's eyebrows lifted.

"It's not a half-bad idea. It's not perfect, and we'd have to lay down a lot of groundwork if we're to sell the story to the public, but it has promise."

"You cannot be serious." Violet looked horrified.

Was he?

Yeah, he was. He just wasn't certain his only motive was to give them more time . . . unless you counted the extra time he'd get with Violet. More one-on-ones meant more snarky comments. More javelin-speared glares.

And more opportunities to belly-drag his way onto her good*ish* side.

"I'm completely serious," he heard himself say. "Fake-dating me wouldn't be that horrible. I *am* Alpha of the NAP. It comes with definite perks."

"Perks like people photographing you while you pee. Stalkers scrounging through your trash cans for DNA? You're calling those perks?"

"That was only one photo, and it was in that tabloid less than a day before my people got all the copies pulled from the shelves."

"Oh, well then, yeah. Sign me up." She rolled her eyes.

"Let's give it a try," Linc surprised himself by pressing. "Like your grandmother said, neither of us has any other prospects. Our families have known each other for years. News of our union wouldn't be a complete shock."

Violet looked as if she'd swallowed rusty nails as her gaze landed on her grandmother. "You think this is our only choice?"

"I would never make a decision for you, sweetheart, but I did warn you that we'd have to take opportunities where they came. We need time to figure a way around that arcane Supernatural law, and I think a courting period is exactly the opportunity to do that."

Violet sank down onto the edge of her bed. "I need time to think about it."

"What's there to think about?" Linc asked.

"Uh, *a lot*. In case you haven't noticed, I've gone to great lengths to keep myself and my inabilities *out* of the spotlight. Dating you . . . even fake-dating . . . will put me right in center stage. I'm not like you, O Most Powerful of Alphas. I don't thrive on attention."

He understood her concern. Hell, he'd be lying if he didn't admit the human half of his brain thought this was a bad idea.

But his Wolf?

That furry bastard was all in, and practically salivating.

7

Let's Make a Deal

Evidently Vi hadn't hit her weekly max on bad ideas, because the second Harper mentioned hitting up Claws, the new club that had opened downtown two weeks earlier, the *no* that hovered on her lips magically turned into a *yes*.

Her acquiescence had surprised no one more than Harper, but her best friend had jumped on the lapse of judgment and dragged her on a daylong shopping excursion where Vi spent way too much money on things she'd never wear again unless held at gunpoint.

One such thing? Tonight's outfit.

Vi yanked on the kerchief dress and wished for a time machine so she could talk her past-self out of the purchase. The halter-style top exposed a ridiculous amount of cleavage and the back bared everything right down to the curve of her ass. Thank Goddess the hemline—in comparison—ended modestly an inch above her knees. If it hadn't, she would've given girls' night thirty minutes before feigning cramps and heading home to her comfortable sweatpants and Mr. Fancy Pants, her Maine coon.

"Tug at the dress one more time and you'll be left standing there in your bra and panties," Harper warned.

Looking babe-a-licious in a silky little red number that hugged her curves to perfection, Vi's bestie stepped forward when the line moved, already making come-hither eyes at the security guard manning the door.

Tonight, Harper put the *seduction* in succubus, so much so that Bax, who never once glanced at either of them in a sexual way, had given her an appreciative once-over when she'd stepped out of her apartment.

Vi mumbled, "Since the back of this dress hits my ass, I'd only be in my panties."

Harper's head swiveled her way. "What about the pasties we bought?"

"Technical malfunction."

"In other words, you couldn't figure out how to put them on?"

"Even watched a YouTube tutorial. Pasties aren't for a woman with my boobage. I did MacGyver myself a pretty wicked tape bra, though. Let's hope I don't sweat. The slightest bit of moisture and the girls will go swingin' free. Be on the lookout."

Bax choked on his water.

Vi clapped him on the back. "Swallow, then breathe, Bax. Swallow, then breathe."

"Stop talking about bras and pasties and swinging . . . girls . . . and I won't have an issue," he muttered.

"You may be an angel, but you're far from a saint. You've seen your fair share of ladies' underthings," Olive's voice chimed.

Vi glanced to Harper, thinking one of them had boob-dialed her sister, but a second later, Bax's gaze shifted over her shoulder, his eyes wide.

Her baby sis stood there in the flesh, sporting a sleek sapphire jumpsuit that made her blue eyes pop behind her glasses. Vi squealed.

"You're here!" She dragged Olive into a hug that nearly toppled them both. "Wait. Are you really here? You haven't found a way to clone yourself or something?"

"I haven't quite figured that spell out yet without causing some serious repercussions, so this is all me." Olive dove in to hug Harper, but notably didn't reach for Bax, despite the angel's gaze being adhered to the deep V of her cleavage.

Linking arms, Vi kept her triplet close. "Not that I'm in any way complaining, but weren't you feet deep in a dusty old book emergency?"

"I did what I had to do there and brought the rest back with me." She glanced away as she needlessly pushed her glasses higher on her nose.

Violet read her sister's body language. "Rose asked you to come back, didn't she?"

"No! I mean, she didn't ask me in those exact words. She may have insinuated that with her time being stretched between Prima prep and the Tiger King, you may need some sisterly support with your new Magic woes in the coming weeks."

"And she told you about that law the Council dug up." Olly didn't deny it. "I still don't even know what I'm going to do."

"I hate to be the bringer of bad news," Olive interjected, "but what choice do you have? I did some research on the flight home, and that snooty demon Councilman wasn't wrong. The Witch Codex doesn't say the *Prima* must form a Witch Bond. It says the *Firstborn* of the Triad."

"Guess there weren't any magicless Firstborns until I came around. Gee, I love being so damn special," Vi grumbled.

Harper stole her other arm. "First, we know you're not magicless, because you put the NAP Alpha in a magically induced nap for *hours*."

People in front of them in line stole quick glances over their shoulders.

"Eyes forward. There's nothing to see here, folks." The succubus glowered until they went back to their own conversations. "And secondly," she added, "your grandma won't feed you to the wolves. She'll figure out something."

Oh, she figured something out, and then Lincoln had run away with the idea. *Fake-date Lincoln Thorne.*

All day, Vi had gone back and forth about whether to do it. She'd barely survived dating him when they were naive teenagers, and they'd only been together for one hot second. Doing it again as seasoned adults?

Disaster waiting to happen.

"Let's make a few rules for tonight," Vi suggested. "No talk about Supernatural laws, Witch Bonds, or broody Alphas who may or may not have been recently knocked unconscious."

"You four staying out here all night?" The thick-necked demon bouncer manning the line looked at them impatiently. "Name, or get lost."

Harper put a little extra sway in her hips as they stepped up. "Harper Jacobs. I should be on the VIP list, along with special guests."

He ran his gaze over his clipboard before memorizing her ID. When he glanced back, he didn't bothering hiding his appreciation of her cleavage. "Well, *Harper.* I hope you and your friends have a great time tonight."

"We will." She flashed him a small wink. "Maybe when you get off you can see to it yourself."

"I just might do that."

Both Vi and Olive laughed as they stepped into the club.

"What?" Harper pretended to be affronted. "He's cute . . . and did you see those muscles? I bet he doesn't need the jack when he changes a tire."

"This is New York. No one needs to change a tire," Vi pointed out. "Plus, he's probably working until close."

"Your point?"

"By the time he's allowed to leave his post, you'll already be wrapped around someone equally as hot."

"Only some*one*? You think this place will be that dead? I was hoping to make it a Venus-and-David night."

This time, they all chuckled, Bax shaking his head at their antics. Harper, no doubt, was dead serious. No, she didn't have sex with anyone, being a virginal succubus and all, but as she'd said many times in the past, there was a whole long list of fun waiting to be had that didn't involve technical intercourse.

Clubs were a dime a dozen in New York, even those that boasted of having something others didn't. But Claws actually fulfilled the promise. Rustic open-flame chandeliers, spelled not to do more than flicker, hung from the rafters of the vaulted ceilings, and professional dancers standing on elaborately decorated pedestals high off the ground swayed to the loud, heart-pumping music.

Bax whistled as his gaze slid over the bar. It took up the entirety of the back wall and wrapped around the corner. "How did you score an invite to this place again?"

"I'd love to say I used my succubus charms, but in reality, I stopped this little Yorkie from running out in front of a cab and his very appreciative dog-mom happens to be the co-owner. I secured myself a spot on the list for life." Harper beamed proudly. "She *really* loves her dog."

"This place is wicked," Olive shouted in Vi's ear.

"It's definitely something," she agreed.

"No, I mean I sense something." Her sister scanned the room, searching for something Vi couldn't see.

She reached out with her own brand-new, unpredictable Magic, but it sparked and fizzled like a lame firework.

Olive pointed to the far corner. "Over there. Succubi."

Sure enough, three sex demons, their eyes hazed over in mid thrall, focused on different areas of the club. As close as she was to Harper, Vi had never seen her best friend feed, so it was difficult to say if the succubi were actively munching on the club's partygoers, or if they were responsible for the few couples currently pushing the boundaries of public decency. While neither was necessarily against the law, they definitely straddled its perimeter.

"Keep close," Vi warned.

Olive, always the most careful of the three sisters, nodded.

Bax left them to get the first round of drinks, and the girls circled the dance floor in hopes of finding the perfect spot to let loose. They found it on the second level, where it wasn't nearly as crowded.

"Let's get out there, bitches—er, witches!" Harper dragged them to an open space.

Lifting her hands and swiveling her hips, Vi forgot all about the precarious state of her taped-up boobs and lost herself to the steady thump of the music. One song turned into another, and soon she barely registered the tempo changes.

It felt good not to worry.

It felt good not to think.

It felt good not to feel.

It felt good to enjoy time with her sister and her friends and with the three succubi in the corner who were most definitely throwing a little bit of their Magic into the crowd.

✦ ✦ ✦

Owned by a shifter couple from Linc's Pack, Claws drew people from every corner of the city and the surrounding suburbs. People waited in line for hours in hopes of being let inside.

Linc didn't have those same feelings. He came when Adrian dragged him out, his Second-in-Command eating up the atmosphere by the shovelful. They'd arrived less than three minutes earlier and the bastard had already waved to no fewer than two dozen people and stopped to chat with at least half that number.

Adrian said goodbye to yet another of his many admirers and

flagged down the bartender. "Don't look at me like that, man. More people would stop to talk to you if you erased that 'fuck off' stamp that's permanently tattooed across your forehead."

"Yeah, but if I do that, people will stop and talk to me, and expect *me* to talk to *them*. It'll be a whole big talking thing," Linc joked dryly.

Adrian laughed. "You're fucking hopeless. Look around, my friend. You're surrounded by attractive women and your gaze hasn't lingered on a single one of them. Why did I bring you here tonight?"

"Beats the hell out of me. Maybe because you like to make me miserable." He accepted the beer from the bartender and took a long sip. "You know this isn't my scene."

"No, but do you know whose scene it is? Dozens of single, available women who'd be thrilled to have the attention of the NAP Alpha. Let loose. Relax. Maybe you'll find your mate on the dance floor."

Linc wasn't tempted in the least to dip into his best friend's world. His thoughts drifted to a certain mouthy witch and wondered what she was doing right then.

He hadn't told Adrian about what had happened in the alley, or about the Prima's suggestion and Violet's immediate refusal to even entertain a fake-dating ruse. Hell, she damn near laughed him out of her apartment before he'd heard the underlying reservation under all the indignation.

Thinking they couldn't pull off the guise of a soon-to-be-mated couple wasn't the sole reason for her hesitation. Just like him, she sensed the pull between them when they were in close proximity, and it probably scared the shit out of her.

It sure as hell made *him* uneasy.

She shrugged it off because it required a huge degree of trust in the other person . . . and he'd already shattered her trust once. Violet Maxwell wasn't the type to forgive and forget, and on the far-off chance that she did forgive him, no way would she forget—or let him forget—what he'd destroyed.

Another one of Adrian's fans approached him and Linc used the distraction to his advantage, silently signaling his departure, and walked the club's perimeter solo. Beautiful people occupied every inch of the converted building, but other than a cursory glance, his attention didn't stay on any of them longer than a few passing seconds, and his inner Wolf didn't give anyone even that long.

He'd made a full loop around the club, wondering if Adrian would consider his time out in public time served, when his inner beast stirred.

He stopped a few feet shy of the DJ's stage, his gaze tracking up the stairs leading to a second-floor dancing balcony. Hanging left and right next to the scenic overlook and . . . there she was.

Violet, her dress revealing a tantalizing amount of skin, was turned toward him as she swayed to the beat of the music. Her hair, swept up in a sexy updo, revealed both the gentle slope of her neck and the intricate tattoo on her shoulder. Red heels emphasized her legs, making them look damn close to a mile long.

Her friend Harper and Olive danced on either side of her. All laughing. All smiling. But it was the smile on Violet's face as she turned toward her sister that took his breath away, and damned if he wasn't a little miffed he hadn't been the one to put it there.

He got snark and bark.

A smile? No.

Not unless she laughed *at* him.

Happy Violet danced in a slow circle toward the edge of the balcony. As if she sensed she was being watched, she glanced down and her eyes caught his.

Her mouth moved in a silent curse. Linc chuckled, and the sight of his humor spurred her into movement. She said something to her friends and was gone before he blinked.

He'd barely made it up the first two steps when she barreled down, stopping on the perch above him, which put them at eye level. "What the hell are you doing here?"

He eased them off to the side of the staircase to let someone pass, staying close to her so he didn't have to scream. "Probably the same reasons as you."

"You're trying to get your mind off a certain demanding wolf shifter who also happens to be a pain your ass?" It didn't look like she was joking. "What a coinky-dink!"

"Dance with me?"

Her eyes widened and she looked a split second from fleeing. "Lincoln, I—"

"I'd like to speak with you about how we left things." And a huge part of him wanted to get her alone, and against him. Hell, she'd used his real name, and hadn't referred to him as "Alpha Thorne" or "Wolfman," so that was a good sign.

His eyes never left her face as he held out his hand. *"Please."*

"This music isn't exactly conducive to chitchat."

"Leave that to me." He took her hand, his fingers automatically entwining with hers as he steered them through the crowd and over toward the DJ.

A few requests made, he selected a secluded corner and spun her more fully into his arms, his palm settling on the bare curve of her back.

Her brow furrowed in confusion.

"Wait for it." Two seconds later, the upbeat techno tempo was replaced with one that was much slower . . . and more seductive. "There we go. Conversation-friendly."

She looked at his shirt, his chin . . . everywhere but square in the eye. "Did you finally come to the conclusion that my gran's idea is a monumentally bad one? Even the idea of *fake* dating is ridiculous."

"We'll have to agree to disagree."

That did the trick. Her eyes, stormier than a summer night sky after a wicked squall, snapped up to his. "Everyone will see right through it."

"I don't think you realize the effect you've had on me ever since I was a pup, princess." His thumb, nestled securely against the small of her back, caressed her soft skin until she shivered.

His inner Wolf damn neared purred at their physical closeness, and if he didn't know any better, he'd say her skin was heating beneath his palm. She trapped her bottom lip between her teeth and examined his face carefully while he did the same.

Contrary to Adrian's belief, Linc wasn't a monk. Women enjoyed him and he enjoyed them, but he'd never once been as enamored with someone as he'd always been with the woman in front of him. Not even close.

But he'd also never fucked up with anyone as badly as he had with Violet. "How can I convince you that we can do this?"

Her free hand tentatively settled on his upper arm. "You want the truth?"

"Always."

"It's not that I don't think *we* can't pull it off. It's that I don't think *I* can."

He winced. "Wow. Okay. I don't consider myself a vain guy, but I'm not gonna lie. That stings a bit."

She rolled her eyes. "I wasn't questioning your level of attractiveness, Wolfman. You're practically wet-dream fodder. Don't go searching for compliments."

He grinned. "Then what's the problem?"

"I don't know if I can trust you," she said, confirming his earlier suspicion.

His smirk vanished. That was worse than her not being able to fake an attraction to him. He stopped dancing but kept her in his arms.

"Violet, you've got to know—that night . . ." His throat tickled in warning. "I didn't mean to . . ."

Slowly swelling, his tongue became a mushy mass of useless muscle in his mouth.

"I know it was a long time ago," Violet took over. "And I know we were two stupid kids who didn't know anything about anything. I should let it go and move on. But I can't deny that if I agree to this fake-date arrangement, I won't be able to help thinking about the other time I counted on you and you didn't come through. If this goes *well*, I have three months to figure out what my next step is. If this *backfires*, I'll end up Witch Bonded a week from now to some sixty-five-year-old warlock whose favorite pastime is polishing his amethyst collection."

Linc strained through the swelling of his vocal cords until he finally growled in defeat. ". . . I'm sorry."

Fucking Gregor.

"I hear your concerns, and you have no idea how much I wish I could take them away." He eased them back into a slow sway, keeping her close. "But all I can say is that if you decide to do this with me, I'll do my damn best to ensure you get all the time you need to figure out your situation with the Witch Bond."

She studied him as if trying to read his sincerity, and he didn't push. He wanted her to know he was fucking serious. She wasn't the only one who didn't want to see her Witch Bonded to some asshole who didn't deserve her.

"*If* I agree to this fake-date-to-fake-mate scheme, there will be no fake platitudes," Violet demanded. "No murmuring sweet nothings in my ear, or popping up with surprise flowers at my workplace. It will be a *business* arrangement."

Linc lifted his brow. "Shouldn't I be the one warning you I don't do hearts and sonnets?"

"Why? Because you think you're too damn irresistible? Please. I have plans for my life, and even though they're a little foggy at the moment, I know they don't involve being mated to a shifter who has no desire to be mated."

"And how do you know I don't want to be mated?"

"Because you're cutting it damn close to your own deadline. Has there ever been an Alpha who pushed the Elders so far?"

"Not many." Gorgeous *and* smart. "But it's not that I don't want to be mated. It's that I won't enter a Mate Bond unless it's with my True Mate."

"Your *True* Mate? Really?"

A heavy dose of ironic humor tilted up his lips. "Do I detect a little disbelief in your tone, princess?"

"Well, yeah. You don't exactly strike me as the—"

"Romantic type?"

"I was about to say the believing-in-fairy-tales type, but that works, too."

"Your grandmother found her True Mate, didn't she? Who's to say mine won't fall into my lap?"

Violet smirked.

"Why do I get the impression you're laughing *at* me and not *with* me?"

"Because it's obvious you've never heard the story about how my grandmother ran into my grandfather. I mean that literally, by the way. She was driving without a license and nearly ran him over. She broke his leg and his collarbone and dislocated his elbow. She was *not* one of his favorite people for a long time. There was no falling in love—or laps—at first sight."

He laughed with her. "I didn't know that. How have I not heard that story?"

"Didn't you ever wonder why she doesn't drive? She hasn't gotten behind the wheel of a car since the day she plowed him down."

"I thought it had something to do with her eyesight."

"Nope. She has better vision than most twenty-year-olds." Violet's shoulders relaxed and she blew a strand of dark hair from her eyes. "You know this whole plan of hers could implode in about a million different ways, right? If the Council finds out I have

Magic, we're screwed . . . me more than you, but I can't imagine you'd be their favorite person if they think you helped me hide it."

"They won't find out, but if they do, I'm a big boy. I'll handle them. Just like I'll deal with the Elders. But Edie was right. We don't have the luxury to not give it a try."

"I can't believe I'm about to agree to this . . ."

His hand flexed around hers as he brought their dancing to a stop. "Does this mean we're doing it?"

She sighed. "Like Gran said, it's not like I have any front-runners."

A grin eased onto his face. "Do you want me to drop down on one knee and ask you formally?"

"Do. Not. Dare." She sent a panicked look around them as if he'd been serious . . . and maybe he had been. "No soft murmurs."

"My lips are sealed." He mock-zipped lips.

"No flowers."

He wrinkled his nose. "I'm allergic, anyway."

She hit him with one more rule. *"And no sex."*

Linc's gaze, which had previously dropped to her mouth, shot up to her eyes. "No sex?"

She shook her head.

"Nothing?"

"Not between the two of us. And not between us and anyone else," she clarified. "If I'm putting myself in the public eye, I refuse to become headline fodder when some paparazzi photographs you butt-ass naked in a hot tub with one of your flavors of the week."

"What you're saying is, you want both sexual and nonsexual monogamy for the duration of our agreement?"

"Is that a problem for you?" Her purple eyes twinkled in challenge. She thought he'd never agree to it.

"Deal. No sex . . . but when you want to change the no-sex-between-us rule, I'll be happy to oblige."

For the first time in his life, he'd thrown Violet Maxwell off guard, and judging by the pink flush creeping up her chest and into her cheeks, he'd also put one hell of a wicked image in her head.

Hell, he'd put it in his, too.

Violet cleared her throat. "So it looks like we're doing this. Congratulations, Wolfman. You're officially fake-dating the Not-So-Magicless Maxwell."

She'd never been magicless to him. Even when she hadn't been in possession of her Magic.

8

Murder in the First Degree

The back storeroom at Potion's Up had the same magical properties as Mary Poppins's carpetbag. There was no other way to explain why, for every crate of vanilla-flavored vodka Vi counted, three more showed up. At this rate, she'd finish inventory sometime between tomorrow evening and never.

She should've finished an hour ago, and would've, if she hadn't lost count on the tequila. And the rum. And she'd been pretty close to finishing the gin selection when thoughts about a certain broody Alpha distracted her to the point that she lost count.

Three separate times.

Had she really agreed to fake a relationship?

When she'd woken up that morning, she'd thought it had been a weirdly vivid dream brought on by too-spicy guacamole, but Lincoln had texted an hour later, and then called two hours after that. It wasn't long after the second voice mail that she'd put her cell on silent and stuffed it in her back pocket.

Ignoring him wasn't one of her finer moments, but she needed a little more time to adjust to the idea of diving back into the dating pool. Her last foray could barely be considered dipping a toe. "Dating" the Alpha of the North American Pack was the equivalent of slathering herself in chum and cannonballing into shark-filled ocean deeps.

And that was before factoring in their last go-round.

A loud stomach growl reminded her she hadn't eaten anything since the PowerBar she'd scarfed on her walk into the bar ten hours ago. She needed to do something about that before her stomach turned cannibal and digested itself.

"Violet Ann Maxwell!" Harp's voice boomed a second before the storeroom door slammed open. "Witch, where are you?"

"Same place I've been all damn night," Vi muttered as her best friend rounded the corner, dumping her purse onto one of the racks.

Harper studied her through narrowed eyes. "Start dishing."

"About . . . ?"

Her vivid green eyes narrowed even more. "I knew there was something more to 'He was just saying hello' when Mr. Sex on Legs showed up at Claws. I didn't want to call you a stinking liar before, but I am now, *you stinking liar.*"

Vi wasn't in the habit of keeping things from her friends, but the truth refused to spill from her tongue. The last thing she needed was her friends being charged as an accessory or something if the witch's brew hit the rotating ceiling fan.

"Why am I getting yelled at?" she questioned cautiously.

"Because you must have had a pretty damn interesting conversation with Mr. Sex on Legs that you didn't tell me about, and we both know withholding that kind of information is illegal in this friendship."

"What makes you think Lincoln and I had an interesting conversation?"

"Because Alpha Thorne opened the door for me when I walked in just now, and the first thing he did when he saw me was ask about you."

Vi nearly dropped a case of wine coolers. "He's here? At Potion's Up?"

"Yep."

"Lincoln Thorne."

Harp wiggled her eyebrows. "Guess he wanted to finish that *conversation* you guys had at the club."

Vi glanced down at her skinny jeans and Potion's Up tank, which, thanks to a washing machine mishap, was about two sizes too small. She tugged the hem as close to her belly button as it would reach, but one shrug of her shoulders and it rode right back up.

Hex Me.

Harper chuckled as if she knew what Vi was thinking. "Honestly, you wore less at Claws." She plucked something from Vi's hair that looked suspiciously like a spiderweb. "There. Now you look a little less Halloweentown. Go get 'em." She smacked Vi's ass and shooed her out of the storeroom.

It didn't take long to find him. Following a half dozen stares, she tracked Lincoln to a corner booth.

"What are you doing here?" she hissed the second she was within hearing distance.

He gestured to the seat across from him. "Want to join me?"

"I'm working."

He glanced at his watch. "According to Harper, you should've gotten off a few minutes ago."

Gotten off. She quickly banished the wild images flying through her head, but they didn't go far. "Well, I didn't. I have a few things to finish up and I don't know how much longer it'll be."

Lincoln sighed, obviously not believing her, and with good reason. Shit. *Can wolf shifters really smell a lie?*

"We should talk about how all of this will work. Is it really something you want to *wing*?"

"'This'?"

"Our agreement. Rules and requests. Dos and don'ts. And just so you know, one of my top expectations is that you won't ignore my calls and texts."

Violet bristled. "And just so *you* know, my top rule is that you won't be a thorny pain in my backside, because I do—and will always—have a life outside of our *agreement*."

He stood, never taking his eyes off her as he closed the distance between them. He stopped just shy of touching her, but damn . . . her body vibrated as if he'd run his hands over every inch of her skin.

"Fair enough." Linc nodded. "But that proves exactly why we should talk sooner rather than later."

"You mean now?"

He arched an eyebrow. "Now seems as good a time as any. I can wait until you're done with whatever it is you have to do."

He wouldn't give up until he got his way. "Fine, but this means you're feeding me. I'm so hungry right now I could eat dog food."

She threw him a pointed look.

His mouth twitched. "I'd love to take you to dinner."

"I need to run into the back and grab my things. I'll meet you out here?"

"Sounds good."

Ignoring his panty-melting smirk, and Harper's small chuckle as she passed the bar, Vi headed toward the back. After running her signature across the inventory sheet, she tucked the clipboard into the hanging wall mount, grabbed her satchel, and headed toward the rear exit without breaking her stride.

The crisp autumn air hit her full force before the door even slammed closed behind her. Planning on jumping on the subway two blocks up, she turned left and came to a dead stop.

Lincoln leaned casually against the hood of a Jeep, legs crossed, and damned if that smirk wasn't still on his face. "You look surprised to see me. Oh, wait, you told me to wait for you inside, didn't you? Damn. Guess it's a good thing I got confused." He rounded the passenger side and held the door open. "We should feed that stomach of yours before it registers on the Richter scale."

Annoyed he'd read her so easily, she slid into the surprisingly modest Wrangler and scanned the interior while waiting for him to climb into the driver's seat.

"I don't think I've ever heard you this quiet." He shot her a quick glance as he steered them out of the alley.

"You have a Jeep."

"Do you have something against all-terrain vehicles?"

"Not at all. Whenever I flirt with the idea of getting a car, I usually picture something like this. I just didn't take *you* as a Wrangler guy. Figured you either had a car service, or that you'd drive something more pretentious . . . like an Aston Martin Vantage."

He chuckled. "Adrian bought one of those not long ago. It's cherry red."

"Because of course he did."

"And I do occasionally use a service, but mostly for special events. Any other time, I like to be the one in control . . . and not only when it comes to modes of transportation." He winked.

If she hadn't been so busy telling her lady bits to cool off, she would've rolled her eyes at the innuendo. The temperature inside the Jeep rose ten or more degrees, causing sweat to collect between her boobs.

She looked out the window at the passing city and tried not to think about a bossy-in-the-bedroom Lincoln, but the more she tried not thinking about it, the more she did. At least until her stomach growl practically became a third person in the car.

She had just opened her mouth to tell Lincoln to pull over at the next place that boasted anything crispy, juicy, or, hell, edible, when he pulled to a stop in front of an attractive brownstone.

Vi peered out, confirming her suspicions. They were in a residential Brooklyn neighborhood. "This doesn't look like someplace with tacos."

"In a few minutes, it'll be someplace with whatever food you want." He rushed around the hood to open her door, but she was already stepping onto the curb.

She'd walked into the pages of a magazine. Tall birch trees lined the street like an army of well-kept soldiers, and garden-level doors, tucked beneath long, wrought-iron-handled steps, gave the quaint street a romantic, old-timey New York City feel.

Vi stared up at the closest brownstone, which had a crafty wreath decorating the vivid red door and a sprawling woven welcome mat.

Lincoln stood next to her, a smirk dancing on his lips as he watched her reaction. "Does it pass your inspection?"

"You live *here*?" Vi heard the doubt in her own voice.

He chuckled, leading the way up the steps as he dug in his pocket for the keys. "My name's on the lease. Figured if I own it, I may as well live in it."

"I thought the Alpha of the North American Pack would have a penthouse suite in a Central Park high-rise or something."

"And again, that would be Adrian." He pushed open the front door and stepped aside. "After you."

The nineteenth-century—or older—building was as gorgeous inside as it was charming outside. Rich cherry hardwood floors stretched throughout the parlor, and more naturally accented the arched entrance to each room. She slowly walked through the front hall, glancing at a long line of framed black and white photographic art on the wall.

"Do you want food first, or a tour? Or you can take a self-guided look around while I get dinner started," Linc suggested, as if sensing her curiosity.

"You'd let me wander around on my own? That's mighty brave of you. Aren't you afraid I'll stumble onto something I shouldn't? Like your porn collection?"

He chuckled. "I have no secrets."

If only that were the truth.

Lincoln seemed to realize where her mind had gone, because

he dropped his keys on a small foyer table and nodded toward the back of the house. His kitchen was an eclectic mix of modern comfort and old charm, from the sleek tiled backsplash to the refurbished gas stove.

"You can have your pick of salmon, chicken, or we can go spaghetti. Lady's choice." He rifled through the fridge, giving her a prime view of his denim-clad ass. When she didn't answer right away, he glanced over his shoulder, catching her mid-ogle.

She ignored his knowing smirk. "You're cooking? Are you serious?"

"I never joke about food, princess. And I'm trying not to be offended by the fact that you're so surprised I know how to operate an oven. If you don't trust my cooking, there's always takeout. The Thai place a few blocks away delivers."

"Which will get food in my stomach quicker?"

"I can have salmon ready in fifteen."

"Sold. But if I get food poisoning, I know where you live now, so . . ."

Lincoln Thorne is about to cook me dinner. Harper would have a field day with that information.

As magnificent as the view was, she felt weird standing around doing nothing. "Is there something I can do to help?"

"Can you make a salad?"

"Sure. How long do I heat it up and at what temperature?" At his worried expression, she snorted. "Yeah, I'm pretty sure I can manage a salad."

Between Lincoln's massive size, her unfamiliarity with his cabinets, and the notoriously compact space of New York City brownstones, they bumped into one another more than once as they worked to put food on the table.

It was so plainly domestic, she chuckled—until she remembered daydreaming about this exact scene fourteen years ago, moments before realizing she and Lincoln Thorne could never happen.

✦ ✦ ✦

Sometime between arriving at Linc's place and their first bite of salmon, the easy chuckles and Violet's light banter stopped. He was still trying to pinpoint what he might have said or done to change their easygoing back-and-forth when she popped the last bit of peppered fish into her mouth and let out a pleasure-filled hum.

"Liked it?" He grinned, already knowing what she'd thought of the meal thanks to her soft, appreciative noises. He'd been half hard from the moment he'd poured the first glass of wine.

"It was much better than the bowl of ramen I would've made for myself."

"Next time, when we're not on a time crunch, I'll throw some steaks on the grill that will practically melt in your mouth."

"So there'll be a next time?"

"We'll be dating. It would be more than a little odd if you're never seen coming and going from my house."

"Yeah, I guess you're right." But she didn't sound happy about it as she sat back in her chair with a defeated sigh. "You haven't changed your mind about this?"

"Why would I have changed my mind?"

"Because you came to your senses?"

He moved his chair closer, his hand reflexively reaching out across the table to take hers. He stopped at the last second, not wanting to make her bolt. "Why are you so adamant this won't work?"

"Have you met the two of us?"

"Yes, and I'm a big fan of both."

Vi snortled, rolling her eyes.

"I'm not saying it'll be easy," Linc added.

"Gee, you think?"

"I do, which is why we need ground rules and expectations in place. More than no soft murmurs, no flowers at work, and no sex . . . which I'm still open to negotiating."

Pink rose into her cheeks.

From his pocket, he tugged out the list he'd carefully constructed earlier in the day and handed it to her. "Here's a few ideas I pulled together. We can add to it or take away anything you don't think is necessary."

Violet read it and laughed. A full minute later, she was still laughing.

He folded his arms across his chest and waited for her to wipe the tears from her eyes. "I take it you have a problem with something?"

"Some*thing*? Try all of it!" She tossed his bullet-pointed suggestions on the table, and on seeing his face, finally dimmed her smile. "Oh, you mean that wasn't a joke?"

He cocked an eyebrow, waiting for her to elaborate.

"Five dates a week, starting tomorrow? Who in their right mind goes out on dates five nights a week, other than Harper? I have work, and I have the KCC, and a necessity for *sleep*. And let's not forget I'm about thirty-two years behind schedule in figuring out that pesky little thing called Magic. Five nights isn't doable for me in this lifetime, or any other."

He leaned his elbows on the table. "Then what would be?"

"One."

Lincoln barked out a laugh. "One public appearance a week is hardly enough to put us in the public eye the way we need to be. It's vital that we look like we're making a serious trek to a Bonding Ceremony."

"Fine. *Two*."

"Four."

She glowered. "I could *maybe* swing three—but not every week, and only with advance notice—and I'm not talking about an hour. At least two days. That's my final offer. And it's not like we can start tomorrow and bust out three or four dates right out of the gate."

"And why not?"

"Because we haven't laid eyes on each other in years. Don't you think it'll look a bit odd if we're suddenly inseparable?"

She had a point. "So what do you suggest?"

"You seem pretty adept at being everywhere already—maybe we manufacture a few run-ins, so when we finally do go on our first date it won't be as shocking as it would be otherwise."

There was the barely veiled insinuation that people wouldn't believe them as a couple, and he didn't like it one damn bit.

"My volunteering at the KCC would help with that. Think you can go a few minutes without growling at me?" Linc challenged, and like he'd hoped, her lips curled into a grin.

"I don't know. Think you can go longer than five minutes without pissing me off?" Vi teased.

"That seems like a pretty tall order."

"Especially for you. So this is all you wanted to hash out? Our number of weekly dates? That could've easily been talked about over the phone or text."

"There's one more thing I wanted to talk about in person to make sure we're both on the same page. *Physicality.* I'm on board with your no-sex rule. But shifters—in general—are pretty physical beings. We touch. A lot. Will you be okay with that? I don't want to do anything that will make you uncomfortable."

Her gaze flickered down to his mouth and back, making him suck down a groan.

"What kind of touching are we talking about?" Damned if her voice didn't drop a few octaves.

"Nothing that would be considered public indecency." *Unfortunately.* "But things normal couples would do. Standing close, intimate whispers, hand-holding, and, depending on the event or situation, maybe a few public PG-13 kisses. And if you're okay with that, there's also the question of if you can refrain from flinching or grimacing while it's happening. Most women enjoy being touched by the man they want to be with for the rest of their lives."

He waited for her answer with bated breath.

It definitely wouldn't be grimaces *he'd* be fighting to hold back. Once upon a time, she'd liked his touches, and while they'd never gone the full-naked-Monty as teens, they hadn't been innocent.

But that was then, and this was now. Time and circumstances had changed them both, and as much as they needed this to work, he needed her comfortable with this plan every step of the way.

She finally nodded. "I think I can handle that."

Finally satisfied they were on the same page, Linc stuck out his hand. "Then we have ourselves a deal. I think this is the start of a beautiful friendship, Violet Ann Maxwell."

She took his hand reluctantly. "Or the beginnings of murder in the first degree."

9

Whiskers & Kittens

Twelve hundred and one. That's how many hours Vi had been at the bridal boutique searching for Rose's perfect Bonding Ceremony dress, and neither their mom nor Rose appeared to be losing steam anytime soon.

With a sharp gasp, Christina threw her hands to her chest. "I think this might be the one. What do you think, Rose? Is it?"

Rose did a half spin in front of the mirror, her face scrunched up as she contemplated the corset-style bodice and supersized princess skirt. "I don't know. It's nice, but . . ."

Violet barely suppressed a soft groan. Olive, the only one close enough to hear, chuckled before burying her nose back in her book.

That made at least fifty dresses and twice as many *nice, but*s, and with no end in sight, Vi contemplated flinging herself into a mound of silk and tulle and never coming out.

Olive, ever the practical sister, closed her book and eyed the rack of dresses the boutique owner had brought into the room. "Maybe if we knew exactly what you were looking for, we could help."

"Something formal, but not ostentatious, and it can't look like everyday wear, either," Rose answered.

Their mother agreed with a serious nod. "Absolutely not. Not only is this your Bonding to the European Alpha, but you're the next Prima. Expectations need to be met."

"You could always wear a fur dress," Vi muttered. Judging by Christina's scowl, she hadn't been as quiet as she'd thought. "What? It wouldn't be real!"

"Is this a joke to you?"

"A joke? No." She nodded to the mint-green embodiment of the word "hideous" her mother called a bridesmaid dress. "All humor was sucked out of me the second I put this on my body."

"You're not being very supportive of your sister, Violet Ann. This is a big deal. The least you could do is act as though you're happy for her."

"I *am* happy . . . as long as it's what she wants."

Rose stared at her as if she had two heads, and after a quick glance to their mother, her brown eyes shifted back. "This is what I've prepared for my entire life."

"That's not remotely the same thing. Just because it's what's expected of you doesn't mean it's what you want." Steam could've poured out of their mother's ears, so Vi continued, "Can you honestly tell me you're excited about becoming the side piece to a notorious French playboy?"

Christina sucked in a quick breath. "What your sister understands that you don't is that sometimes service and responsibility comes before our own petty desires. It's expected for a man in Alpha Bisset's position to be in the papers. At his level, nothing goes beyond scrutiny."

Olive snortled. "Especially when he's naked in a hot tub with three equally naked women."

"I'm just worried about my sister's happiness. Is that a crime?" Vi demanded.

Christina glanced around the room as if making sure they were alone. "Maybe instead of needlessly worrying about your sister, you should be worried about yourself and what you plan to do when your three months is up."

"I'm not worried," she lied. "The Council gave me time to weigh my options, and that's what I'm doing."

"And how are you doing that?" Unlike their mother, Rose's question was weighted heavily in concern. "You've spent your entire life avoiding the Supernatural community. If you'd like, I can help. Make a reintroduction or something."

"Thanks for the offer, sis, but I'm covered."

For the first time that day, Rose wasn't focused on the mountain of dresses. "I don't mind. While working with Gran, I've met a lot of people all over the country and beyond. And I bet if I asked him, Valentin would include you in some of his Pack activities and—"

Vi held up a hand to stop her sister. "I love you, Ro, but that's not necessary. I'm good."

"You need to put yourself out there. Date. Shop around. You don't want to be stuck with someone who's the absolute worst for you."

It was on the tip of her tongue to ask what made Valentin *her* perfect match, but she swallowed the question. "I totally agree, but I meant that I don't need help because I'm already seeing someone."

Everyone froze. Rose. Olive. Their mother, whose look of surprise nearly made Violet laugh. Eyes widened. Mouths dropped. "You three could look a little less shocked. It's insulting."

Olive looked hurt. "You're dating someone and you didn't tell me?"

"Why didn't you bring him to the Bond Announcement?" Rose asked.

And here it goes . . .

"Because he was already there," she answered Rose first, then, turning to Olive, added, "And it's still pretty new. We're not ready to tell our families. Technically our first date isn't until this Friday, but—"

"He was at the party?" Christina asked. The wheels could practically be seen turning in her mother's head. If her mystery man had been invited, he was *someone*. "Who are you seeing?"

Vi shifted anxiously. Did she want to do this? Once the words left her mouth, there was no turning back.

"Vi," Rose interjected, eager to hear the answer herself. "Who in Goddess's name are you dating?"

"Lincoln Thorne."

Doused in silence, the only thing heard in the room was the sharp tick of a nearby clock and her own thundering heartbeat. She considered making a complete one-eighty and turning it into a joke, but Christina beat her to it, breaking out into laughter that tousled her long blond hair.

Olive frowned in disapproval at their mother, and Rose stared, a little slack-jawed. At first, Vi couldn't blame her mother's disbelief, but then it chafed her nerves.

Why the fucking hell not? Yeah, she may have been a supernatural fuckup in her formative years, but she was an awesome freakin' catch. If anything, people should be shocked she'd consider giving *Lincoln Thorne* the time of day.

Sparky—as if agreeing—heated up her inner core.

Propping her hands on her hips, she waited for Christina to finish.

Tears collected in the corners of her mother's eyes. "And you said you couldn't conjure any humor wearing that dress. Goddess, Violet, thank you. I hadn't realized how long it'd been since I laughed."

Rose reached for their mother's arm. "Mom, I don't think she's joking."

"Of course she's joking. How could she possibly be—" Christina looked Vi's way and immediately stopped. "Oh. My. *Alpha* Thorne? Alpha *Lincoln* Thorne, from the North American Pack?"

"The one and only." *Thankfully.* No way could the world—or she herself—survive more than one of him.

"Sweetheart, I know your sister's impending Bonding is stressful for you, as was finding out about that ridiculous law regarding Firstborns, but to bring an innocent man into your jokes? You're better than that. You're a Maxwell."

She was done with dress shopping and everything that went along with it. "Well, this Maxwell has been dress shopping for way too long and needs to plan for her joke of a date tomorrow night."

Thankful she still had on her jeans and tank beneath the hideous dress, she unzipped the silky abomination and let it hit the floor. She kissed Olive goodbye and pulled Rose into a hug. "If you find the dress that doesn't make you say 'nice, but . . . ,' text me a pic. But I'm warning you right now, I am not wearing that tea leaf to the ceremony."

Violet grabbed her messenger bag and headed out into the Manhattan afternoon.

Despite the fresh air, she forced her breathing to slow before she hyperventilated right there on the sidewalk. Through the shop window, her family was already in the throes of conversation, dissecting her out-of-the-blue announcement. The store owner hovered nearby, not even pretending not to eavesdrop.

It wouldn't take long for news about the Magicless Maxwell to spread through the Supernatural community like wildfire. The wolf was definitely out of the den.

✦ ✦ ✦

Sweat rolled off Linc's forehead, dripping into his eyes. It took all his willpower not to wipe the offending moisture away, but to do so would be a show of weakness, and if there was anything Lincoln Thorne was not, it was weak.

Hell, he'd grown up beneath Gregor Thorne's roof, and not once during his tenure under his father's rules had he ever felt this level of stress. Not while handling headstrong dignitaries, or fending off supernatural skirmishes.

Not even bringing shifter society into the modern age.

This was the most difficult challenge he'd ever faced, and he wasn't sure he was coming out the other side alive . . . or, at the very least, the same person.

"Run that by me one more time . . . to make sure I understand." Linc prayed he'd heard the eight-year-old wrong.

Misha stood in front of him, her little hands propped on her hips, reminding him of a much smaller version of Violet. She sighed, her frustration palpable. "You bet us that we couldn't have the tables cleaned in less than fifteen minutes. We did it in ten. It's time to pay up, Alpha Thorne."

"And what's the cost again?" He put the last of the basketballs back onto the rolling cart before giving the little witch his full attention.

He and Adrian had shown up for their volunteer shift at the KCC, and it had been nonstop since the second they stepped through the doors. How Violet managed to keep the place running so smoothly was beyond him. He was tired, sore, and covered in mystery stains he didn't know how the hell he'd gotten.

"We're having a fashion show . . . and you're our headliner," Misha repeated.

That's exactly what he'd been afraid he'd heard.

"While I accept that you won and that you're cashing in, I'm a little busy." Linc treaded carefully. "Maybe Harper can—"

"She's on snack prep in the kitchen . . . and your smiley friend said he wasn't the one who placed the bet and you're on your own."

Adrian, that rat bastard. Knowing he wasn't getting out of this, Linc reluctantly let the little witch lead the way. All he could do was hope it wasn't as bad as it sounded.

It wasn't.

It was way, way worse.

The clothes for the fashion show didn't come from Uncle Jim's closet or Great-Aunt Edna's cedar chest. Whoever donated them had either worked on a Hollywood film set or was heavily into cosplay, because there was everything from superhero capes to a golden Roman centurion breastplate. Linc reached for a plastic pirate sword and tri-cornered hat, but before his fingers even made contact, both were pulled out of his reach.

"That's mine," a five-year-old demon admonished him with a warning look. "I'm always the pirate. You have to pick something else."

Linc quickly relinquished his claim. "It's all yours, Captain Jack. What do you suggest I pick . . . in your professional opinion?"

Misha slapped a headband into his hand and immediately giggled. "Here."

It wasn't just a headband. It was a *cat-eared* headband—fuzzy black fur and all.

A few kids stopped, waiting to see what he'd do next. So he did the only thing he could.

He tucked it behind his ears and grinned. "How do I look?"

"Like you're missing something." Misha tapped her finger against her mouth. "Oh! I know!" She rummaged through the large trunk before tugging something out with an excited "*Purrfect!*"

"Is that . . ."

"A tail!" She grinned wickedly. "The strap goes around your waist to keep it in place and then you kind of . . . flick." She demonstrated, swinging her hips from side to side as if she was wearing a hula hoop. "Like a cat."

He lifted a quizzical eyebrow. "I'm not so sure that'll fit me."

"The belt's stretchy. It'll fit."

And damned if it didn't. After Linc secured his ears and tail in place, one of the other kids pushed him into sitting on a nearby box to get his "show face" on, and then it was runway time.

With music playing from someone's cell phone, they each sashayed down an aisle made of construction paper while the others stood on both sides, oohing and ahhing and snapping pictures like the media. Linc joined in the fun until it was time for him to strut his feline stuff on the catwalk.

Laughter filled the room as he executed a near perfect three-quarter turn and, on his second run, ended his pose with a low "meow."

Pretty soon, it wasn't just the kids laughing.

Harper and Adrian stood in the open doorway, his friend yanking out his phone and taking a series of photos and the succubus releasing an ear-piercing wolf whistle. But it was the third person's reaction that drew Linc's attention.

Violet's look of disbelief morphed into full-blown laughter.

He completed a third run before meeting a contemplative Misha by the makeshift stage. "What do you say, Miss Sharma? Obligation fulfilled?" Linc held out his hand.

The little witch accepted the handshake with a giggle. "You're pretty fun for an Alpha."

"That's high praise coming from you."

"I know. And yep, you're done." She bounded away with a skip and joined her friends.

Linc left his cat ears and tail on, because why the hell not, and headed toward Violet and the others.

"That needs to be worn at the next Pack meeting." Adrian ducked when Linc took a playful swing at him.

"If I find a video of that anywhere on social media, you'll get more than a demotion."

One of the kids called Harper over, and of course, where the succubus went, so did Linc's Second-in-Command. Left alone with Violet, he could still see the laughter dancing in her eyes, which had now lightened to a near silver.

She fought to contain her laughter. "You took a bet, didn't you? Let me guess—clean-up time?"

He stopped stroking his tail. "How did you . . . wait a minute. Was I played?"

"Mm. Like a violin. It's Misha's way of hazing new volunteers. She lays down a bet, does a little hocus-pocus to speed up the cleaning process, and voilà. Bet won. I should've warned you, but I'm kind of glad I didn't."

Grinning, Linc stepped closer. "You are, are you?"

"Yep. Those eyeliner whiskers bring out your eyes." She palmed his jaw, her thumb rubbing against his cheek as she peered at him through her dark lashes.

Fuck him. He momentarily forgot how to breathe. A few seconds. A minute. It was enough time for him to get light-headed before she stepped away.

His inner Wolf rumbled in displeasure at their distance, but Linc reined him in. "I thought you had the day off to do something with your sisters."

"I do. I did. Dress shopping for Rose's Bonding Ceremony."

"And how did that go?"

"My mother was there, so about as well as could be expected." She glanced around, making sure they were alone. "I may have let it slip that we have a date tomorrow night."

He waited for more. "That's it?"

"Well, yeah. It's not how we talked about it coming out in the open, but now they know and—"

"Are you having second thoughts about this?" He reached for her hand reflexively, and this time, she didn't pull away. "I know you don't like lying to them, but it won't be for forever. Think of the alternative."

Violet snorted. "*That's* not happening while there's still breath left in my body."

"Which means your family would've found out about us eventually. It's not a big deal. So we're still on for eight?"

"Eight what?"

"Our date. Eight o'clock still works for you?"

"Oh." A pink hue rose to her cheeks. "Yeah, still works."

The gym door slammed open, startling Violet and putting Linc on alert. He reflexively shifted to stand in front of her, protecting her from the unknown threat—but it wasn't an unknown.

Isaac Ziegler, red-faced and sweating, lasered his dark, beady eyes on Violet. "Do you care to explain the meaning of this?" He held up a piece of Thorne Enterprises letterhead in a fisted hand.

"I'm not exactly sure what you're referring to," Violet said honestly.

"Who the hell did you talk to, and what the hell did you say?"

"I—"

Forgetting about his cat ears, Linc cleared his throat and glared at the human. "If that's your termination letter, then I'm the one you should be directing your questions to."

Ziegler turned to look at him.

It took a few seconds for the now former director's eyes to widen in recognition. "You're the Alpha?"

"I am, and I also happen to be part of the Supernatural Council, which dictates where and how Council funds get appropriated. That includes funds for employment. That letter you're holding came directly from my office. Violet had nothing to do with it."

"I've given this center my best for the last six years."

Linc raised an eyebrow. "Your best? Really?"

"There's been some challenges, but—"

"When I pay someone's salary, I expect that person to do their job. In the last month, you've been to the KCC a grand total of four times . . . and it's questionable whether or not those were four full days, as it appears you don't keep very accurate time cards."

"I have duties that take me off—"

"Off-site? An eighteen-hole golf game at the Westchester Country Club isn't what I call a business expense. If I were a real bastard, I'd be suing you for repayment for work you've never done."

Ziegler's face bypassed red and went straight to fuchsia. "You can't do this."

"I can, and I already did."

"And who will run the center?"

"The same people who've run it while you were MIA, and who've done an incredible job of it. And if Violet and her volunteers require any further assistance, I'll be available to help."

Ziegler spun to Violet. "You vindictive bitch. This is all your doing, isn't it? You had your eyes on this job from the first day you started."

A low growl rolled from Linc's throat as he stepped between them, letting his Wolf's eyes flash through his regular golden brown. The warning did the trick. Violet's former boss clamped his mouth shut.

Adrian appeared next to the doorway, studying the scene. "Everything okay in here?"

"Escort Mr. Ziegler out of the KCC."

"You'll regret this." Ziegler turned his scowl at Violet. "And you'll *definitely* regret this. I promise you that."

"Get him the fuck out of here, Adrian."

Adrian took Ziegler's arm. "Let's go, man, because I can say with all certainty that Linc's bite is definitely worse than his bark, and right now he looks like he wants to take a nice big chunk out of you."

The asshole's protests echoed down the hall as he was escorted out of the building.

"Did you say I'll be running things here at the KCC?" Vi shot him a questioning look.

Linc wasn't sure what the right answer was here, so he went for the truth. "Yes? I know I should've discussed it with you beforehand. If it puts too much on your plate, I'll look for a full-time replacement, but in the meantime—"

"I'll do it."

"You're sure? I know you have Potion's Up and—"

"Honestly, I've done the job for the past few months, and we've gotten a few more volunteers in the last week, so it'll be doable."

"Then the job is yours for however long you want it." He couldn't stop from smiling. "See—we work. We've been in a room together for more than five minutes and we didn't come to blows."

Mouth pulling into a smirk, she playfully tugged on the end of his tail. "Guess I can't yell at a man in cat whiskers. But when you wash them off? No promises."

She turned to leave, pausing at the doorway. "Oh, and Wolfman?"

"Yeah?"

"See you at eight tomorrow." She threw him a wink that made him half hard, and disappeared from view.

Unable to fight his growing grin, Lincoln absentmindedly played with his cat tail. Yeah, it was a fake first date, but damned if he wasn't looking forward to it as if it were the real thing.

10

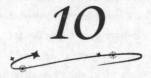

Big-Witch Panties

Vi tried canceling the date with Lincoln on six different occasions, but every time she picked up her cell, she put it back down.

Why?

Hell if she knew.

There was no way this wouldn't end in a disaster worthy of an apocalypse movie. It was *Lincoln*. Bane of her childhood existence. Teenage heartbreaker. Mr. Moody, Broody, and Way Too Drool-Worthy.

Mr. Fancy Pants rubbed against her ankles, dropping her attention to his twenty pounds of fluff. "I should cancel, right? There's leftover pad Thai in the fridge and it would be wasteful to let it spoil."

Fancy answered with a loud *meow* that sounded more like a baby cry than cat talk thanks to his growing deafness.

"I'll take that as an agreement. Let's go cancel ourselves a fake date with a wolf shifter. I'd much rather spend the night cuddled with you anyway."

Before she picked up her phone, her front door opened and a steady stream of footsteps clamored into the miniscule foyer.

"The cavalry is here!" Garment bags stacked a foot over her

short stature and a large duffel braced over one shoulder, Harper sauntered into the apartment.

"You know I gave you that key for emergencies, right?"

"Babe, this *is* an emergency. The fashion kind."

Rose strolled in next carrying two tackle boxes. "And the hair-and-makeup kind."

Olive brought up the rear, closing the door behind her. "And the moral-support kind."

Her sisters and best friend dropped their loads on her bed and studied her with a critical eye.

Vi shifted uneasily. "Why are you all looking at me like you're about to throw me on a cold metal slab and dissect me?"

Rose tapped a well-manicured fingernail on her chin. "We're not dissecting. We're triaging. What do you think, Harp? A detoxifying exfoliating mask followed by some light moisturizer?"

Gently pinching Vi's chin between her fingers, Harper tilted her head left and right. "Maybe not so light on the moisturizer. Those pores are begging for hydration. And we need to resuscitate that hair ASAP. Good thing we brought the AED supplies, because we all know the only thing she has in her bathroom is a single broad-toothed comb and a drawer full of hair ties."

"Hey! I have scrunchies, too." Vi tossed her a half-hearted glare, which went ignored.

Olive picked up the small gift bag on Vi's end table. "What's this?"

She snatched it away. "A gift . . . for Lincoln."

All three women stopped what they were doing.

Rose's eyebrows lifted toward her hairline. "You bought the man a gift? For taking you to dinner? His gift is the honor of your presence and your time."

"Hell yeah it is." Harper tried snatching the bag, but Vi tugged it away, sticking it back on the end table.

It wasn't a real gift. It was a joke, and one she'd regretted pur-chasing the second she'd brought it home. Hoping to change the direction of their attention, she asked, "So what's first?"

That was all she needed to say to get them back on track.

Harper and Rose escorted—aka *dragged*—her into the bath-room with strict orders to shower, shampoo, and depilate *every-where*. She shaved her legs and underarms, but defiantly left her lady bits alone. Lincoln Thorne wasn't getting anywhere near there anytime soon—or ever.

Not wanting the girls to be unsupervised for long, she moved quickly. It was the only speedy thing about date prep. For the next two hours, she was buffed, polished, waxed, and rewaxed. By the end of it all, she felt more like a car than a witch.

"Let's talk shoes!" Rose dove excitedly into the bag she'd dropped on Vi's bed and pulled out two identical balance-defying contrap-tions.

Vi shook her head. "You can put those death stilts back in the bag. There's no way they're touching my feet."

"But—"

"No. In the bag. Now."

"Let's just—"

"If they don't strangle my feet to death, I'll die from the fall when I trip and roll my ass down a flight of stairs." She propped her hands on her hips. "In the bag, Rose Marie. I'm not kidding."

Harper rescued the shoes, clutching them to her chest. "You've got to wear them! They're Jimmy Choos! If I had these shoes, I'd be wearing them naked in bed, while doing laundry. Hell, I'd wear them while scrubbing my freaking toilet."

"Then feel free, but I'm not. Lincoln liked me enough to ask me out while I was wearing normal people shoes, and so I think I'll make do with sensible flats."

All three of them shared different versions of "the look," but Vi wouldn't budge. Folding her arms across her chest, she mentally dared any of them to continue the argument.

"Fine." Rose relented with a sigh. "But if you're not wearing the Jimmys, you have to wear one of the dresses Harper brought. No excuses."

Her best friend's eyes lit up.

Vi snuck a wary glance at the bulging garment bag on the bed. No way did she want to fight with industrial-strength pasties again, but she trusted Harper—at least 90 percent of the time. And she didn't have much choice. She was outnumbered.

"Deal." Vi finally agreed. "But you all need to wait on the other side of the screen."

Harper snorted. "It's not like we haven't seen the goods before."

"That's the deal. Take it or leave it."

Rose frowned, not pleased. "We'll take it, but you need to show us *every* dress. No sliding it halfway on, shaking your head, and taking it off. Every. Dress. *We're* the ones with voting power."

"Whatever. If I don't get dressed soon, I'll end up wearing this damn towel."

They snickered, but listened, trudging into the living room while she got out the first dress option. It wasn't bad, closely resembling the dress she'd worn to Claws, but because Lincoln had already seen her in something similar, the fashionistas on the other side of the privacy screen vetoed it.

Six dresses later, she slid into a black cocktail dress that reminded her of the white one worn by Marilyn Monroe in the iconic vent scene. Its deep plunging neckline had a built-in bra, and a cute red belt puckered the dress at the waist before flaring into a flirty skirt that dropped to an inch above her knees.

In Harper's world, it was a parka.

In Violet's, it was practically perfect.

Turning in front of the mirror, Vi checked out her exposed back and sides. Once she was confident she didn't flash too much side boob, she paired the dress with a chunky red necklace from her jewelry box and slipped into a pair of wide-edge spool heels.

"Clock's ticking," Harp said impatiently.

Vi stepped into the living room.

One by one, her sisters' and Harper's mouths dropped.

She flattened the full skirt and mentally prepped herself for the comments. "Is it that bad? I thought I was onto something this time."

Olive slowly walked around. "You are . . . wow, Vi. You're always beautiful, but you look like a retro pinup girl."

Rose nodded her approval. "Definitely wow . . . even without the Jimmys."

Violet rolled her eyes. "I don't think Harper's the only one who would wear them while naked."

Her sister's lips twitched. "And you'd be correct in that assumption."

They all laughed, right until the knock on the door.

Vi's stomach turned into a bowling ball. "He's right on time."

With a mischievous smirk plastered on her face, Harper practically bounced to the door. "Let's hope he's punctual in all avenues of life, if you know what I mean."

Olive, a confused frown on her face, glanced to Rose. "What does she mean?"

Rose and Vi both chuckled, and Vi answered, "Sex, Olly."

"What does sex have to do with being punctual?"

"Everything," Vi, Rose, and Harper said at the same time.

The succubus opened the door, and there stood Lincoln. Wearing a dark suit with no tie, the first few buttons of his white dress shirt undone, he looked every bit fancy casual. His jacket hugged his broad shoulders perfectly, and his hair was in fashionable disarray, almost as if he'd combed his fingers through it a few times.

A nervous habit?

Goddess knew she had her own nervous tics, but she couldn't see why *he'd* be nervous about a simple dinner date.

His gaze skirted past Harper, past her sisters, and finally stopped—and froze—on Vi.

He soaked her in from head to toe, and even though he hadn't stepped into the apartment, her body shivered as if he'd stroked her with his bare hands. And it wasn't the only thing that had come alive. Her Magic, almost as if sensing her heightened response, flipped around in her lower abdomen.

"Should I be increasing the number on the reservation from two to five?" Lincoln teased with a coy smirk.

Vi eased Harper to the side. "Not necessary, because they're all heading back to their own places."

Harp nodded emphatically. "You're right. We'll be tucked snugly into our own beds, which means the one here will be open and available, and if I'm not mistaken, with very recently laundered sheets."

Vi's face heated. Sometimes she wished she could disown all of them, at least temporarily. "You ready to go? Please?"

Mr. Fancy Pants threaded through Vi's ankles with a low *meow*.

"And who do we have here? Looks like you have a big, bad protector," Linc mused.

"You got the 'big' part right." Fancy looked up at Linc, as if sizing him up, but as Linc reached out to scratch his head, Vi intercepted his hand instead. "He's not a big fan of men."

"Or anyone whose name isn't Violet," Harper muttered.

"I think it has something to do with his owners before I rescued him. I don't think they were always the kindest to him."

"Then I'm glad they don't have him anymore."

Keeping hold of her hand, he reached his other toward Fancy to let him sniff. The fluffball's nose twitched and wiggled, and with one final glance up at Lincoln, he wholeheartedly threw his body weight against the outstretched hand.

"Well, I'll be a horny succubus. It took that furbeast a full year to let me pet him," Harper grumbled behind Vi's shoulder. "Traitor."

Lincoln gave Fancy one last pet before standing, his hand still holding Violet's. "You ready to go? Have everything you need?"

A small purse was shoved into her free hand courtesy of Rose, and a second later, Olive did the same with Lincoln's gift-wrapped surprise. "Looks like I'm all set."

Harper waved as Vi and Lincoln headed toward the elevator. "You kids have a good time! Don't do anything I wouldn't do! Actually, on second thought . . . go bananas."

Vi chuckled as she and Linc headed out to start their fake first date.

There was nothing her best friend wouldn't do.

✦ ✦ ✦

He couldn't take his eyes off her. At first, because her beauty damn near took his breath away, and then in the car, because she'd gotten too quiet and he'd needed to make sure she hadn't bailed at a stoplight.

He'd been shocked she hadn't called him to cancel, but he'd also been relieved. He told himself it was because the sooner their relationship was out in the open, the less he had to worry about the Elders lying in wait.

That was a lie. If he saw this date only as an opportunity to put them in the public eye, he wouldn't be struggling to find things to say. And he sure as hell wouldn't be worried about how stupid he'd sound saying them.

Or worse, how boring.

Pack and business—they monopolized 100 percent of his life. He didn't know how to do much else, and while this date was technically linked to his plan to better his Pack, his nerves told him it felt like a hell of a lot more.

Thirty minutes later, they navigated their way through the sea of tables at Le Petit, Linc's hand splayed on the bare skin of Vi's lower back as they followed the maître d'. The French restaurant was where people came to be noticed, and it worked.

People looked their way as they passed, a few leaning over to whisper to their tablemates.

Violet's spine stiffened, and the sweet lavender scent he knew was her underlying Magic invaded his senses. He slid his arm more securely around her waist, holding her close. "You okay?"

Her purple gaze met his as she rescued a stray lock of hair from her eyelashes. "There's a reason I signed up to be part of the stage crew for every high school musical. I don't like the spotlight."

She joked, but he wasn't fooled. She was nervous.

"And here I thought you didn't want to play opposite me as my love interest—because, if you remember, I was nearly always the leading man." He flashed what he hoped was a disarming smile.

The maître d' stopped at a private corner table. "Will this do, Alpha Thorne?"

"This is great, Pierre. Thank you." Linc pulled out Vi's chair, but before she could sit, someone called his name.

From across the restaurant, an older couple headed their way. "Fuck me sideways."

Vi snorted. "Good friends of yours, I presume?"

"Of my father's. Frank and Idina Trent." His strained smile said the rest as they approached.

"I thought that was you, son," Frank boomed loudly. "I'm sorry . . . *Alpha Thorne*. Still not quite used to the little boy who used to trail around your father being the Big Man himself."

Hide from him is more accurate.

Lincoln smiled politely. "Frank. Idina. It's been a while."

Frank had the nerve to chuckle. "Things have been rather busy. That's why we're in the city . . . to mix a little business with a little more pleasure."

"You'll be in town for a while, then?"

"We are. We're renting a condo uptown for a month or two."

"Good. You'll be here for the mandatory Pack meeting in a few weeks."

Frank's smile tensed. "Yeah, I heard about that from a bear friend of mine, but I can't be sure I'll be available. Business, you know."

"I'm sure you'll figure something out." Linc's Alpha powers skittered over his skin and into the air. He didn't use them often, much preferring to reason with his members, but there was no reasoning with his father's friends. When Linc had first banned Blood Matches, the Trents had been the loudest voices in opposition, and they still were.

Idina was the first to lower her eyes. Frank took a little longer to submit—but he did. "Yes, Alpha. We'll be there."

Violet watched everything play out, shifting at his side.

Her movement caught Idina's attention. "You look familiar."

"This is Violet Maxwell. Violet, Frank and Idina are members of the North American Pack—as you've probably already deduced by our conversation."

Violet smiled politely. "It's nice to meet you."

"Maxwell. Why does that name sound familiar?" Idina's mouth dropped in recognition a moment later. "You're the Magicless Maxwell! Am I right? I recognize you now. It just took me a while. You're the one who shunned Supernatural society. Or did they exile you because you didn't have any talent? I think I heard once that your family banished you."

"I can assure you that I haven't been shunned, exiled, or banished . . . by Supernatural society or my family," Violet answered tightly.

Idina did a piss-poor job of hiding her disappointment. "That's a blessing for you, isn't it? Back in the day, anyone unable to fulfill their fated potential was swiftly handled. It's how things were done."

"Then I guess it's a good thing we're no longer *back in the day*."

Idina bristled, as did her mate. Frank shot Linc an expectant look, waiting for him to reprimand Violet for her tone, but he did the exact opposite. Shifting closer to her, he settled his hand on her lower back in a show of support and let a smirk curl on his lips.

Frank huffed. "I don't know who you think you are, young lady, but—"

"Oh, I'm Violet Maxwell. You know, the Magicless Maxwell, as your wife so rudely pointed out. And while I've stepped aside as the Prima Apparent, I'm still very much part of my family . . . which includes my grandmother. The Prima. You may know her as the woman who's made great strides in dismantling some of those archaic belief structures from the past that you speak of."

Frank took a daring step forward. "Now, wait a damn minute—"

Linc's smirk faded immediately as he blocked the older shifter's advance. This time, the growl rolling from his chest wasn't so quiet . . . and it didn't come from his inner beast, but from *him*.

"*You* wait a damn minute, Frank," he warned, his voice hard.

"You're letting someone like her speak to an upstanding member of the NAP this way? This is outrageous!" Frank's eyes bulged.

"What's outrageous is your behavior, and I'm not sure how you can consider yourself an upstanding member when you haven't shown your face at any of the last six Pack meetings," Linc said, keeping his voice low. "And yes, I will allow Miss Maxwell to say her piece, because as you well know, my feelings on Supernatural society as a whole align quite well with hers."

Idina clutched her pearls. "Your father's turning in his grave right now at what you've made of the Pack."

"Honestly, Idina, I hope he is."

The older woman gasped, and Frank looked seconds away from passing out.

"Now, if you'll be so kind as to leave, I'd like to salvage the remainder of the night I have planned with the beautiful woman at my side."

Red-faced and fuming, the couple turned and hustled away, muttering to one another in hushed tones as they left the building. Linc mentally counted to five before turning toward Violet, not sure what he'd find.

Instead of the pissed expression he'd expected, she studied him as if he were something under a microscope she was trying to figure out.

"Do I have something on my face?" He'd meant the joke to lighten the mood, but she didn't laugh.

"Did you seriously mean that?" she asked.

"I meant everything I said, but which 'that' are you referring to specifically?"

"All of it."

"Yes." Linc held her chair for her before taking his own seat. He'd no sooner sat when their waiter came over to collect their drink orders. When they were alone again, he continued. "I think that while some traditions are important, it's up to us as a society to choose which ones belong and which ones should see their end—like the Witch Bond. Just because something is the way it's always been done doesn't make it right. Our history—both Norm and Supernatural—shows us time and time again that our ancestors hardly ever got shit right, and not in the way they should have."

"And the part about your father?"

Linc stiffened at the mention of the bastard who'd tried raising him in his own likeness.

Violet's cheeks flushed. "Never mind. It's none of my business. Forget I said anything. We're not actually here to get to know each other again."

"I could never forget anything that comes out of your mouth." And he—surprisingly—didn't *want* to forget what she asked. "I meant what I said about Gregor, too. He was both a two-legged monster and a four-legged one."

Violet's eyes shifted to her lap and back to him. "You didn't tell me the worst of it—about him."

It hadn't been a question. When Linc and Violet had gotten close their senior year, he'd admitted what lay behind his father's public mask. He hadn't told her all of it. If he had, she never would've been able to close her eyes in sleep again.

Linc held his breath, thinking for a moment that she was about to bring up the night she'd witnessed the Blood Match.

"No," he finally admitted. "It's not something I wanted you to be part of. It's not something I want my Pack to be part of anymore, which is why I'm fighting so hard to dissolve the Elder Board. They're the last remnants of my father's time. If I snuff out their power with the Alpha vote, we'll be that much closer to making sure people like my father can't control anyone again."

She looked like she wanted to say more, and hell, so did he. But if they stayed on this topic of conversation much longer, there'd be no recovering what was left of their first official date.

He nudged his chin to the small bag he'd seen her carry inside. "I gotta admit, I'm curious about what's deserving of so much tissue paper."

Violet cocked a dark eyebrow. "That was quite the segue, Wolfman."

Grinning, he shrugged. "I try."

A pink hue rose up on her cheeks as she handed over the bag. "Like Gran always says, wear it well."

"Wear, huh? Did you get me . . ." He plunged his big hand into the paper. ". . . *cat ears*?" He blinked twice as he registered the decorative headband, complete with black fur and sequins, and burst out laughing.

Violet failed to suppress her chuckle. "The kids wanted to give you a little something."

"Have they picked out their next target?"

Vi nodded, barely withholding a grin. "Misha's determined to get Adrian to wear a unicorn horn before the end of next week."

Linc laughed again, the gesture feeling foreign. "If there's anyone who could pull that off, it's that little witch. She could take over the world if she chose."

"Pretty sure one day she will."

They talked through appetizers and entrées, and continued their back-and-forth straight through to dessert. Humorous jibes and banter replaced biting retorts. By the time dinner was done two hours later, Linc had laughed more than he had in years, his good mood only dimming when they stepped out of the restaurant and straight into the bright flashes of the paparazzi.

News traveled fast.

Photographers snapped pictures from left and right, a few managing to get too up-close-and-personal. Keeping his arm firmly tucked around Violet's waist, Linc guided her through the horde to where the valet waited with his car.

"Alpha Thorne!" A reporter from *Supernatural Times* shoved his recorder an inch from Violet's face. "When did you start dating a Maxwell witch?"

This question sent up a flurry of others.

"What would your Pack think of their Alpha wooing the Magicless Maxwell?"

"Do you two plan on forming a Mate Bond?"

"Is she your True Mate?"

Lincoln ignored them all, gently easing Violet into the passenger seat before pushing his way through the aggressive crowd to get to the driver's side. The second he slid into his seat, he revved the engine and pulled away, sending photographers scurrying in all directions.

Paparazzi was something he dealt with on a daily basis. He was used to it, but Violet's hands, clenched tightly in her lap, told him she wasn't.

He shot her a concerned look. "You okay over there?"

It took a few thunderous heartbeats before she nodded.

"Can you say something so I know you're not lying?"

"Does that happen often?" Her voice was barely more than a whisper. She cleared her throat before continuing. "I know I teased about you not picking out an avocado without being photographed, but I was joking."

"It happens enough."

As Linc navigated the streets back to her apartment, he snuck her more than one concerned glance. By the time he pulled up in front of her building, she hadn't made a single wolf joke. It was eerie as hell.

"I'm sorry," he apologized.

She turned her purple gaze his way. "For what?"

Linc scrubbed a hand over his face. "Frank and Idina. The photographers. All of it. Contrary to what you may think, I'm not completely obtuse. You shied away from this life for a reason, and here I am making you step right back into it."

"I shied away from it because I thought I'd be able to fly under the radar and live my life the way I wanted it. Guess what? It didn't work. And you're not *making* me do it. I could've said no. I'm getting as much out of this as you are."

He opened his mouth to apologize again, but she clamped her hand over his lips.

"I may not like dealing with all the Franks and Idinas of the world, or the greedy photographers, but a small part of why this is creating such a commotion is because I chose to lie low. I'm done lying with my belly on the ground."

Linc gently removed her hand from his mouth, and chuckled. "Was that a dog reference?"

"Maybe." Her mouth twitched into a delectable smirk. "But something you said tonight reminded me that I'm not the type to sit back and hope things will magically work out for the better. If I don't want to be pushed into a Witch Bond, I have to prove I don't need one."

He grinned. "That almost sounds suspiciously like a plan, Miss Maxwell."

"It's the start of one. It's time to be a Maxwell and pull up my big-witch panties."

Fucking A. Hearing her mention her panties sent his brain to places it had no business traveling.

Not without some degree of difficulty, he tore his mind away from the mental image of her underwear and nodded. "Point made."

This time, she didn't protest when he insisted on seeing her to her apartment door.

Her keys jingled in her hand. "Well, Alpha Thorne. Thank you so much for the fake date. I had a good time."

"Like handing pretentious shifters their asses? Or was it the untouched escargot that did it for you?"

She wrinkled her nose in disgust. "I'm more of a food truck kind of girl compared to cultured snails—but the bread was freakin' delicious. And yeah, handing pretentious shifters their asses was pretty fun, too."

"Noted for next time."

His attention dropped to the sight of her bottom lip trapped between her teeth, and damned if he didn't want to free it with his own lips and see if it tasted as good as it looked. Her gaze flickered to his mouth and back, and that did it for him.

As if magnetized, his body leaned closer, Violet resting her hand on his arm as she met him halfway. The softness of her lips was practically on his when a neighbor's door opened and closed, reminding them that until that very moment, they'd been alone and a mere lip-pucker away from kissing.

They both froze.

Violet swallowed audibly, her voice breathless. "I should go inside."

He nodded, and forced himself back. "No snails next time. Promise. I'll talk to you soon."

"Good night."

Linc tucked his hands in his pockets as she stepped into her apartment and closed the door behind her.

"Aren't you leaving now?" Her voice sounded muffled.

"Once you flip the locks."

"Are you kidding me?" Her temper flared through the few inches of wood, bringing the distinct lavender scent of her Magic.

He waited pointedly.

Releasing a heavy sigh, she flipped the lock into place. "There. I'm safe and secure. You can leave now, *Wolfman.*"

With a grin on his face, Linc damn near skipped back to the car, and it wasn't because of the restaurant, or that he'd finally taken Adrian's advice and lightened up. It had everything to do with the company.

And he hoped that with their first official fake date out of the way, Violet Maxwell hated him a little bit less.

11

Bite Me

It was one of *those* mornings . . . the kind where you woke up to the realization that you'd broken your record of hitting snooze twelve times. Where you finally dragged your carcass out of bed and into the shower only to be blasted with ice-cold water. The kind where you looked for your house keys everywhere—including rifling through a disgusting trash can—only to find your twenty-pound cat lying on top of them.

If Vi hadn't received six SOS texts from Harper requesting snack backup, she would've climbed back into bed and called it a day. But the kids needed their afternoon yogurt, and with their up-coming camping trip to Cheesequake State Park and the growing call to make s'mores around the campfire, she had no other choice than to do a grocery store run.

Hell hath no fury like two dozen kids without their favorite sugary treat.

Vi navigated the busy supermarket with the sole focus of getting the goods and getting out. Unfortunately, everyone else in New York City had the same idea. By the time she finally located a basket, an eerie tingle of awareness blossomed across the back of her neck.

The same thing had happened when she'd had lunch with Rose

and Olive two days ago, and again last night on her commute home from Potion's Up. Each time—including this one—she hadn't been able to pinpoint the source.

Blaming her paranoia on her latest *Stranger Things* binge watch, Vi passed a burly man with an empty cart and headed for the dairy section. A tall woman stood in front of the cheese, two different products in her hand as if she couldn't choose.

Vi felt the woman's pain as she glanced down at the million different yogurt choices, and reached for her phone to call Harper.

"Why are there so many yogurt flavors?" she asked when her best friend answered.

"Because variety is the spice of life, sweetheart."

She dumped a few cartons of vanilla into her basket. "Strawberry or blueberry?"

"Strawberry . . . and don't think saving the day with dairy will get you a reprieve from dishing about Mr. Sexy Pants," Harper warned. "I'm dying for details about the *date*."

"I thought you called him Mr. Sex on Legs."

"He's that, too."

"Maybe I haven't said much about our date because there isn't much to say," Vi lied. "It was a date. He picked me up. We ate. He brought me home."

. . . where they'd been a hairsbreadth from kissing each other senseless.

Maybe.

Harper wasn't the only one itching for details. Rose and her mother had texted about it on a daily basis, and even Olive brought it up on their last phone call. But talking about the fake date meant admitting how much she hadn't hated it.

An entire evening with Lincoln Thorne, and she hadn't considered throttling him once, had even enjoyed herself—with the exception of dealing with two entitled shifters.

Vi put another carton of yogurt in her basket and headed toward the crackers. That damn tingle was back. She whipped around, catching a brief glimpse of a black sweatshirt not unlike the one the burly guy had worn.

Unease knotted her stomach, but everywhere she looked, no one paid her any attention.

"*Hello*," Harper drawled from the other end of the line. "Are you okay? You're even more evasive than usual."

"I thought someone was following me, but . . ." Vi chuckled nervously, feeling silly. "My lack of sleep has officially come back to bite me on the ass."

"Are you sure that's what bit you on the ass? Because I have it on good authority that a lot of shifters are into a little bite play and—"

"Oh my Goddess, will you stop? Lincoln did not bite me—on the ass or in any other location!" She laughed her way to the checkout, where the twentysomething behind the register raised a decoratively pierced eyebrow. "Sorry. My best friend doesn't get the whole boundaries thing. It's a constant struggle."

The woman shrugged noncommittally and rung her up. "She's not wrong, though. Shifters love a little nibble. Vampires, too, although they're more tactful about where they put their mark."

"How did you know she said . . . ?"

The cashier suggestively rolled her bottom lip against her two slowly elongating canines. *Vampire.* "Shifters aren't the only Supes with impressive hearing." With a little wink, she handed Vi her bagged items. "And if you're not into letting the shifter sneak a little taste, I volunteer myself as tribute. I love a little witchy snack."

"Do it!" Harper screeched in her ear. "Vampire venom is *literally* orgasmic!"

Vi ignored her best friend. "Thanks, but I'm currently on a fang-free diet . . . both shifter and vamp."

"Can't blame a woman for trying. Have a nice day."

"You too." Vi pocketed her receipt and stepped out onto the busy Manhattan sidewalk.

Rush hour was already heavily underway. She sidestepped right, nearly crashing into oncoming foot traffic. A half step left, and she almost fell head over ass into a pile of trash heaped on the sidewalk.

"As much as I adore your tenacity, Harp, I've evidently lost the ability to walk, talk, and navigate. We'll pick up this conversation when I get to the center?"

"You better believe we will, witch. I want it in verbal surround sound."

Vi stuffed her phone into her back pocket. From the other direction, a broad-shouldered man bumped into her, spinning her around with the force. She opened her mouth to hurl a scathing reprimand when her gaze slid past him, picking out the burly guy from the grocery store.

They both froze, staring at one another. It was almost comical until she registered what he held in his hand. *A camera.*

Seeing her notice him, he snapped a picture and quickened his pace, sweat beading on his forehead the faster he moved.

"Son of a witch's tit," Vi cursed.

She dodged and weaved, throwing an occasional glance over her shoulder. Every time she increased her pace, so did the guy behind her. Cars moved through the intersection ahead, and unwilling to stop and give him time to catch up, she hung a left at the corner.

Sweatshirt Man followed.

"What the freaking hell does a witch have to do to get rid of you?" she murmured.

Hailing a cab during rush hour was on the same level as winning the Mega Millions lottery. She looked around for other options when her gaze landed on a bike share kiosk.

"I can't believe I'm about to do this." Quickly swiping her credit card, she yanked out her assigned bike, looped her bags on the handlebars, and prayed to Goddess she didn't run into a building, person, or car.

It had been way too long since she'd ridden a bicycle. Wobbling unsteadily down the street, she nearly crashed into three hydrants before finally getting the hang of it. With each block she passed, her paparazzi admirer got smaller and smaller. The jerk lifted a phone to his ear, his arm waving wildly, annoyed she'd given him the slip.

"And that's what I call the Witch Slip." Vi giggled.

Two cars zoomed past her, making her weave unsteadily in her lane. She'd just gotten her bearings when a third car roared up from behind and lingered alongside her. She waved the car ahead, but it didn't go.

She waved again. "Pass, already!"

Instead, it kept pace with her.

Vi glanced up to see the woman from the dairy aisle steering with one hand, an expensive-looking camera occupying the other.

"Say cheese!" The paparazza immediately snapped a series of pictures.

Vi wobbled. "Move over! You're too close!"

The woman ignored her, firing off more pictures. The car drifted into the bike lane, clipping Vi's shoulder.

"I said back off, lady!"

Click. Click. Click.

Up ahead, construction tape cordoned off an area of road with a gaping hole large enough to swallow an entire car, but the photographer was too busy snapping pictures to notice.

Click. Click. Click.

"Look in front of you!" Vi pointed to the roadblock. "Stop!"

The woman finally looked, and slammed hard on the brakes, swerving her SUV directly into Vi's path. Vi had two options— hole or coffee cart—and while they both sucked, one sucked a hell of a lot less.

Her front wheel hit the curb, and Vi was airborne, careening straight into Carl's Coffee Cart in a tangle of steel, wheels, and limbs.

"Shit. Are you okay, lady?" The older gentleman manning the cart hovered over her. "That was a pretty bad spill. I can't believe that driver didn't stop."

Sure enough, the SUV was nowhere to be seen.

"Yeah, I'm okay." She pushed into a sitting position and hissed as pain shot down her arm and into her hands.

"Let me take a look at those." A uniformed EMT dropped to a crouch in front of her, carefully removing the twisted bike from around her legs. "We saw your tumble from across the street. You've got some slick defensive driving skills."

"Evidently not slick enough." She plucked a stone from her palm and grimaced. "But I'm fine. Just a little battered and bruised."

"Why don't you let me and my partner check you out?" The paramedic flagged down another guy across the street, gesturing for him to bring a med bag.

"That's not necessary. It's a few scrapes that I can deal with at home."

The coffee cart man stepped forward. "I saw her hit her head on the edge of my wheel. I don't know if I would trust what she says right now. She could have a concussion."

"No, no. I'm okay." Vi pushed herself to her feet and groaned, but not because of her head.

Vanilla and strawberry yogurt now coated the street and sidewalk, and there was no sign of the s'mores fixings anywhere. The surrounding crowd grew, first by one person, then another. A teenager pulled her phone from her pocket and started taking a video. An unsettled feeling formed in the pit of Vi's stomach.

The EMT touched her elbow. "We really should take you to Mount Sinai to get looked at."

"I really am fine, and I'm running late, and—"

"You'll be running even later if you collapse in an hour because you have an undiagnosed concussion or worse. We'll get the chair out of the back of the bus and wheel you up. Look, you can refuse treatment, but you'll have to sign a waiver, and then if anything pops up later down the line, your insurance won't cover it."

At least a half dozen cell phones were turned toward her.

"For the love of Goddess, fine. I'll go, but I'm not using the wheely thing."

"It's protocol."

"And it's also not happening." She stared him dead in the eye. "Not in this lifetime or in any other."

He must've sensed her seriousness. "Then let's go."

She walked with him to the ambulance across the street, where they didn't give her any choice but to sit on the gurney inside. While his partner drove, the paramedic cleaned and dressed the cuts on her hands. Remembering Harper was expecting her, she pulled her phone from her back pocket and cursed at the cracked screen. It woke up long enough for her to shoot off a text telling Harper to send someone else out for the afternoon snack run.

"Luck must have been on your side today, Miss Maxwell. Things could've ended a lot differently if you hadn't landed where you did." Applying a last piece of tape over her bandage, the paramedic flashed a supportive smile.

"Yeah, I guess you're right. Wait . . . how did you know my name? I didn't tell you. Did I?" *Crap.* Maybe she *had* hit her head.

The EMT's gaze flickered away shyly. He looked like he was about her age, maybe a little younger. "I recognized you from the paper . . . with Alpha Thorne. I'm a member of the North American Pack."

Vi wasn't sure whether to be concerned or pleased with being recognized off the street, and while that had been the goal she and Lincoln hoped for, it also meant there was no going back.

✦ ✦ ✦

The two Elders from Linc's Pack stared at him as if the weight of their gazes alone could crush him. It was the third time in the hour-long visit that their inner bears had challenged his Wolf and failed.

He had to give them props for not giving up.

They'd arrived at Thorne Enterprises under the guise of concern for a Pack in California whose homes were dangerously close to a breakout wildfire. The Pack was fine; Adrian had flown out there to personally ensure evacuation went smoothly, and was already back. This was only another attempt by the Elders—the third in as many days—to sniff out information.

It was obvious they'd heard rumors about the impending Alpha vote, and it didn't take a nuclear physicist to know Bisset was behind the information leak.

Linc decided to play their game for now. "I'm honored that you and Elder Cho are so concerned for my future, Jane, but I'm not worried."

"That makes one of us." Jane Goodman, leader of one of the biggest bear dens in northern Virginia, frowned. "It's simply unheard of for an Alpha of your line—of *any* line—to push the envelope in this way. And I won't lie, a few of our Elder colleagues from the other Packs are less than thrilled. Our recent meetings have been quite . . . irritable."

Linc almost laughed. The bear Elder had a great poker face, but she signified the exact reason the Elders' control needed to be dissolved. One of his father's former mistresses, she treated her own local Pack as badly as Linc's father had treated his.

He exchanged a look with Adrian, who stood by the door, fighting off a smirk until his cell vibrated with a text. His SIC glanced at the caller ID only to dismiss it with a small shrug and tuck it into his back pocket.

"Well, Jane, I wouldn't want your Elder colleagues to worry over nothing, so I'm happy to inform you that my plan isn't to remain a bachelor much longer," Linc lied.

Elder Goodman's mouth opened and closed. When she failed to say anything, Elder Cho took over. "You're to be mated? With who?"

Adrian's cell phone buzzed again. "Excuse me while I step out and take this."

"I haven't asked the lady the question yet," Linc said, turning to the older man. "We're still early in our relationship, but I'm hopeful. As for who, I'm sure if you keep your ears open, the Supernatural grapevine will fill you in on everything you need to know."

His best friend burst back into the office. "Alpha Thorne . . . a word?"

He followed Adrian into the corridor, about to drag his friend into a hug for getting him out of the room.

"It's Violet." Adrian's words halted any kind of affection.

"*What's* Violet?"

"She's been taken to Mount Sinai."

The hair on the back of Linc's neck lifted as his Wolf pushed against the surface, sensing his sudden rush of fear. He turned to his assistant. "Marie! Get rid of the Elders."

"What do you want me to tell them?" Marie called after him.

"Make something up." He stalked to the elevator, Adrian at his side. "Start talking. Now."

"We received a call from an eagle shifter who works emergency services in Midtown. He brought Violet into the emergency room about an hour ago."

"An hour ago, and I'm just being told now?" A low growl rolled from his throat. "Why did she need the hospital? What happened?"

"I'm still in the process of confirming it, but it may have been paparazzi related."

"I want it confirmed, and then I want the name of the photographer responsible. Going after me is one thing. Going after her to the point of injury is something different."

Linc's friend didn't disagree, or question his sudden urge to bash heads. By the time they reached the lobby, his car had been brought to the front of the building. Twenty minutes later, he squealed to a stop in front of Mount Sinai and hopped out. They could tow the damn thing or take it for a joyride. He didn't care.

He rushed up to the balding demon behind the registration desk. "I need to see Violet Maxwell. She was brought in through emergency services sometime within the last two hours."

The man typed away on his computer, not sparing him so much as a quick glance.

Linc barely refrained from reaching across the counter. "Violet. Maxwell. Where is she and what condition is she in?"

"Are you family?" The demon still didn't look at him.

"No, but—"

"No familial relationship, no information."

"That's not acceptable."

The attendant finally peered up at him over the rim of his glasses. "Mister, I don't care if you're Alpha of the NAP or the freakin' Tooth Fairy. I'm not giving out patient information."

His Wolf nearly burst his way to the surface right there in the hospital lobby, stopped only by the heavy hand that landed on his shoulder. Adrian steered him away, gently nudging him toward a Staff Only door on the left. A doctor pushed through it from the other side and stepped into the waiting room. Linc caught it before it closed, and slipped into the inner sanctum of the emergency room.

Doctors and nurses in scrubs hustled up and down the corridor, some pushing equipment heavier than themselves while others attended to the army of alarms echoing throughout the ER.

Linc tuned it all out and listened for the one sound he wanted to hear—Violet's voice. Pushing out with his sensitive hearing, he turned corner after corner, his Wolf growing more anxious the longer he searched.

"You guys look ridiculously busy. I feel bad taking up a bed," Violet's melodious voice reached him two halls later.

"We'll get you out of here as soon as we can," someone replied. "But—"

"As soon as the doctor looks over your MRI and clears you, I'll get your discharge papers printed pronto. I *promise.*"

Violet's frustration put a relieved smile on Linc's face. If she could still give the nurses a hard time, she was more than fine.

Leaning against the wall outside her room, he waited for the nurse to leave. "Is she trying to make a run for it?"

The older woman—a human—startled. "Since before they brought her in, from my understanding. You're with her?"

"I am."

"You think you can keep her put for about thirty minutes while I light a fire under the doctor's behind?"

"I'm definitely up for the challenge." He pushed off the wall, more than ready to see her. "She's okay?"

The nurse patted his arm. "She's fine, honey. Her pride's more wounded than she is."

He let himself digest that piece of information before he knocked on the door. Violet's surly "come in" beckoned him into the room.

"What in Goddess's name are you doing here?" she demanded.

"Would you believe me if I told you I'm a candy striper?" His tease deepened the witch's frown.

"They don't have *candy stripers* in hospitals anymore. It's not 1952 . . . and you didn't answer my question."

He ran his gaze over her ripped jeans and up to the large bandages covering each palm. On the left corner of her forehead, she had a Ping-Pong-ball-size bump.

"What happened?" Linc demanded gently, irritation rolling his stomach into a hard knot.

She pushed herself off the gurney and drilled him with a "back off" look when he stepped forward to help. "I asked you a question first. Why are you here? *How* are you here?"

"I drove."

"*Linc*," Violet growled.

His lips twitched. "You haven't called me that in years."

"I'll call you other names if you don't answer my question."

To refrain from reaching out and touching her, he perched himself against the counter. "I'm the NAP Alpha, princess. Not much happens in my territory that I don't know about."

"When you say 'territory,' you better be talking about this city and not me."

He smirked, knowing it would piss her off, and it did. She approached *him*, fire lighting up her eyes until a faint, misty glow seeped out from beneath her bandages.

Lavender was quickly becoming his favorite scent.

Her shoes bumped his and she stopped. "Let's get one thing straight right now. Make sure your wolfy ears are open, because if I have to say it a second time, things will not be pleasant for you."

"Wolfy ears are open and listening."

She drilled a finger into his chest. "When I agreed to this ridiculous plan, I didn't agree to you peeing on my leg, or whatever it is you do to mark your *territory*."

"I wouldn't dare." He kept a straight face—barely.

"Good—because I own every inch of my own territory."

"Of course you do."

"Exactly."

"But the release of bodily functions isn't necessary to stake my claim, princess. The paparazzi did that for me by taking all those pictures of our first date." Slipping his hand over hers, he guided her finger-drill away from his sternum . . . because damn that hurt. "And to answer your question, a new Pack member notified Adrian about the incident, thinking it was something I'd want to know . . . and he was right."

"Freakin' EMT . . ." Vi muttered about HIPAA and ethics.

"I answered your question. Now it's time for you to answer mine. *What happened?*"

Both his and Vi's gazes dropped to where his thumb was reflexively stroking the back of her hand. He waited for her to pull away, but instead, she eased closer, dropping her free hand onto his chest. Linc's Wolf hummed his approval at the contact.

"Something tells me you already know." She lifted a brow in challenge.

"I got the abridged version on the way over, but now I want the unabridged."

As Vi recounted her run-in with the photographers, Linc's anger rose, his clenched jaw threatening the well-being of his teeth. He pulled away, dragging his hand through his hair as he paced. This had happened because of him and his bright fucking ideas.

"Will you stop with the brooding? You're making me a little woozy," Violet claimed.

He stared at her, aghast at the smile on her face. "You're joking right now? You could have been seriously hurt."

"There could also be a freak blizzard in Arizona, but you don't see me watching the Weather Channel to catch a glimpse of Jim Cantore."

"This isn't a joke."

"You're right. It's not." Grabbing his arm, she tugged him to a stop. "I'm not letting a few pushy photographers stop us from doing what we have to do, and honestly, I'm offended you think I'm some delicate flower who wilts at the first sign of heat."

Linc snorted. "A flowering cactus, maybe, but you're no daisy."

"*Lincoln.*"

"Fine. You're right, but being a cactus doesn't mean we can't take precautions."

She studied him through narrowed, distrustful eyes. "I'm not going to like what you're about to say, am I?"

"You'll hate it with every fiber of your being."

"Then maybe we should go a different route."

He shook his head. "Can't do it, princess. When things heat up between us, the paparazzi and anyone else angling for a story will only get braver."

"You're giving me a *babysitter* . . ."

"That's not what I'd call it."

"What would you call it?"

"A witchsitter."

12

Magic for Dummies

Vi focused on the *Magic for Dummies* manual spread out on her lap and tried—and failed—to ignore the swish of the cat clock ticking away the seconds.

Tick-tock. Tick-tock.

Time-running. Out-soon.

She contemplated *accidentally* blasting it off the wall, but since it was one of Olive's most prized possessions, she settled for sending it an occasional hard glare.

The better part of her morning had been spent losing the feeling in her ass and poring over Magic how-to books written with ten-year-olds in mind. Evidently ten-year-olds who were better versed in Magic than she was, because she'd yet to make a single spell work and didn't have much hope for future attempts.

"How's it going over there?" Olive didn't take her eyes off the aged text she'd been scanning over for the last hour. "I can practically smell you thinking."

"That's probably still the burnt plastic from your bobblehead." Vi grimaced at the misshapen blob that had once looked like her sister's idol, Jane Goodall. "I'm still determined to replace that, by the way."

"Good luck with that. It was one of only a hundred ever made."

With a frustrated sigh, Vi closed her book. "Maybe this is a waste of time. Maybe we're doing this all for nothing and the Council's right. Maybe I do need a Witch Bond."

Olive finally dragged her attention away from her desk. "Do you really think that or is this your frustration talking?"

Vi tossed the magical text on the pile with all the others. "No, I don't think that, and yes, I'm frustrated. I'm trying to learn thirty-two years' worth of Magic in three months, and Sparky is being a diva, picking and choosing when it wants to make an appearance."

"Sparky?"

"If men can name their penises, I can name my Magic."

Olly raised her hands in mock surrender. "You just need to work with *Sparky* enough so you're not leaving a Magic residue behind wherever you go. You'll get it. And I'll find a loophole to get you out of this Witch Bond. It's out there. It'll just take a little time and ingenuity to find it."

Vi glanced at the text in front of her sister. "And some dusty old books written in languages no one speaks anymore?"

Olive smirked. "Exactly. This law has been around for a long time. We won't find the answers we need in anything pubbed during Gran's lifetime, and probably not for centuries before. You're forgetting she was subjected to this stupid law, too."

Vi *had* forgotten. The large difference in their scenarios was that Edie had found her True Mate in Jethro McAllister, their grandfather. Forming an eternal magical bond hadn't been a sacrifice for them. They had had fifty-five blessed years together before cancer stole him away.

Loud voices raised in anger sounded right outside Olly's office.

"What the Hex . . ." Vi flung open the door to find Bax nose-to-nose with the broad-shouldered bear shifter who was serving as Lincoln's witch-sitter of the day.

"What the hell is this?" Bax demanded, not taking his attention off the man in front of him.

"That's a Leo. He's my protection detail." Whom she'd been blessed with for the last very long forty-eight hours. "Leo, this is a Bax. He's my best friend. You can let him inside."

"Why the hell do you have a protection detail?"

Leo answered, "She was assaulted a few days ago and the Alpha would like to ensure it doesn't happen again."

Bax's eyes flew open. "You were fucking assaulted? By who?"

Vi grimaced. "Doesn't swearing get you angel demerits or something?"

"Violet . . ."

The bear shifter crossed his arms over his broad chest. "His name's not on the preapproved list. No name. No entry."

"That's because . . ." She thought on her feet ". . . he's my Guardian Angel."

Leo bounced his gaze from her to Bax. "Then he should be demoted."

"I'll take that under consideration." Before Bax could square off with the shifter, she hauled him into the office and closed the door.

"Your Guardian Angel? If I were ever assigned to you, I'd hand in my resignation right on the spot," Bax joked dryly.

"Hardy-har-har. GA clients are confidential, right? There's no way for Leo to find out if you are or aren't, and as my best friend, you technically *are* mine."

"Technicalities will bite you on the ass one day . . . if your wolf shifter doesn't do it first."

Violet tossed her hands in the air. "What is it with people envisioning Lincoln biting me on the ass?"

He chuckled, his gaze veering toward Olive, who stood ramrod straight, her attention shifting from her dusty books to the hot, tatted-up angel. Vi caught her sister visually objectifying Bax's broad chest and wiggled her eyebrows suggestively. Olive blushed.

Oblivious to the admiration, Bax perched his ass on the edge of the desk. "I'm used to things changing when I head out of town for assignments, but Lincoln Thorne, Vi? How the hell did *that* happen? And what's this about an attack?"

"It wasn't an *attack*. It was a run-in with an overly eager paparazza who evidently sucks at driving a car while taking pictures. And Lincoln is . . . new."

Bax stared at her with those all-knowing angel eyes.

She tried not to fidget. "What have I said about those freakin' eyes? Put them away!"

"You *really* suck at lying, babe."

"I do *not* suck."

"So you admit you're lying?"

She blustered. "No! That's not what I meant. Stop twisting my words. What are you doing here, anyway?"

Olive shifted nervously. "I asked him to do me a favor, but I thought he'd shoot me an email or something. I didn't think I'd get a personal visit."

Vi glanced between her sister and best friend. "Does someone want to clue me in?"

"I've been trying to get my hands on some texts from the Celestial Archives because I think they could point us in the right direction, but since Bax is bookless, I'm guessing my request was denied."

Bax flashed her an apologetic smile. "Sorry, angel. I tried. I explained the situation to the archive curator, but her hands are tied. The edict comes from way above her . . . like . . . *way* above."

"No witches." Olive dropped back into her chair with a defeated grumble. "It's not like I'll go Willow and try to annihilate the world. Those texts could potentially solve countless world issues, but *no* . . . can't let anyone without wings near them."

Olive's rant continued, shifting from the Celestial Archives to mutterings about inaccurate historical documentation and angelic scribes. Vi snapped her fingers in front of her sister to get her attention and not only got it, but also a plume of purple mist and golden sparks.

"Holy shit!" Bax pushed off the desk, ready to dive beneath it if necessary.

Vi glanced at her now normal hand. "I don't get it. I have literally tried to dim a lightbulb for an hour. I don't try, and *there's Sparky*."

"That was one of the things I hoped the Celestial Archives could tell us," Olive admitted. She grabbed a book from the stack on her desk. "This diary belonged to a twelfth-century Franciscan monk, a vampire who made some pretty heavy insinuations that a Firstborn's power isn't gifted from this earthly plane."

"Translation, please?"

"He thought the power was gifted from the heavens." Bax made a face, which Olive saw. "What? You don't think so?"

"It was the twelfth century. They weren't above putting farm animals on trial for murder. You should take whatever you find in that diary with a grain of salt."

Vi's mouth dropped. "Seriously? Like pigs and roosters and stuff?"

"Like anything big enough to kill a human." He turned to the youngest Maxwell. "You had a hunch—and it was a good one—but the archives won't get you what you need."

"If only I could look at them myself and come to my own conclusions," Olive flung back.

Bax glowered at her, his jaw muscle ticking. "If it'll make you feel better, I'll call in a few favors and ask around, but don't count on it turning anything up."

"I'm doomed." Vi collapsed into the chair. "Finding this loophole is next to impossible. It's eleventh-grade AP Algebra all over again."

"Except you can be tutored in algebra. It's too bad you can't get a Magic tutor and show-and-tell the Council how you don't blow shit up."

She mulled over Bax's words before jumping to her feet and

planting a noisy kiss on his cheek. "You freaking genius angel-man! That's it! I can *show* them that a Firstborn doesn't need a Witch Bond in order to control his or her powers!"

Olive nervously bit her bottom lip.

Vi read the doubt in her face. "You don't think I can do it."

"It's not that." Olly glanced at melted Jane Goodall. "It won't be easy. Like you said, you've been without Sparky for thirty-two years. That's a lot of time to make up for."

"It is, but I don't have much choice. Not that I doubt your ability to find miracles, but what happens if three months pass and we're no closer to finding that loophole? I'm screwed. *And* Witch Bonded to someone with an incurable case of halitosis." Vi prepped to drop to her knees and beg. "What do you say, Olly? It's an educational challenge. Think of it as magical boot camp and you can be the one who screams in my face and runs me ragged."

Olly didn't look as against the idea as she had a second ago. "Do I get to wear camo and blow a whistle?"

"If it helps, you can wear a sexy catsuit and use a megaphone."

"Rose will want a piece of the action. If there's an opportunity for her to tell someone what to do, she'll jump at it."

"So you'll do it, Sergeant Maxwell?"

"I won't go easy on you because we shared a womb for eight months," Olive warned.

"I wouldn't expect you to."

"And you're not to question my tactics. If I tell you to rub peanut butter in your hair and chant to the red moon while naked, I'll expect you to do it."

"Oh-kay." Vi nodded, withholding a laugh. "I may look at you weird, but consider it done."

Bax cleared his throat. "Where are you guys planning on having this magical boot camp? It's not like the city is overflowing with spaces large—and secluded—enough to contain any accidents."

"Leave that to me," Olly demanded. "I'll find us the perfect place. Away from the general public. Big enough to work in but not too big for a cloaking ward."

"Cloaking?"

Olive gave her a *duh* look. "Do you want the Supernatural Council to sniff out your Magic usage and put an end to this before it's even begun?"

"Cloaking ward it is."

"Not to rain on your picnic, but . . ." Bax gestured to the office door ". . . what are you planning on doing with Winnie the Pooh out there?"

"Hex me. You're right." Vi racked her brain, but came up blank. "I'll dust off a few tactics from the teenage vault and see if any of them can be applied to overbearing shifter bodyguards."

Good thing she and her sisters had been pretty creative in their rebel years, because it would take nothing short of genius to get Leo to unwittingly abandon his post.

❤ ❤ ❤

Linc had barely walked into the office when Adrian was in his face. "Where the fuck have you been? I've called you six times."

"All in the last six minutes, which is how long it took me to walk into the building and get up here. What's up?" Walking past Marie's desk, he dropped her favorite tea by the phone and accepted her enthusiastic thank-you.

"*What's up* is that Alpha Asshat is here, and he brought Benson and Flores."

Linc stopped abruptly. "Say that again."

"You heard me. Fuckhead rolled in here with a shit-eating grin, looking like the tiger who'd eaten the canary."

Extra time with the Alphas meant additional chances to solidify their positions in the upcoming Elder vote. That would usually be a good thing—especially more time with Benson. But not if Bisset had herded them here. The bastard was up to something.

"How long have they been waiting?"

"Too long. Benson started pursing her lips about ten minutes ago."

Fuck. That was the first sign her patience had worn thin. Next up was the finger drumming, and no Supe or Norm wanted to be in a room with her when her annoyance ratcheted up to the level beyond *that*.

They headed off to the conference room.

"Any idea what this is about?" Linc asked on the way.

"Wouldn't say. Just planted their asses and demanded to see you."

"Yeah, but we have audio in that meeting room, so . . ."

"You think I'd eavesdrop on private conversations without their knowledge?" At Linc's pointed look, Adrian chuckled. "Yeah, you're right. Bisset's banking on surprising you. It's about the Elders. They heard about Goodman and Cho's recent visit and it's making them a bit antsy."

"And I'm sure they had a little tiger helping that along," Linc murmured. "That pussycat won't be happy until he gets my Council seat."

"And he thinks he's a shoo-in, considering he's just months away from securing a Mate Bond with the Prima Apparent." Adrian tugged him to a stop in front of the door. "You have to go in there with a clear head. Do not fuck around."

"My head is clear," Linc barked, his Wolf pushing closer to the surface.

Adrian gave him a pointed look. "I don't think so. That furry bastard is holding loaded dice and he'll toss them the second he has you in the position he wants. Lose your shit in there, and you risk losing what credibility you have with Flores and Benson. Calm, cool, and maliciously calculated. If there was ever a time to hone your inner father, this is it."

"If I were my father, I'd go in there in my animal form and rip Bisset's throat out." Loosening his tie, Linc reined in his Wolf. "Let's show the cat where the litter box is."

All eyes turned their way as they entered the room.

Bisset, sitting on the far end as if he were a king, grinned. "Guess it's better to show up late than not show at all."

"Had I known I was getting a visit today, I would've cleared my calendar." Linc shook the two other Alphas' hands before leaning against the edge of the oblong table. "What can I do for you today?"

Flores flicked a quick glance to Gertrude Benson, the Australian Alpha. "We heard about your visit with the Elders, and we're concerned. I'm sure we don't have to tell you that they could make things extremely difficult for our Packs—and us—if we're not careful."

"Everything's fine with the Elders. We're still on track to make our official vote in a few weeks."

Benson's steely gaze practically drilled through him. "I'm extremely allergic to the term *fine*. More often than not, it's hiding a total clusterfuck beneath its rather dull surface."

Linc chuckled, liking the Alpha's no-nonsense attitude. "I'm not usually a fan of it either . . . especially when it comes from the women in my life. But in this instance, I mean it. The Elders *were* concerned—and perhaps a little suspicious—about my prolonged bachelorhood, but I assured them—"

"What exactly does that mean?" Bisset sounded flippant, even a bit hostile. While he'd grinned when Linc first entered the room, he wasn't smiling now.

Good. That meant Linc was on the right track. "It means that I'm dating someone very special to me, and while it's in its beginning stages, I'm hopeful it will become a lot more."

And hell if that didn't have a ring of truth to it . . .

Vi *was* special to him, and always had been—and he was damn hopeful their budding friendship continued to grow. Into *what*, he didn't know.

"You're soon to be mated? With who?" Bisset glowered.

Linc couldn't help but prod him with a grin. "Let's say that if all goes well, we might be brothers-in-law, Val."

Although the Australian Alpha was harder to read, after a few more minutes of questioning—and Linc remaining calm and collected—Flores and Benson seemed appeased. For now. Adrian led them back out to the main office, but Bisset lagged behind.

He held Linc's gaze in open challenge, the daring move stirring Linc's Wolf. "Can I help you with something else, Valentin?"

"You think you're quite the chess player, don't you? Well, I assure you, whatever game you're playing won't end how you'd like."

"I wouldn't place bets on that."

"Oh, I would. And when this all blows up in your face, I'll be there to sweep away the smoke . . . and snatch up your Council seat. We'll see how far you get with your shifter-friendly, love-and-hug society then."

Linc chuckled. "Let's play into your delusion for a hot second and say you take over my seat on the Council. You're one voice of five. How much damage do you think the others will let you do to me? Unless you think that by Bonding with the Prima Apparent, your one voice automatically becomes two."

Bisset glared.

Bingo.

Linc smirked confidently. "You're about to Bond to a Maxwell witch. Nothing and no one could make them do something they don't want to do. Just a little FYI, in case you were hedging your bets on Rose being a submissive little Alpha's wife."

Bisset's eyes flashed silver, signaling his tiger was dangerously close to the surface.

"*You're* the one who should be careful about the games you're playing," Linc warned. "I may be known as the *unconventional* Alpha, but I assure you, my father's blood still flows through my veins. Cross me, and you sure as hell better take me down all the way. Now get the hell out of my office."

Bisset pushed past Adrian on his way out.

"Was it something I said?" he joked dryly.

"It was a lot of somethings *I* said. I'm actually glad he showed up today."

Adrian's eyebrows lifted into a surprised look. "Yeah? Why?"

"Because he wouldn't have done it unless he was scared things weren't about to go his way."

That meant they just needed to stay on track and keep the momentum going. Keep reassuring the Alphas. Keep building plans for the switch of power once the Elder Board was dissolved.

And keep his eye on the time so he wasn't late picking up Violet for date number two.

13

Nothing Says "Romance" Like Rental Shoes

Violet waved to Misha and her mom as they left the KCC and walked down the block toward home. As much as she loved that the center's numbers grew every day, she couldn't wait to get home and out of her clothes, which, thanks to an overzealous hug during a craft project, had glittered handprints on the back.

Tide To Go could only do so much.

Vi unlocked the front door and turned at the sound of rumbled music.

Lincoln's Jeep sat at the curb, and Wolfman himself leaned against the passenger side, his hands tucked into the pockets of gray dress pants.

Buttoned shirt.

Tie.

She smacked her forehead. "We had a date."

He smirked. "Which you obviously forgot."

"No, no. I didn't forget." She glanced to her ripped jeans and T-shirt. "Okay, yeah. I forgot. I'm sorry . . . and seeing as I'm in no condition for anyplace as remotely civilized as Le Petit, I'll have to pass tonight."

"You're standing me up?"

"Standing up implies I was a no-show. This is more of an

I'm-not-fit-to-be-around-people-in-public-unless-we're-going-to-a-bowling-alley excuse." He studied her so long she got antsy. "What?"

"Is that your only hesitancy about going out tonight?"

"Yeah."

He pushed off the car and opened the door. "Then leave the where to me."

She shot him a look of disbelief. "You seriously still want to go out? I look like I just dove headfirst into a hot tub filled with glitter bombs. I don't even want to be seen with myself."

Lincoln released a bone-tired sigh, and for the first time since seeing him sitting at the curb, she looked beyond the blatant physical yumminess and to the exhaustion bracketing his eyes. "Can I be honest with you, Violet?"

No. Yes. Maybe.

"Sure," she said hesitantly.

"I've had one hell of a fucking day, and the only reason I got through it without ripping someone's head off their shoulders was knowing I'd see you tonight." Clearing his throat, he failed to hide the cute pink coloration on his cheeks. "I was counting down the minutes."

He was embarrassed.

Vi bit the inside of her cheek to stop herself from teasing him. "Okay."

His surprised gaze met hers. "You trust me?"

"Is there a reason I shouldn't?" Not counting the million and one she could list off the top of her head . . .

"No."

"Then yeah. I'll trust you—as long as it doesn't involve cultured snails. But don't come whining to me if the paparazzi snaps pics of us and the headline tomorrow reads 'NAP Alpha Dates Zombie Girl.'"

"No snails." A low chuckle rolled from his chest as he tucked a strand of hair away from her face. "And I'd be fine with that head-line, because you're one hell of a gorgeous zombie."

His hand lingered, knuckles stroking her cheek. Vi's stomach somersaulted, and her Magic perked up its head—if it even had one. In a desperate attempt to preempt any explosive fireworks, she slid into the passenger seat and meditated like a champ until he climbed behind the wheel.

"So Lincoln Thorne had *A Day*, huh?"

He glanced toward her as he navigated their way through the city. "*A Day?* Is there a definition that goes with that?"

"A Day: When the thought of peopling automatically steers you to the nearest liquor store, or in Olly's case, bookstore. For me, my go-to is my couch with all seven seasons of *Buffy*."

He grinned. "And in my case, homicide?"

"You mentioned decapitations, so homicide seems like a good fit."

He chuckled. "Then yeah, I most definitely had A Day."

"Do you have them often?"

His smile slowly vanished. "Often enough."

"Do you want to talk about it?" She wished she could take back the question the second it left her lips.

This was how she'd let her guard down fourteen years ago.

Back-and-forth jibes slowly transformed into full-fledged dis-cussions doused heavily in sarcasm . . . and then *real* talks. Curi-ous questions and serious answers. The more she'd gotten to know Teenage Lincoln, the more she'd liked him.

Vi lucked out. The coy smile lifting the corners of his mouth told her he hadn't taken her question too seriously. *This time.*

"Violet Maxwell, are you attempting to have a civilized conver-sation with me that doesn't involve threats of physical maiming or questioning my manhood?"

"I was, but now I'm not so sure that's a good idea. Maybe we should stick to what we do best." She smirked.

Humor once again lightened his eyes. "Thanks for the offer, Dr. Phil, but right now, the only thing I need is to not think about anything at all."

They pulled into a public garage and parked. Lincoln tossed his suit jacket in the back seat and rolled up his sleeves. His arms, corded with thick muscle, gave Vi flashbacks to what it had felt like to be cradled in them.

Way too hot for her own good, she fanned herself with her shirt.

"You okay?" He spotted the flush in her cheeks.

Next to go was the tie, and Goddess help her, he undid his top few shirt buttons, revealing the edge of his collarbone. *Clean up on parking level two.* "It's . . . uh, a little warm . . . out here. Don't you think?"

She hadn't realized she'd licked her lips until Lincoln's rumbly chuckle disengaged her eyes from his body and drifted back to his grin. "Are you done objectifying my body? It's okay if you're not. I'll wait."

"I wasn't objectifying it." At his disbelieving snort, she added, "I was appreciating the scenery. There's a huge difference."

He rounded the hood and, sliding his fingers through hers, gently eased her to his side. "It's okay, sweetheart. Objectify me anytime you want."

She'd definitely take him up on that, but for now, she let him lead the way.

They headed back to the street, where they hung a right and walked half a block. "Are you telling me where we're going?"

"Still not a big fan of surprises?" Mirth danced in his eyes as he suppressed a grin.

"As a general rule? No. Not since Gran tried passing off mashed cauliflower as potatoes a few Thanksgivings back. I still haven't recuperated."

"I pride myself on giving a lady what she wants, so . . ." Stopping, he nudged his chin to a brightly lit neon sign on their right.

"*Glo-Bowl?*" She bounced her gaze from the basement bowling alley to the expectant shifter. "You're taking me bowling?"

"You said you weren't dressed for fancy French cuisine, and to be honest, I've had enough French things this week. Except maybe French fries, so . . . what do you say? Are you up to our next dating challenge?"

"Rental shoes and sticking my fingers in dark holes where a million others have done the same? Turn the French fries into cheese nachos, and you have a deal."

"Then let's do it."

It had been years since she'd stepped inside a bowling alley. The last time had been before she'd hit double digits, when her grandfather had snuck her and her sisters out of the house— unbeknownst to their mother—and taken them to Rock-n-Bowl.

Loud music blared on the overhead system, amplified by the loud drone of voices and the steady thunder of pins falling. Violet soaked it all in, and couldn't help the giggle that escaped when the attendant behind the counter gave them second, third, and fourth looks as they paid for their shoes and picked out their balls.

Lincoln snatched a bright purple one off the rack and held it out to her. "This one seems fitting. Violet for Violet."

"It's an eight-pound ball."

"And?" He looked confused.

"Do I look like a ten-year-old to you?" She nudged him away to scan the heavier balls, picking, instead, a fourteen pounder with an elegant swirl of midnight blue and gold. "This one should do the trick."

"That's a pretty—"

She shot him a glare.

"Good choice." He grabbed the heaviest ball for himself and took both their picks to the ball return before plopping in front of the computer to input their names. "We should make this night even more interesting . . . if you're up for it. How about a bet?"

Tying her shoes, she caught the mischievous glint in his eye. "What terms are we talking about?"

"Winner chooses the time, location, and activity of our next date."

"Winner's choice?"

He nodded. "No limits. Anything's fair game."

She lifted an eyebrow. "That's a dangerous declaration, Wolfman. I have a pretty wicked imagination. I'm not sure you know exactly what you'd be getting yourself into."

"You're not the only one with a wicked imagination, *princess*." His body heat wrapped around her like a cozy blanket as he stepped close, sticking out his hand. "Up for it?"

"You're on."

The second her palm touched his, Sparky stretched its legs and arms, and when Lincoln's eyes flickered molten gold, giving her a glimpse of his Wolf, her Magic damn near did a jig.

They stared at each other, neither of them willing—or able—to move. Except closer. Her shoes brushed against his just as someone nearby dropped their ball with a heavy *thud*, reminding them both how *not* alone they were.

"We should . . ."

"Yeah." Lincoln cleared his throat and stepped away first. "You're up, Red. Best two out of three claims victory."

Red? She looked up at the overhead game screen and laughed. "Red Riding Hood and the Big Bad Wolf?"

His eyes gleamed wickedly. "I thought it was fitting."

He wasn't wrong. It took three full turns—and epic fails—for Violet to finally shrug off the aftereffects of whatever connection had zinged between them a few minutes ago. On her fourth, she stood centimeters from crossing the foul line and prayed to Goddess she'd knock down at least one pin.

"You want a few pointers?" Lincoln taunted from the bench. "I don't mind sharing my wisdom."

"I got it handled." She held the ball to her nose, lined up her shot, swung, and released. A snail could've made it to the pins faster. "Hex me."

"You sure I can't be of assistance?"

"Never been surer of anything in my life." The second her ball reappeared on the belt, she took her stance back on the line, and waited.

And focused.

And . . . sighed.

Tossing a look over her shoulder, she caught Lincoln's gaze on her ass. "Can you take your eyes off my bum long enough to give me a few pointers?"

"I make no promises." He damn near glided over the floor like a predator stalking its prey, stopping behind her. He dropped his hands to her hips, gently turning her back toward the lane.

"The key"—his cheek brushed hers as he spoke—"is picturing a string from your ball to the lead pin. While you hold that image in your head, swing the ball back and release it straight."

"Shouldn't I do one of those fancy hook things where it curves?"

"Let's focus on the basics before attempting tricks. Picture the string."

At the brush of his lips against her ear, she sucked down a needy whimper.

"Keep your eyes focused on the pin."

Lincoln caressed her arm into a slow drop, the gentle touch immediately bringing goose bumps to the surface of her skin.

"Swing . . . and release."

Vi sent a prayer to Goddess, pictured the string, swung, and let go. This time her ball possessed more pizzazz than it had on her previous attempts, hitting the pins with a loud *crack*. They blasted apart, leaving only one remaining upright.

"I did it!" She flung her arms around Lincoln's neck. "It worked! Hell's Spells, I actually did it!"

"Hell yeah, you did." He spun her off the ground. "It's the string thing. Works every time."

Vi slowly registered the firmness nestled against her stomach, and on reflex, her body shifted closer until two inches, maybe less, separated their lips.

She wanted Lincoln Thorne to kiss her more than she wanted those cheese nachos. Her lips tingled in anticipation, and so did her Magic, hovering beneath the surface of her skin, electrically charging every cell in her body in preparation.

Lincoln's eyes shifted from brown to gold, letting her know she wasn't the only one having difficulty keeping her Supernatural side under wraps.

He groaned. "You're fucking killing me right now, princess. It's difficult being a gentleman when you're looking at me like that."

"Sometimes gentlemen are highly overrated." Her eyes, hooded heavily in lust, flickered to his mouth.

Did I mean that to sound like an invitation?

Without a doubt.

Somewhere a few lanes over, someone called out their names. More than a half dozen people had their phones trained directly on them.

"Do you want to give them something to record, Wolfman?" She lifted to her toes and waited for the quick swoop of his mouth, but instead of pulling her closer, Lincoln stepped away.

✦ ✦ ✦

Not kissing Violet right then and there took Herculean willpower of which Linc had not thought himself capable. While part of him knew he'd done the right thing, the other half called him an idiot.

Their deal's foundation relied heavily on these outings and small, witnessed PDAs. People needed to believe they were on their way toward a Bonding in a month. But at some point during the night—hell, maybe even before he'd picked her up—this had stopped feeling like a show for the public and started feeling like a real date.

And hell if he didn't want to end it like a real date.

With a real kiss.

Just them. No damn cameras.

Linc wrestled with the silent admission for the rest of the night, and by the time they reached her place, he still didn't know what the hell to do about it.

What did she expect when they said their goodbyes? What did she want?

He sure as hell knew what *he* wanted to happen at her front door, but their no-sex rule tanked that idea, and not to mention, he half expected her friend and sisters to throw open the door as they reached her apartment.

When they didn't, nervous anticipation tied his tongue.

"Did you—?" she asked at the same time he said, "I want—"

She nudged him, a small smile flirting her lips upward. "You go."

"Ladies first." He shoved his hands deep in his pockets to keep from fidgeting. "Did I *what*?"

"Back at the bowling alley, you said something about being a gentleman. What did you mean?"

He cocked an eyebrow. "I would've thought the hard-on I was sporting for half the night would've clued you in."

"And yet you didn't kiss me when I practically flashed you a glaring green light. Aren't people supposed to think we're together? There were dozens of cameras pointed in our direction. It would've been a perfect moment."

Exactly. "They are, and you're right, there were a lot of phones."

"So why didn't you kiss me?" She waited expectantly for him to answer, and when he couldn't find the words, her eyes dimmed with an unnamed emotion. "You know what? Never mind. Forget I asked."

She turned to unlock her door.

"Violet, I—"

"No, no. It's okay." She waved him off, voice tense. "Kissing me is something you need to psych yourself up for, not a spur-of-the-moment thing. Consider me informed. I'll try not to blindside you with the threat of my lips again."

"Hey." Cupping her elbow, he turned her toward him.

"It's *fine*, Lincoln. You don't need to explain yourself."

The hurt in her eyes said otherwise. "I didn't want our first reunion kiss to be for anyone's entertainment but our own."

Fuck, he hadn't meant to be quite so blunt.

Violet blinked slowly. "You didn't want to kiss me because we were in front of people? But that's . . . that's the whole point of these dates."

"I know. And I wish I could explain it, but I can't. I've been trying for the last few hours."

Five seconds.

Ten.

He waited not so patiently through the silence, shifting awkwardly on his feet. "Aren't you going to say something?"

"Yeah."

"And that would be . . . ?"

"There aren't any cameras around right now—so why the hell aren't you kissing me?"

Fuck if he knew.

They moved simultaneously, their bodies clashing in a tangled slant of mouths and hands. Linc cradled the back of her head and hauled her closer, but he didn't have to swipe his tongue against her lips to request entry. She opened for him automatically, gliding her tongue along his in a kiss that rocked him down to his core.

Raw energy crackled in the air, drawing their bodies so close a piece of paper couldn't have fit between them. Linc's inner Wolf pushed his way toward the surface, but he held him back, unwilling to share the woman steadily dismantling their control.

With a soft whimper and a shift of bodies, Violet's back gently hit the wall—and then all gentleness went out the fucking window.

They touched.

They devoured.

The longer their bodies—and mouths—remained fused, the more the air sizzled.

Hooking her leg around his, she tugged him between the V of her thighs. "I wish I wasn't wearing jeans right now."

Linc dragged his mouth down her neck in a series of gentle nips and licks. "I really wish you weren't wearing *anything* right now."

"I wish we *both* weren't wearing anything." Violet's soft palm slid beneath his shirt.

Linc's chuckle ended with a groan as she rolled her hips against the erection straining behind his zipper. One more hip swivel, and he'd come in his pants like a randy teenager. "Just say the word and we'll go inside and take care of that ASAP."

Focused on navigating his mouth down the column of her neck, it took Linc a moment to realize that the string of curses flowing from her mouth weren't sexual invitations, and it took another to realize why.

Magic engulfed them.

Not a toe, or a fingertip. A fine, purple mist—the source of the growing heat—fully encompassed them like some kind of magical cocoon.

"We can't do this." Body trembling, she pushed away.

The Magic cloud disappeared with a heavy *whoosh*, making them both sway on their feet.

"That was . . . something." He struggled to catch his breath, his chest heaving from the heavy make-out session.

"*That* was a reminder we shouldn't be doing this." Violet nibbled her swollen lower lip. "I'm sorry, Lincoln, but—"

"Don't apologize." He cut her off, rescuing her tortured lower lip with his thumb. "Don't apologize for something you don't want to do. Ever. Especially when it comes to sex and your body."

"I didn't say I didn't want to do it. As a matter of fact, I think me climbing you like a jungle gym in my hallway proves I do . . . but this won't end well."

"It doesn't have to—"

"Get complicated?" She let out an abrupt laugh. "It *always* gets complicated, and that's before factoring in our past. There's too much riding on this for us to muddy the waters."

Linc dragged his hand over his face, unsuccessfully willing his hard-on away. "You're right."

"You agree with me?" She looked surprised.

"I don't *want* to, but I do . . . so you can put the weapons away." He nodded to her fisted hands, still pulsating with purple energy.

"Shit. Shit, shit, shit." She fanned her hands. "I wish these things had an on/off switch."

He reached for her but she yanked back, eyes wide, and held up her glowing hands. "Last time these babies got like this, they melted a brilliant scientist."

Two doors away, an older woman, her head covered in curlers, poked her head into the hall.

Violet whipped her hands behind her back. "Hey, Mrs. Powers. Sorry, were we too loud?"

"Oh, Violet, dear. It's you. No, no. I thought Mr. Ansari locked himself out of his apartment again. He gave me his spare key after the last time."

"Nope. Just me."

"You okay, dear? You look a little flushed." The neighbor drilled Lincoln with an appraising look. "I have one of those medical alert doodads. One press of a button and a stampede of heroic men and women will be on their way."

"Not necessary, Mrs. P., but thanks for the offer."

The older woman pierced Linc with one final look before disappearing back behind her door.

Violet had already opened hers, turning in the doorway. Her hands were back to normal as she played with her keys. "I'm sorry we couldn't do something a little fancier than Glo-Bowl."

"Don't be sorry. I had good time."

"*Sure* you did."

Bothered by the fact that she didn't believe him, he reached for her hand. Static sparked where their skin touched, and in an instant, that magical charge rushed back. "I mean it, Violet. I enjoyed every second . . . even when you almost magi-cuted me."

This time she chuckled, slowly sliding her hand away from his. "Good night, Wolfman."

"Sweet dreams, princess."

She disappeared behind her door, and the *thunk* of a dead bolt immediately followed. "There. Safe and secure. You can go home now."

"What makes you think I didn't already?" he joked.

"Because I can practically hear your caveman mind working overtime on the other side of the door. Good *night*."

He whistled his way toward the elevator. As he reached Violet's neighbor's, the door whipped open.

The older woman stood at the threshold armed with a wooden rolling pin and a sharp glare. "I didn't want to say anything before, but I will now. You treat that girl right, or I'll make you *poof* so fast your handsome head'll spin. You hearing me? I know people who make things happen."

Lincoln nodded seriously. "I hear you loud and clear, Mrs. Powers. And I have no intention of mistreating Violet."

"Good." With a parting look and a *harrumph,* the neighbor disappeared back inside her apartment, the door rattling on its hinges as she slammed it shut.

Violet touched the life of every person with whom she came into contact. Her family. The KCC kids. Mrs. Powers. *Him.*

Hurting her was the last thing he wanted, but personal experience had taught him that shit happened despite best intentions. He needed to be vigilant. Alert. And maybe start crossing his fingers, eyes, and toes that history wasn't doomed to repeat itself.

14

Ass Ointment

Olive would forever be Vi's lifeline phone call if she were ever on an IQ game show. Rose, with her ability to flip her witch switch at a moment's notice, was the perfect person to get your lazy building super to finally fix the AC. And Vi was the Maxwell with the bright ideas.

Right then, she was prepped to turn in her Bright Idea Badge.

For any given field trip, they'd never gotten more than ten or eleven permission slips, but evidently the lure of sleeping on the hard ground in the middle of a New Jersey forest was too good an opportunity to pass up.

Twenty-four school-age city kids on a two-day camping trip.

"Gotta love the smell of bug spray and glue in the morning." Harper stepped up to the bus with Rose and Olive at her side and Bax bringing up the rear. They each had a bag over their shoulder, and in Rose's case, two.

"I can't tell you guys how thankful I am for this. I figured we'd get more takers than our usual field trips, but I didn't expect this many for a fall trip."

Bax waved off her thanks. "Not a problem. In twelve hours, I won't even know they exist. I brought the expensive vodka."

"Oh, good. Wait . . . what?"

"Relax, I'm kidding." He winked, grabbing the girls' bags and tucking them into the bus's bottom storage. "I brought the cheap stuff."

He stepped away, laughing hard, as she smacked his ass with her clipboard.

"So . . ." Harper waited expectantly.

"So . . ." Vi played innocent. "It'll take us about one to two hours to get to the park, so let's make sure everyone uses the bathroom before we head out. I'd like to keep the one on the bus for emergency use only."

Harper glanced at her sisters. "Is she being oblivious on purpose?"

"Yes," Rose and Olive said at the same time.

She knew exactly what the succubus wanted to hear. She'd made the mistake of telling her best friend that she and Lincoln had a second date, and Harper had been relentlessly trying to get details ever since.

"I don't know what you want me to say." Another parent dropped off their kid, and Vi crossed their name off the list.

Harper sighed. "For starters, you can go into explicit detail about what kind of kisser he is. I have my theories, but I want to know how close they are to reality."

What kind of kisser?

Good. Great. But it wasn't as if she still felt the tingle of it against her lips two days after the fact. Oh, wait. She did.

A smile slid onto her face.

Harper's eyes widened. "Oh, you little holdout! If I didn't love you, I'd hate you for keeping us in suspense."

Rose grinned. "So I'm taking it the date went well?"

"I'd say things went better than well. Look at her. She's glowing." Harper waggled her eyebrows. "You did the hanky with Mr. Wolf's panky, didn't you? Did you levitate the bed with your new

Magic? Ooh, you broke the frame. I did that once—not during actual sex, of course, but there's this position—"

"We didn't break the bed." Vi shushed her best friend. "We just . . . kissed."

But it sure felt like a lot more.

"It must have been one hell of a kiss to bring out your sparkles."

Vi glanced down to her hands before realizing Harp meant in general, not her Magic.

"Where *is* Lincoln?" Rose glanced down the sidewalk. "Didn't you say something about him and his SIC chaperoning, too? We told everyone seven, right?"

"Uh, yeah. But I'm not sure he'll be showing." Her gaze slid toward Leo.

Wearing mirrored sunglasses and a frown, he stood by the front of the bus like a gargoyle, glowering at anyone who got close. She'd already had to tell him twice to tone it down. A bunch of eight-year-olds didn't have plans to throw her ass in a windowless van.

The bear shifter's presence was a stark reminder Lincoln wasn't around.

She'd almost called him last night, but chickened out. Their date had not only left her with a case of lady blue balls, but a slew of unanswered questions she wasn't sure she was prepped to have answered.

Where in hell had that kiss come from? Or more accurately, her all-encompassing craving for it? And could she call it a *kiss*? It had been a whole-body—and soul—experience, and one Sparky had clearly enjoyed, too.

It was better that he no-showed for the trip. A two-day nature experience with two dozen kids wasn't exactly the time to get distracted, and Lincoln Thorne was a distraction in the purest sense of the word.

Vi glanced at her watch and noted the late time. "We better get moving. Hey, everyone! Zip the lips, you little monsters, and pay attention. Before we—"

"Hey, Miss Violet," a little Norm boy chirped, "are we eating cheesecake when we get there?"

"We're not *eating* cheesecake," someone answered. "It's *called* Cheesequake. We're eating s'mores and stuff."

"Sorry, no cheesecake this trip," Vi chuckled, "but there will be some pretty delicious treats in our future. Make sure you give your bags to Bax, and he'll get them into the bottom of the bus. Did everyone use the bathroom?"

More than one child exchanged worried looks.

Harper saw them, too. "Everyone who needs to drain their balloon, with me. Then we need to get this bus a-rollin'."

Harp was right. If they didn't leave soon, they'd run into rush hour, and she did not want to be stuck in a tunnel, in bumper-to-bumper traffic, with twenty-four overexcited kids.

The kids were loading onto the bus and beginning the extremely important decision-making process of choosing their seatmates when Bax slipped past. "All packed and ready."

She grabbed his arm. "Hey. Are you sure you can handle twelve boys on your own? Maybe Rose can ask Valentin if—"

Bax's face twisted into a look of disgust.

"You're right. That's probably a waste of time."

"For Valentin Bisset, 'camping' is a three-star hotel."

Vi snorted. "You give him way more credit than me. But still, there's quite a few troublemakers coming with us. The girls and I can take some of the load, but there may be things that call for testosterone."

"You realize I was once a troublemaker, too, right?"

"*Once?*"

He cracked a smile. "I have it covered, babe."

With a small wink, he made his way to the back of the bus, where the kids instantly made it their road-trip goal to get him to show off his wings. Vi was chatting with the bus driver about best routes out of the city when Harper returned with the remaining kids . . . and a huge smirk.

"I found a few stragglers." Harper claimed a seat farther back, not pausing to elaborate.

"Stragglers? What do you . . ." Her question died on her lips as Lincoln stepped onto the bus, Adrian behind him.

"You wouldn't have left without us, would you?" Duffel bag draped over his shoulder, Lincoln disarmed her with a killer grin.

"I wasn't sure you remembered."

"Not remember?" Adrian smacked his friend on the shoulder. "This guy was banging on my door at four o'clock this morning."

"Because I knew you'd forget to pack, and I was right." Linc challenged with a smirk, shifting his attention to Vi. "Adrian needs constant prodding. He'll be late to his own funeral."

"Well, you guys made it on time. Go ahead and find an empty seat." And then with a final head count, they were on their way.

"Seat buddy?" Lincoln tossed his bag onto the floor and slid toward the window. He patted the spot next to him. "I promise I don't bite unless it's with permission."

Even with him against the window, the bus was small enough that their legs pushed against each other as she sat next to him. "So . . ."

He looked at her expectantly, but all the questions about their date—and the post-party—died on her lips the second a little face peeked through the crack in the seats in front of them. The young boy giggled and turned back around.

"You sure you're prepared for this, Alpha Thorne?" Vi asked. They'd barely pulled away from the curb, and the kids' conversations had already gotten more animated.

"I think I can handle the woods and tent living for two days. I *am* a wolf shifter."

"It's not the rustic living conditions I'm talking about."

From somewhere behind them, someone threw a wadded-up paper snowball. It landed on Lincoln's lap with a wet *plop*. The shifter looked confused before grimacing as he audibly questioned what it had been wet with.

Smothering a laugh, she took it to the garbage can before reclaiming her seat. "*That's* why I asked if you're ready."

"Because of supersized spitballs? I've helped out at the community center a few times now. I think I've proven I can hold my own."

"You can read to six five-year-olds like a boss and jump into your car and head home. This is twenty-four kids for the next *consecutive* thirty-six hours. The only time you'll get to yourself is when you go to the bathroom . . . and even then there's a buddy system so no one ventures out alone."

"I run an entire continent of shifters, some of whom have made it known they'd love to rip my throat out at the first possible chance." He kicked out his legs as far as they could go, which wasn't far in the cramped seats. "I still got it covered."

Vi hid her disbelief behind a small smile.

As soon as they cleared the city perimeter, the kids went from excited to bundles of pure energy. Lincoln changed seats to sit sentinel near a group of boys who'd dared another to hang half his body out the bus window, and three seats away, Rose broke out the Prima voice.

Thanks to navigating past an auto accident, the two hours to Cheesequake State Park felt like twelve. But once they rolled through the front gates, they checked in easily, and less than an hour later, reached their home for the next two days.

The campsite had more than enough room for everyone to spread out their tents, with a large firepit center stage and a handful of picnic tables at which to eat meals and work on nature projects. With sleeping arrangements made back at the center and a firm no-tentmate-swapping policy in place, the first thing the kids did was erect their sleeping quarters.

Seeing Vi struggling with the weight of a large cooler, Lincoln hustled to her side and took it out of her hands, tucking it beneath the shade of a tree. "Thanks. I think Harper went a little extra with the drinks."

"Explain this tent situation again." He nodded to where a group of kids were in deep discussion on best locations. "You're letting them figure things out themselves?"

"They know where they're allowed to put them. Everything else is to foster teamwork. When they lay their heads down tonight, they'll be proud that they did it together. Isn't that why you want to build a shiftocracy?"

Lincoln busted out a laugh. "A shiftocracy?"

She chuckled, dropping a box of paper supplies on a picnic table. "Isn't that what you're trying to do? Transfer the power from one to give it to all."

"Pretty much. And speaking of shiftocracy, I had a surprise visit from three of the other Alphas."

"Is that good thing?" Vi leaned against the picnic table.

"Usually any time with them is a good thing, but this time?" He shrugged, standing next to her, their shoulders brushing. "Pretty sure Benson, the Australian Alpha, hates me with every fiber of her being."

Vi chuckled. "I'm sure it's not that bad."

"She moves to the opposite side of the room whenever I enter it."

"Did you sniff your pits? Maybe she's trying to keep her lunch down around your wolfy BO."

Lincoln laughed. "Are you telling me I stink, princess?"

Only in the most delectable way, Vi thought.

They fell into an awkward silence. She liked talking to him. Hearing about his plans for the shifters fascinated her, and also put her in awe. Eliciting major change sometimes took generations, not to mention the significant degree of risk required. Not only was he making it happen in less than one, he'd put a hell of a lot more than his reputation and his position on the line in the process.

And she wanted him to know she recognized the hurdles he'd overcome to get the Packs where they were today.

"About that kiss—" Lincoln began.

"I snuck in to watch a Blood Match," Vi blurted at the same time.

She watched him uncertainly as he stared off into the distance. That sexy jaw muscle worked overtime, flicking wildly as he clenched his teeth. Bax did the same thing, and it only happened when he struggled to keep his shit together.

"I knew it was illegal for outsiders to see," Vi admitted softly. "I just . . . have no excuse. At least, not a good one. You'd acted cagey the whole week leading up to graduation and I thought . . ." She took a deep breath. ". . . I thought you were having second thoughts about leaving Athens. Turns out, I was right."

She snuck a look at him.

"You're not going to say anything? Tell me it was a stupid thing to do—of which I am fully aware. Hell, I knew it back then, but I was too worried about you to care."

A low grumble rolled out from Lincoln's throat, but it wasn't a growl. "That was dangerous . . ."

"I know. Sometimes I think about how lucky I was not to get caught, and I . . ." She shivered. "What would have happened if one of your father's men had found me around the corner? He didn't like me . . . and he never hid the fact that he didn't like the idea of us together. I'm pretty sure he only tolerated me because of Gran."

Lincoln's eyes closed briefly before turning toward her. Heat and something else she couldn't identify flickered gold, signaling his Wolf was close to the surface.

She got the hint.

"You know what? Don't tell me." She pushed off the table, immediately forcing the thought from her mind. "Some things are best left in the dark, right?"

A squabble broke out between two of the kids, and Vi excused herself to deal with it. She wasn't sure what had possessed her to bring up that night, except that for a few brief moments, it had almost felt like old times . . . back when she'd been young, fun, and kinda-sorta in love.

Rose approached her thirty minutes later. "Okay, what was that about?"

The kids were joyously picking up dried twigs to use in the firepit for that night's sweet treat, oblivious to the surrounding adults.

"What was what?" Vi feigned innocence.

"I know an intense conversation when I see one, and that made *me* antsy."

"Maybe you sat in some poison ivy when you took the girls to the bathroom. You could have a rash on your ass. Have Olive check that out."

"Someone has a rash on their ass?" Olive approached, hearing only the tail end, and reached for the first-aid kit hanging off her shoulder. "I have ointment for that."

Harper popped up next to her. "Who has an ass rash?"

"Rose," Olive answered.

"You should check that out for her. You have ointment, right?"

"I do *not* have an ass rash," exclaimed Rose.

The four of them looked at one another and laughed. When the tears dried, Olive announced, "Oh, by the way, I found the perfect spot for our magical boot camp. Spacious. Secluded—by New York standards. And the best part, it already looks a magical tsunami hit it, so when Sparky pulls a Magic Gone Wild, no one will even notice."

Vi glared. "Thanks for the vote of confidence, sis. Gives me the warm tinglies. So when are we doing this?"

"Day after we get back? If you can manage to get your guard bear to hibernate or something."

"I have a few ideas. We'll see what works best in the moment."

She usually did her best work on the fly.

❖ ❖ ❖

Linc had needed to shift in the worst way after his conversation with Violet. Not the one about shiftocracy, or even the questioning of his personal hygiene.

Blood Matches. That Blood Match.

Claws tearing apart his insides, his inner Wolf had demanded he tell her everything. But he'd nearly lost control when she admitted she'd done it because she'd been worried for *him*. That she'd risked her life because he'd done something to make her question how much he cared.

So many things he'd wanted to say, and all he'd managed to croak out was a grunted "That was dangerous."

No shit, Sherlock.

Timmy, the waist-high eagle shifter he'd met his first day at the center, bumped into the back of his legs, tearing Linc's attention away from his pity party. "Whoops. Sorry, Alpha."

"Don't worry about it."

"Hey, wait for me!" Timmy tore after his friends as they all headed back to the camp, excitedly talking about their run and already plotting their strategy to convince Violet into letting them take another.

Linc chuckled. He'd been the same way at their age. It didn't matter if you flew high above the treetops or sank your paws firmly into the dirt—time in your animal form always came with freedom that was difficult to find anywhere else.

When they returned from their run, the campsite buzzed with

activity, kids talking excitedly while prepping for their first official campfire meal.

Violet plucked a small twig from a young wolf shifter's hair as the ten-year-old walked past. "You all look very happy . . . and very dirty."

"That was the *best*, Miss Violet!" Timmy's broad smile barely fit on his narrow face. "Alpha Thorne walked me through how to shift to my bird and back and it was *so* much easier than all the other times I tried! *And* I didn't fly into a single tree! I mean, I had that one close call, but there was no actual contact!"

Violet wrapped the little boy in a side hug. "I'm glad you didn't give yourself a concussion, and your aunts will be too. Why don't you go with the others to get cleaned up? We'll be sitting down to eat in a bit."

"Sure thing." He skipped away, his red hair bouncing.

"That was nice of you to help Timmy." She turned her eyes to Linc. "He hasn't had an easy time of things lately and I know it meant a lot to him."

"I can't help but be curious . . ."

"Why he has such a problem shifting?" She read his mind. "His parents were killed in a hunting incident when he was six."

Linc's smile melted away. "And by 'hunting,' you mean . . ."

"The Eliases were out for a post-dinner flight in their animal forms when someone decided to spend their evening shooting eagles for sport. Timmy's lived with his mother's sister and her wife ever since, and while they adore him, they're Norm. They can't . . ."

"Help when it comes to shifting problems," Linc guessed.

Violet's gaze drifted over to where the little boy stood back from the rest of the kids, waiting his turn to wash up. "It's one of the reasons he comes to the KCC . . . to socialize more in the shifter community."

"Timmy's lucky he has you to make sure that happens."

"You mean the center."

"The KCC wouldn't be what it is to the kids if you weren't part of it, Violet. Do you think Isaac ever gave it the same focus that you have while you've volunteered?"

She didn't dispute him, and cupping his cheek, she smiled and plucked a dried leaf from his hair. "Looks like the kids aren't the only ones who could use a little cleanup, Wolfman."

He ran his hand over his hair with a chuckle. "Probably not. I showed a few of the younger kids how to stalk up behind a rabbit."

Violet's smile fell. "You let them hunt a defenseless rabbit?"

"What? No." He chuckled. "We pounced on Adrian. We pretended *he* was a rabbit."

As much as he didn't want to end their conversation, he also didn't want to continue smelling like a forest floor. Excusing himself to do a quick washup, he ducked into the tent where he'd left his belongings only to find someone else's stuff, his own nowhere to be seen. "What the . . . ?"

"Your things are in the one on the end, along with your friend's." The angel glared at him from a few feet away, his tattooed arms crossed over his chest.

"Who moved it?"

"I did. This is the only single tent we brought, and someone who showed up on time should use it." Bax turned to leave.

Lincoln should've let him. Instead, he followed. "What the hell did I do to piss you off?"

"Guilty much, Thorne?"

"Not guilty. Perceptive. I was reading body language before I could walk, and yours is telling me I should consider sleeping with one eye open. I'm taking a stab in the dark and saying it's Violet-related."

The muscle in the angel's jaw ticked wildly. *Bingo.*

"Look, I'm sorry if I'm stepping on toes . . ." Actually, he wasn't sorry in the least. The thought of anyone laying claim to her in such a way made him not only want to step on toes, but heads, spines, and any other body part that would cause irreparable harm.

"Stepping on toes?" Bax challenged. "Is that what you think you're doing?"

"Or a wing. However you want to describe it."

"You think I don't like you because I have feelings for her?"

"You mean you don't?"

Anyone with eyes could see he and Vi were close, and Linc would be lying if he didn't admit it bothered him. Hell, he and Vi weren't even a real item, but the jealousy ripping through him definitely was.

Bax glanced around as if making sure no little ears could hear them. "*Fuck no.* Violet's like a sister to me. It's the big brother in me that wants to rip your head off your shoulders."

"For doing what? Breathing?"

"Something's off with the two of you. I haven't figured out what yet, but there's a change in the air when you're near each other, and unlike Harper, I don't think it's pheromones."

"So because your angel sense is tingling, you're planning my decapitation?"

"You're using her, Thorne. Something's not right about this entire situation, and I'm not sitting back and pretending otherwise."

A flash of anger raised the hairs on his arms. "Do you think so little of your friend that you can't imagine me being interested in her without ulterior motives?"

"I couldn't love Violet more than I already do. She deserves nothing but the best. That's not you. No offense."

A low growl rolled from his throat. "When you say 'no offense,' it's a sign that what you said is pretty damn offensive."

"Then it's a good thing I don't care if I offend you or not. You're the North American Alpha. There's only one person that'll get hurt in the end, and that's not you."

"I have no intention of hurting her—on purpose or otherwise."

Bax stepped closer, putting them nearly nose-to-nose. "For your sake, that better be true. If she ends up becoming a Lincoln Thorne casualty, I'll tear you into pieces and fly your body parts to opposite ends of the earth. A jigsaw champion wouldn't be able to put you back together again, much less all the king's men. You get me?"

He nodded. "I get you . . . but you should also know that if you come between me and Violet, there won't be enough pieces of you for anyone to even attempt to reassemble. Do *you* get *me*?"

And fuck if he didn't mean it.

They stood in a standoff, neither one of them willing to back down first. Linc's Wolf itched to be let out and get their point across himself, but eventually the angel stalked away to where Violet stood talking to a small group of kids.

And that's where the bastard stayed for the majority of the night. He may as well have pissed on her leg, which was why, two hours later, Linc was surprised to find the spot next to her empty when he glanced through the crackling fire.

Grabbing a plate of untouched chocolate and graham crackers, he headed her way. "This seat taken?"

She peered up at him through her thick lashes, a small smirk pulling up her lips. "It'll cost you that chocolate bar."

"Small price to pay for the best seat in the house." Claiming the spot, he stretched his legs out in front of him and eyed the charred marshmallow she attempted to crush between two crackers.

He laughed. "Is that a marshmallow or a volcano rock you're about to put in your mouth?"

She paused with her creation an inch away from her lips. "Have your fun, but this is the only way to eat a s'more. It gives it a smoky, earthy flavor—something I'd thought you'd enjoy, being a nature lover and all."

"Oh, I'm a nature lover, but I'm also partial to keeping my original teeth as long as possible. The only way to properly roast a marshmallow is until it's golden perfection. Toasty on the outside and gooey on the inside." He popped a sugar cloud on a stick and hovered it a few inches above the flames. "The secret is keeping it *away* from direct contact with the fire. Too close, and you get . . . volcano rock."

"You do you, and I'll do me." Her gaze fastened on his, she took an oversize bite of her charred treat and moved her jaw at a snail's pace. At some point, something crunched. "See. *Yum.*"

He barely suppressed a smile. "Good, huh?"

"The best." Tears sprung to her eyes as she tried to swallow and failed.

Laughing, he handed her his spare napkin and chuckled harder when she turned away to spit out her treat.

"That was way worse than I remember."

"Try this one." He held out his perfectly toasted marshmallow, expertly sandwiched between two slabs of already melting chocolate and two graham crackers.

"I can't steal yours."

He cracked it in half and held one out to her. "Now we both get a taste of perfection."

"If you insist." She took a bite, and this time, a real *yum* rolled up from her throat.

Linc's cock twitched, egged on by every sexy lick, nibble, and moan. He strategically shifted his pants. "Good?"

"This is freakin' delicious. I've seen the error of my ways." A small dollop of chocolate clung to the corner of her lip.

"You have a little something . . ." Linc touched his own mouth.

"Here?" She rubbed, missing the spot.

"A little to the left."

She wiped again. "Now?"

She'd managed to smudge it more.

"May I?" After getting her nod, he cupped her cheek and dabbed the chocolate spot away with his thumb.

"You get it?"

Yeah, he got it . . . and damned if he didn't want to keep touching her.

It had been two long, excruciating days since he'd had his first taste of her mouth, and it was killing him not to close the distance and taste it again. Violet. Marshmallow. Chocolate. And all.

Vi oh so gently tilted her cheek deeper into his palm.

So soft. So inviting. Their bodies leaned forward as if attracted by magnets, but with less than two inches before full contact, those magnets were ripped away.

"Miss Violet!" Misha bounded up, oblivious to what she'd interrupted. The eight-year-old's determined look bounced between them. "Can we tell ghost stories now? My brother told me that on Boy Scout camping trips, they always tell spooky stories, and I think we should do that too."

With a slight blush rising to her cheeks, Vi shifted her attention to the young witch. "I'm not so sure it's a good idea. Some of our group are pretty young. They may get scared."

"I already talked to everyone and they all agreed to it."

Violet didn't look convinced. "I'm not so sure that—"

"Oh, please, please, please. I'll tell the older kids not to go too scary. *Please*, Miss Violet! I swear I won't try to con any more volunteers into any bets, *please*!"

He gently bumped his shoulder into Violet's. "Come on, Miss Violet. How often do these kids get to tell each other spooky stories around a real campfire?"

"Exactly!" Misha nearly jumped out of her shoes in excitement.

"Fine," Violet finally gave in with a sigh. "But nothing with any blood or gore."

Misha squealed so high only dogs—and wolves—could hear, and ran off to tell her friends the good news.

Violet's mouth twisted into a warning smile. "When the kids

come knocking on my tent because they're too scared to fall asleep, I'm sending them to yours."

"They'll be more than welcome. It's not like I'll be doing much sleeping with Adrian snoring all night. The guy may be a lion, but he snores louder than a damn grizzly bear."

Violet's laugh eased a smile to his lips. But Linc secretly wished that if anyone showed up at his tent because they couldn't sleep, it would be her.

15

Magical Shingles

For someone who turned into a six-hundred-pound bear, Leo the Guard had a suspiciously witchy aptitude for showing up out of nowhere, and when least expected.

A day after their return from Cheesequake, Vi had made it two subway stops before he casually entered her car and made himself comfortable in the open seat across from her. On her second escape attempt, he was leaning against the front of Olive's apartment building before she'd even stepped into her cab.

Today, two hours before she planned on meeting Olive and Rose, he had promptly parked himself in front of her building's elevator. Enough was enough. It was time to nip this shifter in the bud.

Vi yanked her apartment door open.

Down the hall, Leo immediately snapped to attention. "Miss Maxwell. You okay? Do you need anything?"

"Nope." She poised to knock on Mrs. Powers's front door. "Just visiting my elderly neighbor for some tea and cheek-pinching."

He nodded and stepped back into position as Mrs. Powers answered. "Violet! What a nice surprise! What can I do for you?"

"It's funny you should ask that, Mrs. P." She slid a coy look toward Leo before whispering, "Can I use your fire escape?"

Goddess love her neighbor. She didn't even bat an eye as she stepped aside. "My escape is your escape."

With a small wave to Leo, Vi disappeared inside her neighbor's apartment and fired off a quick text to Rose, instructing her to pick her up around back. By the time she'd finished tea with Mrs. Powers, her sister's Audi had pulled around the corner.

Rose stuck her head out of the window and laughed as Vi navigated the rickety fire escape. "Do I want to know why you're sneaking down your *neighbor's* fire escape?"

"Because the city still hasn't replaced my fire ladder and I don't fancy breaking an ankle . . . or my whole body."

"Hey, whatever works."

"Desperate times. Inventive measures." She dropped to the ground and wiped her hands on her jeans before climbing into the passenger seat. "Where's Olly?"

Rose nudged her chin to the GPS. "Already there putting the protective wards in place."

"She's going all out for this, isn't she?"

"Are you kidding? This is a puzzle she can't solve, and it's driving her up the wall. When she's making you run magical laps, remember that you're the one who put this idea into her head."

"And what will you be doing while she hones her inner drill sergeant?"

"I'll be watching the fallout."

Violet smacked her sister's leg playfully. "Thanks for the pep talk, witch!"

"I mean that I'll be there for moral support!" Rose laughed. "*And* to clean up the mess you leave behind. Besides, it was either be your backup or deal with Bonding Ceremony stuff. This won, hands down."

"*Deal* with?" She studied her sister's profile. "Shouldn't it be something you're *happy* to prepare for, not *have* to?"

Rose, Queen of Blank Expressions, clutched the steering wheel in a white-knuckle grip, the only sign her triplet held something back. In true Prima fashion, she never *burdened* anyone else with her problems.

"You know you can talk to me, right?" Vi reminded her gently. "I'm not saying I won't tease you relentlessly, but I'll always listen, and if there's anything I can do . . ."

Rose's eyes remained glued on the street. "I know."

"But you won't tell me what's going on."

"Why bother you with it when I can handle it on my own? Besides, between your Magic flare-ups, the Council forcing you into a Witch Bond, *and* the new man in your life, you have enough stacked on your plate. I'm not piling on more."

It was on the tip of her tongue to deny that Linc was *the new man in her life,* but she couldn't. She wasn't sure *what* he was. They had an arrangement, a deal with certain expectations . . . but none of those included searing-hot kisses against her front door and suggestions of nakedness.

And not to mention, she missed him. Two days apart felt like two years.

Most people didn't miss their business partners, or mentally scold themselves for sticking to their own no-sex rule—and she'd done the latter at least a dozen times in the past twenty-four hours.

Magic Boot Camp couldn't have come at a better time. She needed a distraction, and both her and Lincoln had to focus on their reasons for making the deal in the first place.

Thirty minutes later, Vi's eyebrows flew into her hairline as the GPS announced their arrival at Olive's "perfect place." "Whoa. An empty sports stadium wasn't available?"

Actually, a sports stadium would've been smaller.

Dumpsters piled high with used construction materials sat outside the long-forgotten sewing factory, and what windows weren't already broken or boarded up were caked with blackened grime.

Large. Dank. Ominous. The place screamed "horror flick" more than "boot camp."

The iron front door opened with a loud squeal and Olive stepped out, wearing a big grin and a plastic whistle around her neck. "Isn't this place perfect?"

"It's . . . big."

Olive shrugged. "We need space."

"For what? To duck and cover?"

"Exactly. And this place is so abandoned, even the rats don't come here. But as an extra precaution, I spelled it to repel anyone who doesn't already know the address."

Olive had gone all out, dividing the inside into three distinct areas. Self-defense dummies occupied the far left, and set up on the right were a half dozen targets a lot like the ones they'd used at archery camp. Meditation candles and a cushioned mat sprawled over the third, smaller area up front.

Vi knew her sister was incredible, but she'd outdone herself. "I can't believe you did this in such a short period of time."

Olive brushed off the compliment with a small shrug. "I haven't found a loophole in that damn law—*yet*—so getting your magical mojo in shape is the least I can do."

Vi warmed her palms. "Then let's figure this out. Do I stretch and run laps or something?"

"We're waiting for reinforcements."

Before Vi asked who, the heavy iron door slammed open, and in walked Harper and Bax.

The succubus smacked the angel in the stomach. "See! I told you our girl would get away this time! Mr. Broody Wings didn't think you'd give your guard bear the slip, but I had every faith in you. As always."

Bax snorted. "Is that why you made a spa appointment in an hour? Because you thought she'd make it?"

Harper stuck her tongue out at him.

Vi glanced back to her sisters. "Not that I don't love having all my favorite people in the room, but why the audience?"

Olive dragged her over to the self-defense dummies. "Because while Rose and I are studying your magical currents, Bax and Harper will coax Sparky to come out and play."

"Coax it out?"

"You're not walking around the city leaking all over the place. Ninety-five percent of the time, it's MIA, right? Something about Potion's Up and the alley triggered flares, and we need to figure out what it was."

"There may have been a few other times . . ." Vi admitted warily.

All eyes turned to her.

"Who? Why? Where? And when?" Olive asked.

"Who—with Lincoln. Why—beats the hell out of me. Where—at my apartment door. When—after our last date."

Everyone stared, waiting . . .

"When we kissed, I kind of put us in a big purple bubble."

Olive looked contemplative. "How big are we talking?"

"Like a human-sized hamster ball? It took me a minute to notice it, but when I did, it went haywire before disappearing like someone sucked it up with a vacuum."

"Interesting. Okay. We can work with this. All we have to do is re-create that moment." She slid her gaze to Bax. "Do you think you could—?"

"I am not kissing Baxter!" Horror lifted her voice a few octaves. "No way. No how. No. That's . . . *ick.*"

Folding his massive arms over his chest, Bax shot her an offended look. "I'll have you know I'm a fucking phenomenal kisser."

"I'm sure you are . . . just as I'm sure you've never kissed anyone who's seen you eat a peanut butter–coated cucumber. It's not happening."

Harper pressed a noisy kiss to her cheek. "Fine. I volunteer. Pucker up, cupcake."

Vi chuckled. "Thanks for the offer, but I don't think we'd get the same result. As much as I love you both, you're not—"

"Lincoln Thorne," Bax finished, all too aware of her thoughts, and not thrilled with them. "That Alpha you ran into at Rose's party was him, wasn't it?"

"Yes, but this isn't *him*. At least, not all of it," she added before anyone got a bizarre idea like calling Lincoln to join the party. "He wasn't around when Sparky materialized in the alley. It was me, the girl, and her jerkface ex. Lincoln showed up after I went all glowy."

Olive pushed her glasses higher on her nose. "Maybe your Magic isn't necessarily connected to Linc, but to emotional surges. Fear. Excitement. *Stress*. It's like shingles."

Vi arched an eyebrow. "You're saying I have magical shingles?"

"I'm saying that unless you strip away all emotions and walk around like a witchy Vulcan, you need to put a leash on it. Not *just* a leash, but a muzzle, a collar, and an electrified fence. If you don't exhibit more control than anyone *ever*, there's no way the Council will entertain the idea of letting you off the hook for the Witch Bond."

"Aren't you a fountain of good news . . ."

But Olive was right. Controlling her Magic wasn't enough. She needed to *own* it better than any witch before her had ever done. Even Edie.

"Where do we start?"

Three hours later, Vi was sorry she asked. Panting and doubled over, she wiped away the sweat dripping into her eyes. It stung and blurred her vision, but it didn't prevent her from reveling in the fact that as rough shape as she was in, Bax and Harper looked five times worse.

The angel and succubus lay on the mat-covered ground, and Bax emitted a slight wheeze with every exhalation. Harper, face-down on the floor, looked like she was already sleeping.

Vi dropped to the ground between them. "This isn't working. I'd take off my bra and wave it as a white flag, but I'm too tired to reach around and unclasp it."

"No!" Olive bounced on the balls of her feet like a cheerleader. "You almost had it that time! Our efforts just need a little CPR."

Harper groaned. "*I'll* need CPR if we keep this up much longer. As it is I'll be crawling into Lace and Leather to get a recharge."

Vi chuckled at the mental image of her best friend dragging herself into the sex club on her hands and knees.

Bax and Harper had been her supernatural sparring partners for the better part of the past three hours. Harp, as a succubus and master manipulator of emotions, easily mimicked Vi's fear from the night in the alley, but Bax hadn't been so lucky. Someone had to play the threat in their magical reimagining, and he'd been chosen.

"You sure you're okay?" Vi inspected his charred shirt. On their last run-through, Sparky had nearly singed a few important bits. "That last bolt thing—"

"Got a little too close for comfort?" He snorted. "Yeah. Remind me to bring a fire extinguisher next time."

"Next time?" With a grimace, she pushed herself into a sitting position and found her two sisters with their heads bowed close together, murmuring. "Please tell me we're not doing this again. I don't have many friends. I can't afford to magically zap the ones I do have into nonexistence."

"Aw, you do love us." Harper unsteadily climbed to her feet and, reaching out a hand, helped drag Vi to hers. "And I think Bax's scorch burns prove there's more work to be done."

"Harper's right," Olive agreed. "With a little more practice and daily meditation, you'll rein in your Magic no problem . . . or at least condition it not to attack first, behave later."

Rose nodded. "And you have to work on not treating it like an accident waiting to happen."

"Are you serious? It *is* an accident waiting to happen! Were you napping for the last three hours?" Her gaze skittered to where her cell phone lay blasted into a hundred pieces.

There was no fixing that, even with great customer support.

"What time is it?" She grabbed Bax's arm, checking his watch. "Crap. I have to get out of here before my guard bear lets the wolf out of the bag. I also need a shower, ibuprofen, and a nap . . . not necessarily in that order. If I could, I'd do it all simultaneously."

"But we've only been at this for three hours!" Olive complained. "We could do another round of meditation if you're too physically strung out from the magical work."

"See, sis. I see your lips moving and I hear noises coming out of your mouth, but my brain is too tired to compute." Pulling her triplet into a hug, she burrowed her nose into Olly's sweet cinnamon-scented hair. "Thank you for doing this, but I'm not superhuman like you. I need a break."

"Fine. We can go again tomorrow."

"I'll be at the KCC all day and then I'm at Potion's Up all night. Maybe Friday?"

"Aren't you seeing Mr. Sex on Legs?" Harper waggled her eyebrows. "Maybe that's why you were a bit off tonight. I know *my* Magic gets a bit twitchy the longer I go without some hanky-panky. You need to ring yourself up a booty call."

"I don't need a booty call. And actually, I don't know when Linc and I are seeing each other next. Our schedules haven't really synched since we got back."

They'd tried, but just as they'd been interrupted every single time they'd been alone at Cheesequake, something always seemed to pop up when they made plans. Maybe Harper's booty call suggestion had merit. Maybe they just needed not to plan, to go with the flow instead. Then they could actually find a few minutes to do more than video chat.

Vi said her goodbyes to Harper and her sisters, each of whom

204 ❀ April Asher

tried making her feel better about her complete and total failure.
She loved them for it, but it wouldn't change the fact that she could
meditate until she was the picture of serenity itself and still leave
scorch marks on the earth.

Riding home on the back of Bax's motorcycle, Vi didn't care
about any of it. She held on tight, savoring the wind whipping
against her cheeks, and lost all her negative thoughts by the time
they arrived at her building.

Vi climbed off the bike and handed him back his helmet.
"Thanks for the ride. I . . . what's wrong?"

His gaze fixed on something behind her, Bax shut off his bike
and followed her onto the sidewalk. "I think I'll stick around for
a bit."

"What are you . . . ?" Her Magic, which should've taken a
twelve-year hibernation thanks to magical Boot Camp, woke up,
dowsing her entire body in awareness.

Lincoln leaned against her building, so still he could give a living statue in Central Park a run for their money. He made no move
to come closer, his hands shoved deep into his pockets and his eyes
flickering from hot human brown to striking wolfy gold.

Hex me.

"Maybe we should head over to my place . . ." Bax's hand banded
around her elbow, ready to lead her back to the bike.

"And do what? Stare at the bare walls? No offense, but your
place is a little too Spartan for me. Thanks for the ride home, but
I got it from here."

He didn't so much as blink. "I'm not so sure you—"

"Bax." She patted his chest affectionately. "Go guard someone
who can't guard themselves. I'll be fine. He's basically an oversized
puppy."

"You heard her, angel." Linc pushed off the wall and closed in
on them. "It's time for you to go."

"Will you shush?" Vi spun around to face him, her annoyance

kicking up her Magic level a few notches. "If I'm not in the mood for *his* overprotective nonsense, I'm *really* not in the mood for yours."

Linc's eyes burned hot as he came to a stop less than an inch away.

"What the fuck happened here?" Despite a low, rolling growl, his touch was feather-soft as he swept a thumb across her cheek. "You have a cut."

"Something probably kicked up while we were on the bike."

"You sure about that?"

Bax shifted closer, his chest practically bumping into her back. "I don't think I like what you're insinuating, *wolf.*"

"And I know I don't give a damn, *angel.*"

They sandwiched her between them as they threw piercing glares at each other over her head.

Vi sighed, tired. "I love my curves too much to risk becoming pancaked, so you guys go ahead and have your penis-measuring contest without me. Tell me who wins. On second thought, don't."

She slipped out from between them and headed to her building.

"Better hurry, Thorne," Bax taunted. "I don't think she's in a holding-the-door mood and she's damn fast for someone with short legs."

Vi smirked. She *did* move fast—when she wanted, or when shopping with Harper and Rose and had no choice but to keep up or be left behind in the shoe department.

With a curse, Lincoln followed, barely catching the building's front door before it shut. By the time he stepped inside, she was already up the first flight of stairs, and when he finally reached her apartment, her door was already halfway open.

"Violet . . ."

"Not until we're inside. There are ears everywhere."

On cue, Mrs. Powers's door clicked shut.

He waited until they stood in her small foyer before whirling around on her. "What the fuck were you thinking sneaking off like that?"

"First, I didn't sneak." She dropped her keys on the TV stand and went to the kitchen to grab a bottle of water.

Lincoln followed. "So you didn't crawl out of a window like a teenager?"

"No, I climbed down a fire escape like a responsible adult, but that's not the point."

He folded his arms across his broad chest. Damn, he looked sexy standing there all pissed off and growly, and . . . Vi dragged her thoughts out of the gutter with a reminder of why she'd resorted to sneaking out a window.

She took a swig of water and faced him, glare for glare. "I don't need a walking shadow twenty-four hours a day. Personally, I don't think I need one at all."

"Well, that's nonnegotiable, because we already saw what the paparazzi is willing to do to get a scoop, and it'll only get worse the deeper we get into this arrangement. Eventually, it won't only be paparazzi. There are a lot of people out there who aren't exactly members of the Lincoln Thorne fan club."

She snorted. "Now *that* I believe."

"You think this is a joke?" Linc's eyes flashed gold. "If the Elders get wind of what myself and the other Alphas are planning, what do you think they'll do? Come after *us*? No. No, they follow my father's rule of law, and that means they'll go after every person we care about."

For each one of Lincoln's steps forward, she took one back, until she'd walked her ass into the counter. Not that he'd hurt her. Lincoln Thorne may be many things—arrogant and pompous and a huge hothead—but he wouldn't hurt a fly or a woman.

He braced his hands against the counter on either side of her hips, effectively caging her in. "What do you say to that, princess?"

"That you better not piss off the Elders prematurely." Vi ignored the magical heat swelling in her body and stared him down.

"Why do you insist on making this as difficult as possible? Sometimes you do things that—"

"That what?" Her gaze dropped to his mouth, which was now less than an inch away.

Ever since their first kiss, she'd dreamed of a second. Literally. In her sleep-dreams. In her daydreams. And in her sex-deprived imagination, they were alone and naked.

"Sometimes I do what, Wolfman?" Vi wet her bottom lip in an attempt to soothe her suddenly dry mouth.

Lincoln's attention flickered down to watch the movement. "Sometimes you drive me right up to my breaking point."

Her body hummed as he dipped his nose to the curve of her neck . . . oh so close but not touching. "I've spent years building control over my Wolf, and you walk back into my life and he's like a horny, temperamental pup all over again."

Her mind shut off.

"Nothing I say or do appeases him." Linc gently nipped her shoulder before kissing away the slight sting. "Because I'm not giving him what he wants. What *we* want."

Vi's heart skipped a beat, her chest heaving as if she'd finished the New York City Marathon. "What do you want?"

"*You.*"

Sparky jumped right on board.

Magic hung heavy in the air, coils of purple and gold energy licking over every surface of her skin. A tendril flickered out as if reaching for Lincoln.

"I take back the rule," Vi whispered before she thought about it too much.

She wanted to touch Lincoln Thorne more than she wanted her next breath. She wanted to feel his hands on her, wanted to bask in his heat and roll around *on* him. And when she looked into his golden-flecked eyes, she saw her own needs staring right back at her.

✦ ✦ ✦

In the hours since Leo had informed him that Violet had given him the slip, both Linc and his Wolf had been near out of their minds. And now that she stood in front of him, smelling like a lavender-infused wonderland, he wasn't so sure he hadn't projected the words he wanted to hear into his own head.

He gripped the counter until his knuckles popped from the pressure, because if he didn't, he'd touch her. "I need you to clarify what you mean, Violet. I need to be one hundred percent certain we're talking about the same—"

"Lincoln." Her warm palms slid up his chest and cupped the back of his neck. "I revoke the no-sex-between-us rule."

That was all he needed to hear.

Grasping her hips, he tugged her into a searing-hot kiss. Her hands dove into his hair and held him close—as if he'd think about pulling away. Not this time. He only came up for air when his chest burned from lack of oxygen, and even then, he kept his mouth on her skin, nibbling and kissing his way from her mouth down the sensitive column of her neck.

She bared her throat to him with a breathy sigh.

"Keep making those sexy little noises and I'll fuck you right here against the counter, princess." With a low growl, Linc nipped her earlobe and savored her corresponding shiver.

"And that's a problem why?"

Tipping her face toward his, he answered, "Because I've waited nearly half my life for this moment, and I plan on it being a marathon, not a sprint."

He hadn't meant to blurt it all out like that, but it couldn't be helped. And he couldn't seem to care. It was true. He'd lost count of how many times he'd pictured them together throughout the years, and now she stood in front of him in the flesh.

No way was he about to rush things.

A myriad of emotions flashed through Violet's periwinkle eyes, too fast to be deciphered. "This has to stay as uncomplicated as possible. Do you think we can do that?"

"Princess, if it means I can take you somewhere significantly more comfortable than a kitchen counter, I can and will do anything."

"My couch is pretty comfy and it's only six feet away."

"That'll work."

Their mouths and hands worked into a frenzy as he walked them backward toward the sofa. By the time her legs bumped into it, Violet already had his shirt halfway off. Linc grabbed the back of the collar and yanked it the rest of the way.

"Hell's Spells, I love it when guys do that." She dragged his mouth back to hers.

"If you can think about other guys right now, I'm not doing my job."

"Then by all means, make me forget."

"Oh, I plan on it."

Gentle quivers slipped through her body as he lifted her shirt inch by inch, trailing the backs of his knuckles up her torso. Her breathing hitched, but as her lace-covered breasts came into view, it was *him* who quaked.

"Fuck me, Violet. You're perfect." He took one cloth-covered nipple in his mouth, instantly feeling it harden against his tongue.

"We still have way too much clothing on."

He chuckled. "I couldn't agree more."

With a coy grin and quick fingers, she unhooked the clasp of her bra and tossed the lacey white contraption on top of their shirt pile.

What little poise Linc still possessed vanished. "You're right. The underwear has to go."

He dropped to his knees and, keeping his gaze locked on her, slowly slid her jeans and panties down her legs in one slow glide. She kicked them away, and in a matter of seconds, his own jeans were gone, and the condom from his wallet was out and rolled onto his throbbing erection.

"No more teasing." She dropped back onto the couch and hauled him on top of her. "I need you. Now."

Her wetness, perfectly aligned with the tip of his cock, tempted him like nothing else.

Violet rolled her hips, lifting them to meet his. "Lincoln . . ."

He took a deep breath in an attempt to get a handle on his control. "You're making it damn hard not to sink inside you and take you right here and now."

"Good."

"Not good. I want to take my time. Taste you—"

"You can have a buffet later. I wanted you inside me ten minutes ago."

Fuck if he didn't want to give the lady exactly what she asked for. Anchoring his knees on the couch, he hooked her legs over his arms, gripped her hips, and pushed into her in one solid thrust.

Violet mewed below him. "Hell's Spells, Lincoln. Don't you dare stop!"

"Baby, I'm just getting started." He pulled out slowly, nearly giving himself double vision, and slammed into her again.

Within seconds, he set a brutal pace that had them both breathless and panting. The only sound in the room, other than the faint squeak of the couch, was the sweaty clash of their bodies.

Every kiss. Each touch. Pleasure swirled not only between them, but around them.

Electricity crackled in the air.

Linc's Wolf howled high into the metaphorical sky.

And when their bodies simultaneously found release, Linc knew there was no way things weren't about to get complicated . . . and he didn't care in the least.

16

The Universal Gesture

Vi couldn't wipe the smirk off her face, and after Harper hurled a fourth calculating look her way during their shift at Potion's Up, she'd tried. *So damn hard.* Naked time with Lincoln the night before kept working its way into her subconscious, making it nearly impossible not to grin.

Hesitant Vi, who had been reluctant about taking the no-sex rule off the table, had been replaced by Voracious Violet, who'd experienced so many toe-curling orgasms it felt like she'd competed in the annual Crunch-a-Thon down at the gym.

Nope. She welcomed her orgasm-induced sore abs and couldn't wait for the next workout.

Harper's tray thunked down on the bar, startling Vi out of her postcoital daydream. "This is me waving the white flag of surrender. If you don't tell me what put that smile on your face, I will spontaneously combust."

"Please don't." Gage dumped a tub of ice into the freezer chest and drilled the succubus with a warning scowl. "I'm still cleaning all the nooks and crannies after the last time someone combusted in here. This place is now a combustion-free zone."

Harper ignored their boss with a roll of her eyes. "I mean it, Vi. You've been prancing around here with that satisfied grin on your face since you walked through the door. *Prancing.* You're not a prancer."

She shrugged. "Maybe I'll take it up."

Especially if sexy time with Lincoln wasn't a once-and-done deal. They hadn't discussed it with all the orgasming they'd done, nor after the breakfast Violet-buffet she'd given him that morning, but she had hopes.

As images of their goodbye kiss played through her memory, her lips twitched into another impish smirk.

"Do not play coy with me, Violet Ann Maxwell," Harper warned, glaring at her with narrowed eyes. "I *invented* coyness. You have sexual mojo pouring off you like freaking Niagara Falls. I could feed off it right now and not hit up the club for an entire month. And just so you know, levels don't get that high from being horny."

Gage released an exasperated sigh. "Can't the two of you go a single shift without one of you mentioning the word 'horny'?"

"I can." Vi jabbed her thumb at Harper. "But this one has a serious issue."

Harper scoffed. "I don't have an issue."

"You have a one-track mind, Harp."

"I know. I'm saying it's not an issue. I fully embrace my constant state of horniness. And honestly, I'm a little disappointed in you, Gage. If I were a man, you'd pat me on the back and cheer me on to my next conquest."

Muttering about lacing his next pint of O-negative with Pepto-Bismol, the vampire disappeared into the back room.

Harper leaned on the counter, the move amping up her cleavage. "Come on, Maxwell. Give a succubus girl something . . . *anything* . . . to feed on. Just a little snack to tide me over until I get the full-Monty story."

Vi chuckled. "You can keep hoisting your boobs up until they become a second chin. A Maxwell doesn't kiss and tell."

"Keep your secrets. It doesn't matter. I already know your little glow 'n' show has to do with a certain hot Alpha."

"And how do you know that?"

"Because I spent an hour on the phone with Bax last night talking him out of going back to your apartment and neutering a wolf." Harper hopped onto a bar stool. "Don't tell him I said this, but if forced to place a bet, I'd place all my money on your Alpha. Bax is all sort of angel badass with the long hair and tattoos, but Lincoln's *literally* an animal. He's animalistic by nature—which is why shifters are one of my favorite Supernaturals."

The bar door opened. Vi turned to welcome the newest customer, but her vocal cords seized.

"What's wrong? You look like you've seen Freddy Krug—" Harper followed her gaze, and her look of curiosity turned to shock. "Fuck me with a dildo. What the hell is your mother doing in Manhattan? I thought she never ventured more than a foot outside of Tribeca when she came into the city!"

"She doesn't." Which was why Vi's alert level rose to DEFCON 1.

She debated the likelihood of getting to the storeroom without being detected, but like the well-trained witch she was, Christina Maxwell found Vi as if she was marked with a magical tracking beacon.

"It's too late. I've been spotted." Vi clutched Harper's hand. "If you're my best friend, you won't abandon me right now."

"Technically, I share that role with Bax, and if you want to get more technical, you've been best friends with your sisters since you were womb-mates. So I'm like the third best friend, once removed . . ."

"Harper."

Vi's mother assessed the bar with unmasked distaste. "Violet. I see you're still working here."

Out of habit, Vi tucked a strand of purple hair behind her ear. "Well, you did find me here, so . . ."

Christina frowned before passing a sly glance to a still-trapped Harper. "Heather. You're looking . . . well."

"Thank you, Mrs. Maxwell." Harper smiled, not bothering to correct her. They'd met many times through the years, and while Harper had tried to correct her in the beginning, Christina still called her a different H-name on every single run-in. "If you two will excuse me, I have a retirement party to inebriate."

"Harp." Vi shook her head gently.

"Sorry, sunshine, but duty calls."

Her horrible best friend left them alone.

"Can I get you something to drink?" Vi asked her mother.

Christina glanced at the collection of colorful bottles along the wall and the cauldron Gage kept at the ready. "I don't suppose you have any vintage Dom?"

"No, but we have all the other major men—Jim, Jack, Johnnie, and Jose."

"Then let's bypass the drink and skip to why I'm here. I wanted to speak with you."

That sounds ominous. Flicking a glance to the nearest customer, three stools away, Vi grimaced. "Phones are great for that kind of thing. You dial. You talk."

"And they can also be ignored. I much prefer a more direct route. It's too important to leave to chance."

"Is Gran okay?" Vi asked, immediately worried. "Dad?"

"Your father's fine, and your grandmother is her usual ornery self. My concern's for you."

"Me? I'm not following."

"You can only imagine my complete and total embarrassment when Mrs. Bender approached me at a dinner party the other night and brought up this dreadful article about you being involved in a hit-and-run with the paparazzi. A hit-and-run!"

Vi blinked. It looked like her mother. Wore the same pinched expression. The concern coming out of her mouth threw her off, though. "I'm fine. It wasn't—"

"Paparazzi following you, Violet. You told me there'd been one date, but you're involved with the North American Alpha to the point that media is following your every move, and you didn't see fit to tell your own mother? I do not appreciate being blindsided like that."

And there's the real Christina . . .

"*And* I have it on good authority you've been spotted around town together *several* times. And in a . . . *bowling alley.*"

Vi arched her eyebrow at her mother's disgusted tone. "It wasn't a brothel, for Goddess's sake . . . although that *is* a good idea for our next night out."

I did win our bowling bet, after all.

Her mother wasn't amused. "Sometimes I wonder where I went wrong with you and Olive."

Vi bit her tongue.

"At least Rose isn't hell-bent on making a mockery out of our family . . ."

And tongue released. "That's because she's too busy going after what *you* want and she's forgotten all about *herself*!"

Christina looked taken aback. "Excuse me?"

"I'm not so sure I can anymore, *Mother.*" Christina visibly winced at the title used in public. "Now, did you come here to remind me how short I fall on the Christina Maxwell List of Acceptable Qualities, or was there another purpose?"

Christina huffed. "Well, before that little bit of unpleasantness, I was about to suggest you bring Lincoln to the house for a family dinner. But now I demand it."

"A *family* dinner? With which family? The Singhs?"

"Ours. Next Saturday. And you're bringing the Alpha. No excuses."

Horror at having to attend one of her mother's notorious dinners was only magnified by the second request. "I'll go, but I'm not bringing Lincoln."

"And why not?"

"Because he can't drop his duties as the NAP Alpha the moment Christina Maxwell beckons him to drive upstate."

"Fine. If scheduling is the issue, we'll make it three Saturdays from now. Your father will be home in between business trips, so he'll be available as well. Do you think that's ample enough notice? It's dinner with your family. It's not as if you're asking him to place his neck on an executioner's block."

No, although that was a pretty good analogy for Vi's enthusiasm level.

Potion's Up's door opened again, and Vi's Magic instantly rolled over as if expecting a belly rub. This time, she wasn't the only one who sensed the charged atmosphere. Everyone in the bar—Christina included—turned to where Lincoln Thorne stood inside the door with his NAP Second-in-Command.

His heated gaze locked on hers from across the room, and damned if her stomach didn't flip. They'd agreed to keep things uncomplicated for the sake of their arrangement, and she couldn't wait to uncomplicate things again.

And again.

Too distracted by her suddenly rampant libido, she missed her mother waving Lincoln over until he broke away from Adrian and headed their way. She threw a quick glance at her reflection in the bar mirror and winced at the sight of her lopsided cleavage.

"Mrs. Maxwell. This is a surprise." Charm oozed off Lincoln as he reached for her hand. "Do you come here often?"

"Not in the least." Christina almost seemed offended before she remembered to whom she was talking. A smile slithered onto her face. "I'm surprised it's the type of place you visit, Alpha Thorne. It seems a little . . . kitschy."

"It certainly has its own brand of style." He flashed Violet an obvious wink. "But it's the magnificent customer service that keeps me coming back for more. There's nothing quite like it in the city."

Too thick, Vi mouthed.

Linc grinned wider.

Christina's calculated gleam was back. "I'm glad I ran into you, as it seems my daughter wouldn't entertain the idea . . ."

"Mother, no. I told you—"

"And I told you I'm not taking no for an answer." The older witch turned back to Lincoln. "I'm hosting a family dinner three Saturdays from now, and seeing as you and our lovely Violet have been seeing one another, I'd like to extend the invitation to you as well. As a matter of fact, I insist."

Vi shook her head behind her mother's shoulder. *Say no. No way.*

"I'd love to. Name the time, and I'll make sure Violet and I are there."

Proud of herself, Christina shot her daughter a haughty *I told you so* look. "Marvelous. I'll text the details to Violet. Now, if you'll excuse me . . . sweetheart?"

"Yes, Mother?"

Christina's gaze dropped to Vi's boobs. "Please wear something appropriate for Saturday evening. Rose and Alpha Bisset will be there as well, and we can't have the man rethinking the ties he's about to make to our family."

"Don't wear the full-body leather catsuit. Got it." Gritting her teeth, she waited for her mother's exit. The second her over-processed hair was out the door, Vi spun. "What the hell?"

Leaning against the bar, Lincoln casually dipped his hand into a bowl of pretzels as if he hadn't made a deal with the devil herself. "Do you seriously have a leather catsuit? Because the mental image that's in my head is—"

"What about me shaking my head did you not understand? It's a universal gesture known to everyone. Side to side. Left, then right."

"Would she have taken no for an answer?" He cocked a dark eyebrow and, leaning over the table until their faces were mere inches apart, flicked his gaze to her mouth and back. "Besides, me being invited to the Maxwell family dinner means we're doing something right."

"All it means is that she wants to lure you into her own personal lair before she executes her attack. Have you never watched Animal Planet? It's Predator 101."

Cupping the back of her neck, he guided her already tingling lips to his for a slow, tantalizing kiss. They'd both agreed PDA went hand in hand with their arrangement, but damned if this didn't feel like something else.

Or maybe that was her attempt at complicating the uncomplicated.

His tongue barely slid past her defenses in a soft, searching caress before retreating. A low groan escaped her throat when he pulled away. Not only had she fisted his shirt, but they'd developed more than a small audience.

There wasn't an eye in Potion's Up that wasn't fixed on them.

Gage gave her a silent look of disapproval from the other end of the bar. "Think you could work sometime tonight, Maxwell?"

"I could," Vi teased back, pushing his buttons. "I think the real question you mean to ask is *will* I be working tonight, and the answer is yes."

He scoffed and stalked away.

"Nice guy, your boss." Lincoln chuckled.

"Actually, he's a great guy. This girl he's dating has him on some special diet that's supposed to enhance sexual something-or-other. He's only drinking O negative, which is evidently the equivalent of sucking plain tofu through a straw."

"Sounds delicious. Why don't you grab two beers for me and Adrian so your boss doesn't have reason to get crankier?"

She grabbed two bottles from the chest, flipped off the caps, and pushed them his way. "So why are you here? My mom was right. This isn't your typical hangout spot."

"I'm thinking of changing that . . . and I maybe hoped I could sneak you away when you got off shift."

"Only maybe?" she openly flirted. "I'm closing tonight, so it'll be a while."

"Good thing wolves are nocturnal." He winked and, taking his beers, headed off to his friend in the far back corner.

Vi didn't bother hiding the fact that she ogled his ass as he walked away. Buns that perfect were meant to be admired, and she couldn't wait until the end of her shift so she could both admire and ogle . . . and maybe fondle a bit.

Gage cleared his throat from the other end of the bar.

"Okay! I'm working!"

"Miracles do happen," the vampire muttered.

❖ ❖ ❖

Adrian's shit-eating smirk broadened as the bastard lifted his nose in the air and took a big sniff. "What is that I smell? Is that *love* in the air?"

"I think it's your BO. When did you last give your fur a good shampoo?" Linc slid him a beer before taking the seat across from him.

"A very professional deflection, asshole." Adrian chuckled from over the rim of his drink. "But you're forgetting there's brains behind this beautiful mug. I see what you're doing."

"Yeah? And?"

"And nothing. I wholeheartedly approve, my friend." His gaze shifted toward the bar.

Violet bounced in conversation between Gage and Harper as she filled orders, hands expertly flipping and spinning bottles. *Those hands.* They'd nearly destroyed him last night, and he was already raring to experience that again, his inner Wolf panting in agreement.

"Don't fuck this up." Adrian's sentiment yanked him out of his horny fog. "And don't give me that clueless look. You know what I'm talking about. Don't pull your usual self-sabotage shit, or I swear I'll approach the Elders myself and offer to be their hitman."

"I don't know what you're talking about," Linc lied.

"Fuck if you don't. Look, I won't tell you what to do—"

"You've tried telling me what to do for nearly a third of my life."

"And I plan on continuing the streak until someone comes along who can do it better." His gaze skated back toward Violet. "But seriously, don't be you and fuck this up. I couldn't have picked a better match for you if I'd tried. She doesn't take any shit—especially your special brand of shit—and she's not easily intimidated. Picking someone like Violet Maxwell as your mate would drive the Elders fucking crazy, and I'm totally here for it."

Linc's brow lifted. "I thought you wanted me to play nice with the Elders while we bide our time. Now you want me to piss them off?"

"I think Violet's the best of both worlds. You get a mate, and I get to sell tickets to the show." Adrian leaned back in his seat.

"What show?"

"The first time Violet faces off with Elder Goodman. That would be pay-per-view shit right there. Beer. Buttered popcorn. It would be a thing of fucking beauty."

He snickered, unable to disagree. "She's already proven she can hold her own against people like the Trents. Goodman would be child's play."

"That's exactly what I mean. Who better to help you create change than a magicless witch who's had to fight for every ounce of respect sent her way? No way would she back down from a challenge. Plus, she's a feast for the eyes. If I found someone who could tolerate my sorry ass and looked like your pretty little witch, I'd forfeit the clubs and Mate Bond her in a fucking heartbeat."

Linc's Wolf pushed to the surface close enough to emit a low, dangerous growl. "Feast your eyes somewhere that isn't Violet."

Adrian chuckled, damn near ecstatic. "Interesting . . ."

"What the hell are you talking about?"

"You haven't looked in a mirror recently, have you?"

Linc took a casual sip of his beer, not really tasting it. "Are you saying I have something on my face?"

"I'm saying there's something *in* your face. Specifically, your eyes."

Adrian wasn't wrong. Linc swept his gaze over the bar before letting it rest on Violet. The subtle purple in her hair was a tad more vibrant, the pink hue in her cheeks more noticeable. And damned if her skin didn't look soft as silk, begging to be touched. It was as if she stood in front of him in ultra-high-def.

Linc's Wolf was a hell of a lot closer to the surface than he'd thought.

As Linc cajoled his inner beast to behave, a loud group of men—all Norms—rolled into the bar, one of whom gave Gage a slight chin lift. The vampire flagged down Violet, and after reaching for the cauldron, she and Harper led the new arrivals to the other side of the bar.

Violet flipped and spun bottles, putting on a tableside show before she poured their contents into the oversized bowl. In a matter of minutes, the brew misted up, bathing her face in a gorgeous swirling rainbow of colors.

Linc wasn't the only one mesmerized. All the men in the bachelor party watched in drunken rapture, squeezing in closer to get a better view.

It wasn't long before she and Harper filled a second cauldron and the party did away with any semblance of public decorum and manners. Two men flanked Violet on either side, sending each other lecherous smirks as a third asshole cut her retreat off from behind.

Her polite smile disappeared as she shot the dark-haired guy closest to her a warning glare. He didn't seem to get the hint, instead reaching out and touching her arm.

Linc pushed up from the table, a growl already rumbling through his chest.

Adrian quickly followed, an expectant grin on his face. "Just when I thought tonight was about to be a bust . . ."

Linc's gaze remained fastened on Violet and her handsy admirer. He didn't see the other hulking form who'd also set his eyes on the inebriated asshole until he nearly ran into him.

"Where the hell's Gage?" Bax glowered at the party, where two more guys had now effectively cut Harper off from Violet.

The succubus looked mad enough to spit venom—if that had been a succubus thing.

"He disappeared somewhere in the back, and it appears these assholes—"

"Took it as a free pass."

Violet's angel friend didn't like him, and the feeling went both ways. But Linc's Wolf sensed a temporary ally. "You want to help us show these guys some manners?"

"Does that involve bashing a few heads together?"

Linc's lips twitched. "We can try appealing to their common sense and decency first—"

One of the party guests stumbled into a nearby table. "When are the fucking lap dances starting?"

"—but I don't have high hopes for that going well."

Adrian patted the angel on the shoulder. "Fair warning, this guy's Wolf is chomping at the bit to sink his teeth into somebody."

"You know if we get involved, she'll have a shit-fit, right?" Bax flicked his gaze toward Violet. "I'll get ignored for a few days, but you'll suffer from a major case of blue balls."

Linc didn't doubt that in the least. "I'm pretty adept at talking myself out of most doghouses."

Bax failed to fight off a smirk. "So long as you're not taken by surprise."

The three of them approached the party. The guys on the group's outer edge, more sober than their friends, took one look at Linc, Adrian, and Bax and scurried away. The remaining dozen weren't so accommodating. A burly, bearded redhead went so far as to purposefully step in their way.

"Where do you think you're going?" Big Red puffed out his chest like an inflated peacock.

"Over there." Calling on his inner Wolf, Linc doused the atmosphere in his Alpha powers. "So it's in your best interests to step aside. Now."

A small group of Supes sitting at the bar glanced their way before quickly leaving money for their bill and hightailing it out of the building. Linc's power pushed harder against Big Red, and the man, who must have had a little shifter somewhere in his family tree, grimaced as he fought against obeying.

"Whatever," Big Red growled, stepping aside.

Everyone else was either too drunk or too human to notice the three Supernaturals shouldering their way through the crowd. Adrian broke away to deal with the asshole backing Harper into a corner, which left Bax and Linc to deal with Violet's two drunken admirers.

"You guys have had your fun. It's time to pack up and head out." Linc focused on the beady-eyed bastard with his hand on Violet's arm. "Now."

The human flipped him off. "We'll head out when we're fucking good and ready, and that won't be until we convince our new witchy friend to join us at the after-party."

Violet ripped her arm from his grasp. "And I told you that wasn't happening. I didn't suddenly change my mind after the tenth time you *requested* it."

"Then I wasn't being persuasive enough." He reached for her again, invoking a low, ominous growl not from Linc's Wolf, but from *Linc*.

The asshat tossed a shit-eating smirk his way. "Someone's a little possessive, huh? Do you shifter assholes really pee on the women you think are yours? Is that what's happening here? Did you mark her or something?"

"If you don't walk the fuck away, I'll be marking you with my teeth."

Linc was doing a piss-poor job of holding his Wolf back, and he couldn't bring himself to care. Every shift, breath, and flinch sharpened his senses until all he heard was Violet's galloping heartbeat.

"Lincoln," she murmured, knowing that in his super-state, he'd hear her perfectly. "It's not worth it. Let it alone."

Asshat chuckled. "Yeah, *Lincoln*. Let it alone."

A quick glance right verified Adrian already had Harper away from the group. His best friend gave him a look, silently asking *What's next?*

"Lincoln . . ." Violet's purple eyes practically pleaded.

"Let's go." He held his hand out to her, only for her to be yanked back, a startled cry escaping her lips.

Linc snapped.

Lightning reflexes had him in front of the drunk bastard before anyone blinked. Releasing his grip on Violet, the asshole swung. Linc ducked and retaliated with a heavy punch to the jaw. The Norm stumbled back, crashing into a nearby table and setting off a chain reaction of flying fists.

A free-for-all erupted throughout the bar. Someone hurled a chair toward Linc's head, but a split second before impact, it rained mulch chips.

"What the hell . . . ?"

Violet stood six feet away, glowing palms pointed in his direction, shooting him an award-winning glare. "I told you to let it go! Is your wolfy hearing on the fritz or something?"

Asshat's fist whipped past his face. "Can you yell at me about this later, princess? I'm a bit busy."

Linc clocked the ringleader in the jaw a second time, sending him flying back into one of his buddies. Although they all deserved a good beating, hitting a shifter or a supercharged demon was a hell of a lot different than slugging a Norm. There was a line that couldn't be crossed.

Someone bumped into Linc from behind. He spun, ready to pummel whoever it was, and stopped when he came face-to-face with Bax. Barely winded, the angel acknowledged him with a slight nod, and then they spun out, each prepped to deal with the threats coming up on their flanks.

They never got the chance.

Rising Magic thickened the air, lifting every hair on Linc's body, until in one powerful pulse, an energy wave ripped through the room, knocking everyone on their asses.

The entire bachelor party. Linc. Bax. Adrian.

Everyone who hadn't vacated the building at the first sign of trouble was swept clean off their feet. All except Violet.

Her hair whipping around her as if in the middle of a hurricane, she looked like Storm from X-Men, and Magic was clearly her weapon. It swirled around her body in a protective shield.

"Violet?" His hands outspread, Linc carefully approached.

Her startling purple eyes fastened on him like two gorgeously glowing orbs. "Don't come any closer."

"As you said before, I'm not fond of listening."

Bax cleared his throat. "Dude, you may want to take it up."

"It's okay. It won't hurt me. *She* won't hurt me."

He wasn't sure how he knew that, but he did. He reached out to the nearest purple tendril, and as if it were arms, it wrapped around him and pulled him closer, its power sending a warm, pleasant zing through his body.

Violet blinked as if seeing him for the first time. "Lincoln . . . ? What's happening? How are you . . . ?"

"No clue, but let's put this beautiful display on a dimmer switch. Unless you want word to get to the Council that the Magicless Maxwell is far from magicless."

"I'm not sure I can."

"You're the girl who snuck into a fortified high school to save frogs from annihilation-by-biology-student. You can do this."

She speared him with a hard glare. "This wouldn't be necessary if you had *let it go*."

And there she is . . .

He smirked. "We have this special thing between us, sweetheart. It's called mutual agitation. If I wasn't pissing you off, we wouldn't be *us*."

She muttered under her breath, linking his name with a few colorful adjectives, but her fingers wrapped tight around his as she closed her eyes. He couldn't stop looking at her, in full awe of both her strength and beauty.

Her Magic receded a trickle at a time, and then in a blink, it all rushed back, buckling her knees.

Linc caught her and, pulling her close, ghosted a kiss over her forehead. "You're one badass witch, Violet Maxwell. Remind me to never *really* piss you off."

Commotion and the clang of the door drew everyone's attention to the front of the bar, where police stormed their way inside, a shocked Gage hot on their tail. The vampire released a string of obscenities.

Furniture obliterated. Glass shattered. Alcohol puddled over nearly every square inch of floor. Yeah, it was bad. And when the ass-hole brigade pointed their fingers at Linc, Adrian, and Bax, things went from bad to worse.

17

Three Supernatural Stooges

Plotting the murder of three Supernaturals wasn't something Vi should do while standing in the middle of a busy police station, but it couldn't be helped.

Arrested. Bax, Adrian, *and* Lincoln.

She hadn't laid eyes on any of them since the cops had escorted them out of Potion's Up in handcuffs, and the officer behind the reception desk wouldn't tell her a damn thing. Thirty more minutes and she'd have her nails bitten down to the quick. But as worried as she was, she also hoped the guys' cellmates were tattooed bikers named Hellion, Scar, and Buddy.

Sitting on the lobby bench, her knee bobbed in a nervous twitch she hadn't experienced since her teens. She caught herself, stood and paced, then rinse and repeat.

Her hands were a whole different issue. Ever since her magical shenanigans back at the bar, they kept lighting up like two malfunctioning glow sticks. No rhyme or reason. No warning. Just Sparky saying, *Hello, did you forget about me?*

As if.

Shoving her hands as deep into her pockets as they'd go, she turned, not sensing her grandma's presence until the soothing scent of vanilla wrapped around her like a cozy blanket. "Gran."

Edie's steady hand steered her back to the seat. "Breathe, my dear. This isn't the first time Supernaturals have gotten themselves into a pickle, and it won't be the last."

"How are you even here right now? Did you see it on the news or have a vision or—"

"I answered the phone." The Prima sat next to her as if they were about to have afternoon tea. "Nothing happens to my family or a member of the Council without my being notified. I simply choose whether or not it's something I want to acknowledge."

Vi felt the color drain from her face. "Oh, Goddess, Gran. The Council . . . the second they get wind of this, I'm getting witch-slapped and Witch Bonded."

"They won't get wind of it just yet."

"But all those witnesses . . ."

"All Norms, with the exception of you and your gentlemen friends. It appears what happened to that man from the alley also manifested itself here."

She digested her grandma's words. "They don't remember what happened?"

"They remembered Lincoln and his friends plenty, but your Magic?" Edie shook her head. "No."

Vi practically melted into the bench from relief.

"Now, a little less worry." Edie patted her knee. "The boys and your wolf will be released posthaste and now that the officers have collected enough corroborating statements, the charges have been dropped."

"He's not my wolf, Gran." Vi avoided her grandma's assessing look.

"Really?"

"Yes, *really*. My life is riddled with more than enough problems right now. I don't need to add an unpredictable, moody shifter to the list."

"Ah, yes. About your *problems* . . ." Edie glanced to where Vi sat on her hands in an attempt to stave off the magical current. It worked, but unfortunately, it also diminished the blood flow to her fingers, making them tingle. "What happened?"

"If I knew what happened, I'd explain it to myself in a way that doesn't freak me out."

"Try."

She admitted it all, starting with the presence of the frequent flare-ups and working with her sisters in controlling them. With every piece of new information, Edie's face remained unchanged . . .

Until Vi reached the part about the night's big kaboom.

The older witch's mouth tightened.

"It's bad, isn't it?" Vi worried.

"You should have said something to me before tonight, Violet Ann."

She cringed. Middle name usage was *not* a good sign. "I know. I know, but I was afraid the Council would push up the timeline on the whole Witch Bond thing."

"And if the Council became aware of your powers that's exactly what would happen . . . but *I* am not the Council. First and foremost, I'm your grandmother."

"I'm sorry." Expelling a heavy sigh, Vi dropped her head onto Edie's narrow shoulder. "I thought I could get a handle on it. But no matter what I do to control it, Sparky goes haywire. It's almost like it's taunting me."

"*Control* it? Sweetheart, are you trying to put your Magic back in its little box?"

"Well, yeah. It can't keep leaking all over the place like an incontinent bladder. That's . . . hazardous."

Edie reached over and gave her left knee a firm squeeze. "Sweetheart, I owe you an apology. I've been remiss in my duties not only as Prima, but as your grandmother. Magic—*your* Magic—isn't something to bottle up and stick on a shelf. When it shows, it's for a reason, and it's up to you to figure out what that reason is."

"Because like me, it has the worst timing ever?" Vi half joked.

Edie's mood sobered. "Violet, your Magic *is* you . . . like the heart beating in your chest and the blood flowing through your veins. It's the equivalent of Lincoln's wolf, or Harper's inner demon, or Baxter's celestial call to protect. Have you ever asked Lincoln what happens if he ignores his other side?"

"No." Although she'd witnessed firsthand that he sometimes battled his inner self, too.

"His wolf would rebel. Act out. He'd become more aggressive in the hopes of showing he was an indispensable part of Lincoln's life."

"You're saying my Magic is tired of sitting in the shadows? But why is it pissed off now when it contentedly lay dormant for the last thirty-some odd years?"

"Perhaps it needed the right incentive to get you on board . . . *and* because you, my dear, have so much more strength and control than you realize."

Vi snortled. "Spoken by someone who didn't see me nearly blow up Potion's with a magical bomb. That doesn't seem very controlled."

"Because you were fighting yourself. It wants your acceptance, sweetheart. The two of you need to learn to trust each other."

"Trust it won't run amok and rat me out to the Supernatural Council before I'm ready? How do I do that?"

"That's for you to figure out, bae. But for a witch—and especially a Firstborn in a Triad—trust is the vital ingredient for a fulfilled, happy life. Trust in yourself, your Magic . . . and in others."

"Then I'm pretty much screwed," Vi muttered.

A corner door opened, and the Three Supernatural Stooges stepped into view. Adrian approached the desk sergeant first, reclaiming his belongings before stepping aside to let Bax do the same. Neither man looked too bad. Adrian sported a slight bruise on his lower jaw, and Bax's shirt was ripped at the collar, but other than that, they looked fairly intact.

And then there was Lincoln.

No bruises. No tears. No wrinkles in sight. His hair, in slightly more disarray than usual, was the only evidence he'd even participated in the bar brawl at all.

As he shoved his wallet into his back pocket, his gaze found hers. "Violet."

She didn't wait for them. Turning on her heel, she exited the precinct.

"Violet!" Bax called out. "Hey! Wait up!"

Multiple sets of footsteps followed her at a quick pace.

"Violet! Come on!"

"Not a word, Baxter Donovan."

"But—" He was right behind her.

She spun, finger-drilling him into his hard chest. It hurt her more than it did him, but she didn't care. "Not. A. Damn. Word. Unless you want me to finish what I started back at the bar, in which case, by all means, keep yapping."

All three men clamped their mouths shut.

"Yeah, I didn't think so. If only you'd been that smart a few hours ago."

She headed outside, where her grandmother's car idled in front of the building. Edie ushered all four of them into the back. Normally, the town car was roomy with extra space to spare, but not with the three oversized baboons in residence.

Linc sat directly across from her, his long legs bumping into hers accidentally . . . the first time. Each nudge and bump grew more insistent, but she stared out the window at the passing scenery and ignored them—and him.

"Thank you for getting us out of there, Prima Maxwell." Adrian broke the tense silence first. "It would've been another two hours before the Pack lawyer could've even made an appearance."

"You would've been released eventually," Edie admitted. "The charges against the three of you had already been dropped, but it appeared one of the young gentlemen from this evening had a family member processing the paperwork. They were determined to prolong your release out for as long as possible."

Linc finally dragged his gaze away from Vi. "Whatever the case, Edie, thank you. I'm incredibly sorry for—"

Edie silenced him with the slight raising of her hand. "Did they deserve it?"

"Definitely," all three men said in chorus.

"Then I think a few hours in a holding cell was worth it, don't you?"

Unable to believe her ears, Vi's mouth dropped. "Gran! You're condoning their behavior?"

"There's a time and a place for taking a stand, my dear. Supernaturals wouldn't have the rights we do today if it weren't for the scuffles of the past."

"Revolutions, Gran. *Protests*. Not bar brawls against drunken, horny bachelor parties."

"Revolutionary acts come in all shapes, sizes, and tactical maneuvers."

Realizing they'd been given a free pass in the eyes of the Prima, Bax's and Adrian's shoulders loosened and the two men joked back and forth, replaying the night's tag-team efforts. Lincoln, although sitting easier, didn't join them.

Instead, he watched Vi, his face giving nothing away about what was running through his head. That was fine with her. She had too many thoughts floating around in her own mind. She didn't have the time or the mental capacity to worry about his.

Especially when the car slowed to a stop in front of Potion's Up.

"Thanks, Gran." Vi planted a kiss on her grandmother's cheek and hustled out of the car.

"Thank you, again, Prima," Linc's voice echoed moments before the sound of his steps followed.

"You're seriously giving me the silent treatment right now? How old are we? Five?" he called after her. "And what the hell are you doing back here? Gage seriously can't expect you to finish your shift."

Anger whirled her toward him. "Someone has to help clean up the mess you helped create."

"*I'll* help." Remorse softened the hard angles of his face. "You shouldn't have to—"

"I know I shouldn't *have* to, but I am, because Gage—rightfully—doesn't want you back in his bar tonight. Hell, I'm lucky he didn't fire my ass."

"You didn't do a damn thing." He reached to touch her before dropping his hands at his sides. "Me, Adrian, and Bax? Yeah. But it couldn't be helped. Those guys deserved the ass-beating they got for acting like that, but you? Not your fault."

"Did you conk your head during the brawl, or are you willfully forgetting the fact I created a baby magi-bomb right by the pool table?"

"It wasn't—"

Vi clamped her hand over his mouth. "If you tell me I'm not at fault, I will scream . . . or hex you with a pig's tail. And I have the Magic now to attempt it."

Lincoln trailed his hands down her arms, gently pulling her hand from his mouth . . . and then didn't let go. His fingers wrapped firmly around hers. "All you did was knock a few people on their asses. No harm, no foul."

"*This* time . . . but I don't expect you to get it."

"Then *tell* me."

Mother Nature released the floodgates, rain pouring down in heavy sheets and soaking them through in seconds, but neither she nor Lincoln moved. With hair matted to their heads and water dripping off their faces, they did nothing but stare at one another.

"Explain it to me, Violet," Lincoln finally demanded, "because I *want* to understand. I want to understand *you*!"

"Why? This thing between us has a shelf life, right? It gets your Elders temporarily off your back until you seal the deal with the other Alphas, and it keeps the Council off mine until I learn how to pull off a fucking miracle. So why does it matter to you?"

His gaze practically drilled into hers. "I don't know, but it does. It matters a hell of a lot."

"You want to know what's holding me back with my Magic, Wolfman? *Me.* Evidently *trust* is a key factor in getting my Magic to play nice, and guess what I have a hard time doing these days . . . or any day?"

Tears poured down her cheeks freely, camouflaged by the rain—at least she thought it had masked them, until Lincoln gently cupped her cool cheek, his eyes wolfy gold. "You can trust *me*. If you can't trust anything else, know that you can trust *me*."

Goddess, she wanted to . . . more than she ever thought possible. Her mouth opened and closed, but the words wouldn't come.

"Tell me why you never showed that night," she heard herself demand softly.

Lincoln's face hardened into a look of physical pain. "Ask me anything but that . . ."

"But *that* is why I cried myself to sleep every night for a year," Vi admitted. "It's why, despite it being my favorite spot, I never walked down by the river after that night. *That* is why I never let myself fully trust anyone except my sisters."

A faint growl rumbled through Lincoln's chest. "I can't tell you, princess. I really fucking wish I could, but . . ."

Another wave of tears threatened, but she held them at bay with a sad nod. "I guessed as much, and that's why I told you things had to stay uncomplicated. We're helping each other out, and we can have fun doing it in the process. But that's it, Lincoln. Don't ask me to trust you, because until you can tell me about *that*, it's not going to happen. *We're* not happening."

Before the heat of his stare disintegrated her resolve, she stepped away. "I need to get inside and help Gage and Harper."

Her emotions weren't the only thing knotted up in a jumbled mess. Her Magic swirled beneath the surface, Sparky's disapproval growing the more distance she put between herself and Lincoln.

Don't look back. Isn't that what the movies always said?

But at the door to Potion's, she looked back at Lincoln anyway.

Disappointment glinted in his eyes, bringing an ache to her chest.

In an instant, he slammed his emotionless Alpha mask back into place. "By the time you're done, Leo will be here to see you home safe. Good night, Violet."

She didn't bother arguing as she watched him turn away.

Gran was right. In order to trust in others—and in her Magic—Vi needed to first trust in herself. It didn't come easily.

Gran. Olive and Rose. Bax and Harper. That pretty much summed up the people she trusted with her life—and her heart. But Hell's Spells . . . a huge part of her wanted to add Lincoln Thorne to that list.

She just wasn't sure she was prepped to deal with the fallout.

Good news traveled fast in Supernatural society, but bad news traveled at the speed of light, especially when it involved assault charges against a member of the Council. Even if they were dropped, it wasn't a good look.

Cameras flashed in Linc's face as he navigated his way through the media outside the Council building. Reporters hurled questions they knew he'd never answer. Ignoring them, he pushed his way inside, where it was only a small degree less chaotic.

A few people nodded polite greetings as he headed toward the Council chambers, while others stopped to snicker. All of it rolled off his back. He didn't regret a damn thing about that night—except for how it had ended.

Violet's words were like a scythe to the gut, and while he didn't blame her, hearing it hadn't been easy. And it didn't get any easier with each mental replay.

Linc stepped into the Council chambers and immediately noticed his colleagues weren't the only people in the room. Elders Goodman and Cho sat along the left aisle, and sitting between them was Valentin Bisset. The smug bastard smirked, tilting his head as if saying hello.

An automatic growl rolled up from Linc's throat.

"At ease, Alpha Thorne." Coming up alongside him, the Prima gently threaded her arm through his, steering him away from Alpha Asshole.

"Sometimes I second-guess my decision in banning Blood Matches," Lincoln muttered under his breath for only the Maxwell matriarch to hear.

Her lips twitched as she fought off a grin. "We both know that's not true, but you're correct in feeling as though our visiting European Alpha is overstaying his welcome."

Lincoln dragged his attention from the tiger. "Not so fond of your future grandson-in-law?"

"Let's just say, if Rose were to have a change of heart sometime between now and the day of the Bonding Ceremony, I'd offer to drive the getaway car. Alas, their match was made by my daughter, and Christina knows nothing better than strategic power plays."

"That's very motherly of her."

Edie studied him carefully, the older witch damn near looking through him. "You know why they've summoned the Council here today, don't you?"

"Because good news travels fast in our circles?"

"Because they will stop at nothing to keep what little power they have over you and the Packs."

"You're talking about the Elders."

She nodded. "They know if it were up to you, they would become inconsequential. This is their way of making sure that doesn't happen."

He scrubbed a palm over his face. "For fuck's sake, it's not like I'm banishing them to the ends of the earth. I just want to give Pack members more say. It'll make for stronger, more cohesive Packs in the long run."

"You'll get no arguments from me, young man. Having elected Pack representatives is something—in my opinion—that is long overdue. But as we both know, just because something is the right thing doesn't make it the popular decision, and when something isn't well-received . . ."

He slid a discreet scowl toward Bisset. ". . . the tiger pounces. If that bastard gets my Council seat, he'll *expand* the Elders' control over the Packs and plummet us back into the fucking Dark Ages."

"Unfortunately, I don't think you're that far off."

"I'm *not* losing my seat, Edie. Not now, and definitely not to a shifter like him."

The Prima patted his arm in a show of support. "Then I sincerely hope you have a plan, Alpha Thorne, and it better be a good one."

"Lately, my good plans seem to blow up in my face," Linc said truthfully, adding, "Edie, about the other night . . ."

She waved him off, her lips pulling into a small grin. "No explanation necessary. I'm a firm believer that all things happen for a reason. Work things. Life things. And especially love things."

"I thought we were talking about what happened at the bar . . ."

She winked coyly, taking her seat. "I suppose that little anecdote can be used for that, too, but I said it with my granddaughter in mind. There's one thing you should know about our Violet before you become more invested . . ."

It was on his lips to deny there was any *investment*, but he couldn't. That night on the sidewalk, he'd wanted Violet's trust more than he'd wanted his next breath. "And what's that?"

"My granddaughter has always had a difficult time seeing the strength and power she's always had within."

"And she needs someone to help bring it out?" Lincoln shook his head, doubtful. "I'm sorry, Prima, but I respectfully disagree."

The witch cocked a single silver eyebrow. "Oh? And what is it you think my granddaughter requires? Do tell."

"Someone to believe she can bring it out in herself."

The small smile on the older woman's mouth told him he'd played right into her hands. "That is a very interesting theory. Now to hope there's someone out there strong enough to let that happen."

He'd do it. In a heartbeat.

He'd take great pleasure in having a first-row seat when Violet showed everyone she was the badass witch he always knew she was. He'd be there in an instant if she needed a champion or a shoulder to cry on. Hell, he'd happily get his ass kicked in bowling every damn night of the week if it kept her gorgeous smile in his life.

"If everyone can please be seated," Angel Ramón called the meeting to order.

With roll call done and no other cases on the pop-up meeting's agenda, Elder Goodman quickly took her position at the front podium, her cane thunking on the marble floor.

Linc barely withheld a sigh. The walking stick was no more than a prop. Last week he'd personally witnessed the bear shifter shake a tree to the ground that was twice her animal's girth.

"As the North American Pack representatives on the Elder Board, myself and Elder Cho thank you all for seeing us in these unprecedented times." She paused for dramatic effect. "I wish it was under different circumstances."

Xavier, the vampire Councilman, interjected, "I wish it was when we'd already planned to be in session. What *circumstance* calls for an emergency meeting of the Council?"

"We regret to say that we're concerned for the health and well-being of our Alpha." Her gaze flicked to Linc with fake worry. "We're afraid that with the pressure of his thirty-third birthday on the horizon, and his duties to both his Pack and this Council, Alpha Thorne has overextended himself."

Xavier's eyes slid to Linc for rebuttal, but Edie's warning stare reined in his temper.

Edie turned an unamused glower on the bear shifter. "Can you recall a specific time in which Alpha Thorne has failed to care for his Pack, Elder Goodman?"

"Not specifically . . . but it's quite obvious that Council duties are overshadowing his duties to the NAP. It's simply too much responsibility for a man in his position."

Murmurs rumbled through the large hall.

Prima Maxwell settled them all with a quick command. "And I suppose you're prepared to nominate someone who you feel can handle the responsibility?"

"We are, Prima." Elder Goodman shifted her gaze to Bisset. "We'd like to nominate Alpha Bisset, from the European Pack."

Valentin cleared his throat, fixing his expensive silk tie as he stood. "And I, Prima, wholeheartedly accept the nomination and feel as though it's my duty and my privilege to serve."

Edie didn't look impressed. "While I commend your commitment, Alpha Bisset, nominations only go so far. There's a multistep process that needs to be followed."

Goodman nodded smugly. "Of course, Prima. We understand the importance of making sure the right person is appointed."

The Prima glanced to the rest of the board and, lastly, to Lincoln. "Then this Council will begin the necessary steps to review and validate the request. You'll be notified either of the acceptance or the declination."

"I'm sorry, Prima," Bisset interjected, "but if I may be so bold as to ask when that may be?"

"Actually, you may not be so bold," Prima Maxwell stated coolly, standing from her position at the center table. "A decision will be reached when a decision is reached."

"But—"

"The nomination is made, Alpha Bisset. The rest is out of your hands."

Elder Goodman interrupted with a long train of questions, but Edie was already halfway out the door, the rest of the Council on her heels. Lincoln went last, unable to help throwing a final glance at his two Pack members and the tiger shifter.

Hands were flailing. Voices rose. No one looked happy. The three of them argued animatedly until Bisset glanced Lincoln's way, his jaw clenched so tight it looked a teeth-grind away from snapping.

Linc couldn't help himself. He smiled and, taking a page from Violet's handbook, waved.

Bring it, you furry bastard.

18

Suck a Broomstick

Steeped in history and nestled beneath the Manhattan side of the Queensboro Bridge, Guastavino's vaulted tile ceiling and forty-foot-high windows provided the perfect backdrop for schmoozing rich Supes and Norms out of their money, and Linc's assistant made it all happen.

Marie had taken their morning coffee conversation about Timmy's difficulty shifting and the need for a mentorship program, and surprised him two days ago with not only a concept for the Children at Play Project, but a venue, guest list, and instructions to behave himself at the inaugural gala to raise funds for the venture.

He'd been behaving himself . . . for the most part. Now he savored victory's spicy cinnamon scent and the frustration bracketing Bisset's eyes.

As if sensing Linc's attention, the tiger bared his teeth at him from across the room and stalked away from where he'd been speaking with the Asian and South American Alphas for the past thirty minutes.

Linc chuckled.

"I told you to behave." Humor shone on his assistant's face as she stepped up to him, a glass of wine in hand.

"I'm behaving."

"Not causing trouble and behaving are two incredibly different things."

"Behaving's boring. Admit it. You like it when I'm a little naughty." He flashed her a wink that made her chuckle.

Marie shook her head. "Boredom wouldn't be an issue if you had your gorgeous witch on your arm. I dropped off an invitation."

He knew.

He'd seen Violet's name on the list, right alongside her grandmother's and sisters', the members of the Council, and anyone else from the Supe and Norm communities who had pull and extra money to burn.

Linc forced his smile to hold. "Violet has a lot of responsibilities that she probably couldn't get out of. You did practically plan this thing in an hour."

But more than likely, she was avoiding him.

They hadn't spoken since the night in front of Potion's Up two days ago, and while he'd left a message *personally* inviting her to the gala, he hadn't heard back. He hadn't expected to, remembering their original deal regarding advance notice for large events.

A business arrangement with no-strings fun.

That's what she'd demanded, and while he may have jumped at the chance when their plan was first hatched, it turned his stomach now. He wanted her there. Standing at his side. And not because it made it easier to later strip her naked and have a repeat sex-fest performance.

All the possibilities happening in the room were largely inspired by her and the children at the Kids' Community Center, and he wished she could see it. That's why the children were invited, and why, after an hour at the main party, they'd head across the street to attend a much "funner" party of their own.

"Alpha Thorne." Gertrude Benson, the Australian Alpha, stepped next to him. "This is quite the event."

Marie excused herself, leaving them alone.

"It is," Linc said politely. "I wish I could take the credit for it, but it was all my amazing assistant's doing. I just had to show up."

"Good for you for having people on whom you can count to come through for you."

Although she was smiling, the Alpha's words were loaded with hidden meaning. "I'm definitely lucky . . . but there's something else you want to say."

"Handsome and smart . . . just like your father."

"I am *nothing* like my father," Linc nearly growled.

Benson assessed him with a critical eye before nodding. "No, I suppose you're not. And not to speak ill of the dead, but when one lives his life the way your father did, it usually ends that way, too. I appreciate you taking great measures to ensure that doesn't happen."

Linc watched her carefully. "But?"

"But . . . I can't help but be concerned if it's for the right reasons."

"You don't think I want to end centuries' worth of needless bloodshed? Of authoritarian 'leadership'? Is that why you haven't given me a firm answer, or even a direction, as to where your vote will go on the Elder matter?"

"It's without a doubt that I believe the Elders' ancient beliefs need to go. I'm concerned about what happens once they do." She pierced him with a hard, weighted stare. "Once the Elders are disbanded, their power will fall to the Alphas. And as we both know, power is a dangerous commodity. Even the best of people get drunk on it. It wouldn't take much for *us* to become the things we're working to eradicate."

"And that's why once the Elders are gone, we keep moving forward. We shift our way of doing things. We shift it *to* the Packs. We give our people a say in who gets to lead them."

"You'd be able to do that? You're a young, powerful Alpha with your entire life ahead of you. Would you be able to give up that level of influence to step aside and let another lead?"

"If that's what the Pack wants? Then yes. I would."

She studied him as if trying to sniff out a lie, but she wouldn't find one. Yes, he enjoyed being Alpha. It was what he had been born to do, but it wasn't *all* he was meant to be. Did he want to step down? No. He hoped like hell his Pack saw his commitment to them and wanted him to stay.

But he wouldn't stand in their way if they chose someone else.

"I guess I have a lot to think about, don't I?" Benson questioned, obviously not expecting an answer. "If you'll excuse me, I saw one of the children toting around blue cotton candy, and I'm determined to find some for myself before the night is over."

Linc watched her go, right back to not knowing which way she leaned. He replayed their conversation in his head over and over again, wondering what he could say or do to put the older Alpha's fears to rest, but he came up blank.

The best he could hope for was to be honest with her and not give her a reason to doubt his motives or his determination.

Get inside without falling over the hem of her dress—that was Vi's goal the second she'd stepped out of her grandmother's town car and onto the lavish red carpet leading into the Children at Play Gala. Her black floor-length A-line gown with dual side slits made it more of a challenge than normal, but now that they were inside and away from the dozens of photographers lined up in front of Guastavino's, she breathed a little easier, not as worried about flashing someone her unmentionables.

At least until she remembered her odds of running into Lincoln at any moment.

Marie's note on the invitation had made it impossible to skip the event. She *had* to go. It was for the kids, and if her presence convinced one person to hand over a dollar, her anxiety was well worth it.

But that didn't mean she wasn't nervous. The last time she'd laid eyes on Lincoln, she'd told him she couldn't trust him not to break her heart, but that wasn't entirely true.

What scared her was that she *could* see herself trusting him.

Her imagination easily conjured happy images of them laughing as they had during their impromptu bowling alley date, or snuggling after a particular sexalicious sex-fest. But not far behind those mental pictures came the *other* ones.

Ones of her alone, waiting for a Lincoln who never showed. Of crying herself to sleep for another year straight because the man she cared about didn't have the decency to *tell* her why he no longer wanted to be together.

Teen Violet had survived a Lincoln heartbreak because at eighteen, she hadn't known what she was missing. But now? After their business deal, and their not-so-fake dates, and the kisses, and the multiple orgasms?

Adult Violet's recovery from a Lincoln heartbreak would require a hell of a lot more than an ice-cream-and-*Supernatural* marathon.

"You okay?" Rose remained next to her even after Edie excused herself to speak with one of the other Council reps. "You look a little . . . expectant."

"If 'expectant' means I'm realizing I should've taken Olive up on her offer to hang out with her and Dean and Sam Winchester, then yes. I'm very expectant."

"And does your urge to spend time in front of a television involve a certain sexy shifter?" Concern lined Rose's face as she threaded her arm through Vi's and led the way through the room.

"What would the Tiger King say if he heard you talking like that about Adrian Collins?" Vi teased.

"We both know that's not who I meant. It doesn't take Olive's genius IQ to figure something's going on with you and Lincoln. You came with me and Gran instead of him."

"And you came with me and Gran when I'm sure Val is around here skulking and sulking."

"Not nearly the same thing."

A cold sweat broke out across Vi's forehead, making her regret not swiping a little deodorant under her boobs. "Fine. We had a disagreement the night of the"—she mimicked an explosion—"and we haven't talked since."

"From what Gran told me, those guys in Potion's had it coming. They're lucky it was Linc, Adrian, and Bax. If they'd messed around with the wrong Supernaturals, they wouldn't have gotten off so free and clear . . . or physically intact."

Vi sighed. "Yeah, Gran didn't seem too bothered by it, either."

She *almost* told Rose that her and Lincoln's rift wasn't about the drunken jerk-turds, but it was easier to let her believe that than tell her the truth while crowded into a room with the city's elite.

"So now you know why *I* came with Gran," Vi pointed out. "Now, tell me why you quickly deflect the subject whenever I mention Valentin."

Rose opened her mouth to deny it.

"Don't give me the Prima-in-Training runaround. I wasn't groomed for the role like you, but I had a seat in the sidecar. If this Witch Bond isn't what you want, then don't go through with it."

"I'm the Prima Apparent, Vi. I have to."

"Like hell. You're forgetting that the reason *I'm* being coerced into a Bonding is because the law *technically* states it's a requirement of the *Firstborn*. Remember? The curse of the Maxwell Dud strikes again."

Rose's mouth opened and closed, as if second-guessing what she'd been about to say, and then dropped her voice to a whisper. "We both know you're not quite the dud they think you are. Maybe I'm not meant to be Gran's successor. Maybe it's *you*."

Vi snortled. "Did you not hear about me nearly taking out an entire city block? Or forget the time I nearly electrocuted the shifter I'm—uh, Lincoln."

Hell's Spells, had she almost said *falling for*?

No.

Maybe.

She didn't have time to think about it because her little sister of two minutes looked ready to throw up.

Vi tugged her to a gentle stop. "Ro, do you not *want* to be Prima?"

Rose's brown eyes darted away and back. "I thought I did, but . . ."

Never in their thirty-two years had she ever seen her sister look so unsure. "You need to tell Gran."

"I can't do that! Olive has no desire for the role, and if you don't want it—"

"Exploding. Bar," Vi enunciated. "A large part of me will always wonder what it would be like to fill Gran's shoes, but I came to grips with the fact that it wouldn't be me a long time ago. My Magic not being as MIA as we thought doesn't mean I'm suddenly Prima material."

"We're working on your control."

"And as Gran pointed out the other night, control isn't my only issue." A headache blossomed to life behind her right temple, but Vi reached out, taking her triplet's hand. "If you don't want to Bond with Valentin, don't. Mom will get over her disappointment eventually, and until that happens, think of the years of blessed silence you'll have because she stopped talking to you."

Rose smiled wanly. "I wish it were that simple."

"It can be. Everything can be simplified if you're willing to do it."

Wow. She almost sounded like she knew what she was talking about. She almost sounded like *Gran*.

"That's great advice." Rose's gaze flickered over her shoulder. "And I think you should start taking it . . . right about now."

Vi didn't have to search the crowd when Rose turned her around. She found Lincoln immediately. In sexy disarray, his hair contrasted with the clean lines of his fitted tux, and the scruff on his jaw hinted he hadn't used a razor in a few days.

His heated gaze ran up and down her body before he gifted her an appreciative smile that enflamed her cheeks so hot, they nearly melted off her face.

After saying something to the person standing next to him, he crossed the room.

"Would you like an ice cube to put in your panties?" Rose's murmured question hauled Vi's thoughts out of the lusty trench, but barely. "I can see if I can get my hands on an entire tray."

"If it isn't two-thirds of the Maxwell sisters. You both look gorgeous tonight. Although that's not much of a surprise." His attention bounced from Rose to Violet, and held.

"You don't look so bad yourself."

They stared, neither of them moving until a large flux of people had Lincoln wrapping an arm around her waist and shifting closer. She nearly sighed on contact, Sparky waking up enough to let her know that she was there and that she approved.

She.

Taking advice from Edie, Vi vowed to treat her Magic as if they were the same, yet separate. It wasn't too difficult a task, considering Sparky had an obvious mind of her own, and a huge-ass attitude.

"There you are! Finally!" Valentin forced his way through a nearby couple, his hard gaze bouncing from Lincoln to Rose. "When you said you'd be arriving with the Prima, I didn't realize you'd be so late."

Rose instantly donned her Prima face, strained smile firmly in place. "The gala opened its doors less than forty minutes ago. I hardly call that late. Did you need something . . . dear?"

Oh yeah. *Trouble in Paris.* Once she was alone with her sister, there *would* be a talk.

"I need you to stand by my side while I speak to Julius Kontos and Xavier Hastings." Valentin looked smugly at Lincoln. "After all, I have to get to know them better since I'll be taking over Alpha Thorne's seat on the Supernatural Council."

Lincoln tensed at Vi's side.

"What did you say?" she asked.

Valentin sneered. "Did Lincoln not share the news? The Elders put in a formal request for Alpha Thorne to step down from his position."

Hurt Lincoln hadn't told her, she threw him a glare. "You're letting him shove you out?"

"I'm not letting him—or the Elders—do anything." Linc shifted his piercing gaze to Valentin. "And I have no intention of stepping aside."

The tiger shifter snorted. "You won't have much of a choice. Perhaps you should have played nice with the Elders instead of making enemies of them."

Vi bristled. "Are these the same Elders who teach their children to be bullies and believe they can use their power to take advantage of others? Because if so, I'd be very honored to be the first person to tell you to go suck a broomstick."

Rose covered her laugh behind a cough, but Lincoln didn't bother. With a chuckle, his hand tightened on her hip in a show of support.

If Valentin Bisset had the power to throw javelins with his eyes, she'd be a kabob. His Alpha powers brushed against her skin like ants on parade, trying to will her into submission.

Sparky wasn't having it, and neither was Violet.

Holding his gaze, she kept her body lax, even lifting her chin to show she wasn't about to cower. *I could stand here all day, Pepé Le Pee-Yew.*

He backed down first, his face red and livid. "*Rose?* With me."

Her sister released an annoyed sigh, and turned to Violet,

mouthing a soft *I'll explain later* before she followed him to the other side of the room.

Lincoln's arm hauled her closer against his chest. "That was fucking sexy as hell. For a second, I thought you were about to blast him next door."

"For a second, I considered it, although next door is still too close for my liking."

They shared a look and laughed. In that moment, she forgot about the awkwardness between them and instead, focused on how right it felt being in his arms. She opened her mouth to issue an apology for what she'd said at Potion's Up, when two party-dressed kids tore around the corner and screeched to a stop next to them.

"Miss Violet! Alpha Thorne!" Timmy, his hair sticking up in the back, beamed excitedly, Misha by his side. "Did you hear they're taking us to a sock-hop across the street? A sock-hop! I can't wait!"

Violet fixed his hair. "I'm pretty jealous. That sounds like a lot of fun."

"Do you think you'll hop around in your bare feet?" Linc asked.

Misha rolled her eyes. "It's called a *sock*-hop, Alpha Thorne . . . but if you want to put it to a bet . . ."

Lincoln laughed. "Sorry, but no. I learned my lesson betting against you. But I'm pretty sure Adrian is around here somewhere. You might be able to sucker him."

And speak of the devil—Adrian strolled through the crowd, talking and smiling.

"Will you come with us?" A wide-eyed Timmy tugged on Lincoln's arm. "Please? That way he won't suspect anything."

Lincoln looked to Violet.

"Go." She ushered him on with a chuckle. "I know you're dying to see him in a unicorn horn."

Vi's face threatened to crack from smiling as she watched Lincoln escort the kids over to the oblivious lion shifter.

An older woman came up to her side, her gaze following Vi's. "He seems at ease with the kids."

She recognized the woman as Alpha Benson, and with her was one of the NAP Elders, Jane Goodman. It was showtime, and Vi was an act of one.

"He is," she replied to the Australian Alpha. "And the kids are taken with him, too."

"Is that so?" She sounded a bit surprised.

"They look forward to his shifts at the KCC so much that we rotate his helpers of the day so everyone gets a turn."

Elder Goodman look bewildered. "Shift? Do you mean he's *working* at the center?"

"'Working' implies he gets a paycheck. He and his Second, Mr. Collins, volunteer a few times a week."

Benson turned back to give Lincoln a thoughtful look. "I hadn't heard that."

"Why would you hear about it?"

Benson gave her a little smile. "Usually when an Alpha does something as benevolent as working with children, it's flaunted around news channels for everyone to see. They're ploys to increase popularity."

"Then I feel very sorry for those Alphas, and for the people who'd accept a hollow gesture like that—but that's not Lincoln. He enjoys his time with the kids because he's invested in their future. He wants them all to have the childhood that he didn't have growing up . . . which is a large part of why we're all at this gala tonight. Right?"

Benson's mouth twitched into a smirk. "You don't sugarcoat things, do you?"

"My grandmother always says sugarcoating things makes them easier to swallow, but it doesn't change their base ingredients."

"Your grandmother is a smart woman, and so, it appears, are

you." Her gaze skirted back to Lincoln, who now had no fewer than six kids surrounding him and Adrian.

Goodman cleared her throat. "If you don't mind me asking, Miss Maxwell, when is the big day?"

"I'm sorry?" Lincoln and the kids had temporarily distracted Vi.

"Your Mate Bonding? We're fairly close to Alpha Thorne's thirty-third birthday now, and myself and the rest of the Elders have yet to hear a formal announcement." The Elder waited expectantly. "Unless the two of you aren't as serious as he's led us to believe . . ."

"We are," Vi said automatically. Hell's Spells, had she sounded too eager?

"So there's a date?"

"Not one that we agree on." Vi prayed her smile looked genuine. "And don't get me started on the venue. Although being here, I think I've found the perfect place. It's gorgeous."

"I see."

Witch-shit on a broomstick. Goodman didn't believe her.

A million thoughts fired through Vi's head, all of them geared toward not screwing things up for Lincoln. "But my move-in day is in two days."

Stuff me in a cauldron and turn it on high.

The Elder looked curious. "You're moving in together?"

"I'm hoping to get settled into Lincoln's brownstone before flying to Sydney for Alpha Benson's grandson's birthday party— which we're both excited for, by the way."

Please believe it. Please believe it.

"Then I look forward to hearing about that date soon." Goodman nodded before both she and Benson moved on to their next victim.

The night went up and down from that point onward, and the children were eventually whisked away to their own private sock-hop across the street. Every time Vi attempted to get Lincoln alone, another well-meaning citizen came up to give their support to the Children at Play Project. It was a good problem to have, but Vi needed to get him alone.

ASAP.

An hour later, she grabbed his hand and dragged him through the lower lobby of Guastavino's before shoving him inside a maintenance closet.

Lincoln teasingly eased her closer. "I've always dreamed about sex in a broom closet."

"We're moving in together," she blurted.

He blinked. "I'm sorry, what?"

She paced as far as the small closet allowed. "Alpha Benson and Elder Goodman came around, and Goodman kept asking questions about our Bonding date and whether we'd set one, and I could practically *see* her sniffing for something fishy and it just spewed out of my mouth . . . like verbal diarrhea."

"That we're moving in together."

"It was either that, or give her an actual Bonding date, so I chose the lesser of two evils."

"It's okay, I—"

"No, it's not okay!" She flailed. "Something's going on with Rose and Valentin, and then he pisses on your Council seat and claims it for himself?"

"Are you—"

"Done? No." She whirled on him, drilling a finger into his chest. "How could you not tell me that furry bastard is trying to weasel his way onto the Supernatural Council?"

Linc waited five seconds, and then an additional two. "You're done now? Can I speak?"

She narrowed her eyes. "*Lincoln.*"

He grasped her hand before she chiseled her way to his spine. "First, I don't know why I didn't think of you moving in sooner. And second, he only made the seat-grab yesterday, and since I wasn't sure where things stood with us, I didn't tell you."

She went quiet. Hell, they both did, their breathing the only sound heard in the room.

"About the other night at Potion's . . ." Vi started.

"You don't need to explain anything, and I don't want to hear something that isn't true. You don't trust me. That's just reality. I'm not saying I like it, or that I'll stop trying to earn it, but I don't want you to say it until you're sure you mean it."

Vi leaned against the edge of a low table with a heavy sigh. "I told them we were moving in together before the Alpha's grandson's birthday party. That's less than a week away. What are we going to do? If it doesn't happen, the Elders will get antsy again and start asking—"

"Then we do it." Lincoln scooted closer, gently easing himself between her parted thighs as he cupped her chin and tilted her face up toward him. "We'll sublet your place so it's there for you afterward, and we move you into the brownstone."

"And Mr. Fancy Pants?"

"Bring him. I'd never tell you to leave him behind. Plus, I think the fluffy little monster likes me."

"But what if—"

He silenced her with the soft pad of his thumb. "This is a constantly evolving situation, princess. We'll deal with things as they come, and we'll deal with them together. Now, a serious question for you, because I'm not sure I can wait until you move in to find out for myself . . . do you wear sexy satin pj's to bed or nothing at all?"

"Neither. I wear flannels plastered with little yellow ducks drinking coffee."

Lincoln chuckled, hauling her to the edge of the table. He kissed the corner of her mouth, then her jaw.

"Not every woman owns a satin nightie, you know." Vi leaned into his touch with a breathy sigh. "And sleeping naked is only done by someone who's never rolled over midsleep and nearly ripped off a nipple."

"Well, we can't have that. I happen to love your nipples exactly where they are." With a sexy growl, he took her mouth in a breath-stealing kiss that would've quaked her knees if she'd been standing. "Goddamn, I've wanted to feel you in my hands for fucking days."

She reflexively rolled her hips against the hardening bulge behind his zipper.

"Dress." Clarifying her point, she opened her legs wider and grabbing his butt, brought his body closer to hers. "I'm wearing an easy-access dress, which you should definitely take advantage of sooner rather than later."

Lincoln nipped and kissed his way down the curve of her bare shoulder. "Do you want me to make you come, princess?"

"Would you like an engraved invitation, or written directions?"

"Do you think I need directions?" His hands slipped beneath the layers of fabric, knuckles brushing up the gentle curve of her thigh and pausing at the edge of her panties. "Is this what you want, Violet? Do you want me to touch you right here?"

She squirmed closer. "Lincoln . . ."

He rolled his thumb over her cloth-covered clit. "Or is this what you had in mind?"

"Damn it, Wolfman." She released a feminine growl. "You know damn well where I want your hand and what I want you to do . . . so get busy."

He pushed his fingers into her already soaked pussy, and after a few hard thrusts of his fingers and a couple of swipes over her clit, she came undone in his arms. He swallowed her cries with a kiss, and she couldn't bring herself to pull away until her head spun.

"Hell's Spells," Vi's voice shook as her body slowly recovered. "That was . . . wow."

Lincoln ghosted his lips over hers in a soft kiss. "Watching you come is my new favorite hobby."

A commotion in the hall cut off her snarky retort. "What the hell's happening out there?"

Vi rushed to put her dress back to rights before they stepped into the chaos, Lincoln leading the way. A massive crowd was beelining for the building's front entrance.

"Did someone pull a fire alarm or something?" Vi searched for her sister and grandmother in the mob of perfectly set hairdos, but didn't see them.

Linc entwined their fingers. "Stay close."

They followed the mass exit and found Rose on the curb, her mouth covering her hand as she stared in horror across the street.

Bright orange flames engulfed one of the buildings next door. Sirens blared in the distance, but with no one there to tame it, the fire was going wild, smoke billowing high into the night sky.

Vi scanned the temporarily untouched structures surrounding them when her heart stalled. "Lincoln, where were the children having their sock-hop?"

She looked up at his horror-stricken face, and she *knew*. So did Rose. Her sister took off way too fast for someone wearing five-inch heels.

"Rose! Wait!" She started to follow.

Lincoln tugged her hand gently, worry distorting his handsome face. "Violet . . ."

"I'll be fine." She squeezed his fingers. "But I need to go help my sister. Make sure the police and firefighters know the children are inside."

Clasping the back of her head, he pulled her into a hard kiss. "Be careful."

"Careful is my middle name." She winked and ran after her sister, weaving in and out of the growing crowd of spectators.

She found Rose a few feet from the building, arguing with one of the first police officers on the scene.

"Look, I already said no," the cop said staunchly. "No one is getting into this building unless they're wearing NYFD gear. Now get back to the other side of the street or I'll have one of my friends escort you there."

"We don't have time for this," Rose muttered. "Sorry, Officer, but a witch has to do what a witch has to do."

Vi's triplet blew a confusion hex right in the man's face. His eyes instantly glazed over as he leaned a little heavier on his squad car.

Vi's mouth dropped. "Did you just . . ."

"It'll only last a few seconds." Rose took off toward the building, calling over her shoulder, "You coming or not?"

"Hey! *I'm* the sister that's supposed to have the bad ideas! I don't like this role-reversal thing!"

The second they stepped through the front doors, they slammed into a barrier of thick black smoke. Fire licked up the walls and across the ceiling, too extensive for the minuscule spray from the overhead sprinklers. In a few minutes, things were going to get toasty.

"Over there!" Vi pointed to the center of the room, remembering from the *Magic for Dummies* book that when dealing with Elemental Magic, being as close to the epicenter as possible was important.

They scaled fallen beams and carefully walked over busted glass. Finding the safest spot, Rose closed her eyes and called the Elements. Debris fell down around them, and more than once, Vi shifted them aside to avoid a precariously hanging piece of ceiling.

Slowly but surely, the flames above their heads receded.

"It's working!" Vi shouted over the roaring alarms. "Keep going! The flames are getting smaller!"

Rose nodded and continued. The longer she performed the spell, the more she swayed on her feet . . . until Rose's knees buckled.

Vi caught her and carefully lowered her to the ground. She looked too damn pale. "You can't keep going. You'll Magic yourself unconscious before you even make a dent."

"You do it."

No way did she hear Rose right. "I ca—"

"I *know* you can do it. You just need to diminish the flames a little bit and give the firefighters extra time to get here and evacuate the kids from the higher floors. I'll stay with you." Rose trapped Vi's shaking head between her palms. "You're the Firstborn, Vi. You're the fucking General Leia Organa of witches."

"Then why do I feel more like Jar Jar Binks?" At her sister's stern glare, Vi took a deep breath and immediately coughed, her lungs filling with smoke.

She closed her eyes, and this time, she didn't call her Magic. Sparky was right there, ready to get her Leia Organa on.

Magic pulsed through her veins.

Through every muscle.

Through each atom.

Magic poured out of her like a powerful, raging river, and by the time it slowed to a steady trickle, the only things in the room were Rose, Violet, and a whole lot of bewildered firefighters without any flames to fight.

19

Zap Me

Two days fly by when you're recuperating from a slight case of smoke inhalation and the release of a magical tsunami. Vi's slightly sore throat was the worst of her injuries from the fire. Everyone safely evacuated. No loss of life. According to the fire marshal, Rose's quick thinking and expert action had saved many lives.

Yep . . . Rose's.

To everyone except their immediate friends—and Edie—the Prima Apparent was the she-ro responsible for extinguishing the four-alarm fire. The fudged news got Rose a new slew of adoring fans, and Vi made it to move-in day without being forced into a premature Witch Bond.

Everyone won.

Under the guise of subletting her apartment, Vi had left a few things behind at her studio, knowing if she forgot anything important, she could always make a quick run across town. All she needed within easy reach were the necessities.

Clothes—check.

Cat—check.

Toiletries and personal items—check.

Her *great*-grandmother's cast-iron frying pan—check.

Bax came down from the master bedroom, where he'd taken the

first of her two boxes of clothes. "I don't trust a man who has silk sheets. It's sleazy porno-guy type shit and it's eerie as hell."

"He doesn't have silk sheets." *Wait . . . does he?* "Why are you inspecting Lincoln's bed, anyway? Why are you inspecting anything?"

"So I shouldn't tell you I found his Red Room of Pain and Pleasure?"

Vi grabbed a pillow from the couch and lobbed it at his head. He laughingly dodged it, disappearing back outside.

At some point after their jailbird experience, Bax and Lincoln had formed an unlikely friendship, the glare tally dropping at least 75 percent. While it made move-in day more bearable, it also meant they sometimes outnumbered her.

Just as she'd done on her first visit, her friends had oohed and ahhed over Lincoln's immaculate brownstone when they'd first arrived, Bax even threatening to make use of the large home gym that took up the entire garden level.

Vi was pretty excited about that, too. To stumble off a treadmill without having witnesses? *Priceless.*

For now, she stood in a sea of brown boxes and contemplated where to start.

"Where do you want these?" Rose asked, distracted, as she and Olive walked in with boxes labeled "Kitchen."

"Kitchen would be my guess." Vi got an eye roll for her smartassedness.

"What's up with all the cooking things?" Olive thunked her box on the counter and eyed the upscale double oven. "I highly doubt Lincoln Thorne lacks kitchen tools. He probably has things Rachael Ray hasn't even heard of."

"But they wouldn't be *my* kitchen things. Lincoln being able to afford gadgets doesn't mean he has them. He's a bachelor. I can't see him busting out a zester."

Two corded arms wrapped around her from behind seconds before Lincoln's mouth nudged her ear. "No, but I have a pretty kick-ass espresso maker."

His bearded scruff tickled her neck. "See, he doesn't have a zester . . . and I bet he doesn't have a garlic press, either."

"No zester. No press. But there's a bread maker beneath the island that I haven't touched since I bought it." He nestled closer. "Bax took the last box up to Harper. Now it's a matter of unpacking."

Vi held her breath. "What was the last box?"

"The last of your clothes. Why?"

"And where's Harper?"

"In the bedroom."

"You left her alone with my clothes?!?" A foreboding sense of horror flooded through her.

"Should I not have—?"

Taking the stairs at a sprint that would do an Olympian proud, Vi burst through the bedroom door and got a sweater to the face as Harper—succubus-deep in Lincoln's walk-in closet—did Goddess only knew what to her belongings.

Clothes flew out at an alarming rate . . . another sweater, her favorite jeans. They landed either on the floor or on the bed, one garment after another.

Vi picked up the clothing trail. "What the hell do you think you're doing?"

"Moving is a perfect time to purge your closet." There went her yoga pants. "I wish you had let me do this before you packed." And a Yankees tank top. "You could've saved yourself some backbreaking work." Vi's jumpsuit with pockets that she wanted to be buried in sailed over her head, nearly landing in the garbage pail.

Vi scooped it all up and deposited it on the dresser. "If I threw out every article of clothing you didn't like, I'd be walking around in my underwear."

Harper poked her head out of the closet, her nose wrinkling

in distaste. "No, you'd be naked, because I hate your underwear. Ninety percent of it was made with your grandmother in mind."

Spoken like someone who hadn't seen Edie Maxwell's choice of undergarments, but she didn't want to scar Harper for life. Five years after her own run-in with Edie's lacey thong, the image was still etched into her retinas.

Approaching her friend as carefully as she would a dangerous animal, Vi rescued a second pair of yoga pants. "Harper, I love you, but step away from my stuff."

"But—"

"Back away from the yoga pants. Nice and slow."

Harper pouted. "You're killing my fun."

"And you're killing my Fabletics collection. If you want something to do, you and Bax can run over to the pizza shop on Union Ave and get us all dinner."

Her best friend's eyes lit up. "You mean that cute little dive next to Ladies & Gents? I heard that pizza is amazeballs . . . but they can be a little slow. We may have to wait for it."

"Good thing there's a strip club next door." Vi smirked.

"It's a *gentleperson's* club, and if you'd come with me the last time I dropped in you'd have seen some exceptional dancers."

The distraction worked. After Harper and Bax left to grab the pizza, reality slowly sunk in.

A few dates—that's all this was supposed to be. Dinner. Maybe a movie or a walk through the park. She'd never intended family gatherings and move-in days with friends. What was next? An *actual* Bonding?

At the thought of it, Vi waited for panic to set in, but it never came.

If she were honest with herself, she could almost see herself living here.

With Lincoln.

For *real*, not to keep up appearances.

Magic's tingling warmth swelled up from her core. Purple and golden sparks wound around her fingertips, and she playfully danced her Magic around her palm before calling it back like she had the night of the fire.

Olive watched her. "You're getting pretty good at that. Have you been practicing since the warehouse?"

"Some, and I've come to the realization that my Magic is as temperamental as me," Vi half joked.

Linc came out of the kitchen, a water bottle in his hand. "What warehouse?"

Olive mouthed an apology.

"That night I gave Leo the slip and you couldn't reach me?" *The first night we had sex.* "Rose and Olive were putting me through magical boot camp. To get my Magic into shape. It didn't go well."

"She killed the big bad cell phone. And Bax had to go home and bathe in sunburn aftercare ointment." Rose sat on the end of the couch, calling Mr. Fancy Pants onto her lap.

"Harsh, sis." Vi chuckled.

"Harsh, but true."

Linc's gaze settled on Vi. "You've been practicing?"

"Trying. Gran said some things the other day that made me rethink my entire approach."

"It must be working, because you extinguished that fire pretty damn quick." Pride flickered in his dark eyes. "It was badass."

Yeah it was, and she smiled at the compliment, feeling her cheeks heat.

"You did Leia Organa that fire," Rose pointed out. "There was no hesitancy. One moment the fire practically licked at our heels, and the next . . . *whoosh*. Gone. You called the Elements so much faster than I've ever done."

"Beginner's luck."

Olive exclaimed excitedly, "We need another boot camp!"

"You can use the gym downstairs," Lincoln offered. "I'll shove a few of the machines against the walls. It isn't a warehouse, but you'll have plenty of room."

Olive clapped her hands. "Perfect!"

"No, not perfect," Vi declared. "Are you forgetting the damage I caused at the warehouse? Broken windows? Broken phone? Decapitated sparring dummy? I highly doubt Lincoln wants his gorgeous home to get condemned."

Rose waved her hand dismissively. "You said things seemed clearer after your talk with Gran. New approach. New outcome. And hello . . . *fire*."

"I succeeded in not blowing something up *one* time. One time does not make a habit."

Lincoln took her hand and drew her close. "If you're that nervous about bringing down the building, I'm sure your sisters could put protective charms on the walls. But I don't think you'll need them."

The sensation of his thumb stroking along the inside of her wrist flipped her stomach and her reservations.

"A reinforcement spell." Olive was already nodding. "We'll put it on the ceiling, too. We can't forget the ceiling."

Vi was losing the battle. "But what about a target? Unless Lincoln has a sex doll tucked in a closet somewhere, we don't have one."

"Use me," he suggested.

"*I decapitated the last one.* Unless you're a chameleon shifter with the ability to regrow your head, it's not just a horrible idea, it's a lethal one. I'm not going to prison for murdering the North American Alpha. I barely dodged that bullet once before."

Cupping her chin with a hooked finger, he tilted her face up to his. "I trust you. It's about damn time you trust yourself, too."

Sweet Mother of Goddess, this time it wasn't only her stomach that flipped. Her ovaries ovulated right then and there, heat warming her entire body the longer he held her gaze. In typical

Sparky fashion, her Magic swirled within and, being the hussy she was, zipped straight to her womanly bits.

They all wore her down.

Treadmill off to the side and protective charms in place, Rose and Olive walked her through a series of meditation techniques meant to relax her body and calm her mind. They didn't work well, both her body and her mind hyperaware of Lincoln's presence nearby.

Rise and shine, Sleeping Beauty. It's time to put on a show, but not put anyone in the hospital. Think you can handle that?

Her Magic charged forward like a broken dam, buckling her knees. Lincoln stepped forward, but with a flick of her wrist, she held him at bay. "I got this."

And she did. Sparky ignited every cell in her body. Colors brightened and everything focused . . . including the twin balls of purple energy hovering above her open palms.

"Fucking gorgeous," Lincoln muttered.

Rose circled around her slowly. "How do you feel?"

Nervous.

Excited.

"Alive," Vi admitted.

"What else?"

Magic flowed through her veins and soaked into her muscles. "Strong. I feel really, really strong."

"Good. Now shoot a bolt of energy right in front of Lincoln's feet."

Vi's eyes snapped to her sister. "Absolutely not. I happen to like his feet. They're sexy . . . as sexy as foot-fungus carriers can be."

Lincoln stepped closer with a chuckle. "Let her rip, sweetheart. I'm right here in all my sexy-footed glory."

"Do you remember the last time I threw a magical bolt at you? No, you don't. Because I knocked you unconscious."

"Let's go, Maxwell. Unless you're . . . chicken?" He smirked.

"Tell me that's not a *Back to the Future* reference." He cocked up a dark eyebrow. "Fine . . . but don't say I didn't warn you."

Her Magic charged like a laser beam and, at the barest mental suggestion, zapped the floor inches shy of where he stood, leaving behind a charred spot of melted plastic.

"Yes!" Olive fist-pumped.

"You did it!" Rose beamed excitedly.

Lincoln tapped himself on the chest. "Now, zap me head-on."

She laughed . . . until she registered his seriousness. "No way."

"You can manifest the power to be exactly what you want it to be. Instead of burning a hole into the ground, give me a little shock."

"And if that shock stops your heart? Do you have an AED under the sink I don't know about?"

"Not needed. You'll do just fine."

"You don't know that."

"I do because I know *you*." Determination and Lincoln's inner Wolf peeked out through his golden-flecked eyes as he stepped forward. "*Zap me*."

Vi stepped back, and he countered with another one forward. "You don't know what you're asking."

"Sure I do. You don't want to be Witch Bonded? Prove you don't need it."

"Not right now."

"If not now, when?" he taunted her.

Rose cleared her throat. "Lincoln, maybe—"

Keeping his attention on Violet, he shook his head. "The Council won't wait for you to be comfortable, princess. One day soon, they'll make edicts you won't like and you have to be prepared to fight for what you want. That won't happen if you don't push yourself now. *Do. It*. If you want to be the only one with a say in your future, you'll damn well electrocute my ass right now."

Like hell will I let anyone dictate my life!

With a curse and a mini prayer to Goddess, she slung her Magic into Linc like a cannon. The impact hurtled him back ten feet before he landed with a heavy *thud*.

"Don't be dead! Do *not* be dead!" Dropping to his side, she gently patted his face. "Wake up! You cannot do this to me, Wolfman! I swear to Goddess, if you die, I'll find a necromancer to bring you back so I can kill you again. Wake up, Lincoln! Come on! I need you."

"Need me, huh?" His eyes flickered open a second before a knowing smirk spread over his face. "I always knew your bark was worse than your bite."

"You were playing *possum*?"

She reached out to smack his chest. He caught her hand and pulled her on top of him. One roll later and she was beneath him, their mouths less than an inch away.

"I wasn't playing," Lincoln denied. "In case you couldn't tell, I hit the mat pretty damn hard. It took a moment to catch my breath . . . and then you were saying sweet things about needing me. I wanted to hear more."

Her annoyance melted as he tucked a strand of purple hair behind her ear. "Did I hurt you? For a second there I thought you sprouted wings like Bax."

"No wings, and it didn't hurt in the least. It was like a warm pulse . . . pretty close to what's happening now."

Sure enough, Magic enclosed them in a bubble of swirling shades of purple and gold. From the outside, Rose and Olive circled them, their mouths moving, but with no sound. It was as if they'd been muted.

"I can't hear them. Why can't I hear them?" Vi asked.

"Guess you wanted us to be in our own little world, and I can't say I'm sorry about it. I've wanted to get you alone all damn day. I just didn't think it'd happen like this."

"And this isn't hurting you?" She had to make sure.

"*Very* much the opposite, princess." With a subtle shifting of hips, the evidence of how much it *wasn't* hurting him pressed against her stomach.

Her gaze dropped to his mouth. "My sisters are right outside this little bubble."

"They won't always be." Their kiss started gentle, and at the moment she let herself sink into it, he pulled away with a grin. "The troops are getting restless . . ."

Sure enough, both sisters were waving their hands in the air in an attempt to grab Vi's attention.

Vi let the magical dome fall away, and the second she did, Olive was pulling her into an excited hug.

"*I cannot wait* to get to the office and consult my books."

✦ ✦ ✦

As much as Linc enjoyed hanging out with Violet's friends and family, he couldn't wait to get her all to himself. All her things put away, pizza almost entirely consumed, he absentmindedly stroked her arm as conversation slowly morphed from the vampire inaccuracies on *Vampire Diaries* to a serious discussion of why men's pockets were so much deeper than women's.

And then Rose made a confession that froze everyone to their spots.

"Our mother did *what*?" Nestling closer to him on the couch, Violet gawked at her sister as if she'd admitted to being a cannibalistic serial killer.

"It wasn't Mom," a grim-faced Rose corrected. "*I'm* the one who signed the Bonding Agreement."

"Which you never would've signed if it weren't for Christina. Is this what you were so tight-lipped about the last week? Rose Marie! You should have said something!"

Linc glanced from person to person before settling back on the woman nestled against him. "What's a Bonding Agreement, and why does everyone look like the world's about to end?"

Violet distractedly played with his free hand. "It's a legally binding document—which my highly intelligent, overachieving, and overplanning sister *signed*—that states that as long as she's expected to be Prima, she has to form a Witch Bond with Pepé Le Pee-Yew."

He shot Rose a surprised look. "You can't break off the engagement?"

"As long as I'm the next Prima? No. There's no breaking it." Rose sipped the beer in front of her, then, as if realizing her fate, took a much longer draw. "As much as I wish I could throw the blame on someone else for this, I can't. Mom only made the introduction. I was the one who didn't see the scum beneath the shiny surface until it was too late."

"I imagine that's exactly what he was betting on," Linc said dryly.

Rose nodded and tipped her head back, draining her drink.

"I didn't know this kind of thing existed," Linc admitted.

Bax snorted. "Look at the big bad Councilman who doesn't know Supernatural law."

"Like you knew about it until ten seconds ago," Vi chastised her friend. "It's a Prima thing that's not common knowledge even in witch circles. Edie didn't have one because Grandpa Jethro was her True Mate."

Lincoln's business brain kicked in. "So what I'm hearing is that all Rose needs to do to get out of hitching herself to Bisset is refuse to be Prima. No Prima title, voided contract, no Bonding."

Rose looked to Violet, and Violet looked to Olive.

The youngest triplet nodded. "That would do it. But then who would be Prima?"

Silence fell over the group, the scratching in Fancy Pants's litter box the only thing heard for at least ten seconds . . . and then all three sisters talked at once.

They seemed to have no problem following their overlapping conversations, but hell if Linc could figure it out.

Sticking his fingers into his mouth, Bax whistled the trio into silence. "Please remember that not everyone here is a member of the Magical Triad."

"Sorry," the sisters said in unison, wearing varying versions of sheepish smiles.

Bax failed to hide his amusement. "So before your grandmother and her sisters, there wasn't a Magical Triad in close to a hundred and fifty years, right? Supernaturals managed fine without a Prima for well over a century. I'd imagine we'd be fine without one again."

"But were we fine?" Vi's voice sounded skeptical. "Shifter feuds. Clashes between vampires and human hunters. The Angel Wars. The only Supernaturals who weren't at war with anyone else were the demons, and that's because they were constantly at war with themselves. It was a shit show until Gran showed up."

Everyone sobered, knowing she spoke the truth. Everyone looked—and acted—as if they'd aged twenty years. A minute turned to ten, then ten to fifteen.

Harper stood, first to break the silence. "Now that my Ladies & Gents buzz has been officially killed off, it's time for me to head out." She tugged Violet into a hug. "Christen every room the second we're out the door. Just disinfect all surfaces before we visit again because I am not eating on an ass-table regardless of how hot you both are."

Violet snortled and said her goodbyes, hugging Bax and each of her sisters. The angel even offered Linc a handshake before following the girls out.

For the first time all day, Linc and Violet were alone.

As she bent to pick up empty pizza boxes, he slid his arms around her waist and nuzzled his mouth into the curve of her neck. "Not that I didn't enjoy hanging out with your family, but I've wanted you naked and under me since I woke up this morning."

"Now that we live together, you can have me every morning until our charade ends and we go back to normal."

Charade.

Normal.

Despite it explaining their deal accurately, those words chafed both Linc *and* his Wolf. They'd fooled everyone into thinking they were headed toward a mating, making each other a part of the other's life.

But wasn't that happening for real?

Seeing her things hanging in his closet would take adjusting to, but he liked them there. Just like he couldn't wait to get a whiff of her shampoo in a hot, steamy bathroom, and he ached at the thought of waking up in the morning with her pliant body wrapped naked against his.

Or fully clothed and wearing flannel duck pj's. He wasn't particular.

He told himself this was all *fake fun*, but neither the man nor the wolf in him seemed to listen.

"What do you want to do now that we're alone?" Linc dropped onto the couch and tugged her onto his lap. Her legs straddled his as she shifted closer.

"I have a few ideas. Ninety-seven percent of them require nudity."

He slowly guided her mouth to his. "You have the best fucking ideas."

"I do, and I'm full of them right now." She drew her shirt over her head and tossed it aside.

He cupped a lace-covered breast and played with the already pebbled nipple. "I can't wait to get my mouth on you."

"Just your mouth?" Vi teased.

"To start with . . . and then you'll get my hands."

"And then . . . ?" She nipped his shoulder before nestling her head onto the curve of his neck.

"And then . . ." The rhythmic sound of her breathing tickled his skin. "Violet?"

Nothing.

"Vi?" He brushed aside her curtain of hair and pressed a kiss to her cheek.

She'd fallen asleep on him. Literally.

"Guess we're taking a rain check on the nudity." He chuckled and took Violet to his bed, where someone—probably Harper—had left an unopened box of Magnum condoms and an extra-large bottle of lube.

After he tucked her snugly beneath the covers, she mumbled sleepily and pulled him behind her into a spoon formation. He went willingly, curling one arm over her waist and holding her close.

This feels nice.

Feels right.

And that warm, electric current pulsating to every point of contact sure as hell didn't feel like a charade.

20

Playing Hardball

Vi wasn't a wake-up-at-the-butt-crack-of-dawn-and-exercise person. Instead, she adopted a listen-to-your-body's-circadian-rhythm approach to physical fitness and errand running. Most days, her rhythm didn't start until nine in the morning, and after working the closing shift at Potion's Up, sometimes ten.

That morning wasn't an exception.

Yesterday's moving day had drained her both physically and mentally, and according to the note left on the pillow next to hers, had *not* been a dream. *Make yourself at home.*

She hoped Lincoln meant it, because after tugging her hair into a ponytail and shoving her feet into sneakers, she'd spent the better part of the afternoon and early evening doing magical push-ups in his gym.

With no Lincoln to serve as her target, she concentrated mostly on meditation exercises and graduated to simple spells she'd seen her gran perform countless times growing up. Elemental Magic was definitely the easiest for her to handle.

She'd ignited and extinguished more than a dozen candles at once, created a mini wind storm that played with Mr. Fancy Pants, pushing his cat toy around the room. And she'd summoned her inner ice princess, freezing cups of water in a quick finger snap.

A few short weeks ago, she was the Magicless Maxwell. Today, she was *The Boss*.

At that thought, Sparky whipped her hair around her head until it looked like she'd been caught in a tornado.

Vi laughed. "Oh, relax. I didn't mean it. *We're* the Boss."

The front door's alarm disengaged, and a few minutes later, Lincoln descended the steps.

"Please tell me one of your sisters swung by and put the protection charm back up." Tossing his suit jacket and keys on one of the exercise machines still tucked into the corner, he flashed her a teasing grin.

Vi turned in time to see him shuck his tie and roll up his shirt-sleeves. Arm porn was definitely a thing, because the sight of his muscular forearms sucked away all the moisture in her mouth.

"For your information, Olive walked me through the process over the phone and I erected the charms myself. *And* I did it successfully on the first try. What do you say about that?"

"I say I need to kiss you." Sliding his hand into her hair, he dragged her into a hot, slow kiss that left her knees quaking. "Have you been practicing all day?"

Head still in a kiss fog, she nodded. "I took water breaks."

"When was the last time you put something in your body that wasn't liquid?"

"This morning?"

He gave her a disapproving look.

"We'll run up and eat in a second. First, I want to show you what I've been working on." She dragged him to the center of the room and, once he was in position, handed him an uncapped water bottle. "For the demonstration."

He raised a sexy eyebrow. "Spring water?"

"Just hold it."

Mr. Fancy Pants scurried away as Vi reclaimed her spot in

the center of the floor. Clearing her mind, she nudged her Magic awake. *Let's have some fun, Sparky* . . .

The bottle's contents lifted, one drop at a time, until it hovered over their heads . . . and then she nudged her Magic into motion. Water spun in artistic aquatic swirls before transforming into a simple orb. It morphed from an orb into a heart, and after swirling around again, took the shape of a howling wolf.

Lincoln's Wolf.

"Violet." He watched in awe. "This is amazing. How are you doing this?"

"Beats the hell out of me, but it's pretty cool, right?"

Water Wolf stalked around him, lifting higher and higher until it sat on its haunches while suspended over Lincoln's head. He realized his predicament a split second before she dropped the spell—and the water—on top of him.

Rivulets ran down his shocked face, dripping off his chin.

She giggled. "You look a little wet. You should probably change your clothes. On second thought, don't. I like the wet look."

"You think that was funny?" He advanced toward her, slowly unbuttoning his wet shirt.

"Immensely." She edged backward a step, then two. "It went way better than I imagined. And did you see how much the wolf resembled yours? I'm a magical Rembrandt."

"It was incredible." Another step closer.

She lifted her hands in surrender. "No more magical pranks. I promise . . . if you get rid of that evil glint in your eye."

"There's nothing evil glinting in my eye, baby. It's a guarantee." A playful growl rolled from his throat as he leaped. He caught her around the waist, easily lifting her off the ground.

Vi laughed. "It was a joke! Where's your sense of humor, Wolfman?"

"Drenched. Like the rest of me."

She laughed harder. "Put me down, or I'll have to take the gloves off. I'm not above playing dirty."

"Dirty, huh? That doesn't sound half bad to me."

We'll see about that.

Relaxing deeper into his embrace, Vi wiggled against the forming erection pressing against her ass, and when Linc emitted a soft groan, did it again.

"Playing hardball, little witch?"

"It's not the only thing in the room that's hard."

Gently dropping her back on her feet, Lincoln braced her hands against the wall. The brush of his mouth against her ear sent a hot rush of desire through her body. "Do you enjoy hard things, princess?"

"I enjoy *your* hard things." Damn, was that her breathless voice?

To make sure there was no misunderstanding, Vi squirmed, pushing her body closer to his. She wasn't sure where this brazen, sex-deprived alter ego had come from, but she wasn't about to question it now.

"And I'd really like to enjoy it *now*."

A low, sexy growl rumbled through Lincoln's chest a split second before her body was airborne, tossed over his shoulder in a fireman's carry.

"Ugh, you're getting me all wet, Wolfman." Vi couldn't help but giggle.

He smacked her ass playfully. "Not yet, but I intend to."

✦ ✦ ✦

Linc took the stairs two at a time, his craving to be buried inside Violet growing with each step. By the time he reached the bedroom and gently placed her back on her feet, his plan to go slow had evaporated.

She yanked his mouth to hers, and in a heated frenzy of lips and tongue, he walked her backward until her legs bumped the mattress. "You have no idea how bad I want to throw you on that bed and have my way with you."

"So why don't you?" She undid the last two buttons of his shirt and pushed it off his broad shoulders. It had barely hit the floor before she shoved his pants down his legs, boxer briefs and all.

Pre-come beaded on the tip of his cock, and as if he wasn't far enough gone, she wrapped her soft hand around him and squeezed.

Linc reflexively pushed himself into her hot grip. "Get naked, and get on the bed."

With mischief glinting in her eyes, she slowly took off every article of clothing and crawled onto the king-size mattress, giving him a delectable view of her bare backside. She looked coyly over her shoulder. "Like what you see?"

"You're practically begging for a bite on the ass. You know that, princess?"

"I keep hearing about this biting thing. I'm starting to think it might be worth a try." Her mouth twitched, and damned if he didn't get harder.

Linc grabbed a condom from the bedside table and had no sooner rolled it into place when Violet lay on her back, her body spread out like a delectable buffet. He forced himself to slow down as he climbed over her, trailing both his hands and his mouth over every inch of her soft skin. Her knee. Her inner thigh. Careful to avoid the dampness between her legs, he brushed his mouth over the curve of her hip, and higher. Purple wisps of Magic rose to meet his touch.

"Are you seeing this?" He reached out to touch a curling tendril and it playfully wrapped around his hand before slinking away.

"Guess Sparky needs you as much as I do." Vi's hooded gaze nearly melted him on the spot. "Don't make me wait anymore, Wolfman."

He needed her too much to make either of them wait.

Dropping a soul-destroying kiss to her mouth, he buried himself into her in one hard thrust. Then he dragged himself to her outer rim and did it again, the two of them working in tandem to build a slow, arduous pace that made them both breathless and sweaty in seconds.

This time, it wasn't only the pleasure that swelled.

Calling to his Wolf, Violet's Magic filled the room with its crackling energy.

It lay beneath them.

It hovered above them.

It hugged them on all sides until they erupted in a simultaneous climax that left them both winded and sated, and his Wolf internally chanting *mine*.

His.

Theirs.

He was falling head over heels for this woman . . . or maybe he'd never gotten back up after last time.

21

Baddest Witch on the Block

Hurricane Violet stormed through her grandmother's front door, bypassing the empty front rooms of the two-story log home, and made a beeline for the back of the house. And yes, she knew Rose and Edie's exact location, because she'd detected their Magic before the Uber turned down the driveway.

That's right.

She'd *sensed* them. Like some freakin' magical bloodhound, she'd tracked them to Athens, New York, and more specifically, to Edie's workroom and home office.

"Have both of you lost the ability to answer the phone?" She stood in the doorway, her hands mounted on her hips. "I've tried reaching you two all damn day!"

Huddled over Edie's desk, Rose and Edie glanced up from the dusty text in front of them.

Her gran glanced at the nearby clock. "It's only ten in the morning, sweetheart. *All* day?"

"It felt like a week." Vi dropped her things and her body into the corner chair.

She'd been up for hours, unable to get last night out of her head. She'd had memorable sex before. Okay, so she'd had *regrettably* memorable sex. But that wasn't last night. Last night was . . . hell if she knew.

It sounded corny to say *magical*, but that's exactly what had happened.

Magic.

Rose handed her a cup of Edie's specially brewed calming tea. "You look like you need a cup of this . . . or a gallon."

"Which is larger . . . a vat or a gallon?" She accepted it and took a test sip. "You know what? It doesn't matter. I couldn't relax if I swam in an Olympic-size swimming pool filled with this stuff."

"It's better than ripping your hair out, which it seems you're about twenty seconds away from doing, so drink up."

She took another sip, wishing it was laced with the whiskey with which Edie spiked her eggnog. "What does it mean when you see fireworks during sex?"

Both Rose and Edie stilled.

"I'm not talking metaphorical fireworks here, either. I'm talking a sparkling, multicolored light show that puts Disney's Illumi-Nations to shame." Vi hit her sister with a pleading look. "Is that a Magic thing? Because while it felt amazing at the time, I'm pretty freaked out right now."

"You saw fireworks when you and Lincoln . . ." Rose glanced at Edie.

The older witch chuckled. "Honestly, girls, I had your mother . . . and a mate. I know sex exists."

"So . . . ?" Vi urged them to say something. *Anything.*

Sparky swirled beneath the surface of her skin, and didn't have any intentions of leaving. No rushes or surges . . . she was just *there*.

Rose cleared her throat and shook her head. "I can't say I've ever had fireworks with Valentin. Or anyone."

"No one?" Vi's voice cracked. "Like . . . maybe a single magical ember?"

Rose's look of regret dropped Vi's head to her hands. "I *knew* things were going too damn perfect. Just when I thought I was getting a handle on this Magic business, it'll all fall apart now. Lincoln and I leave for Australia tomorrow, and then three days after that are the Alpha vote and his birthday. Right as we come down to the wire, things are flipping upside down."

"I'm not so sure you don't have a handle on this Magic business, Vi." Rose sat on the arm of her chair and squeezed her shoulder.

"Did you not hear me when I said I leaked Magic all over Lincoln and myself while we . . . ?" She waggled her eyebrows.

"Heard that part, thanks for the mental visual. My point is that you're not leaking Magic *now*."

"But she's there . . . waiting."

Edie's eyebrow cocked. "Waiting?"

Vi couldn't put it into words. It was like her Magic anticipated something. "I don't know how else to describe it. What if I haven't made as much progress as I thought? That birthday party will be littered with Supernaturals, not to mention the Elders. I can screw things up for both Lincoln *and* myself in one display of sucky luck."

"You could always make your appeal to the Council *now*," Rose suggested.

"I might have considered it right after riding the high of the fire, but now? When I have no idea what Sparky finds so damn interesting?" A sinking sensation settled in the pit of her stomach. "There's a million ways that could backfire on me and then I'd be in the same position I'm in right now . . . or a worse one. What if they push me into an *immediate* Witch Bond? Or coerce me into a Bonding Agreement? Or—"

"Or force you to become Prima," Rose added offhandedly.

Vi and Edie sent her simultaneous looks, but the middle triplet shrugged unapologetically, nursing her own cup of tea. "What? It's not out of the realm of possibility. Is that not something they would do?"

"I couldn't do that to you, Ro. It's not right. *You're* the Prima Apparent."

"What isn't right is a Secondborn being Prima," Rose muttered under her breath.

Gran watched them both carefully. "What are you saying, Rose? You don't want to be Prima?"

Vi squeezed her sister's hand in a show of support. "*Tell her.* She'll understand."

Rose set her cup on the table and stared Edie in the eye. "I'm not sure I want the job, Gran. And I *know* I don't want to be tied to Valentin Bisset for the rest of my life and beyond."

"Why haven't you said anything before now?"

"Because honestly, I *did* want it. Before anyone realized Violet's powers didn't manifest, I can't tell you how many times I wished I could be in her position—and then I *was*. It was exciting. But as the years went by . . . I don't know how to explain it. I'm not certain it's who I am. I'm not . . . *Prima*."

Edie's pensive expression gave no clue as to her thoughts. She sat quietly, hands folded on her lap. If there were ever a time to take up telepathy, this was it, but they all sat in silence.

"Can she do that?" Vi finally asked. "Can she say 'not it' and step down?"

Edie reached for her own tea. "Honestly? There's no precedent for any of this."

A headache blossomed behind Vi's eyes. "The Maxwell Dud fucks everything up yet again."

"This is not on you, Violet."

"It sure as hell feels like it. If I hadn't bottled Sparky up in the first place, Rose wouldn't have been forced to pick up my slack, she wouldn't be contracted to marry a barbaric, chauvinistic tiger king, and I wouldn't be falling in love with a wolf shifter who already broke my heart once!"

Hell's Spells, was she falling in love with Lincoln freakin' Thorne?

Again?

Evidently a modestly decent GPA doesn't represent someone's common sense, because she wasn't sure that she'd ever fallen *out* of love with him. They still had that undeniable connection, and yet it felt different.

It felt like . . . *more*.

It was a realization that would've freaked her the hell out if she didn't already have a steaming pile of witch shit backing up the pipes.

"There's got to be a way for Rose to step down without upending magical society," Vi stated. "It doesn't seem fair that the Council can force her into a role she doesn't want."

"Technically, they can't. Magic itself gifts a Prima her power, not the Council. Not even me, as the current Prima. The reason the Council intervened with your Triad was because—"

"I was a dud."

"But you're not anymore," Rose pointed out. "You have Magic, Vi. And it's only grown in power the last few weeks. I can feel it. Olive can too. You're a walking witchy power source, and the reason you're not blowing shit up anymore is because you and your Magic are finally becoming one. Maybe that thing Sparky is waiting for is for you to realize who you are."

"What? *Prima?*" Vi lifted a skeptical brow. "Even if I am learning better control, that's a huge jump—like the distance from Earth to Mars. I was magicless for thirty-two years. I'm in no shape to become Supernatural society's *It Witch*. Right?"

Edie's slight shoulders shrugged. "That's not up to me, my dear. Or Rose. Or even you. The only opinion that matters is Magic's. I won't bring this up to the Council, because frankly, other than the reigning Prima sitting as Council Chair, this has nothing to do with them. You still have two months until you reach the end of the Council's reprieve. I suggest you take that time and continue working with your Magic. See where it takes you. Even if you prove that you, as the Firstborn, don't need a Witch Bond to anchor your powers, Supernatural law is a sticky enough wicket that the Council could argue a *Prima* does."

Vi groaned. "I could prove that I'm the baddest witch on the block and can control all my badassery, and it's *still* not a guarantee I won't end up Witch Bonded to a seventy-year-old warlock with halitosis."

Rose chuckled. "Do you really think Lincoln would let that happen?"

Honestly, she didn't know.

A heavy ache throbbed in her chest that had nothing to do with Sparky. They weren't True Mates, and if Alpha Benson didn't pull through with the final Alpha vote, she wasn't sure Lincoln wouldn't accept the Elders' mate pick so he could continue fighting them from the inside.

Changing Pack life into a shiftocracy was what he wanted more than anything . . . and more than anything, she wanted him to get what he wanted.

22

Alpha Asshat

Linc paced the length of the hotel suite, sat on the couch, and immediately resumed pacing. Nerves weren't something he usually experienced, and yet he hadn't felt much else since first picking up Violet and jumping on the plane to Australia.

There'd been no ass-busting or jibes, and she hadn't once called him Wolfman during the entire twenty-one-hour flight. Big events weren't her thing, and the Alpha's celebration definitely constituted *an event,* one for which both Supernatural and Norm dignitaries came out in droves. But his gut told him that it wasn't the scale of the party on her mind.

Call him paranoid, but it seemed her change in mood stemmed from their last night together.

The night.

The night he had questioned if it was possible to feel more connected to a person than he was to Violet, and admitted that he couldn't picture it. *That's* why he couldn't take his mind—or his worry—off her. He was scared that the intensity of their growing relationship had terrified her right out of his life.

"I hope this is okay."

He spun around as she stepped out from the bathroom and stole his ability to breathe. "You're . . . wow."

She smoothed down the spaghetti-strapped sundress, the light, silky fabric showcasing her tanned, bare legs. "It's not too casual? I listened to Rose on what to wear to a kid's beachy birthday party that wasn't *just* a birthday party. This was what we came up with."

"You're perfect." He scanned her from head to toe, drinking in every glorious inch of her. "Absolutely perfect."

Her smile wavered.

He pulled her flush against him, his Wolf rumbling in his chest, determined to show her how perfect she was to them both. "Do we really need to go to this party?"

A small smile returned to her lips as she skated her hands over his shoulders. "While I would love nothing more than to hide away in this room, my sister will come looking for us if we don't show."

"Did you tell her our room number?"

"Nope. It would take her at least an hour to realize we weren't there, and maybe thirty minutes to scare the front desk into giving up the info. Think you could have your way with me in an hour and a half?"

He brushed a feather-soft kiss over her mouth. "Sweetheart, I don't think I'll ever be done having my way with you."

He hadn't meant it the way it sounded . . . or maybe he had.

Regardless, he'd spooked her, her body stiffening ever so slightly before gently pulling away. "As tempted as I am to dive into that cozy-looking bed, I didn't spend nearly forty-five minutes getting into this strapless bra to stay in a hotel room. And then there's the fact you have an Australian Alpha to woo."

"You're seriously asking me to give up naked time with you to hang out with a bunch of pretentious shifters?"

Her smile didn't quite reach her eyes. "I'm questioning my priorities, too."

He almost said to hell with his priorities. As much as he wanted sexy time with her, he also wanted time *with* her. To be near her. To soak in her scent and feel her body next to his. That could happen naked or while curled up on the couch watching HGTV.

He didn't care.

Those childish feelings he'd had when they were kids had morphed into something he'd never expected . . . and it all began with a snowball to the face.

With his palm resting on the small of her back, they left the hotel and headed toward the beach party. Violet drifted back into silent mode.

He sent her an inquisitive look. "Will you tell me what has you on edge?"

"I'm not on edge."

"If you clutch my hand any tighter you'll break bones in your hand . . . or mine."

"Sorry." She unraveled her fingers from his, but he gently tugged her back.

"That wasn't a complaint, princess. It was an observation." He pulled her to a stop on the torchlit walking trail. The glow of the flickering flames caressed her cheeks, emphasizing the half-hidden worry glinting in her eyes. "Talk to me. Tell me what's happening in that gorgeous head of yours."

She nibbled on her lower lip. "It's just . . . there's a lot riding on tonight. I don't want to mess it up for you."

He searched her face, and while he sensed nothing but truth in her words, he knew it wasn't quite everything. "No one's messing this up. It's practically in the bag. All you have to do is enjoy the party and be yourself."

She didn't look convinced.

"Give me a safe word."

She chuckled. "A safe word for what? I thought we already decided we had to make an appearance at the party before we participated in any naked-time."

The bonfire festivities blew in from the beach. Conversations. Music. Laughter. But all Linc could see or hear was the witch right in front of him looking like she was ready to bolt.

"Just pick a safe word. When you say it, I know to get you the hell out of here. Whenever you want."

"You can't disappear, Lincoln. Alpha Benson—"

"I can and I will, if it's what you need. So . . . safe word. How about yellow? Or Red. Or . . . underwear?"

"You're ridiculous."

"I'm cautious—how about 'broomsticks'?"

"Broomsticks?" She failed to contain a laugh. "Why would anyone talk about broomsticks at a shifter event? Or any event outside of a Halloween party?"

"Exactly why it'll make the perfect safe word." He curled his arm around her waist and held her close to his side as he turned them back toward the bonfire. "Broomsticks it is. Say it at any point during the night, and I'll have you back in our suite, naked and below me, in a heartbeat."

Violet's laughter eased the constriction that had squeezed his chest.

They made it three or four steps before someone from his Pack stopped to exchange pleasantries. She took it all in stride, smiling and shaking hands at every introduction as they slowly made their way to the waterfront gazebo.

"I don't know how you do it." Violet stretched her jaw when they finally found themselves alone for longer than five seconds.

"Do what?"

She nudged her chin to all the people. "Them. My cheeks already hurt and we've been here less than ten minutes. How do you deal with knowing half of them are only nice to you because they want something? Gran makes it look easy, too."

"Spotting the opportunists comes with practice." Something in her tone had him looking at her a bit longer. "Are you afraid some-one's taking advantage of you?"

"No. No, I'm just wondering if I could ever be that astute."

"I have my Wolf to fall back on, and he's a better judge of char-acter than I am. I'm sure your grandmother says the same about her Magic."

Violet finally grinned. "You're right. She does."

"About damn time you two showed up." Adrian popped up next to them, brushing a welcome kiss on Violet's cheek before clap-ping Linc hard on the shoulder. "I would've sent a search party if I didn't think they'd return scarred for life."

Violet scanned the beach and gazebo. "Have you seen Rose? I sent her a text a while ago, but she hasn't replied yet."

"I did," Adrian said carefully. He quickly averted his eyes.

Violet didn't let him get away with it. "She's with Alpha Asshat, isn't she?"

Linc's Second grimaced in apology. "Yeah. And from the looks of things, it's not pleasure in paradise. You could cut the tension between those two with a dull spoon."

"I should find her and make sure she's okay."

"Do you want a second pair of hands?" Linc offered, attempting to keep his face blank.

She blinked before her delectable mouth eased into a knowing smirk. "You think I need backup when I'm with my sister?"

"It wasn't Rose I was concerned about."

"Who are you trying to protect? Me or Valentin?" Her grin widened. "You know what? It doesn't matter. I think I've proven that I can hold my own with broody Alpha shifters. I'll be fine." She patted his chest, not bothering to hide her amusement. "Go woo an Alpha. I've got Rose covered."

"Fine." He exchanged a nod with the guard hovering six feet away. "At least take Leo with you."

"Isn't he supposed to be *your* security detail?"

"My Wolf is my head of security. Leo's here for you."

Violet brushed a soft kiss over his mouth. "I'll let you have your way now, but you're making this up to me later, Wolfman."

He chuckled at the return of his nickname. "I'll make it up to you all night long, princess."

She smirked, and with a crook of her finger to her guard bear, went in search of her sister. Linc's gaze tracked her across the makeshift dance floor and onto the sandy beach. She may not like these kinds of events, but you'd never tell by the way she welcomed each person who approached her.

"Earth to Lincoln. Come in, Lincoln." Adrian waved a hand in front of his face.

"What?"

His best friend chuckled. "You look at her like you're a man dying of thirst and she's a tall glass of cool water."

"Your point?"

"Nothing. I'm just glad to see you've finally seen the error of your ways. True Mates are a great fairy tale, but reality has some perks, too. I don't think I've ever seen you this happy."

He *was* happy. He'd never *been* this content.

Whenever he wasn't with Violet, he longed to see her, and when she finally stood in his line of sight, he couldn't force himself to look away. And when she was in his arms? He couldn't shake the feeling that he was *home*.

True Mate or not, nothing felt as real or as right as what he experienced with Violet. He wasn't falling in love with her—he'd already crashed headfirst. No warning. No protective gear. But while his heart was full with excitement, reality snuck in, snatching it away.

Violet deserved everything she ever wanted, and he already knew that what she wanted most was the truth. He'd never be able to tell her what had happened fourteen years ago, and while she might eventually forgive him, there'd always be that divide threatening to swallow them whole.

"This wasn't supposed to happen," Linc admitted aloud before tearing his gaze away from where she'd disappeared into the crowd. Grabbing Adrian's arm, he steered them to a secluded area of the party where they wouldn't be disturbed. "All this was supposed to be a no-strings, uncomplicated business arrangement."

Adrian looked puzzled. "What the fuck are you talking about?"

"I took your advice. Violet was saddled with the Witch Bond law, and I needed a potential mate to shake off the Elders' suspicion about the Alpha vote. We both got something out of this. Real feelings weren't meant to be part of the equation."

"You're telling me that you're not together?" Adrian look astounded, then angry, then confused. "Yeah, no. I don't buy that. I've had a first-row seat for how you look at each other, and it's not like business partners, my friend. You're in love with her."

"I'm not sure it's enough. Actually, I know it's not." Fuck, that weight was back on his chest, wrapping around him like a boa constrictor. "I can't give her what she deserves. And then there's the vote to think about. If Benson doesn't side with me, I have to make a choice: step down, or . . ."

"Cave to the Elders' demands?" Adrian's eyes widened. "Are you shitting me right now, man?"

"I can't help my Pack if I'm not in a position of power to do so."

A familiar, goading laugh made both Linc and Adrian turn.

Bisset, grinning from ear to ear and hands shoved deep in his pockets, looked like the tiger that ate Little Red Riding Hood. "This makes more sense than what the two of you tried passing off for the last few weeks. A supernatural con, huh? Kudos."

"Watch it, Bisset." Linc growled.

"Watch what? Your reputation go up in flames?" The tiger shifter chuckled. "Gladly. I'll give you credit, though. I almost believed that little charade you had going with the Maxwell Dud.

Although it never occurred to me that you'd *both* be using each other. I figured she was that good a lay that you couldn't keep your distance. You had me thinking for a hot second that I picked the wrong sister."

"I won't warn you again." Linc's Wolf, close to the surface, deepened his voice. "Watch what you say."

"Oh, I will. And you can watch me tell the Elders how far you're willing to go to make them disappear. I think they'll have a few things to say about that, don't you?" Bisset smirked. "And I bet the Supernatural Council would love to hear about one of their own conspiring with a Firstborn to pull the wool over their eyes as well. I wonder what the punishment would be for a young witch like Violet."

Linc's bones cracked as anger ripped through him. His muscles vibrated, his Wolf demanding to be let out.

How dare Bisset *threaten* Violet? How dare he *talk* of her?

Adrian's demands for him to calm down were easily muted as the need to protect Violet consumed him. Linc's Wolf burst free. Human one second, a wolf the next, Linc's not-so-inner beast immediately locked his sights on their target . . . and he wouldn't back down until he tasted blood.

✦ ✦ ✦

Vi scanned the crowd, hoping to catch a glimpse of her sister, but came up empty. An alarming number of people had worn seductress red to a one-year-old's beach birthday party.

She lifted onto her toes in an attempt to make herself taller. "Hey, Leo? Can you use your spidey sense to sniff out a miserable witch who's trying really hard not to hex her fiancé with a case of genital warts?"

Not even an exasperated sigh.

She glanced back to make sure her shadow was still behind her, but he'd stopped walking, his gaze turned toward the gazebo. The bear shifter looked rattled.

"Are you okay—?"

Rose appeared in front of her like a puff of fairy godmother Magic. "There you are!"

"Hex me to hell and back." Vi clutched her chest.

"Get back to Lincoln. *Now.*"

Her sister's panicked eyes brought all jokes to a standstill. "What's wrong?"

"He'll get himself locked up in Supernatural jail if he kills Valentin in an unsanctioned Blood Match. That's what's wrong."

"An unsanctioned . . . Hell's Spells, I leave him alone for one fucking second." She turned to run her way back down the beach and tripped. Cursing her sandals, she spun back to her sister. "Fairy godmother me back to him. Quick."

"You can—"

"I don't have time to be all experimental and shit, Ro." Vi reached out for her sister's hand. "Let's give someone else a heart attack for once."

Their hands brushed against each other and they blinked into nonexistence and back again twenty yards from where she'd left Lincoln. Beastlike snarls and human squeals guided her the rest of the way.

Those who weren't watching the show in morbid fascination had run away from the oversized black wolf and the massive tiger the way one might flee Godzilla, and she didn't blame them.

Bared teeth snapped and loud, threatening growls rolled from their throats as they met in a hard clash of furry bodies. She winced as Bisset got a good swipe to Lincoln's hind leg, but her Wolfman didn't so much as bat an eye, his own paw reaching out in immediate retaliation.

Vi's Magic pushed its way to the surface.

Not in anger.

Or fear.

Or from nerves.

It rose with the pure, unfiltered need to protect *their* Wolf . . . hers and her Magic's.

There was no way this didn't end badly. If Lincoln lost to Bisset, the bastard would make sure it was a death sentence, and if Lincoln bested Alpha Asshat, they'd have more problems than Witch Bonds or Elder agendas.

Wolf Lincoln and Tiger Bisset rolled on the sand, nearly colliding with a group of spectators. As the two animals came to a stop, Lincoln hovered over the tiger, his massive jaws clamped on the other shifter's throat.

Tiger Bisset lay on the sand, his furry chest heaving. Immobile. One false move and he'd tear his own jugular out, and he knew it.

"First time I'm glad for something being anticlimactic," Vi muttered as Linc's Wolf backed away with a slight limp.

He shifted into his human form first, his linen pants and shirt bloodied and shredded. "It's over. You're not worth my time."

Valentin transformed next, swiping away the blood collecting at the corner of his mouth. "You're fucking pathetic, Thorne. Can't follow through with anything. It's one reason of many why you have no business being on the Council. You're a disgrace not just to the North American Pack, but to all shifters. You're not half the Alpha your father was."

Sparky hurtled herself against Vi's mental walls, itching to be released. *Hell's Spells, what is your problem?*

Sweat broke out across her forehead as she tried withholding her Magic. "You're right. He's a hell of a lot more. You're on dangerous ground, Val. I'd stop while you're ahead."

And before her Magic really did blast him into next week.

The tiger shifter's gaze swung toward her. "It isn't me who's on dangerous ground, sweetheart. Do you know what happens to witches who defraud the Supernatural Council?"

Rose dropped a supportive hand on her sister's shoulder. "No one wants to hear your voice. Stuff it."

Bisset looked from her to Lincoln and back before releasing a sinister chuckle. "You mean you didn't tell your own *triplet*, Violet? Why don't you go ahead and tell her now. Tell everyone about the con you and Alpha Thorne tried running on everyone."

Vi's breath hitched. How could he know? How *did* he know?

"I heard it from the Alpha's own mouth. Isn't that right, Thorne?" Bisset was out for no less blood than when he'd been in tiger form. "Didn't I hear you tell your Second-in-Command that if your little coup against the Elders failed, you'd have no choice but to take the Mate they chose for you? Well, guess what? You've failed, and if the Elders don't know about your little trickery yet, they will very soon."

Take the Mate the Elders *choose for him?*

Vi's and Lincoln's gazes interlocked, and as her trembling heart slowly registered what was happening, she couldn't tear herself away from Lincoln's apologetic eyes.

Pain and guilt swirled in their golden brown depths, but there was also truth. He'd rather Mate Bond with someone he *knew* would be all wrong for him than choose her.

Until that very moment, Vi hadn't realized how badly she'd wanted that role, and now that it had been ripped away from her, it felt like her entire heart was shredded along with it.

This was why she hadn't wanted to make their deal. There'd only ever been one way for things to end between them, and the soul-splitting agony tearing her heart apart was her punishment for thinking otherwise.

Lincoln stepped forward with a soft whisper. "Violet, I—"

Stepping back, she shook her head. "You're right. We were nothing but a business arrangement, and now that we're no longer in business, you need to do what you need to do."

She couldn't escape fast enough, and as she turned, one tear turned into two, then two into three. She'd made it a handful of steps when the floodgates opened and her constricted lungs made it difficult to breathe.

Lincoln's heavy footfalls crashed into the sand, following her. "Violet! Please wait—"

The magical dam she'd erected around both her heart and her Magic shattered. In a single torrent, Sparky poured out of her, flooding everything in her path and slamming into her biggest threat.

Lincoln.

He catapulted in the air as if hit by a Mack truck, landing a good twenty feet away, and this time, Sparky didn't retreat. She swirled around Vi like a protective shield, daring anyone to get close.

Guess the cat's out of the bag now, huh? More than a dozen cameras were aimed her way, recording the show for posterity—and probably the Council.

So much for taking her full three months.

Lincoln's gaze held hers as he slowly pushed to his feet. He didn't look angry. He didn't look scared.

He looked . . . defeated.

"Stay away from me, Linc," Vi murmured, knowing he'd hear despite her barely whispered words. "It's best for everyone if you just stay the hell away from me."

She chanted it to herself on her walk back up to the hotel, hoping that if she said it enough, she'd eventually believe it.

✦ ✦ ✦

With every step that Violet took away from Linc, the vise around his heart constricted until it became nothing but a pile of dust. He sank to his knees, his gaze fixed on her as she disappeared. He didn't care about the low murmur of voices, or the shit show that would soon follow.

All his focus was on the woman who'd walked away and taken his heart with her.

Seeing the hurt in her eyes and knowing he was the one who put it there destroyed him. He *loved* her. So damn much he couldn't see straight. He couldn't think straight. He couldn't sense the threat looming behind him.

A magical bolt whipped past his ear a split second before Bisset's gleaming claw would've made contact with his jugular. The bastard flew backward, landing dangerously close to the blazing fire.

Both her eyes and hands damn near glowing, Rose Maxwell stepped forward, glaring at the tiger shifter. "Consider this your official notice that the Bonding Ceremony's canceled."

"You don't have a choice, witch," Bisset snarled, his lips barely moving. "We have a legal document. You belong to me."

"I'm a third of the Maxwell Triad. I belong to no one but myself. If you come at me or my family again, I'll neuter your pussycat without even blinking. Do I make myself clear?"

Members of his Pack helped him up and then Bisset was scampering away, leaning on them heavily for support.

"Thank you, Rose." Linc turned to Violet's sister. "I—"

With a flip of her hand, the Prima Apparent magically sealed his mouth shut for a hot second as she speared him with her death-ray glare. "I don't know what the hell went on with you and my sister, but I do know I've never felt pain come from her like I did tonight. And you're the one who put it there."

"I never meant to—"

"Intentions don't matter, Linc. Actions do. I always thought you were better than what you showed everyone tonight. I'm sad I was wrong . . . sad for you, for your Pack, and most definitely for Vi. She deserves a partner who loves as fiercely and completely as she does . . . right to the fiber of their heart, body, and soul. If that's not you, stay the hell away from her, or else that little zap she gave you in the alley will be a tickle compared to what Olive and I will do to you. You mess with one Maxwell sister, you mess with the Triad."

Rose released her hold on him and followed the path Violet had taken back to the hotel.

Linc stood alone on the beach, most of the party having retreated closer to the hotel. Alpha Benson stood on the boardwalk with an unamused look on her face, then turned away.

Everyone did. One by one, with the free show over, the guests slowly returned to the party.

Adrian was the only one headed his way, his hands tucked into his pockets and no sign of his usual teasing smile anywhere in sight.

He turned to his best friend. "You going to chastise me, too?"

"Nope."

"You're giving up the opportunity to dish out an 'I told you so'?"

"Yep."

"Why the change in MO?"

"Because you're standing in a pile of rancid, sunbaked shit, my friend. You'll need all your reserve energy to get yourself out of it. Energy . . . and a fucking backhoe."

"I'll handle the Elders . . . and deal with the Council. Violet shouldn't suffer for something I encouraged."

"I'm not talking about them. I'm talking about the *real* challenge in front of you. I'm talking about figuring out how to get the woman you're in love with to let you out of the fucking doghouse you built for yourself." Adrian clapped him hard on the back. "You thought changing the inner workings of shifter society was hard? That's child's play compared to what you're up against with Violet."

He was right. An apology wouldn't cut it. Begging wasn't enough. Flowers were worthless and, knowing Violet, would either end up in the trash or shoved up his backside.

He needed to show her that his trust in her went far beyond anything that could ever be explained. That his belief in her would never waver. That it didn't matter if she wasn't his True Mate . . . she would always and forever be the most important person in his mind, heart, and soul.

23

Boozy (Ice Cream) & Buffy

Vi tried not to wince at her reflection in the mirror and failed miserably. Dark circles lingered under her eyes, and it wasn't poor lighting giving her complexion a sallow, ashen hue. She looked like an extra for *The Walking Dead* and no amount of makeup nor an expertly pasted-on smile could hide the pain festering beneath.

It wasn't the ache you got from sitting in an uncomfortable chair, or breaking a rib. It didn't even come close to what she'd experienced after subjecting herself to one of Rose's Spin classes. This pain was so much worse, her entire chest threatening to cave in on itself as if her heart no longer occupied its usual space.

Maybe that's why she could barely breathe.

Maybe the piercing pain beneath her sternum was the fragmented shards of her heart.

She ran her brush through her hair in an attempt to vanquish the rat's nest that had taken residence, and deemed it the best it would get without a magic wand before padding barefoot into the main room.

Everything came to a stop. Conversations. Bodies . . . at least until Rose, Olive, Harper, and Bax all turned toward her in unison.

Under normal circumstances, she would've cracked a joke about

Stepford friends, because they all wore the same on-edge expression, as if they were about to walk across a bed of nails.

Harper elbowed Bax with a softly muttered curse. "I told you we should've brought the boozy ice cream. Call and have it delivered."

"I don't need boozy ice cream, Harper." Vi's smile wavered.

Before she and Rose had even touched down at JFK early this morning, Olive and Harper had grabbed her belongings and Mr. Fancy Pants from Lincoln's place and brought everything back to Vi's studio. It should've made her feel better. She should've felt comfortable. At home.

Yet something was missing.

"Will you all stop looking at me like I'm about to break?" Vi flounced down on the couch and folded her legs beneath her. "This isn't a big deal. Lincoln and I made a business arrangement and now it's done. End of story."

Bax dropped down next to her and flung an arm over her shoulder. "You still suck at lying."

Harper snorted. "Which is why I can't believe you kept this secret for so long."

Everyone leveled her with looks.

"What? It's nothing short of a miracle!" Sitting on the coffee table in front of her, Harper reached for her hands. "If you don't want boozy ice cream, we'll go straight to the real stuff and have a booze-and-*Buffy*-marathon night. We'll skip the episodes where Angel leaves town . . . and the time she sends him to hell. Oh, and all the later episodes with Oz in all his furry-man glory."

Vi's chuckle morphed into a pathetic whimper. In a split second, she was surrounded on all sides.

Bax dragged her into a firm side-hug, and Harper, with a death grip on Vi's hands, shifted so close she practically sat on her lap. Olive came around the back of the couch and hugged her from behind. Rose was the only one not in the huggle. She paced the room, wearing a determined look Vi knew all too well.

"Take whatever plan that's running through your head and forget it," Vi demanded of her triplet. "Like I told you on the plane, this is no one's fault but mine. I'm the one who agreed to this."

"When *did* you two hatch this plot?" Harper asked. "Was it before or after you put him into a magical coma?"

"After, and it didn't sound like a bad plan at first. It gave us both a little breathing room and time to figure out what to do next. I never anticipated . . ."

Olive finished her sentence. "Falling in love with him."

Hell's Spells, she *had* fallen in love with him.

She'd tripped, fallen, and let it surge over her head like enthusiastic love-soaked quicksand. At some point she'd stopped seeing Lincoln as the obnoxious thorn in her side and instead started seeing the Thorne who always made her laugh, whether on purpose or at his expense.

The man who challenged her.

The man who accepted her.

Vi dropped her head to Bax's shoulder with a groan. "I'm a walking cliché in a paranormal romance . . . except this story doesn't have a happily ever after."

Rose looked contemplative as she sat on the edge of the couch. "Are you certain there can't be?"

"Were you not at the same party I was? If he doesn't get the Alpha vote, he's prepared to Mate Bond with whatever she-demon the Elders dig up. It was all business with us. I'm the idiot that got her signals crossed and fell in love with the man."

"This probably isn't something you want to hear right now, but I'm not so sure it was all business for him. The things he said . . . the way he looked at you when you left. He was a man who realized he'd lost something pretty damn special."

"I was a means to buy himself extra time. There's nothing else for me to do except sit here on my ass and wait for the Supernatural Council to summon me—because we all know that's coming." Her sister opened her mouth to argue. "Enough about me. What are *you* doing about that mating agreement with Alpha Asshat? He doesn't strike me as the type to let bygones be bygones."

"He's not . . . so I guess I need to buy myself some time, too. But I'm not marrying that creep. Not in this lifetime, or in any other."

"I wish I was strong enough to make it all go away for you." Vi sank farther into the couch. "Goddess, I'm a train wreck. I can't have unbelievable, soul-quaking sex with a guy without falling head over heels in love with him. I can't stop Sparky from going rogue. I can't get you out of the mess with Alpha Asshat *because* my Magic went rogue." She wiggled her sock-clad feet. "I can't even find a matching pair of socks. I can't do anything right these days."

"You did one thing right." Harper tugged her cell phone out of her back pocket and automatically dialed. "You made friends with people who don't listen when you say you don't need boozy ice cream. Prepare for brain freeze, my dear, because we're getting toasted on cake-batter-vodka-martini sherbets."

Vi wasn't sure how she'd lucked out having people around her who would stick with her through her darkest times, but she wasn't about to question it. Grabbing the remote, she brought up the *Buffy* pilot and cocooned herself into Bax's side. "Make sure you get a couple pints. *Buffy* had a pretty long run, and there was a lot of Angel angst."

❖ ❖ ❖

Violet's stuff was gone. Linc hadn't expected anything different, but the reality of it hadn't hit him until he'd walked into the brownstone to find it devoid of anything that reminded him of her.

Drawers were emptied and her kitchen gadgets reclaimed. The chair next to the window where she'd sat curled up with a book each morning had been dragged to its former position in the corner, the sweatshirt she'd commandeered as her "reading hoodie" folded up and placed on his bed.

Their bed. At least, it had been for the past few days.

Her flowery scent still lingered everywhere, or maybe it was an olfactory hallucination to help him deal with the fact that he'd fucked up and had no idea how to un-fuck it . . . or if he even could.

Rose's words on the beach had haunted him the entire flight back stateside. Violet *did* deserve someone who loved her as fiercely as she loved those around her. Hell, she deserved more, and it took the threat of losing her *again* for him to realize that that's what he wanted to be.

Hers.

Someone knocked on his front door. Linc ignored it. Adrian had called no less than a dozen times in the last fifteen minutes and threatened him in his last ten voice mails. He probably decided to make good on his promises of kicking his ass in person.

Linc turned thirty-three tomorrow evening, and there was no way he'd gotten all the Alpha votes. Not judging by the unhappy scowl Benson had thrown his way when he'd left the hotel last evening to catch his flight.

The knock came again.

"Go the fuck away, Adrian." Linc growled. "I'll deal with the Elders and the Alpha vote tomorrow. I'm not in the mood."

The door swished open, and a second later, in strode one of the last people he expected to see. "Edie . . . what the hell are you doing here?"

The Maxwell Prima glided through his foyer as if she hadn't magically picklocked her way into his house. "Put your eyes back in your head, young man. This can't wait until tomorrow . . . mood or no mood."

"Prima, I—"

"I'm not coming to you as the Prima. Right now, I'm here as Edie Maxwell, grandmother of the woman you have seriously messed things up with. But once *she's* had her say, *then* you'll get the Prima." She pointed to his couch. "Now, sit and open your little wolf ears."

He sat as instructed.

"Good." She dumped her purse on his coffee table and shot him the grandmother of all glares. "Would you care to explain how the hell the two of you made a mess out of what should've been a fundamentally basic and easy-to-identify phenomena?"

Linc opened his mouth to ask her what she meant.

The Prima didn't wait for his answer. "I'll tell you where you went wrong. You kids these days are so focused on what you *don't* have that you fail to realize what's right in front of your fool faces! I have never, in my seventy-four years on this earth, seen people squander gifts with such blatant disregard."

"Prima Maxwell . . . I mean, Edie," he added when she leveled him a scowl. "I agree I screwed up—"

"Oh, honey. Screwing up is accidentally pouring orange juice into your cereal instead of milk. It's making a U-turn when there's a 'No U-Turn' sign right outside your driver's-side window. What you did—and what Violet did—is not a screwup."

Lincoln stood. "Don't bring Violet into this. *I'm* the one who fucked up. I fucked up fourteen years ago when I gave my father my silence. And I did it again when I agreed to keep things professional between her and me even though I've never once had a professional feeling for her in my body."

"Oh, you don't say," Edie mocked him.

Mocked.

The Maxwell Prima, unarguably the most powerful witch in the world, was openly acting as if he was the stupidest man in the universe . . . and maybe he was.

"You're in love with my granddaughter—yes or no?"

"Edie . . ."

"Yes . . . or no?"

He swallowed the lump in his throat, hesitantly meeting her searing gaze. "Without a doubt, yes. I'm in love with her—so damn much."

"You feel empty when she's not around."

"Yes."

"You feel alive—complete—when she is."

"Yes. I already told you—"

"I'm not finished," she cut him off. "Your Wolf awakens when she's in close proximity, even alerting you to her presence before your shifter senses kick in."

All the time.

"Her Magic calls to your Wolf. When you're together, it wraps around you until it feels as though a missing piece has been put back into its proper place. Two halves become whole. Two souls become one."

Linc couldn't breathe as he stared at the older woman. "What are you saying?"

"I think you know exactly what I'm saying."

Linc's knees went weak, and damned if he didn't get a little light-headed. He knew exactly what Edie was getting at. Part of him had known it all along—particularly his Wolf.

"She's my True Mate." He could barely hear the words as they fell off his lips. "*Violet's* my True Mate. How did I not know this before now? How is this possible?"

"Because until you reentered my granddaughter's life, neither of you had fully embraced your destinies. Up until that happened, all either of you would've felt was a strong desire to be close to the other. A magnetization."

"Our entire childhood . . ."

She nodded. "Was a result of the bond between you, but due to your ages, it's not something you could've easily identified. The two of you simply weren't ready. You had to become the person the other needed."

"But *you* knew."

"I suspected, for many years."

"But you never said anything."

The Prima didn't respond, and Linc's heart leaped to his throat. Fuck. *Had* she said something? Had she told *Violet*? Thinking that was the cause of all the animosity between them growing up made his stomach turn.

True Mates were all about destiny and fate, and Violet Maxwell was all about creating her own path, had been even when they were kids. Had she resented him and the bond between them?

"Edie, did Vi—"

"Violet didn't know," Edie interjected, reading his train of thought. "The link of a True Bonded Pair needs to be exposed naturally and without interference." A flicker of emotion swept across the older woman's face before disappearing again.

"But you did say something to someone, didn't you?"

Grim-faced and with a heavy dose of regret, she nodded. "Your father."

Linc's went statue-still. "Gregor knew Violet was my True Mate?"

"I shared my suspicions with him, and I take full blame for the fallout that came from it. Your father was exceptional at masking his true face, and I regretfully didn't realize it until it was much too late. The damage was done."

It all started to make sense.

The way Gregor had pushed female shifters on him. The lengths he'd taken to put distance between Linc and Violet. It wasn't because she'd been a magicless Firstborn.

"That's why he blackmailed me into compliance. That's why he had his witch mistress at the time hex me into silence. If I had entered a Mate Bond with Violet, he would've lost all control over the NAP . . . and that wasn't something he was ready to relinquish."

Edie didn't confirm or deny. "With your father gone, we can't know his motives for certain, but it's a fair bet. He feared the day you would surpass him in both power and position. Finding—and Bonding—with your True Mate would've done that sooner rather than later."

Linc scrubbed his palm over his face . . . and froze. "Wait. I just told you about that night . . . about the *hex*. How? Every time I've even attempted to mention it—especially to Violet—my tongue literally swells in my mouth."

"Because there isn't anything the Magic of a True Mate can't create or defeat. Once you accepted your destiny, you could no longer be bound."

"You're right, Edie. I didn't just screw this up. I fucked it frontward, backward, sideways. All the damn directions."

Edie chuckled. "Now the real question is, what are you doing to rectify it? Finding your True Mate is something to be honored and cherished . . . and held on to for dear life."

"She'll never listen to me if I talk to her," he said, more to himself than to the Prima. "And True Mate or not, she'll Magic my balls off if I try. I hurt her, Edie. Thinking I could attempt to take a mate who wasn't her hurt both of us."

Words would never be enough to show a witch like Violet Maxwell how much she meant to him. He had to think of something else. Something bigger. Something that would mean more to her than sonnets and pretty words and a public declaration of his undying devotion.

As his mind worked overtime forming a battle plan to fight for his True Mate, the Prima grinned, slowly walking toward his front door.

"Edie."

She turned, one eyebrow raised.

"You said you were talking to me as Edie Maxwell first. What words of wisdom does the Prima have for me in a situation like this?"

"Violet will be summoned to stand in front of the Supernatural Council tomorrow morning. Make sure you're there—and be prepared to dig your way out of the mess you made."

"And what if I'm booted off the Council by then?"

"You're the Alpha of the North American Pack, Lincoln Thorne . . . at least for the time being. Since when do you let something like a misplaced invitation stop you from going where you want?"

She flashed him a wink and left as suddenly as she'd arrived. As the door closed behind her, a plan popped into his head. It had a lot of moving parts, and required a lot of faith—and groveling—on his part, but he'd do that and more to make it happen.

Tugging his cell phone from his pocket, he dialed one of the Lincoln Thorne Hate Club co-chairs. The second the call went through, he didn't hesitate.

"I know you have no reason to help me, but I'm asking anyway. I have an idea where everyone gets what they want."

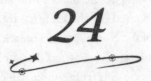

24

Wolfshit

Admitting she'd fallen in love with Lincoln. Realizing it didn't matter one damn bit. The Australia party. The Tiger King. The fallout. Heartbreak.

She was hexed.

It's the only thing that explained the shit-tastic karma that was the last thirty-six hours.

Now a freakin' *summons*. It wasn't that she hadn't expected it, but she hadn't prepared herself to deal with it solo. She stood outside the Council chambers, waiting to be called inside, and everyone who'd previously been on hover mode was now missing in action.

No Rose. No Olive or Bax *or* Harper. All she had was an anxious Christina, who'd caused the vein at Vi's temple to start pulsating within five minutes of her arrival.

"We're here! We're here!" Harper burst through the door with Bax hot on her heels. They each pulled her into hugs. "You got this. Repeat after me: 'I'm Violet Maxwell. I'm a magical badass capable of lighting asses on fire. Literally.'"

Vi chuckled, thankful for the humor. "How long did it take you to come up with that pep talk?"

"She stole it from a self-help podcast she listened to on our way over here," Bax joked.

Harper threw him a scowl. "Where I got it doesn't matter. What does is that it's true. *No one can make you feel inferior without your consent.*"

Vi nearly sobbed with her love for the succubus. "You're quoting Eleanor Roosevelt now? You've grown up on me, Harp."

"Roosevelt?" She looked confused. "No, I'm quoting Joe from *Princess Diaries.*"

Violet pulled Harper into another hard hug. "I love you . . . and hopefully you'll still love me when the Council forces me to Bond with some sixty-year-old badger shifter and I have to move to an island off the coast of Alaska."

"You're not Bonding with some cantankerous badger shifter, I can promise you that."

Vi almost asked her to repeat the sentiment again for extra reassurance when the chamber doors opened. Their heads swiveled as the chamber guard scanned their group.

"Violet Maxwell." His gaze eventually fell on her. "The Council is ready for you."

They all moved as one group.

The guard stepped in their way. "*Just* Violet Maxwell. It's a closed session."

Today is the gift that keeps on giving.

"Go get 'em, tiger." Harper smacked her on the ass. "I mean, witchy. Knock 'em on their asses . . . although not literally. As spry as your grandma is, hip breakage is a serious concern at her age."

Bax held his hand over Harp's mouth, stifling any more pep talk. "You got this, Vi."

She sure as hell hoped so.

Nothing had changed in the Council chambers since the last time she'd been in the room, and as she took the center spot, the Council themselves filed in, her grandmother in the lead. She mentally prepared herself to lay eyes on Lincoln for the first time

314 ❀ April Asher

since magically blasting his feet out from beneath him, but Xavier, the vampire representative, brought up the rear instead.

No Lincoln.

No shifter rep at all.

Vi's gaze flew to her gran, but the Prima didn't give anything away as Angel Ramón called the session to order, pounding the table with a gavel despite the fact that they were the only ones present.

"Violet Maxwell, you've been asked to stand before the Council today as it has been brought to our attention that you have yet to enter a Witch Bond as this Council requested. What do you say in response?"

Vi flicked her gaze to Edie, who nodded subtly. "I say you're not wrong, Councilman. But I'd also add that I was given a three-month deadline."

He frowned, unamused. "That three-month reprieve was contingent on you not being in possession of magical abilities. Multiple witnesses have reported that not only do you possess an affinity for Magic, but that you have a high-level aptitude."

Vi lifted her chin and refused to look away. "Again, you're not wrong, Councilman."

He glowered at her over the rim of his glasses. "Are you being so flippant because you don't understand the severity of your actions, or do you simply not care? May I remind you that the rule of the Firstborn was put in place for a reason?"

"Could you explain that reason, Councilman?" Lincoln's voice ricocheted off the walls.

Heads turned in surprise, Violet's included, as he walked through the chamber doors.

If she wasn't so happy to lay eyes on him again, she'd have been worried. His shirt, rumpled as if he'd slept in it, hung loose, untucked from his jeans, and more than a few days' worth of stubble peppered his jaw.

He stopped a few feet away from the Council bench with not so much as a glance in her direction.

"Alpha Thorne," Ramón tsked, "must I remind you that your participation in this Council is under review? Until a decision is made on your status, your presence is no longer required at proceedings."

"That's too damn bad, because I'm here and I have no intention of being quiet or leaving the chambers." He shot a warning glare to the security guard, who had taken the smallest step forward. "At least not without a fight."

The guard stopped.

Smart man.

"You were about to give the room a reason, sir." Lincoln waited expectantly for the Councilman's answer. "What reason *specifically* is there for a Firstborn to enter a Witch Bond?"

"It is to—"

"Anchor the witch's Magic. Keep it from leveling all of humanity. Yeah, I've heard the stories, too. Pretty sure my mother told them to me before bedtime . . . but that's all they were. Stories."

"That's Supernatural history you're talking about, Alpha."

"It's nothing but a well-fabricated fairy tale someone hundreds of years ago wanted you to *believe* is history."

The vampire stiffened in his seat. "What proof do you have that something we've believed for hundreds of years is nothing but a fabrication?"

"Funny you should ask that, X."

A commotion sounded in the hall outside before the heavy oak doors blew open again, this time admitting not one Maxwell sister, but two. Olive and Rose strode down the center aisle, Olive with a stack of books and—Goddess love her—a mound of paperwork that she plunked on the podium next to Violet.

"What are you guys doing here?" Vi hissed.

"Go with the flow, sis." Olive winked. "And try to keep up."

Angel Ramón whacked his gavel as if his life depended on it. "What is the meaning of this? Does no one understand *closed* proceedings?"

Clearing her throat, Olive pushed her glasses higher onto her nose. "I'm sorry, Councilman, but it was my understanding you wanted proof of Alpha Thorne's allegations?"

His eyes widened marginally. "And you have such proof?"

"What I have right here"—she held up a stack of files—"are transcripts taken from the Celestial Archives themselves. It's a confirmation that the history—and law—of the Firstborn was severely distorted throughout time, and that what we believe today is simply a story steeped heavily in bias and fear."

"That's not possible," Xavier nearly growled.

"Oh, but it is. If I may approach the Council, Prima Maxwell?"

Edie's lips twitched. "Please do, and bring your proof with you."

After tossing a manila folder in front of each Council member, Olive paced the floor like the lawyer she used to be. "What you have in front of you, on the right, are the 'historical' stories to which our mothers rocked us to sleep. Magical Triads. Primas. Witch Bonds. Yadda, yadda, yadda. On the left, acquired from a book in the Celestial Archives, which we know have been kept under strict lock and key from the time they were written, you'll find a very different depiction of Firstborns."

Angel Ramón's eyes flicked up to drill Olly with a hard glare. "And how did you come across this celestial documentation?"

"A scholar never reveals her sources, sir. But as you can see, the two texts are vastly different. One paints Firstborns as powerful but unstable witches capable only of controlling their Magic when anchored to another Supernatural being. The other talks about the responsibility that comes with the power *gifted* to a Firstborn. There's no mention of Witch Bonds. Or anchors. Or instability of any kind. Like in many areas of life, Magic's ability to build up or tear down depends on the motives of the individual wielding it."

"What does this have to do with why we're here today?"

"It has everything to do with it, and it's the reason Lincoln brought me here. The documentation of history is always influenced by the person doing the documenting."

"But those are two varying opinions," Xavier pointed out. "How certain are you that the depiction from the Celestial Archives isn't the one that's skewed?"

Angel Ramón's attention whipped to his vampire colleague. "Because the Angelic Scribes cannot skew history. It's impossible. They document it all. Our faults. Our mistakes. Nothing in the Archives can be fabricated."

Lincoln grinned simply, "Which means the story we were fed our entire lives about Firstborns requiring a tether to another in order to control their Magic is complete and utter wolfshit, and was probably initiated by someone afraid of how that power could hinder *them*."

Julius, the demon representative, scoffed. "You can't be suggesting we simply ignore the way things have always been handled because of your theory."

"While that would be my first choice, I'll offer another suggestion. Test Violet's magic."

Vi's neck nearly spun off her shoulders as she turned her head in his direction. "Say what now?"

He finally looked at her. A perfect blend of chocolate brown and wolfy gold, his eyes softened. There was an entire pool of different emotions swimming in their depths, but not an ounce of concern. "You don't have anything to worry about, princess."

If only that were true.

Ramón looked to Edie. "Can this be done, Prima Maxwell?"

"Of course. With Elemental Magic." Her gran's eyes practically twinkled. *She's been in on this all along.* "Earth, air, water, and fire. They're the hardest Magics to master. Take too much from one, and you seriously deplete the other."

Elemental Magic?

Vi fought to keep a smile off her face as her grandmother turned to her. "Is this acceptable to you, Miss Maxwell? Prove to us that you can harmoniously balance the four elements."

"Sure. And once I do, you'll eradicate the Witch Bond law—for *all* Firstborns. For *everyone*. Now and in the future."

It wasn't a question, and Julius Kontos's eyebrows lifted. "*If* you manage to show us sufficient control, the Council will deliberate on next steps."

"There's nothing to deliberate. Olive gave you more than enough proof. What I'm about to do? It's a courtesy to make you all feel a little better about doing the right thing."

Ramón raised his hand, calling for silence as the vampire and demon representative opened their mouths to argue. "All right, then, Miss Maxwell. Dazzle us. Is there anything you need before you begin?"

She glanced at each of their untouched water bottles. "Unscrew your caps?"

A low chuckle came from Lincoln's side of the room, but she pushed it aside, determined not to mess this up.

Like she'd been for the last few days, Sparky was there the second Vi closed her eyes. *Are you ready to harmonize the hell out of these elements?*

As an answer, Sparky *whooshed* out from her hands. The magical release felt like she'd just taken a huge gulp of fresh air. A smile slipped onto her face as she cleared her mind of everything and everyone—except the connection to her Magic.

Earth . . . Vi opened her eyes.

Gentle vibration rumbled beneath their feet. The uncapped water bottles danced on the Council's desk, bouncing closer to the edge with every small shake. The second they tipped, Vi redirected her Magic.

Water . . .

The spilled contents hovered in a thousand-droplet formation directly in front of the four Supernatural figureheads. The water gently rocked back and forth as if swaying in a hammock.

Air . . .

Sparky swooped up each droplet, swirling them above the Council's heads in an impressive airborne river. The water blob zoomed around Xavier's head, and when the vampire growled out a warning, she brought it back to the center, where she magically morphed it into the same Celtic knot design that was etched onto her shoulder.

And fire . . .

Shocked gasps echoed through the room as Sparky's signature purple energy pulsed from Vi's hands in the form of a magical dancing flame. She altered the size, shaping it into a baseball-size orb of energy, and tossed it through the still-hovering water droplets. In a flash, both her Magic and the water were gone.

Heart thumping in her chest, Vi swallowed a nervously proud smile and waited not-so-patiently for someone to say something. *Anything.*

Olive and Rose dished out two excited thumbs-ups and Lincoln's grin couldn't have grown any wider. She offered him a shaky one in return before turning back to the Council.

"Gentlemen, in case you're having any doubt, *that* is what we call a stable magical connection." Edie beamed proudly. "I'm making the motion to dissolve the Witch Bond law as it pertains to *all* witches . . . whether they possess a magical affinity or not. Do I have a second?"

Vi held her breath while waiting for someone to back her grandmother. Five seconds later, Angel Ramón assented. Then Xavier. And finally, more reluctantly, the demon representative.

"And I, as the not-yet-formally-fired-from-my-duty shifter Councilman, also move to dissolve the archaic law." Lincoln flashed her a coy wink.

"Then let's consider it done. From now on, *all* witches will control their own destiny."

Rose cleared her throat. "If I could add one thing to the Council's docket . . . for *now*?"

"What more could you Maxwell sisters have to say to us today?" Humor laced Ramón's words as he leaned back in his seat. "Want us to declare Fridays International Casual Day?"

"No, sir. I wanted to hand in my formal resignation. I quit."

From somewhere in the rear of the room, Christina muttered about fainting.

Ramón's curiosity piqued. "Did you just say you quit? You can't quit being the Prima Apparent. It's a role that was bestowed upon you by—"

"That's where I'm stopping you, Ramón." Stepping down from the small riser, Edie touched Rose's cheek affectionately before doing the same with Olive. Stopping next to Violet, she turned toward her peers. "This Council doesn't choose the next Prima. That duty falls to Magic itself."

Edie opened her palm. Golden swirls of energy danced off her hand and hovered in the air. "Magic recognizes Magic." The magical ball pulsated, growing ominously larger with each flow and ebb. "Prima recognizes Prima."

"Gran?" Vi hissed. "What's happening here?"

"Magic has already chosen the next Prima."

Edie's glowing orb erupted into a beautiful glitterfest of Magic and rainbows. It rained down on Violet, tickling her skin in a warm, magical snowfall. Sparky burst to the surface to join in on the fun, and the second it collided with Edie's Magic, time stood still.

Everyone outside their two-person cocoon froze in position.

"What the hell is happening?" Vi spun her head around the room before turning her attention to the older woman in front of her. "Gran?"

Tears pooled in the Prima's eyes, the first of her grandmother's she'd ever seen. "You have no idea how proud I am of you, sweetheart. *So* proud. You're destined to do great things. This is your beginning."

"You mean . . . I'm . . ." Vi's eyes widened. "*I'm* the next Prima? How . . . ? Why . . . ? And why would you put Rose through all that pressure and—"

"Everything happened the exact way it was meant to . . . at least until this point. If your sister hadn't undergone the training she did, she wouldn't be prepared for what lies ahead in her own path. Same with Olive." Edie wiped away Vi's fallen tears. "There's a reason you three are so different and yet one harmonious Magical Triad. It was the same for myself and my sisters. You each possess your own greatness, which couldn't be achieved if it weren't for the struggles of the past."

Vi laughed nervously. "You know that sounds ominous, right?"

Edie chuckled. "Challenges are ahead for each of you, but together, you'll be well-equipped to deal with them."

"That doesn't sound any better." Her gaze landed on Lincoln.

This time it wasn't her Magic that fluttered, but her heart. There was so much unsaid between them, and she didn't know if she'd ever find the right words. Just like everyone else, he was frozen in place, his eyes holding a myriad of emotions she couldn't decipher.

"Why did he do this?" she heard herself ask. "Why did he go through all that trouble . . . ?"

"*That's* not my place to share, but it's something for the two of you to share with one another."

"Please tell me that cryptic nonsense doesn't get passed down from Prima to Prima."

Edie chuckled. "You'll be a Prima of your very own making . . . and you'll be a force of nature. I can't wait to be a witness to it."

Edie and Violet's magical cocoon melted away. Time unfroze.

Rose and Olive stormed forward, wrapping her in a Triplet

322 ❉ April Asher

Huggle while their mother immediately assailed Edie with question after question. And in true best friend fashion, Harper and Bax burst through the chamber doors.

"See! I told you!" The succubus nearly tackle-hugged her to the ground. "Violet fucking Maxwell, the badass fucking Prima!"

"I can't quite wrap my head around the last forty-five minutes. I don't even know what to do next, or where to go from here."

"I'll tell you what we're doing and where we're doing it. We're celebrating! At Claws! Tonight!"

Everyone made plans around her, and while she smiled at their enthusiasm, something was missing. Movement from the side of the room caught Vi's attention.

Lincoln stood by the exit, a wary smile on his handsome face. He pushed it broader, but the gesture didn't quite reach his eyes. The sight of his proud sadness conjured a new wave of heartache that distracted her from another incoming Harper hug.

When the succubus pulled away, Lincoln was gone—and he took a huge chunk of her heart with him.

25

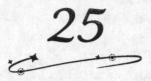

The Witch You Wed

Linc's footsteps echoed down the corridor of Council headquarters. Unlike how it had been for Violet's hearing earlier that morning, the building was now devoid of any media or spectators, the place nearly silent as a tomb.

He'd officially be thirty-three in forty-five minutes, and the Elders weren't wasting a second. They had congregated in the lower levels of the building, and if their basement location wasn't an ominous enough omen, Adrian's frown took it the rest of the way.

"Turn that frown upside down, A. You look like you're headed to an execution," Linc teased.

His best friend gave him a befuddled look. "How could you be joking right now? Of all times?"

"Because when I look back on the day, it was a pretty damn good one."

He couldn't be any prouder of Violet and what she had accomplished. He'd always known she was special, but now others saw it, too. His little ball of purple power would knock the old ways of the Supernatural community on their asses, and then she'd help them rebuild.

Build better. Be better.

"Get your head out of the clouds, man," Adrian scolded, knowing where Linc's thoughts had gone. "Don't fuck this up."

"I have no intention to."

"Good. Because if the Alpha vote comes in—"

"I'm stepping down."

Adrian stopped abruptly. "Excuse me?"

"You heard me. Benson didn't like me before I ruined her grandson's party. There's no way she's coming in with the final vote, and that means I have two options: mate the Elders' pick, or resign from the Supernatural Council and step down as the NAP Alpha." Linc stared his friend in the eye, making himself heard. "I won't Bond with someone who isn't my True Mate, Adrian."

He wouldn't Bond with anyone who wasn't *Violet*.

Adrian groaned. "Think about this. Hard."

"I have. I'll step down, and as my Second-in-Command, you'll become Alpha, and while your position on the Council will only be temporary until a formal nomination process can be done, we'll do whatever we can to make sure your seat holds."

"Dude, your True Mate is—"

"Violet."

Adrian blinked. "What?"

Linc's heart pounded in his chest as he thought about his and his Wolf's perfect match. His inner beast howled at him to go find her, and damned if he didn't want to do just that . . . Elder Board or not.

"Violet Maxwell's my True Mate," Linc admitted. His mouth slipped into a reflexive smile. "I think my Wolf knew it this whole damn time, but with everything going on, I was super slow on the uptake. This Elder shit came between me and my soul mate once already, Adrian. I won't do something that will take her even further away."

Adrian scrubbed his palm over his face before taking a deep

breath. "Alpha Collins, huh? Shit. I didn't have this on my bingo card for today."

Linc squeezed his shoulder. "Think of all the parties you'll be invited to."

"And all the headaches I'll have to deal with when it's *me* trying to woo the Alphas."

Elder Goodman's head poked out from a doorway down the hall. "If you gentlemen would please join us? We'd like to get started."

A few short days ago, this night would've stressed Lincoln beyond belief, but he was at peace with what he was about to do. He had no regrets. Even if Violet never spoke to him again, he'd be happy knowing his heart would forever be owned by hers.

"Thank you for finally joining us," Goodman said dryly, gesturing to the center of the room.

"Thank you for inviting me," Linc joked back.

Fourteen glares looked down at him from their perches. Two representatives from each of the seven Packs sat on the Elder Board, and going by their pinched expressions, all were aware of their Alphas' plans to make them inconsequential.

Goodman's smile was as cold as her heart. "First, I suppose we should tell you happy birthday, Alpha Thorne. You've reached your thirty-third year of life, and as I'm sure you're aware, there is great significance in that date. For the sake of your Pack, and for our traditions, you are to take a mate." She glanced around the room, all for show. "And am I to assume that you don't have your own contender?"

"I don't."

The two Elders on the end exchanged smug looks.

"Then you know that as you've failed to provide your own suitable mate, the Elder Board has the right to choose one for you." Goodman's eyes damn near twinkled.

"No, they don't. Because I step—"

The basement door clanged against the wall as it burst open and five familiar people stepped into the room . . . with Alpha Benson in the lead.

"What is the meaning of this?" Goodman bellowed.

"*This*"—Benson held up what looked to be a bunch of signatures—"is a decree signed by six currently ruling Alphas: Antarctica, North America, South America, Asia, Africa, Australia . . . as well a signature from the European Pack's former Second-in-Command —and new Alpha—Tristan Arnaud. And this means the Elder Board is officially unable to choose any*thing* for any*one*."

Someone dropped the paper in front of Elder Goodman, and the older bear shifter's face contorted as she picked it up. "This is mutiny. This is a coup . . ."

Adrian snickered. "Coup-coup-cachoo, baby."

Linc barely smothered a smile. He exchanged glances with Benson, and the older woman gave him a slight nod.

"Well then," Linc took over, "I guess you have it. By the power vested in the seven Alphas whose signatures you see before you, consider yourselves fully demoted. Should you choose to accept your new roles as Pack members, you'll be accepted. Should you choose not to abide by the Packs' new direction, feel free to let the door hit your asses on the way out."

The fourteen *former* Elders argued and shouted, a few getting in Goodman's face, demanding that she do something.

"Why the change of heart?" Linc asked Benson as the older shifter came up to him and shook his hand. "After your grandson's party, I didn't think I had a prayer of getting you on board."

Benson chuckled. "You're not wrong. You misstepped nearly the entire way, young man. It's a good thing you're only thirty-three, because you have a lot to learn. But to answer your question, *you* changed my mind."

"How?"

"I saw your heart on your sleeve, Lincoln Thorne. First with the children at the gala, and then at my grandson's party. You care not only for your Pack, but for everyone who needs you. But it took a good ass-kicking from your witch to drag my old carcass from my bed and fully embrace it."

Violet?

Linc wasn't sure he'd heard correctly. "I'm not sure what you mean."

Benson's smirk twitched. "You'll have your hands full with that one. She reminds me a lot of my own mate. But before I go, I do have a suggestion, something you should take care of before we sit down tomorrow and make the real work happen."

"What's that?"

"Stop being a wolf's ass and go get your girl."

Linc's Wolf nearly gutted him with his need to get to Violet. *Now.*

"Go." Adrian pointed to the fire stairs. "For crying out loud, put us all out of our miseries and go woo the witch."

Linc bolted, mentally preparing himself to run through the entire city in order to find her, but seconds after bursting out the back door, his Wolf told him exactly where she'd be standing.

Beneath a lamppost, wearing flannel duck pajama pants and rain boots up to her knees, Violet paced on the sidewalk. Her hair fell around her shoulders, ruffling in the cool breeze as she nibbled on the corner of her bottom lip.

"Keep worrying your lip like that and you'll make it bleed," Linc called out in warning.

At the sound of his voice, she spun toward him.

Her eyes damn near glittered as they watched him hesitantly. "Did Benson get there in time? We tried to get here as fast as we could, but . . . did you . . . did you take a—"

"No."

❖ ❖ ❖

Violet wasn't sure what had possessed her to drag herself across the city to the Australian Alpha's New York residence, but she hadn't been able to sit back and let Lincoln potentially make one of the worst decisions of his life. Sparky wouldn't let her, either, practically levitating her ass off the couch and into her galoshes.

She'd told herself it didn't matter what happened, only that she tried. But now, as she watched Lincoln slowly close the distance, she realized it mattered a whole hell of a lot.

His face an unreadable mask of emotions, he prowled closer as if he had all the time in the world. "No, princess. I didn't accept the Elders' Mate Bond, and even if Benson and the others hadn't gotten there in time, it wouldn't have mattered."

Anger burned her eyes. "What do you mean it wouldn't have mattered? Of course it would! You—"

"I was about to step down." Stopping in front of her, Lincoln cupped her cheeks, gently tilting her face toward his. "There was no way I could take a mate that wasn't you, Violet Maxwell."

Moisture welled in her eyes as she fought to keep breathing. "Me? I . . . I don't understand."

"I know." Linc rested his forehead against hers. "But first, you need to know why I didn't show up that night by the river."

Sparky, who'd been going ape-shit for the past few hours, finally soothed at being in his arms. "Lincoln, it was a long time ago and I don't—"

"I *need* to tell you, and you have to hear it. I never want anything but truth between us ever again." He took a shaky breath that matched her own.

For years, she'd wanted the answer, but now? Reality could be so much worse than what she'd built up in her head, but she could see the pain in his eyes, and if telling her took it away, she'd listen.

She nodded hesitantly, her hands clutching his arms for support.

"Gregor *did* know you saw that Blood Match," Linc admitted, "and the reason he didn't come after you was because I bartered with him. My obedience, for your life."

Her heart throbbed in her chest. "Lincoln . . ."

"I wasn't about to let him do anything to you, Violet. But to ensure I didn't go back on my word, he had his witch mistress hex me into silence. I *couldn't* talk about that night . . . to anyone. I've tried so many damn times over the last few weeks to tell you what happened, and each and every time, I couldn't."

He swallowed a heavy lump of emotion. "The only reason I contemplated the Elders' proposal for *one very short* second was because I knew how much that night hurt you. It hurt both of us, and unless I told you what happened, it would always be between us. And princess, I don't want anything between us ever again."

Her eyes roamed his face as she digested the words. "But you're telling me right now. How is that possible?"

Let your Magic guide you.

Sparky pushed her way through her body as if wanting to answer. Her fingerlike tendrils wrapped around both Vi and Lincoln, the Magic guiding them closer, and then in a slow, pulsing, glow, Sparky wasn't the only thing Vi could sense . . .

Linc's Wolf brushed against her mind.

His love caressed her heart.

Vi followed her Magic to the gorgeous purple link binding their souls in an intricate swirl of magical lace and ribbon. Two becoming one.

Realization clicked, and she sucked in a sharp breath, her suspicion confirmed in his golden-flecked eyes. "We're True Mates."

Raw emotion consumed them both as Lincoln stepped closer. "We weren't ready for it when we were kids, but now? I love you, Violet. I am so *in* love with you, and I have been since you pilfered my orange crayon in kindergarten."

She laughed, not realizing she was crying until his thumb brushed away a tear. "You kept stealing my red one."

"I know you don't need to form a Witch Bond, but—"

"Yes."

"Yes, you're aware of that, or yes . . . ?"

"I can handle my Magic on my own, and I know I'll make a kick-ass Prima—albeit a slightly unconventional one. And I know I don't *have* to enter a Witch Bond to change the world . . . but I want to."

Lincoln searched her face. "You do?"

"I do."

"Just to make it clear, you're talking about Bonding to *me*, right?"

"No, to my package delivery man." With a roll of her eyes, she slipped her arms around his neck. "*Yes to you!* I love you, Lincoln Thorne. You've always been the thorn in my backside, but you're *my* Thorne. I don't just want to form a Witch Bond with you. I want to be your mate. Your wife. I want to flip the world upside down and shake things up. And I want to do it while standing side by side."

"Together." He ghosted a soft, barely there kiss over her lips. "There's no walking away. Where one goes, so does the other. In this life and in the next. Violet Maxwell, you're the better half of me."

"I know." She playfully nipped his bottom lip. "I also better be the witch you wed . . . or so help me, Wolfman, Sparks will fly."

"With you, princess, there will always be sparks." Lincoln took her mouth in a kiss they both very literally felt down to their souls.

Sparks *did* fly.

Above them.

Around them.

And consumed them.

Epilogue

When people conjured mental images of heaven, most envisioned angels zipping around a white, cloud-infused wonderland and gleaming pearly gates that twinkled like diamonds. That wasn't Violet's version. Hers involved an evening with her friends, her family, and her sexy soon-to-be mate.

As if thinking about Lincoln magically summoned him, his arms slid around her waist from behind. "You were too far away for too damn long."

"I was gone for five seconds." A grin tugged up the corners of her mouth as she leaned into his embrace.

"Like I said, too damn long." His mouth nuzzled her ear, making her giggle.

Rose appeared from out of nowhere. "Lincoln Thorne, what have you done to my sister? Violet Maxwell does not giggle."

"Maybe not, but the soon-to-be Violet Maxwell-Thorne does." He nipped Vi's earlobe, making her suppress another grin.

Vi studied her sister carefully. "Where have you been? Olive and I looked everywhere for you, but it was like you fell off the planet."

"I didn't disappear," Rose defended herself way too quickly. "I was trying to prevent Mom from harassing Gage too much."

They looked over to the bar, where Christina was behind the counter, giving Gage directions on how to pour drinks *the right way*.

"I know why you wanted to have your Bond Announcement here, but I don't think Gage will ever forgive you." Rose waved when the broody vampire glared their way. He was definitely not a happy vamp.

"It was either here or at the KCC, and the children's center is under too heavy construction right now for that to be safe."

"You could have had it at Guastavino's. They had that opening."

Vi shrugged. "It's gorgeous, but it doesn't feel like *us*. You can use it when you stumble into the man of your dreams."

Rose snortled. "I'm staying man-free for the foreseeable future, but our sister, on the other hand . . ."

They slid their attention to where the youngest triplet was talking animatedly with a cute NYU professor, who, much to everyone's surprise, was none other than the eccentric head of Supernatural Studies—and Olive's date.

Bax sat a table away, glowering in their direction since they'd sat down. Their sister was oblivious.

"I feel like we've stepped into the Upside Down from *Stranger Things*—minus the scary spider creature," Vi admitted. "I'm giggling. Olive's getting her flirt on. Next thing we know, Rose will be having a one-night stand with a sexy stranger in the back room of a seedy bar."

Linc laughed, but Rose's face visibly paled as she shifted her weight from one stiletto-clad foot to the other.

"There's that elusive bastard!" Lincoln released one arm from around Vi's waist and waved to a tall, broad-shouldered blond who'd just turned the corner. "Damian! Get your ass over here and meet the woman of my dreams!"

The hot blond swaggered over to them, a crooked grin on his face. The second Rose saw him, she froze, looking like a deer in headlights.

Lincoln shook the new arrival's hand. "Thanks for coming out for this. It means a lot that you could make it."

Damian released a low chuckle. "When you told me you'd found your True Mate, how could I not? I had to warn the poor girl about getting mixed up with the likes of you."

"Oh, I already know he's trouble. That's why we're getting hitched. We can be trouble together." She held out her hand for him. "I'm Violet, and you must be Damian Adams? I've heard a lot about you."

"Whatever Linc and Adrian told you, don't believe them." Damian grinned mischievously. "I was ten times worse."

Taking in his leather jacket and the wicked gleam in his dark green eyes, she didn't doubt Lincoln's half-demon college roommate one bit.

"*Was?* You're telling me you've suddenly sprouted angel wings?" Linc teased his friend.

"I may not have completely turned my horns in for a halo, but I consider myself a semi-reformed demon."

Vi settled deeper into Lincoln's arms. "Lincoln said you're a vet, right?"

"For creatures big and small. I actually got here pretty quick because I'm taking over Miguel's practice. Turning it into an animal sanctuary. If you're in the market to adopt, I'm pretty sure we can hook you up."

"Did you hear that?" She glanced up at her soon-to-be mate with a beaming smile. "He can hook us up."

Linc groaned, knowing he'd lose the argument about adopting another cat to keep Mr. Fancy Pants company. "Thanks, man. We'll stop by soon and take a look."

Vi snuck a look at her sister. Rose backed away silently, her eyes suspiciously twitchy as they kept flickering over to the gorgeous demon veterinarian.

"Look at me being all rude." Vi squashed her triplet's escape. "Damian, this is my sister Rose. Rose, this is Damian. Lincoln's college friend."

334 ✤ *April Asher*

Rose froze. Damian turned.

Something darkened in both of their eyes as they stared at each other.

Damian's mouth kicked up crookedly, showcasing a one-sided dimple. "Pretty sure we ran into each other over at the bar a little bit ago, but I didn't catch the name, much less make the connection. It's nice to *formally* meet you, Ro."

Her triplet's eyes narrowed. "It's *Rose*."

Damian wrinkled his nose. "I think Ro suits you better."

"Well, I don't. If you'll excuse me, I'm going to go save Gage from Christina." Her sister turned on her heel and stalked away, and damned if she didn't put a little extra sway in her hips.

With a chuckle, Damian excused himself to go in the opposite direction.

Vi blinked, confused. "What just happened there? I haven't seen Rose that uncomfortable since we all wore girdles to the junior prom."

"Your guess is as good as mine, but since Damian's sticking around town, we may find out sooner rather than later."

"Ooh, you think?" She turned and, slinking her arms around his neck, pulled him close.

Sparky stirred from her slumber, swelling like she always did in Lincoln's presence, but this time she wasn't telling Vi that *her* True Mate was nearby.

She was agreeing with what Lincoln said.

Things were about to get interesting.

Supernatural Singles
World Glossary

Alpha: A shifter figurehead who leads a Pack (see *Pack*); the big boss; King of Shifters (in any single designated geographic location).
Example: There's a big difference between being an Alpha *and being an alpha—the former officially being the head honcho, and the latter only thinking he is.*

Angels: Winged beings rooted in religious history. Divided into Celestial, Warrior, and Guardian castes. Don't wear halos; often possess potty mouths.
Example: Just because an angel *can sprout wings doesn't mean he's not wicked as a demon between the sheets.*

Demon: Supernatural being with historic ties to hell.
Example: Even if your CrossFit instructor is a card-carrying demon, *they may not actually have Lucifer on speed dial.*

Hex: A magical curse; can also be exchanged for Norms' four-letter words (i.e., cursing).
*Example: When Violet shouts, "*Hex *me," she's not demanding that someone curse her with a pig's tail. She's expressing frustration.*

Magical Triad: Witch-born triplets; a set of three siblings born into a magical family. A rare phenomenon that leads to Firstborn badassery.
Example: As the eldest in a Magical Triad, *Violet should be a badass*

to rival the badass-edness of General Leia Organa. Instead, she's more like Jar Jar Binks.

Mate: A spouse or partner with whom a shifter has entered into a Mate Bond (see *Mate Bond*). Not to be confused with a True Mate (or with the Australian term for "friend").
Example: Because the Shifter Elders are breathing down Lincoln's collar, he has to pretend-date his way to finding a mate.

Mate Bond: The act of taking a mate. A Supernatural marriage involving one or more shifters; an unbreakable marriage. *Not* an Australian friendship.
Example: Whoever said "A diamond is forever" never heard of a Mate Bond, *the gift that keeps on giving.*

Pack: A community of shifters; a group of Supernatural beings who have both human and animal beings/spirits in personal residence (see *shifters*). A Pack is led by an Alpha (see *Alpha*).
Example: Wolf shifter Lincoln Thorne, Alpha of the North American Pack, *also happens to have an incredible eight-pack set of abs.*

Prima: The leader of the Supernatural Council; the most badass of witches.
Example: If you mess with the Prima, *you get the Hex . . . or, in Violet Maxwell's case, the Disappointed Gran Glower.*

Shifters: Supernatural beings with the ability to turn furry, feathery, or scaly; members of a Pack (see *Pack*).
Example: While some shifters *may be all bark and no bite, there are definitely those that will bite first and ask questions later.*

Supernatural Council: Board of Supernatural badasses; Supernatural Avengers. Protectors of Supernatural law and order. Led by the Prima (see *Prima*), with shifter, angel, demon, and vampire representatives as members.

Example: *After telling Violet she must fulfill an archaic Supernatural law by forming a Witch Bond, every member of the* Supernatural Council *was on her hit list . . . including her grandma.*

True Mate: A shifter's soul mate; one's destined match. The perfect complement to both the shifter's human and animal souls.

Example: *When a shifter finds his* True Mate, *it is a literal interpretation of the* Jerry Maguire *quote, "You* complete *me."*

Vampires: Supernatural being with ties rooted deep in European folklore; the Undead. Those who drink blood as main source of sustenance.

Example: *No,* vampires *do not sparkle or burst into flames while in direct sunlight, and while they do require blood as their main food source, they're quite fond of Italian cuisine. The more garlic, the better.*

Witch/Warlock: A spell caster; a Supernatural being able to wield magic.

Example: *Violet Maxwell may be a* witch *with questionable power, but come at her with one of those green-wart-infested fake witch noses, and she will hex you so hard, your eyebrows fall off.*

Witch Bond: The witch equivalent to a Mate Bond; a witch marriage. Firstborns in Magical Triads are required by Supernatural law to form a Witch Bond to control potentially hazardous magic.

Example: *Violet Maxwell has no intention of letting anyone tell her she must form a* Witch Bond *with some ego-inflated Supernatural . . . and if that means performing magical cardio for twelve hours every day in order to get a better handle on her magic, then so be it.*

Acknowledgments

Most acknowledgments tend to read close to the same: family, friends, agent, publishers, readers. But this isn't an acknowledgment like anything else I've written, just like *Not the Witch You Wed* isn't just *another* of my books.

This is my *pandemic* book. This is the world in which I needed to immerse myself for the sake of my own mental health, and there are so many people who allowed it to happen and accepted it with open arms. My family, always in my corner, and without complaint when I announced it was another curbside-dinner-pickup kind of night. (And thank you to Kid 1 and Kid 2, who kept me constantly laughing, even if it was usually at your father's expense.)

Sarah E. Younger . . . I've called you a lot of things over our years together (all good, I swear). You're not just my agent, but my battle buddy, my homing beacon. You'll never know how much you're appreciated (especially when you listen to my crazy ideas about a New York City paranormal rom-com where supernaturals are out in the open, and say "Go for it!").

Jennie Conway, editor extraordinaire, thank you for your love and enthusiasm for these characters. With your support and guidance, I was able not only to bring Violet and Lincoln to life but to make them shine in an otherwise dark time. Thank you to everyone at St. Martin's for their dedication and hard work in bringing this book into the world. I'm so lucky to have been blessed with an amazing team.

Thank you to Tif Marcelo, Jeanette Escudero, Annie Rains,

and Rachel Lacey. Your friendship and support, guidance, and occasional ass-kickings mean the world to me. Thank you to all my other author friends and my nurse colleagues, who inspire me with everything they do and all that they are. Thank you to all the readers and reviewers and bookstagrammers for going on this wild journey with me.

And thank you to all the strong, fierce, independent women out there who've ever been told to think, behave, or react a certain way and instead stood up and said, "Not today, Satan."

You're all magical.

About the Author

April Asher, aka April Hunt, was hooked on romantic stories from the time she first snuck a bodice-ripper romance out from her mom's bedside table. She now lives out her own happily-ever-after with her college-sweetheart husband, their two children, and a cat who thinks she's more dog—and human—than feline. By day, April dons dark blue nursing scrubs and drinks way too much caffeine. By night, she still consumes too much caffeine, but she does it with a laptop in hand, and from her favorite side of the couch.

From the far left cushion, April Asher pens laugh-out-loud romantic comedies with a paranormal twist, but when she's not putting her characters into embarrassing situations with supernatural entities, she also writes high-octane romantic suspense as April Hunt, her thrill-seeking alter ego.